Praise for Lesley Krueger

"'Steroid Dreams' is just so beautifully written, every sentence poised and funny and intelligent. The prose has a marvellous rhythm, rich with perceptions." —Tessa ￼

*Drink the Sky*

"In its satisfying breadth and women's lives, *Drink the Sky* recalls the novels of 19th century British women . . . not once did I feel like putting this book down."
—*National Post*

"Lesley Krueger adds another richly textured canvas to her gallery with her new novel, *Drink the Sky*. Teeming with the layers of life . . . *Drink the Sky* scrapes away the accretions of civilization to explore questions of social and moral responsibility, revealing human motivation to be at once squalid, beautiful, dangerous, enticing and, like the rainforest canopy itself, ultimately impenetrable." —*The Globe and Mail*

"With tight control of her material and a skilful handling of mounting suspense, Krueger turns *Drink the Sky* into a thriller of admirable precision, an original and provocative novel of ideas."
—*The London Free Press*

*The Corner Garden*

"This writing is a gift of insight, humour and profound slant: new world and old in contagious communication. The vision is so intelligent as to be almost breathtaking." —Linda Spalding, Governor General's Award-winning author of *The Purchase*

"Lesley Krueger has created a marvellous character in Jesse Barfoot, who lights up this fast-paced novel about the startling burdens of youth and age." —Elizabeth Hay, Giller Prize–winning author of *Late Nights On Air*

"[A] powerfully seductive novel about innocence and war."
—Michelle Berry, award-winning author

"Masterful." —*Ottawa Citizen*

"[Lesley Krueger] has perfectly captured the laconic tone of an intelligent teen who can still offer moments of bracing lucidity and keen observation." —*The Globe and Mail*

"A deftly written novel about the parallel loneliness and sordidness of both adolescence and old age." —*Winnipeg Free Press*

"A finely told, patiently unravelled tale of self-examination and self-discovery." —*The Hamilton Spectator*

"A novel rich in history, politics, and philosophy and one that wrestles with issues of displacement, identity and guilt, *The Corner Garden* blossoms slowly into a stunning flower . . . subtle, complex and worth attending to." —*Canadian Literature*

# MAD
# RichArd

## LESLEY
## KRUEGER

ECW PRESS

Published by ECW Press
665 Gerrard Street East
Toronto, Ontario, Canada, M4M 1Y2
416-694-3348 / info@ecwpress.com

LIBRARY AND ARCHIVES CANADA
CATALOGUING IN PUBLICATION

Krueger, Lesley, author
Mad Richard / Lesley Krueger.

Issued in print and electronic formats.
ISBN 978-1-77041-356-6 (paperback)
Also issued as: 978-1-77090-985-4 (pdf)
978-1-77090-984-7 (epub)

I. TITLE.

PS8571.R786M33 2017    C813'.54
C2016-906343-7    C2016-906344-5

Editor for the press: Susan Renouf
Cover images: *Portrait of a Young Man*, 1853, Richard
Dadd (1817–1886). Photo © Tate, London 2016.
Bequeathed by Ian L. Phillips 1984, accessioned 1992

The publication of *Mad Richard* has been generously supported by the Canada Council for the Arts, which
last year invested $153 million to bring the arts to Canadians throughout the country, and by the Government
of Canada through the Canada Book Fund. *Nous remercions le Conseil des arts du Canada de son soutien. L'an
dernier, le Conseil a investi 153 millions de dollars pour mettre de l'art dans la vie des Canadiennes et des Canadiens
de tout le pays. Ce livre est financé en partie par le gouvernement du Canada.* We also acknowledge the support
of the Ontario Arts Council (OAC), an agency of the Government of Ontario, which last year funded 1,737
individual artists and 1,095 organizations in 223 communities across Ontario for a total of $52.1 million, and
the contribution of the Government of Ontario through the Ontario Book Publishing Tax Credit and the
Ontario Media Development Corporation.

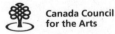

PRINTED AND BOUND IN CANADA        PRINTING: MARQUIS   5   4   3   2   1

RECYCLED
Paper made from
recycled material
FSC
www.fsc.org    FSC® C103567

*Imagination is a strong, restless faculty, which claims to be heard and exercised: are we to be quite deaf to her cry, and insensate to her struggles? When she shows us bright pictures, are we never to look at them, and try to reproduce them? And when she is eloquent, and speaks rapidly and urgently in our ear, are we not to write to her dictation?*

~ Charlotte Brontë

# Bethlem Royal Hospital,

London

*January 20, 1853*

They were bringing the final inmate to the superintendent's office. Mad Richard Dadd the murderer, escorted
from the criminal ward.

Charlotte was already rattled by her visit to the ward for
female lunatics. The shouts and cackles. The sour schoolroom
smell of potatoes, damp woollens, small sins and greater fears.
Many of the inmates were former governesses like herself,
familiar-looking women dressed in uniforms who stood or sat
or paced in a long gallery furnished with workaday tables. She
knew none of them but recognized the type. One freckled
girl pursed her lips and swanned her neck, satirizing an old
mistress the way Charlotte and her sisters had often done at

home. A wire-haired woman shouted loud rhythmic opinions about the Queen, the Queen. No one paid attention to anyone else, and the uncurated noise was discordant.

"Do the mending," one scolded Charlotte as she walked by.

"I don't think I shall," she replied.

"She doesn't think she shall! She doesn't think she shall!"

Screams of over-loud laughter. Sly gazes pecking at her.

Now the door to the superintendent's office opened with a shush, making Charlotte scramble to her feet. Superintendent Hood and her friend Dr. Forbes leapt up just as quickly. An attendant came in, and behind him a man her age, or perhaps a little younger, thirty-five or six.

The famous murderer wore his Bethlem flannels and brown hair down to his collar. When he got closer, she saw pale blue eyes. They said Richard Dadd had been remarkably handsome when he was young, the most promising of his friends, affectionate and modest, an artist of rare talent. Now he considered himself to be a follower of the Egyptian god Osiris, who had ordered him to kill the Devil or devils, which unfortunately had embodied themselves in mortal men.

Dadd's pale eyes frightened her. Charlotte hadn't stopped being frightened since she'd arrived, almost bolting at the gates when she'd realized that she would indeed be entering Bedlam. Yet she was capable of doing what she intended, even though she often knew, as she watched herself do it, that she was making a hash.

"Here you are, Dadd," said Dr. Hood. The superintendent was young for his position, about thirty. Vigorous—evangelical—a reformer of asylums. "You've met Dr. Forbes," he went on, nodding at his fellow physician. "Now he's brought a friend, an author who wished to pay us a visit. Currer Bell, shall we say? Perhaps you'll end up famous, Dadd, if she writes you up in a book."

"It was felt that Currer Bell was a pen name," Dadd said. His words came slowly, but he spoke like a gentleman. "Some indeed speculated that the author was female."

"As you see," she replied, surprised he would recognize the name.

"We bring in magazines," Dr. Hood said, in some pride. He had done that. He had unchained the inmates and decorated the common wards with plants, sculptures, cages full of songbirds. She wouldn't have chosen caged birds herself.

"Shall we sit?" Dr. Forbes asked, and the doctors took their seats. Dadd continued to stand and met her eye.

"The author of *Jane Eyre*," he said. "I wonder if you're here to admit the madwoman in your attic."

He chuckled gently and sat down.

These were the positions Charlotte put herself in. Feeling flustered, graceless and belligerent, she took her seat too long after the others. Her feet didn't quite reach the ground, an absurdly tiny woman in a room used by men. The air smelled of cigars and power. She had no idea how to proceed.

"So you've read the novel then, Dadd?" Dr. Forbes asked.

Both doctors spoke to the madman as if he were a child, although a precocious one. They had placed Dadd's art around the room, paintings he'd done in Bedlam that were based on a tour he'd made of the Holy Land a dozen years before. Shown alongside them were several recent watercolours. King Richard the Second. Robin Hood.

Dr. Forbes had told her that Dadd had been a prize pupil at the Royal Academy, where her brother had aspired to study. But Branwell had never shown anything approaching Dadd's

3

talent. He hadn't even been as accomplished a madman, only threatening murder, and dying of opiates, self-pity and lungs.

Charlotte felt herself vibrate like a trapped sparrow. Governesses in the lunatic ward—madwomen in the attic— her brother's failure before her once again. At night, she was sometimes so torn with longing for the dead she thought that she was mad herself.

She wasn't. She could see that here. Nor was she callous enough for the public life of a writer, forced to tour the enervating sights of the capital by her friends and her own unsettling ambition. Her latest novel was about to be published and she had to start planning the next one. She also had to think about a proposal of marriage she'd received. She loved another man, but her love was beginning to look unrequited. The outside world was a chilly and confusing place. She should probably stop trying and stay home.

Charlotte became aware that Dadd was stuttering as if embarrassed. "D-d-don't read novels," he said.

"A copy of the classics always in hand, eh Dadd?" the superintendent joked.

Without any sign of humour, Dadd pulled a small volume from his jacket pocket and held it up. Juvenal, she saw. The satirist.

Dr. Hood looked even more jolly. "Right you are, Dadd. Juvenal and Shakespeare." He was so supercilious she could scarcely bear it.

"Does being here help you concentrate on your painting?" she asked.

Dadd laughed, a sudden loud burst. "No distractions. Only the distracted," he said, and gave her a slyly intelligent glance.

"This is very awkward, isn't it?" Charlotte asked. "I'm awkward with strangers. I wish I wasn't."

"What do you want to know?" he asked. "How I did it?"

"*No,*" she answered, and struggled a little. She wanted to know whether he'd enjoyed murder, and when he'd first felt himself to be different from his friends. But Charlotte could see that the superintendent wished her to step away from the subject and couldn't muster the bravery to disappoint him.

"More," she said, "your philosophy of art."

Dadd brightened. He walked over to one of his watercolours, the Robin Hood. When he stood beside it, Charlotte could see that his Robin was a self-portrait in doublet and hose.

"I am of the opinion that there is a great deal that is secret in the matter of art," he said, "and that it is explained by one's own second self—which is perhaps as obstinate and vicious a devil as we could desire to oppose. Few can overcome it, hence the dissatisfaction one feels with one's work. There is confirmation of this in the church ritual which says, 'If we say we have no sin, we deceive ourselves.' I believe a strong genius is most likely antagonised by a strong beast or devil." He leaned toward her confidentially. "That is a secret worth knowing."

The two doctors exchanged a glance, but Charlotte said, "I've often wondered where talent comes from. I believe what you say. I believe that each artist is a divided soul. We poor sinners carry whatever talent we have like a burden. But where on earth does it come from?"

"On earth?" he asked sceptically, and touched the painting. She had already noticed that the Robin Hood was a double portrait. The second figure in the composition, perhaps meant to be Friar Tuck, had Dadd's face as well. When she'd looked at it earlier, she'd thought he must have lacked for models and been forced to use the same man twice. Now she was intrigued. Forgetting herself, Charlotte kicked down from her chair and joined him.

"The double nature of human beings was known to the ancient Greeks," Dadd said, touching first one figure and then the other. "The genius was as familiar to them as Christ is with us. The two *intrinsic* natures, you see, were supposed to be always contending for mastery, and after death they were weighed, although art was usually tried in the balance and found wanting. I have somewhere seen reference to this doctrine being well understood also by the Egyptians, as one sees in their paintings."

Mentioning the Egyptians seemed to excite him, and he bounced on the balls of his feet.

Dr. Hood said cheerfully, "No Egyptians, Dadd. Miss Brontë has no interest in Egyptians."

A slip, as Dadd understood instantly.

"Mr. Bell and Miss Brontë. Misses Brontë and Bell." He grew so excited, the attendant loomed up behind him.

"I'm sorry," Charlotte said, touching Dadd's hand, which was broad and fleshy. He looked down as if he considered her touch polluted and pulled away fastidiously. But he was calmer now and went to stand behind his chair.

"My views and those of society are at variance." He spoke with dignity. "My convictions differ from those of other men, and they don't care to make allowances for my views as I do for theirs."

"I'm not sure authors would have anything to write about if everyone agreed," Charlotte said. "Or painters to paint, I suppose."

6

Dadd took her point and gave a shy, confiding smile.

"Once, I was interested in layers," he said. "The layered personality. Layers. Of layers. But that is a, it is a mistake. Doubling. Duality. That's the ticket to, to . . ."

He lost the thread and began humming oddly. When he started to rock backward and forward, Dr. Forbes stood up.

"Perhaps our interview is over," he said. "Thank you, Hood, for your time."

Dadd gave her a look of disappointment. More than that. There was something like agony behind his pale eyes. He's *lonely*, she thought, and wondered why that surprised her.

"I have heard your paintings were once exhibited," she said. "Perhaps they shall be again."

"And perhaps not," Dr. Hood said quickly. "Perhaps they won't leave the asylum, to be pawed over and gawked at."

Dadd ignored the doctor and shambled to his canvases, trying to gather himself.

"Some painters," he said, "the few, perhaps, achieve renown and substantial rewards in their time. Others lag behind. It is with them as with the poets." He gave her a quick, keen glance. "You have read of the poets' feast in Juvenal?"

"I have," Charlotte said, and he fumbled out his tattered volume.

"The rich dishes went to the top of the table," he said, as if she hadn't spoken. "Those at the bottom had to be contented with dry bread. Much of what Juvenal wrote has its counterfeit presentment with us in the nineteenth century. As well as poets, he talks of windows 'barred.' Could it be that there were also madhouses then?"

"I should imagine," Charlotte replied. "Yes, I think you must be right."

"It is not what I intended," he told her.

"What was not?" Charlotte asked. Now she was entirely the clergyman's daughter, hoping to hear the remorse they told her Dadd had never expressed for his crimes.

"What was not?" Charlotte urged. "Please tell me."

But Dadd didn't answer, and the doctor led Charlotte out the door.

# Chatham, Kent

*Where Richard Dadd Was Born on August 1, 1817*

H is oldest memory was of window glass. He was straining to hold himself up, his elbows on the sill, he was that small. He wanted to stare at the green edge of the pane. The window was clear to see through, but where the edge of the glass met the old white frame, it turned mint green. He tried to lick it but couldn't reach, no matter how hard he strained.

A nother memory came from the woods. He didn't know how big he had been, but it came back to him each time he went into Cobham Park, and it had been coming back for a very long time. His boots were kicking through fallen brown leaves, making a rustling papery sound. It was a warm winter day, and the leaves were bright with sunlight shining through a spider's web of branches. A hawk cried above him, and Richard caught something out of the corner of his eye.

It was the hawk's winged shadow flowing across the forest floor in a swift line up the bank. The shadow wheeled for a moment on top of the fallen leaves, jumping as it reached a clod of earth. Then it flowed further up the hill, jerked over a tree stump and disappeared.

N ow Richard was ten years old and hiding in the marshes of the Medway. They were playing Prisoner: a convict escaped from the prison hulks in the river was being pursued by the Army. He was the convict, and sometimes he stayed hidden for a very long time until the others grew bored and stopped looking. When all was quiet, he would sneak back to the hawthorn and tag himself free, and someone else would have to play convict the next time.

They had been given a half-day holiday from the King's School in Rochester, and he'd gone home before commencing Prisoner to leave his top hat on the nail, afraid that it might otherwise get soiled. His father was particular about his top hat, and Richard didn't like to disappoint him.

He also insisted on being called Richard since Dick Dadd sounded like a yahoo. He was named after his mother's father, Richard Martin, and his mother's grandfather, Richard Martin, and all the Richard Martins back into history for nine hundred years. He had the Martin nose, which was repeated all over the Medway, in Chatham Martins and Rochester Martins, Rainham Martins, Gillingham and Gad's

Hill Martins, the same small workable nose on uncles, aunts, cousins and sisters, although his two elder brothers were more in the Dadd line, with a crick.

At the moment, his nose smelled weedy, rank, dungeon water as he crouched close to the sodden ground. Someone was coming, crashing through the bristling reeds, threatening to find him.

"I know you're in here, toad."

His brother Stephen. He crashed so close that Richard could hear him breathe through a thin curtain of reeds. Slowly he rose to a crouch, ready to spring the second his brother spotted him. But luck was with him, and Stephen veered into the marsh, splashing further and further away until his insults grew distant and half-hearted.

"Slime boots!" he swore. "Frog eater!"

Still holding his crouch, Richard skulked toward the hayfield that grew almost to the edge of the marsh, the hay tall and ready for harvest. He had to get home to the hawthorn tree. Stephen wouldn't give up, his ears ready to pick up his rustle, his feet aching to race. Stephen never gave up. He was a dogged, Dadd-nosed bloodhound of a boy, a year older than Richard and soon to be apprenticed, perhaps to an uncle. His reliability meant that more than one uncle had agreed to take him, although Stephen had a secret side, a talent for mimicry almost as good as the players at the Theatre Royal. He could do their grandfather Martin, an ancient shipwright sitting by the fireside whose occasional cry of "And oh the Musselman" puffed from him like pipe smoke.

Richard would not be a tradesman, unlike Stephen and their elder brother, Bob, who was fourteen and already apprenticed to their father, learning to be a chemist and apothecary under their father's sign of the Golden Mortar. They had uncles throughout the Medway practising as chemists and dentists and apothecaries. From what Richard overheard, theirs was a comfortable trade in towns quartered by His Majesty's Army and Navy, with battalions of the King's ragged men jingling through the door all day long, pounds and shillings cascading from their pockets as they begged to be cured of the pox.

But Richard would be a gentleman rather than a comfortable tradesman, which was why his father had entered him as a scholar at the King's School in Rochester. Their family sometimes produced gentlemen, with his father's older brother a naval surgeon, deceased, and a pair of Martins educated as physicians. His father himself was becoming well known for his lectures on geology, and for digging in coal pits and quarries: Robert Dadd, Esquire. Some cockletops laughed at him and issued pamphlets against the museum that made his father's tall forehead go sweaty. Richard didn't suppose he wished to be a physician, but from what he overheard, they thought he was more clever than most chaps. Sometimes his father spoke of Richard being an artist, although his grandfather Richard Martin believed that was a pig in a poke, so there was no telling what would happen really.

For the moment, however, Richard was a convict charged with getting home. Now that Stephen had crashed out of hearing, Richard skulked to the edge of the reeds, scanning the muddy open space he had to cross before he could find more cover in the hayfield. No one and nothing was nearby, and he stepped out easily.

"Flushed!" cried a Tull-like voice.

Piercen Tull rose from the reeds, his face as round as the harvest moon. Startled, Richard turned to meet a pair of small blue

12

eyes half-lost in a pair of freckled cheeks. Not that he was worried. He could beat Fatty Tull any day of the week. Then Tommy Tull popped up beside him: Fatty's small, scurrying, big-eared brother, who stuck to Fatty like a tick. When Tommy bared his teeth, Richard turned, dashing into the hayfield, ducking and twirling a path through the hay, his boots squelching, throwing droplets of water onto the hard-baked ground.

An old cart creaked in pain. "Yuh devil!" a man bellowed. Ahead of them, a farmer was dancing on his cart, fists raised like Jove raining down thunder. When he lowered one arm, the farmer pointed at Fatty, who was crashing through the hayfield behind him, battering a wide swath, breaking the hay like a clumsy, big-kneed, splay-footed heifer. Coursing along beside him was the *rustle, rustle, rustle* of a human rat. Tommy Tull was coming on fast, leaving his brother behind him.

Richard sneezed as he ran. Sneezed again, his eyes squinting shut. When they opened, he saw light up ahead. Bursting free of the hay, vaulting the hedgerow, he tore up the grassy hill toward the hawthorn, boots pounding like a horse's hooves. Glancing back, he saw Tommy Tull just behind him, running with his head thrown back, arms swirling like a windmill.

Sprinting the last few feet, Richard swiped the hawthorn, yelling, "Olly olly oxen free!" Safe now, and feeling sweated, he stopped and arched his back, hands on his waist, trying to get his air.

Tommy Tull had slowed down the instant he yelled, and only ambled up to the hawthorn. Fatty laboured up behind him, breathing as noisily as a bellows, *grunt, haw, grunt, haw*. Stephen joined them from the other side of the hill, and for a while they all kicked dirt at the hawthorn, shaking the last of the marsh water from their shoes. It was a beautifully warm dry day, big clouds billowing across the sky like the cleanest of laundry. They could kick down a mountain of dirt, shake away an ocean of water, left free to roam to the four corners of the known world. Rainham. Gillingham. Chatham. Brompton. Even Gravesend, if they felt a need.

Except—Richard was beginning to sense that his afternoons wouldn't always be this free. Sometimes he could glimpse a door half-open in the distance, a deep room behind it he would soon have to enter. Above the door, a sign solemnly read, *Richard Dadd, Whatever He Shall Be*.

"Perhaps we might go to the rope house?" Stephen asked, as someone usually did. Richard shook his head to clear it and looked overhead. It was near five o'clock by the sun. In silent agreement, the four of them walked over the hill and down again. They would try to breach the rope house at His Majesty's great dockyard, with its rasp of saws audible up and down the Medway, its throbbing hammers and the *thump, thump* of pile drivers. Someone in the family might get them inside, a Dadd or Martin, even a Tull—the Tulls also being family. Grandfather Richard Martin's mother had been a Tull, and a Tullish cowlick, like Fatty's and Tommy's, occasionally shot up on a Martin. It kept them close, made them rough allies, as did the fact that Fatty and Tommy had lost their mother at about the same time as Richard and Stephen, although they'd won that particular contest: the Tulls didn't have a stepmother in her place.

"Baker's bull-dogs, Giles's cats, New-road scrubbers, Troy Town rats."

Fatty started up the chant as he crossed the stile at the bottom of the hill and jumped onto the high road, the rhyme being a list of the Medway's principal educational establishments. The Tulls were students of Baker's school and proud to come first on the list, although Richard politely never commented on the fact that none rivalled the King's School in Rochester. Baker's boys were also particular rivals of Giles's and—teetering at the top of the stile—Richard now saw what Fatty had seen. A white-hatted pupil from Giles's school was ambling down the high road toward them, kicking a stone, left foot, right. As the hat got closer, Richard recognized a scant young Boyes beneath it. They went in for scantiness in the Boyes family.

"Baker's bull-dogs, Giles's cats, New-road scrubbers, Troy Town rats!"

This time they all called it, shouting a challenge. Fists clenched, they stood by the side of the road, waiting for the mouse-haired Boyes to look up. But the Boyes only swerved as he passed them, kicking his stone and keeping his eyes tied to it. Richard looked away in disgust—then did a double-take, spying a length of rope on the verge that would be a useful weapon against stray cats and rabid dogs, pirates and convicts and sailors.

"That's mine," he said, forgetting all Boyeses. Remembering instead, as he bent to pick up the rope, that he'd got a beating that morning from old Reverend Warner of the King's School. Luckily, nobody had seen him wince, although the only one ever likely to have noticed was his mother.

As they strutted down the road, victorious over Giles's, Richard tried to remember his mother. The clink of shipyard hammers sounding in the distance reminded him of the time she had taught him how to light the tinderbox; how she'd brought out the large round tin, which was scruffy inside with rags burnt down to tinder. On top of them were the flint and the clinking piece of steel, formerly part of a horseshoe.

Closing his eyes, he could feel his mother cupped warmly behind him, a sun on his back. She'd taken his hand to show him how to strike the flint edgeways on the steel, and he tried so many times for a spark, they seemed to crouch inside a stench of metal. Finally one of his sparks caught tinder and made a pretty flame. His mother reached behind herself, pushing him forward with her hard round stomach so she could bring out a bundle of matches, each long strip of wood ending in a diamond point she let him touch, scratching at its sulphurous dip of brimstone.

Her hand was over his as she helped him angle the match tip into the tinder flame, and the sulphur sparked to life. Now she had him lean forward to light the kitchen fire, the kindling catching under the logs and crackling as merrily as Sunday's roast. He felt a wizard, doing all that, and could still remember her turned cheek, her smile, her chin and a clean waft of lavender.

Perhaps if she were still with them, his father would already have come to some conclusion about what manner of gentleman Richard would be. His sister Mary Ann said that stepmothers were a distraction, especially one that was a by-blow used by her father as a nursemaid for his legitimate children. His brother Bob had told him not to listen to Mary Ann: their stepmother's parents might have married outside the parish. Not that it was Mary Ann's fault for complaining; these things were worse for sisters. Boys had their fathers and they were all right. Richard imagined that he was all right, although he didn't always feel it, not when the wind howled off the Kentish hills at night and there was no one to sing it away. Even worse were the times when he could scarcely remember what his mother looked like, only her cheek turned aside, although she was supposed to have been a typical Martin. Mary Ann Martin, that was.

A chain clattered down, as loud as a rock slide. They were

16

almost at the dockyard gate, shouts ringing through it, and the long pained whinny of an overloaded horse. A Redcoat stood guard, stiff and silent in his sentry box. Richard was chuffed to recognize the curly haired, freckle-nosed, thick-headed guard who had believed them before when they claimed to be bringing a message for their uncle, and might be convinced again.

Yet between Richard and the guard box was trouble: a fearsome knot of harlots idling there until quit time, frowsy girls in dirty frocks whom the guard should already have ordered away.

"Babes in a wood!" one girl cried, pointing at them rudely. She was a lank-haired piece in linsey-woolsey, one round black eye canted toward them like a gull. The other harlots screeched at her wit, turning and jostling each other, all frayed ribbons and grime. Some of them he recognized, some he didn't. They flowed in and out of town on the tide.

"I knows *them*," another one called, a brown-eyed harlot, tattered in blue. Richard knew her just as well. She was a familiar sight in the alleyways and hayricks, where they had once watched her drunkenly snore away a morning.

"What, them little fuds?" another jeered.

"Got snails up their trousers, an't they?" the tattered one asked, reaching a grubby hand toward Richard. "Want me to stretch out them snail 'orns, little man?"

"Go on. It's slugs," her friend chaffed, shouldering in. "It's slugs, it is. They got little white slugs in them shorty pants."

"Got whelks."

"Got cockles."

"They got peri-*winklers*."

A raw-boned ginger-head lifted her skirts, dancing toward them like a basket of soiled laundry.

"We got oysters. Buy me fine oysters," she cried, the others howling behind her.

"They don't know what we got, Meery," one shrieked, although Richard believed that he did, having sisters. The thought of what they had down there glinted like rainbows on a greasy tide slapping, slapping, slapping ashore. He didn't like the feeling. Stomach clenched, Richard started edging the others toward the sentry, taking charge as he did whenever it was needed.

Beside him, Stephen began to mimic the harlots under his breath. Sloogks, one of them had said, not sounding local. Fuds, Richard didn't even know what that meant. Peri-winklers. As Stephen muttered, the ginger-head seemed to hear, raising her chin at Stephen.

"Wasn't he cheeky? Weren't they all cheeky little beggars, weren't they just?"

"Peri-winklers," Fatty taunted, picking it up. "Sloogks. Velks. Hoo-ers."

With a jeer, a dark-haired girl threw her patten at Fatty, hitting it off his soft round belly so it fell with a clatter in the road. After staring at it for a thoughtful moment, Fatty began to unbutton his trousers.

"Ho! He's going to piss on it, Fan! He's going to piss on yer patten."

Suddenly the harlots were chasing them, the whole be-smattered oyster-ish flock, Tommy snatching the harlot's patten and holding it up like a trophy as they ran.

"Drop that filthy thing!" Richard cried, scared that it had the pox and Tommy would get a contagion. As they raced uphill toward the fort, Tommy pirouetted into the air with rare grace and threw the patten back at the harlots. He was ace at cricket, and as Richard stopped to admire Tommy's throw, the patten made a confusion among the girls, half of them fighting over it, carolling and screeching as a platoon of soldiers pounded out of the fort, *hup-hup-hup*, the first pack of Redcoats herding the screeching harlots back downhill, the second shooing the boys over the crest, so that soon enough, they were sitting in their uncle William Martin's fruitery near Rainham, eating pears.

E arly that evening, trailing back along Chatham High Street, dog-tired and baked by the sun, Richard switched his bit of rope as he passed the Mitre Tavern, where his father sometimes took a cup, switched it again as he passed the printing shop, where Mr. Dadson gave him drawing lessons, and coiled it up before entering his father's shop, where the bell jangled.

"There he is," said his bright-eyed father, who was wiping his counter. He looked over Richard's shoulder as the door slipped closed. "Where's your brother?"

Richard shrugged and slumped onto a high stool at the counter, breathing in the happily caustic scent of unguents and soap and powder with an undertone of cigars. He lay his head on his arms to look up at his father. He saw a few new wiry grey hairs leaping out of the brown to quiver like a halo in the lamplight.

"What have you been up to?"

Again Richard shrugged.

"No lesson with Mr. Dadson?"

"Tomorrow."

"He was under the impression it was today."

"And tomorrow, he'll be under the impression it's Friday," Richard said, before remembering himself and levering up on his elbows. "Sir."

His father only chuckled. "Don't you wish to continue?"

"Yes, I do, rather. Once he gets going, I like it."

"Excellent," his father said, screwing open a jar to give him some taffy. "And what did you see today that you might draw?"

Richard couldn't contain an explosion of air through his nose. Taking the taffy, he grinned up at his father.

"Some strumpets chased us, and one threw her shoe at Fatty, and Tommy Tull picked it up and waved it, and I said, 'Throw that filthy thing away. You'll get a contagion of pox.'"

It was half a question, whether Tommy would really get a contagion that would make his pizzle fall off. But his father only laughed, leaving Richard to slump down again and play the taffy across the counter with his index finger, wondering if adults ever answered your questions, and why they didn't, and how things happened.

"I can't leave yet," his father said, watching him play with the taffy. "You should probably go above. Your mother will be waiting."

*That isn't my mother.* But Richard only made himself shrug again and popped the taffy in his mouth, as his father cleaned the counter, round and round.

# 15 Suffolk Street,
# Pall Mall East, London
*Where Richard Dadd Went to Live in 1834*

A painted dog wasn't precisely like a dog, old Dadson had taught his students back in Chatham. There were conventions, especially in landscapes where dogs were seen at a distance. They should be brown or black, so they didn't pull the eye. They were on their hind legs, with their front paws raised in a way to suggest capering, since art feigned movement. Leaves, dogs, sheep, shepherds: if they looked static, they lay on the paper, as flat as a dead eye.

Now, after more than two years in London, Richard looked down at the mark made by his dropped brush. And hadn't it left the body of a Dadson dog near the edge of his board? Smiling to himself, he added capering legs, hearing again the voice of his first teacher, a West Kent man. *Flut us uh dud oye.*

"What's funny?" Frith asked, getting up to look at his board. His new friend, William Frith. They'd got together to paint in oils, as probationary students at the Royal Academy weren't supposed to, laying out a still life in the Dadd family sitting room. Frith had got nervous and taken out his chalk instead, but Richard didn't care so much about the dicta and prepared his brushes. On the small round table between them were some carefully arranged fossils, a shark's skull, a glass of ruby-red wine that both Frith and Richard kept eying and an old dug-up vase of dried grasses, *nature trés morte.*

"Funny?" Richard answered. "The permeability of time."

"A pronouncement!" Frith cried, before frowning at Richard's dog. "Hardly backed by the performance."

A scrabbling at the door, and his sister's guinea pig hesitated into the room, halting and snuffling, halting and snuffling. Richard's sisters were home, then; the beast freed from its cage. Frith started when he saw it, knocking the nautiloid fossil onto the floor. Screaming, the guinea pig clawed a circle in the parquet like a terrified dog. His father's canaries flapped from their perches, making a dull sound of battered air until the guinea pig finally found its footing, discovered the door and skittered back out.

Not a pig and not from Guinea. A rodent his sister brought back after visiting a girl in Hampstead, he believed.

Ready to apologize for the Daddsian fuss, Richard couldn't help smiling at the expression on Frith's face: the astonished eyes arguing with the polite mouth. He would have to remember facial arguments, and picked up a piece of paper to get it down. Richard had noticed that Frith, being raised in his father's hotel at Harrogate, was less used to encountering drama than the aftermath of drama, or clues to drama. He'd talked about the woman's rags found discarded in what was supposed to be a boy's room; the suicides—surprisingly frequent; the respectable banker arriving with his humdrum wife, then arriving with an entirely different humdrum wife two months later, then again with the humdrum first.

This might lie behind the stasis in Frith's sketches, in pencil and in chalk: the sense of held breath, the lack of living glimmer. Richard offered limited critiques, treatment only, never voicing his diagnosis. *Might you try a touch of white here?* he would ask. He was sure Frith would become what he wanted, but Billy had a row to hoe yet.

The two had become fast friends in January, three months before, when both had entered the Royal Academy Schools as probationers. Frith was a raconteur; Richard the more jokey, more observant and more talented, everybody said. He always sloughed off comments like that, and stopped his father from saying a word, but as he looked around the other probationers—more than just Frith—Richard told himself it was probably true, which was a challenge and a burden, as well as a secret delight.

What he didn't know yet was how he would apply his talent, life being a series of decisions, he was finding, each one increasingly refined. Yes, he would be an artist, and yes, he'd be a painter in oils rather than a sculptor, and no, not of miniatures, although old Dadson had taught him the technique, and of course he would be madly popular, as would Frith, neither of them as crabbed and eccentric as the established RAs, the Royal Academicians who bored them to death with formal lectures.

Richard hadn't got any further than that, even though he'd already exhibited two wet efforts at the Society of British

Artists down the street. His father was behind that, calling on his connections there. His father wanted more than Richard had in him yet, observing his career a little too closely, monitoring his investment.

Unfair to even think that, Richard knew.

"But what do you mean?" Frith said after a silence, even while working away. "How can time be permeable?"

"I was only thinking of the way the past bleeds into the present," Richard said. "What we've been taught as children always animating what we do now. The past never being past and all that."

"Much more interesting if you could prove that the future bleeds into the present," Frith said. "What's going to happen influencing what does. But perhaps that's a bit too mystical for Englishmen."

"Perhaps for most," Richard said. "Although my father's Unitarian."

As his friend laughed, Richard tossed his sketch aside, thinking about the masterpieces he'd seen at Lord Darnley's estate at Cobham Park. He had haunted the collection from the time he'd left the King's School, entry permitted when the family wasn't in residence. In his naivety, Richard had told his father that one of the reasons he liked seeing the paintings was that they showed him the Holy Land where Jesus had walked. His father had smiled and told him that what he was seeing behind the Mother and Child was not Galilee but more likely the view out the painter's window of the Venetian countryside.

"Sixteenth-century Venice," Richard repeated to Frith. "The future bleeding into depictions of the past, not into the past itself."

"Which is why the old-style historical paintings are bankrupt," Frith said. "And why we're going to be different."

Another decision, made with the rest of their new friends, Harry O'Neil and John Phillip and the resplendently named Augustus Egg. They met almost daily in the cast rooms and hallways of the Royal Academy, all of them scruffy aspirants, their hopes, their words, their boasts tumbling over each other like puppies. Frith was their engine of ambition; Richard the glue, their hope, their leader. Impossible to depict the past as it had truly been lived, they agreed, despite what the old guard claimed. So why bother trying? The landscape and portraits and literary subjects they would paint were infinitely more dynamic, a moment brought into focus, if also subtly layered with what had always been true, the present implying the past as one strove for the universal.

Or in the case of literary subjects, as Richard had said recently, on the National Gallery steps, "In the case of Shakespeare and so on, the reverse. The eternal revealing the present. Our present day."

The air was clear that morning after an early March rain, the sun glittering off the gallery's brass doorplates and Egg's highly polished boots, a rare clarity of London light that made Richard think of trips to the Medway chalk pits with his father.

"Rather like the layers in limestone," he added.

"I would call it duality," said Egg, the most educated among them and the most gentle, dark and slight and rich. "One wishes to suggest the past in the present," he said, "and the mystical in the everyday. Depth, not surface."

"But how on earth do you do that?" Frith asked. "I'm speaking of technique."

"Texture. Tone. Chiaroscuro," Egg proposed, starting out bold and trailing into uncertainty.

Behind them, a slow presence emerged from the gallery doors.

"Turning, they saw Turner," Richard murmured. The old man shuffled into the sunlight, short, blinking and irascible. Joseph Mallord William Turner, RA, their occasional lecturer, the venerated master of the sublime and unfocused, someone else they planned not to emulate.

"Explicating. Talking. *Nattering*," Turner said, looking up briefly as he passed. "One does that when young."

Richard was proud of his friends, sufficiently well bred to hold their laughter while the old man shuffled down the steps and out of hearing. Then they broke into guffaws.

"Palimpsests," Egg tried to go on. "Palimpsests," he insisted loudly until they went quiet. "Surely what we're after aren't just reconstructions of the past, but a sense of the past lying under the present. You know. Antique manuscripts scraped and repainted with new layers. Surely that's how one approaches the eternal."

"By scraping?" Richard asked, and paused for their chuckles. "Really, Egg, I insist on layers. You know, or you should. The shell, the white and the yolk."

Groans. Egg's saturnine grin. His finger a pistol aimed at Richard's temple.

*Pop.*


He was thirteen years old the time his father took him to the chalk pit off Berengrave Lane. Richard had left the King's School after yet another flogging from the head-master—and perhaps the memory started there, in the head-master's room, Richard bent over a chair, his trousers down, his bare arse chilly before the cane hit, old Warner walking up behind him. *Snap* and he felt heat instead of pain, and heat, heat, then pain, *snap*, pain. Richard refused to cry, but his traitor knees were trembling.

The Reverend Warner grunted with each stripe, *hunh*, *hunh*. They all knew how much he enjoyed this, *hunh*, the grunt coming up from his vitals even though Richard hadn't done a thing. He had smirked in class, that was all, smirked at what old Warner had said, and now *slash*, *slash*, heat, pain. It was lasting far too long.

A second's indignation and Richard started counting. Pain, one, two, cane goes up. Pause, one, two, then pain.

The next time Warner raised his cane, Richard ducked and made a dash for it, pulling up his trousers as he ran, ankles hampered, half-tripping. Old Warner got hold of his elbow, but Richard jabbed back hard, and dashed if the fucker didn't trip over his feet and tumble over a chair, landing on his clerical knees and making Richard giggle.

Holding up his trousers, he raced out the door, through the classroom and into the garden, bouncing in place as he did up his flies. The boys' noses were pressed against the classroom windows, old Joseph in the garden trimming the lavender, deaf and unmoving, not as deaf as he liked to appear, but deaf at least for now.

Once his flies were secured, Richard was out the gates and into Rochester, and became a boy running as boys ran, swerving around obstacles, adults, until he was safely into the countryside between Rochester and Chatham. Glancing behind him, he saw no pursuit, and doubled over gasping in the middle of the road, his arse beating with pain.

Thunder. Looking up, Richard saw the express bullying toward him. He sprinted aside, pressing against the hedgerow as the horses passed, the swaying carriage, the billow of noise and dust. Afterward, Richard reclaimed the road and limped up Chatham High Street, where soon enough he went inside his father's shop, the bell jangling.

Behind the counter, his father was preoccupied by Mrs. Haberdasher Lambert, a profitable hypochondriac, and gestured Richard toward a stool. Unable to sit, Richard leaned against the wall. His father threw him a glance while dispensing Mrs. Haberdasher Lambert a powder. As the son of a chemist and a King's School scholar, Richard understood both the medical meaning of the adjective "acute," derived from the Latin *acus* for needle, and its secondary use in describing the penetration of an individual who didn't miss a thing.

His acute father observed his acute pain.

The bell jingled a second time as a satisfied Mrs. Haberdasher Lambert left with her powder. His father leaned his elbows on the counter, brows beetling.

"Now, honestly, son, did you deserve it?"

"No, sir. He just likes flogging."

His father beckoned him to the back of the shop, where he lifted Richard's shirt in one fist ready to pull down his drawers.

"But he got you in the kidneys!"

"It hurts like that, please, sir."

"But that's unconscionable!" A moment of silence behind Richard's back, and he added, "I won't be played for a fool."

That afternoon, his father pulled him by the elbow all

the way to Rochester. There he saw Reverend Warner outside the cathedral and steamed toward him like a ship on the
Medway, Richard his dinghy. It was hard for Richard to know
what to feel. There was the pain, and the fact he had not quite
adjusted to changes the architect was making to the cathedral,
the loss of its spire and the change to its profile, which meant
it cast a different shadow than the one his body expected to
be there. That was uncanny, and even though old Warner
didn't frighten him, not very much and not with his father in
front of him, the hair on the back of his neck prickled as they
blocked the headmaster's path.

Without preamble, his father said, "Now really, Warner,
this won't do."

The Reverend Warner looked him over. "I understand, sir,
that you've had a difficult time since losing the second Mrs.
Dadd. But civility remains a virtue and a salve."

In fact, the story of the Berengrave chalk pit might have
started with the death of Richard's stepmother the previous
June, but he didn't like to think about her deathbed, noisy with
screams and odours. His brother Bob had begun referring to
their stepmother as the interregnum, since after their mother's
death, she'd spent four years running the household before
she died herself, at which point their sister Mary Ann reached
the age of sixteen and was able to manage it. In his thirteen
years, Richard had looked first to his mother Mary Ann and
now to his sister Mary Ann, and in between to the late Sophia
Oakes Munk Dadd, who had left Richard with two infant
half-brothers and surprisingly few memories, although she
had once said to him, "The apple of his father's eye can easily
go rotten if he don't take care."

His father answered the Reverend Warner's rebuke with a

satiric bow, although Richard knew that he sincerely mourned his second wife and fretted about the future of his nine motherless children. Richard's brother Stephen had heard him tell their Grandfather Martin that he'd better cut it off than marry again. What in God's name was he was going to do with the nine children he already had?

"But look here," his father went on, before the Reverend Warner could speak. "Beating the boy about the kidneys, that's above and beyond. He voided blood this afternoon. I had to ask the surgeon over to examine him."

This time his father waited for the Reverend Warner to reply and he didn't, looking weasly.

"I wanted my son educated in the King's School and you're running it into the ground. Men removing their boys right and left."

"You're forgetting yourself, Dadd," the Reverend Warner said, with a sudden show of energy. "But then you do, don't you? This museum of yours, these geological lectures, when, in fact, you can boast rather less education than your twelve-year-old son."

"Thirteen," Richard and his father said together, after which his father added, "Then we may consider my boy formally withdrawn from your establishment." Richard didn't quite see the connection but he supposed the gentlemen understood it.

The Reverend bowed. "I will send you notice of your account. Already well in arrears."

"Of course. And I'll send you the bill for Mr. Martin's attendance."

Richard hadn't understood that Mr. Martin would send an account, being family. His head was hurting as much as his arse, trying to understand what was happening between the two men, whose discussion embarrassed him the way he'd been embarrassed by his stepmother haggling over a cabbage at the market fair.

"A surgeon's fee, that's absurd," the headmaster said.

"He thought I was being alarmist until he saw the wounds. His word, not mine."

The red-faced reverend swiped the air, as if clutching for words.

"He saw the *wounds*, sir," his father said. "I'm surprised you have the brass to raise the question of accounts."

That seemed to be their signal to leave. For the second time that day, Richard found himself hurrying across the altered shadow of the cathedral, feeling uncanny but also free, free as a tiger, free as a Medway lark coiling up into the evening sky.

"That took an unexpected turn," his father said. But he sounded satisfied, and stopped in at the baker's to buy a dozen buns for tea.


A week later, they were walking down Rainford Road in the direction of the Berengrave chalk pit, Richard's father having undertaken his education himself. It was a clear May morning, recent showers ended, and they were heading east into a bright sun. In his father's opinion, a boy could choose an acre of ground anywhere in Kent and learn everything from it. Take a spade to a farmer's field and he might dig up a Roman coin stamped with the owl of Minerva—his father had seen one—and this way he would learn that the Romans had settled along the Medway almost two thousand years ago, and that Minerva was the pagan goddess of wisdom, the owl being an eternal symbol of wisdom, and meanwhile conclude that he'd better pursue his study of Latin, not to mention Greek, the knowledge of antique languages being the mark of a gentleman.

Richard already knew these things, but he recognized the fact they constituted an example, and he was happy to follow his father's pleasant lecture down the road.

"Do you hear that?"

His father stopped by some bushes. He whistled up, down. Up, down, mimicking the bird.

"Great tit, sir." Richard still felt larky, freed from school and boredom and flogging. "A teat," he said. "Great teat." Playing a younger boy, and bouncing on his toes as if buttoning his flies. "Teat, teat, bubbies."

"All right, all right."

"It's a silly name. Great tit. Blue tit. Coal tit." And for good measure, "Chiffchaff." Richard felt his voice break and stopped in surprise.

The little birds stopped as well, like candles being snuffed. Richard knew to look up, and picked out a falcon circling.

"Peregrine, sir." Seeing his father's face. "Not this time of year, not here. It has to be a hibby." Correcting himself. "A *hobby* falcon."

"We should consider getting you a spyglass. Or perhaps a gun to take specimens."

"Coal tits the size of my finger." Richard laughed. "Nothing left, I don't think."

"Or a net," his father said. "Then you could draw 'em."

His father thought about this for a moment. "Primarily, you should be drawing," he said, and Richard wondered if this meant he would indeed be an artist. As they walked on, it occurred to Richard that he might have a say in deciding his profession, the way he'd helped decide about the King's School by running away.

"I don't think I should like to be a physician," he said. "Spend all my time around sick people. Or dying."

His father's face went still.

"And I don't particularly care to shoot birds, so I don't think you need purchase a gun. I mean to say, unless you'd like to. I would much rather learn to paint water."

"Water."

"Mr. Dadson says it's terribly difficult to get right. But I think I'd like to."

They turned into Berengrave Lane, where at night four headless horses driven by a headless coachman pulled the carriage of Christopher Bloor as he held his severed head under his arm. The story said he was killed in the lane by men whose wives he'd seduced, and since they'd already been over this, Richard knew his father had no trouble believing in the existence of a local family named Bloor, and didn't see any reason why there couldn't have been a seducer named Christopher who was murdered, more likely by one man than by several. His father even felt it possible that Christopher Bloor's head had been stuck on a pike on the tower of St. Margaret's Church in Rainham at least for the night, the past having been barbarous.

The rest was falderal, an old wives' tale, although if Shakespeare had written a play about Christopher Bloor and his lost head, it would have been elevated to tragedy, Shakespeare having elevated Gad's Hill (where they had family) by choosing it as the place for Falstaff to commit the robbery that began *Henry IV*.

Still, as they walked, Richard crossed one finger over his thumb, not precisely against Christopher Bloor, but because he was thinking of Queen Court. Christopher Bloor rode his carriage down Berengrave Lane from the church to his old residence, always stopping on the way to water his horses in the pond at Queen Court, where the Headless Spinner sat on the roof of the barn. Rainham was a particularly headless place. Crossing your finger and thumb when you thought about Queen Court wasn't strictly necessary, but if you were caught at the pond late at night, you had to cross them on both hands and run past the barn calling, "Saint Margaret, Saint Margaret," making sure you didn't look at the Headless Spinner. If you did, she'd curse you, and one day you would lose your head as well.

Of course, there was a standing dare for boys to go to the pond at night, and once in midsummer Richard had taken it up with Fatty Tull. They'd been brave enough until the sun set, and even when the moon rose ghostly, but when a horse whinnied in the distance and no rider came, they'd known Christopher Bloor was on his way and ran home screaming, "Saint Margaret, Saint Margaret," doubled over like a pair of womblety-cropped Catholics.

On the whole, Richard had enjoyed being terrified. He didn't believe in falderal any more than his father, but without it a boy wouldn't have quite so much fun.

"Analytically," his father said, eying his hand, so Richard uncrossed his fingers. "Analytically, what does it mean to have legends attached to a particular place?"

"I suppose that something happened for the old wives to gossip about. Which means there must have been a Christopher Bloor, and he was murdered."

"Over two thousand years, there have probably been murders on every footpath along the Medway. Why do we remember some and not others? Because," his father said, pausing at the head of the path to the chalk pit, "some places are more important than others. The Berengrave pit was important before recorded time. During the Stone Age, some local denizens would have considered it theirs and others would have tried to rob it, or even fought for its possession."

They were on their way downhill now, under scrubby trees.

"I propose that men died here in robbery or raids, and it would have been in the interest of whoever won the fight to advertise the deaths and arguably their own brutality in order to warn others away from their territory. Cutting off their enemies' heads, you know. Not a man jack wants to lose his. So the ancient Berengrave footpath probably had a dangerous reputation since well before the Romans came. When Christopher Bloor died here, as he arguably did, all the old stories attached themselves to his murder, and he became a warning to stay away from the chalk pit long after the real reason was lost."

Scrambling after his father, Richard mainly heard the word *arguably*. His father's *arguably* had become famous through an anonymous pamphlet about his role as curator of the museum of the Chatham and Rochester Philosophical and Literary Institution, a pamphlet Richard and Stephen had pounced on one evening after their father had laughed too loudly, thrown it on the floor and stalked out to the Mitre Tavern.

". . . which CURATOR," the pamphlet thundered, "possesses a youthful enthusiasm scarcely heard of in a man entered into his forty-second year, his hair now retreated behind his ears by the force of eyebrows permanently raised in astonishment, each day bringing a new Wonder to his sign of the Golden Mortar—a Wonder often carried in the pocket of a seaman newly returned to British shores, who reluctantly agrees to part with his prize in return for a dose of nostrum he hopes will chase away the dose he'd been PRESCRIBED in Taheetee; a Wonder which will soon be entered into the records of the Museum as the fossilized knucklebone of a Houyhnhnm, the pickled nose of a Lilliputian maid and, arguably, the long-lost walking stick of the peripatetic Lemuel Gulliver himself (*arguably* being *arguably* the favourite word of the self-described Gentleman and Mineralogist, ROBERT DADD ESQUIRE)."

"Flint," his balding father said, poking at the face of the pit. "Chalk contains nodules of flint, which the Stone Age tribes used to knap into tools and weapons. Arrowheads and axes. This pit was their armoury. Of course, they would have defended it."

"It's in layers," Richard said. "The chalk."

"Very good. Yes, it was once felt the layers of chalk were leftovers from river drift—layers of sediment laid down in the beds of rivers that changed their courses over time. More recently, it's been proposed that the sediment was, in fact, laid down on sea beds by detritus sinking to the ocean floor. You see what that means, don't you?"

Richard wasn't sure.

"This whole area was once covered by water."

"The Flood," Richard said, getting it. Still examining the layers, he heard a barely perceptible pause from his father, and a change in the timbre of his voice.

"In fact, explorers—even missionaries—are finding that natives around the world tell stories about an ancient flood. What does that say?"

Richard didn't quite understand. "Well, of course, that it happened."

"That a worldwide inundation *arguably* happened, just like Christopher Bloor's murder. The Old Testament story of Noah and his Ark remembers the experience of the Jewish tribes of Israel with what must have been a devastating loss of life. But Noah and his family weren't the only survivors of the Flood, were they? Despite what the Bible says. Other very different tribes all over the world experienced the flood, then picked themselves up and carried on right to the present day. Do you see what I'm saying?"

Richard continued to stare at the chalk face, seeing mainly that his education under his father was going to be very different than it had been under the Reverend Daniel Warner.

"On the one hand, we have a literary interpretation of the historical past in the Old Testament. A myth, as it were. On the other hand, we have geology."

Noah's Ark a myth? Richard's ears prickled like a hare's. His father was a well-known convert to Unitarianism, but he'd never heard him say anything as heretical as this. With any luck, his father wouldn't start saying it publicly, especially in his lectures. He was hugely popular among his backslapping friends and well liked by the common people, but he was already regarded with suspicion by the clergy on Minor Canon Row, and not just old Warner. Educated men called him *jumped-up* for his museum, a *rank materialist* for co-founding the Commercial and Mathematical School and *frankly vulgar* for his fist-pumping support of Reform. When his father stood up at meetings, the gentry would smirk their eyebrows at each other, making Richard shift from one foot to another. He didn't care to be a politician any more than he cared to be a physician. He wanted people to think he was a good chap, no matter who they were.

"See here," his father said, and Richard heard him fumble in his pocket behind him. "Last year, the Scotsman Mr. Charles Lyell published his *Principles of Geology*."

Richard could feel his father offer him the book behind his back. He resisted turning and, when he finally did, found his father looking at him with the abashed, head-ducking expression of a new boy at school wanting to be friends.

"Mr. Lyell estimates the world to be three hundred million years old," his father said shyly, as Richard took the book. "We'll read it together. I could read it for years."

"Does an artist have to be analytical?" Richard asked, examining the spine, the gold lettering.

"An artist should be many things. An artist is *permitted* to be many things." His father looked wistful, then noticed something.

"*There's* luck!" he cried, rapping the chalk with his knuckles. "The edge of an ammonite exposed by the rains. Do you see it?"

Richard did, and they spent the rest of the morning happily chipping out the fossil, his father expounding on Mr. Charles Lyell as the tits sang around them, a hawfinch in the trees, and sparrows, sparrows, sparrows.


The ammonite Richard and Frith were using in their still life was the one he and his father had chiselled out of the Berengrave chalk pit. Before they'd left Chatham, his father had packed up his personal collection and given it to the museum he was leaving behind, the Medway part of their lives over. But he'd been pleased when Richard had asked to keep the ammonite, and allowed the other children to choose keepsakes as well.

Bob's stuffed raven roosted on the top of a cabinet, even though Bob was apprenticed to their uncle Henry Martin in Somers Town and was home only on Sundays. The younger sisters had claimed pretties that Mary Ann grumbled about dusting, probably quite valuable items their father had traded fossils for, a small Greek bust of a lady for Rebecca, and for Maria Elizabeth, an oval Jute brooch neatly framed.

"May I keep the Houyhnhnm's knuckle?" Stephen had asked, and his father's eyebrows pushed his hair back to his collar before he roared with laughter.

"The small-mindedness we're leaving," he said, clapping and clapping Stephen's back as if he'd got something stuck in his throat.

Their father had leased the Golden Mortar so he could buy the Pall Mall water-gilding and framing business from Uncle Picnot, their uncle having decided to run an inn in Leicester Square. Richard had no idea what Uncle Picnot knew about running an inn, aside from being a Frenchman. No more did his harried wife, Aunt Maria, his mother's younger sister.

A bigger puzzle was how his father knew all about framing and water gilding, or perhaps how he'd learned it over the past three years without any appearance of effort.

"Now, see what you've done," Frith said, standing behind Richard.

"Done what?"

"The lighting. The tone. You've made everything darker."

"These things are old. Even wine is old, at least in concept."

"Wine as a concept. You might want to work on that."

"All right," Richard said, reaching for the glass.

"Hey there! I'm not finished!" Frith made a show of batting Richard's hand aside. And then they were sparring, grinning, circling each other, Richard jabbing his fists—jab, jab—Frith jabbing back, both pulling up just shy of contact. They danced around the sitting room. Jab, jab. Jab. As Richard slowly backed him up, Frith stumbled over a foot stool but righted himself and took a swing at Richard.

"An undercut to the gizzard," Richard said, ducking aside.

Outside the door, his younger brothers pounded down the stairs, screaming lustily, their sister Rebecca pounding after them.

"I'll get you!" she cried, as the little boys clattered down to the shop.

"Two-legged hamsters," said Frith, lowering his fists. "Precisely how many Dadds are there?"

"Here?" Richard asked, lowering his. "My oldest brother Bob is apprenticed to our Uncle Harry in Somers Town; you've met him. My younger one, George, stayed in Chatham to apprentice in the shipyards. So nine minus two. The barbarians are the youngest. My step-guineas, Arthur and John. The pig you saw earlier is more of a cousin twice removed."

"All nine living?"

Frith having lost his eldest brother half a dozen years before.

"My father has no idea what he's going to do with the youngers and the sisters."

As Frith nodded thoughtfully, Richard took his chance to grab the glass of wine, salute his friend and drain it.

"Well, you'll be fine, won't you?" Frith asked sardonically, then shook it off and headed back to his chalk.

# The Train Toward Keighley

*February 2, 1853*

C harlotte was relieved to be going home. Visiting Bedlam, the prisons, the Foundling Hospital, the Exchange— doing her tour of institutional London—had left her horri- fied, tender and drained. Her feelings were unusually mixed these days. She liked to think it was a sign of wisdom, but it was probably just middle age.

Looking out the window, she saw a doe course up a frozen hill. A gentleman's residence. The square brick tower of a parish church: a reminder of the latest proposal she had received. Over the years, Charlotte had turned down four pro- posals of marriage, but she couldn't stop thinking about the fourth and latest, despite having been seen off at the station by the man she loved, who had never asked. She had no idea of his intentions, and as the train lurched around a corner, the suffocating heat of the carriage and its jarring thump-thump northward put her on the edge of panic, as if she were trapped inside the palpitations of a fevered heart.

In her new novel, *Villette*, published only days before, Charlotte had done what she knew was a very strange thing, basing one character on the man she loved and another transparently on herself. Charlotte Brontë and George Smith. Lucy Snowe and Dr. John Graham Bretton. Readers would believe through most of the novel that Lucy and Graham would overcome a series of obstacles and marry in the closing chapter. Then Charlotte had done another strange thing, swerving, giving Lucy a new suitor, and meanwhile marrying Graham to an exquisite young lady entirely unlike herself.

Charlotte had mailed George the opening volumes of *Villette* at the end of October. He'd replied enthusiastically, making no reference to the fact Graham was his portrait but asking mildly if Lucy would marry the doctor in the end. Charlotte had written back that she wouldn't, begging an impassioned appeal for the marriage that George hadn't sent. Charlotte had been too busy finishing off the novel to linger on his silence, and consoled herself by assuming he believed she would change her mind. Only after sending him the last pages of the manuscript two weeks later did Charlotte begin to think about the strangeness of what she'd done and wonder what George truly thought.

Post followed post and he didn't reply. Charlotte took up her old habit of walking around her father's dining table in the parsonage, around and around it, wearing an oval into the floor, a channel she could feel cutting through the floorboards, descending so deeply into earth and rock that she was over her head in darkness and didn't see how she would ever get out. She felt trapped, breathless, humiliated—mainly humiliated—and George's eventual reply didn't help. He still didn't say whether he recognized himself in Graham but objected to his character's fictional bride, calling her a namby-pamby, and objected even more that focusing on an alternate suitor for Lucy so late in the story wrecked the shape of the novel.

Charlotte had raised the possibility of a marriage between them as clearly as she could, and George might have answered, *Dearest Charlotte, Graham's loss of Lucy teaches me that I must not lose you.* Instead he criticized her writing.

He had also only offered her five hundred pounds for the copyright of the novel when both Charlotte and her father thought he should have given seven fifty, George Smith being her publisher as well as the object of her affections. He had written to her frequently over the past six years as Smith, Elder & Co. published *Jane Eyre* and her follow-up, *Shirley*, and his letters were personal, even intimate, lighting up her loneliness like Catherine wheels. Now Charlotte wondered if they were only business letters from a publisher trying to jolly a difficult author into writing another book.

George Smith was eight years younger than Charlotte, handsome down to his dimpled chin, and his family was far more prosperous than hers. He couldn't boast her father's education at Cambridge, but he would be a catch for her and he knew it. Re-reading his letter about *Villette* until the creases frayed, she couldn't detect the slightest hint of his feelings as a man. But there was no outright rejection either.

Charlotte knew that George was right, her novel's ending was misshapen. She had started out more or less planning to marry Lucy to Graham, and had seen too late and with a throb of horror how this would look to anyone who recognized the models, or anyone who knew anyone who recognized the models: the whole of literary London, in fact. *Have you read* Villette? *That plain little authoress. She's made poor George Smith* marry *her in print.*

Feeling fevered, Charlotte had switched the focus to Lucy's romance with the foreigner Paul Emmanuel, a double of her French teacher, M. Héger, whom she had loved so hopelessly when she was young. But Constantin Héger remained alive and well in Brussels and just as thoroughly married as he had been when Charlotte had been in love with him. She didn't have the gall to marry him to Lucy either, and left her heroine running a school of her own: a modern woman, fulfilled yet lonely. Charlotte knew her story had lost its symmetry with these swervings, but she couldn't admit this to George, seeing no human way to explain why she'd done what she did.

She also knew it was the better literary decision. Far too conventional to marry Lucy to Graham, or even to fob her off with a foreigner. Charlotte would give every ounce of her success to be conventionally happy, but she also knew the fact she was neither conventional nor happy made her stand out from the crowd—made her famous—and making Lucy just as unconventional gave *Villette* its sole chance of thundering.

Trapped in quiet Haworth, wearing gullies in her father's floor, Charlotte replayed these arguments obsessively, and knew she was going to make herself ill. She decided to go to London, writing George to suggest that she correct the proofs of the novel in place, and hoping that he would say—that she could see—what he truly felt.

C harlotte arrived in Euston Station late one evening at the beginning of January. As the train shuddered to a halt, she let other passengers by her so she could stand at the door of the carriage, needing its height to see over the crowd. Angling her spectacles, she spotted George Smith standing by a pillar. Caught her breath. He was a clothed statue, his trousers of wool almost as fine as his leg and draped provocatively.

George hadn't seen her yet. Charlotte watched him scan the carriages and thought she saw distaste around his mouth. Duty, perhaps. He had a duty to perform. So he knew he was the model for Graham. Of course he did. Charlotte wanted to hide, to flee.

But he had seen her, and gave a forced smile as he pushed past a reuniting family. As he got closer, Charlotte saw a mottled blush rising out of his collar like a rash.

"Here we are." He greeted her with a stiff bow and took her bags so awkwardly he hit one against the carriage door.

Charlotte was always awkward, but she had never seen George less than graceful. She cursed herself for her idiocy in writing about him, for her passion, for what the critics called the coarseness of her novels.

For what she could see from the women of London were her old-fashioned sleeves.

"A pleasant journey, I hope," George said, not quite looking at Charlotte as he helped her onto the station platform. "Except that it never is, really. A supportable journey. As pleasant as these things are capable of being."

"Much like life," she said, and he barked out a genuine laugh, meeting her eye in amusement—and was that admiration?

"I see you've arrived in your usual guise of yourself."

They liked each other. Understood one another. *Let me not to the marriage of true minds admit impediments*, Charlotte thought, gazing up at him. George smiled back warmly, asking in detail about her journey as he beckoned a porter to guide them through the crowd. Outside the station, he won the rush for a cab and half-lifted her inside. It was a dreary winter's night, and as they turned into the road, Charlotte was reminded how noisy London was, the rattle of wheels, the shriek of horses and the high-pitched shouts of the lower orders endlessly selling something or wanting something, like ghosts craving peace. It put Charlotte's nerves up. George was more urbane. As they crossed town, he grew easy, teasing her.

"And the weather in Yorkshire? Is there a polite synonym for dire?"

Soon Charlotte relaxed into thinking she could manage this. She was perfectly capable of spending two or three weeks at George's house under his mother's emollient care. Then they turned into Gloucester Square and she saw his mother holding up a candle at the window. Mrs. Smith was as transparently the model of Graham's mother as her son was of Graham, and the sight of her made Charlotte ill. What on earth was she doing, writing about people then coming to stay with them? It was all she could do to step down from the cab and stumble toward the prosperous house when she wanted to grow a curlew's wings and fly.

The widowed Mrs. Smith and her two grown-up daughters were waiting in the pretty papered sitting room when George brought Charlotte inside. Mrs. Smith was a dark handsome woman and her daughters were accomplished girls and usually agreeable. Now all three looked as stiff as uninhabited corsets, greeting her with forced smiles and averted glances. Charlotte went even stiffer than they, and to her horror, George said he was inundated with business and even at this ungodly hour had to get back to the office—"although I'll see you at breakfast. If you'll forgive me."

The door clicking shut behind him.

"Well," Mrs. Smith said, raising her eyes in frank assessment. Charlotte wondered if she was about to be scolded and bristled. "You'll be wanting some tea."

Mrs. Smith sat Charlotte down and they began a slightly formal civility that continued throughout her visit. One quiet day followed another, Charlotte keeping busy with her proofs and declining most invitations. She'd satisfied her curiosity about London literary society on her previous visits, finding that she came up to Tennyson's elbow, and that Charles Dickens, whom she disliked, decorated his table with artificial flowers.

George continued working such long hours that he usually handed Charlotte over to friends like Dr. Forbes for the few excursions she wished to make: the Bank of England and the Exchange, the prisons of Pentonville and Newgate as well as Bedlam. Yet George was charming over breakfast, which was often the only time of day they met—a supple form hurrying to the table, slinging one long leg over his mahogany chair. Before he'd even quite settled: "Well, *what* have we been up to?"

His eyes remained fixed on her even as he gracefully unfolded his napkin, listening as she told him about the previous day's excursions, the shouts of the Exchange, the silence of the Bank; about poor divided Richard Dadd.

"Can there be such a thing as too much talent?" Charlotte had asked. She had no small talk, but George didn't seem to mind.

"Do *you* think so?"

"Probably. Yes. My sister Emily."

"Tell me more about her."

As her visit extended to a month, Charlotte watched George's obsessive hours begin to wear on him, a muscle ticking at his temple, his eyes grown bloodshot and puffy. She felt tender, wanting to bathe his eyes as she bathed her father's. She also felt a malicious glee to see his bloom fading, making him a better match for her, middle-aged at thirty, and no doubt subject to the same mixed feelings as herself. His letters these past years probably showed as sincere an interest in her well-being as they did in the progress of her novels, much like his attitude toward her excursions. He must have seen that in visiting madhouses and prisons she was *not* trying to satisfy the type of prurience she disliked in others and abhorred in herself. Or, to be honest, not just that. She was also testing the waters, seeing if she could write the type of modern social novel about the desperate condition of the poor that critics cried up so loudly in the press and publishers sold so profitably. Perhaps she could be topical. She might be able to please him.

Maybe he didn't want her to, so he'd have an excuse to drop her.

One minute Charlotte wondered if George worked late to avoid her. The next, she convinced herself that working late meant that his company faced financial difficulties. He might need his famous authoress more than she needed him. George Smith was only a publisher. Charlotte could get another publisher more easily than he could find a new literary lioness. It wasn't an unequal match, or if it was, the advantage was to her. Even the Queen doted on *Jane Eyre*.

The weeks passed and nothing was said, and Charlotte began to suffer agonies. One day, when George excused himself from another dinner, Mrs. Smith shook her head. "My boy's killing himself with work," she said, and Charlotte didn't miss the emphasis. Her *boy*. At least she refrained from asking whether Charlotte's age made her subject to rheumatism. Otherwise, the penny refused to drop, and however much Charlotte wanted George to say—something—he didn't, or wouldn't, or couldn't. No more than she.

One night she had a nightmare. It began in something like the Bedlam ward for women, although it was also a church with stone walls and a ceiling vaulting higher than a cathedral. Charlotte found herself moving among the mad governesses, ghostly blurs against the low opaque windows. Unsettled and anxious, she needed to get past them. As she stumbled toward a door, the room lengthened and narrowed, and soon she was turning corners and climbing up a flight of very high unrailed stairs.

The ceilings were lower here and the walls shiny with marble headstones. She was frightened, feeling followed, and around her the carved medallion faces and letters were coming to life. She turned away and found herself running down a long corridor. Beside her was an insubstantial governess. Two. She didn't know them, but they were also her sisters Emily and Anne, and although they shouldn't have frightened her, she was terrified, moaning as they unfurled their wings and launched themselves skywards, turning into huge white birds that beat the air into shadows above her.

Panting now, Charlotte ran toward an open doorway she knew she couldn't enter. In the square white room beyond it, before a bright square window, a hanged man's feet dangled emptily as his body swayed back and forth, back and forth, slowly swivelling toward her, and she knew that if she saw its face, his face, it would be Richard Dadd or her brother Branwell, and she was paralyzed, unable to catch her breath, suffocating . . .

Charlotte sat up in bed, breathing hard, certain that she had screamed, not in her dream but in the unfamiliar room. She didn't know where she was. Then she remembered that she was in George Smith's house, and her hand went to her throat, terrified that he'd heard her cry out. A foolish, nervous woman. The pulse beneath her fingers beat hard and fast. Charlotte held her breath, listening, and started when the banked coals cracked in the hearth. The house was otherwise quiet. No one was stirring. No one had heard.

Settling back down in bed, willing her heartbeat to slow, Charlotte told herself she was safe. Her bed was warm and soft, far warmer and softer than she was used to, and George was nearby to protect her. In a quick flight of mind, she saw George asleep in his bedroom, and as she smiled at the picture, her heart caught in her throat. *My love.*

Her love lay in bed a few thin walls away, one knee, perhaps, fallen slightly open. It was possible he'd heard her. He might be awake, arms crossed behind his head. Charlotte pictured him sitting up, thinking for a moment, then levering his bare feet out of bed. Leaving his room, he would head down the hallway in nothing but his nightshirt, pausing to listen outside her door, hearing her breathe, breathing in concert, and as she pictured his chest rising and falling, Charlotte's fingers hiked inside her nightdress, where it was already warm and damp as she closed her eyes and saw him opening the door.

S he had to leave the next morning. *Villette* was being published, and Charlotte couldn't bear to be in London when it came out, terrified of reviewers, their snarl and teeth. Too much rode on the book's success. George might even be waiting to see how it did before speaking. If *Villette* proved another sensation, he might *have* to marry her. Or not.

Back at Euston Station, Charlotte looked in George's face for signs of relief that she was finally going, and saw only fondness.

"Well," he said, pressing her hand. Charlotte's heart flapped like a caged bird. Now he had to speak, whether to give her veiled encouragement or let her down gently. But George turned away silently, and she could only watch him hitch up his shoulders and disappear into the crowd.

On the way home, Charlotte sat bereft in her carriage. Her ticket took her to Keighley, where she would be met by her friend Ellen for the final ride to her father's parsonage. Ellen was arriving from her mother's house farther north, and during her week-long visit to Haworth, she would want to analyse every word George Smith had said.

Charlotte wasn't sure that was wise. Nor did she want to talk about her writing, certain that the critics would savage *Villette*, and aware that she could no more follow it up with a social novel than she could fly to the moon. Her visit to London had been a failure—although, she would have to tell Ellen, a pleasant one. For once, she had been allowed to do as she wanted, although her visits to the prisons and the madhouse hadn't given her what she'd hoped.

Yet they'd given her something, even if she couldn't speak about that either. Charlotte's nightmare about Richard Dadd had been a gift. She could only write about what she felt deeply, and clearly she'd been shaken by the consonance between Richard and her poor Branwell. Between the Dadd family and hers. Dr. Forbes had told her Richard wasn't the only Dadd in Bedlam. One of his brothers was held in the incurables ward, a madman if not a murderer. Meanwhile rumours rubbed around London about a sister who had tried to strangle her infant because of its incessant crying. The sister's husband, one of Dadd's oldest friends, was said to have become unreliable as well.

Four members of the Dadd family gone mad. Five Brontës dead before their time. Charlotte's eldest sister, Maria, had been gone long enough that she'd been able to portray her as Helen Burns in *Jane Eyre*. Now she wondered if she could write about Branwell. He'd been gone scarcely five years, but the stories they'd written as children were deep enough in the past that she'd already mined one for her unpublished first novel. Now she wondered if she could make better use of it, taking up a story Branwell had written about the brothers Edward and Willie, a violent man and his victim.

Despite his violent outbursts and the damage he'd done their family, Branwell had seen himself as a victim, and perhaps he was correct. It was a shocking fact that when he'd been employed as a tutor, her brother had been seduced by his rich employer's wife, discovered by her husband, sacked and humiliated. Branwell had loved the woman and blamed their crack-up for his descent into drink and opiates. Her husband had made him a victim. Under this schema, Dadd would be the violent one in anything she wrote, the murderer. Yet perhaps Branwell and Dadd were both these things, violent men as well aso victims, at least of themselves. Double men; more of Dadd's doubling. Charlotte had been given something to think about.

She also knew that taking on such a project would be perilous. The critics already called her unfeminine. Imagine what they'd say if she wrote something that touched on Branwell's adultery or the notorious Richard Dadd. She must, one critic had written, "learn to sacrifice a little of her Yorkshire roughness to the demands of good taste."

What Mr. Lewes had meant, of course, was that he preferred novels to be an escape from the uneasiness of life. He would prefer Charlotte to be an ethereal being, her quill moving lightly across the page as if trailed by a bird in flight. Instead she dug into her paper with her child's fingers and ink-blackened nails and all the force of her plain little body, sucking her tongue and clamping her thighs together warmly, never intending her lovers Jane Eyre and Mr. Rochester to stumble toward a marriage of true *minds*.

*Villette* was her best book so far, despite its faults, and despite the flaying she was certain critics would give her. If they let her, she might follow it up with something even better, a transfiguration of Branwell's story, or Dadd's, or both, that would meld her mature technique with the power she'd first found in herself when writing *Jane Eyre*.

Or not. Success was improbable; continued success so unlikely that courting it seemed like hubris, like folly. Easier to reverse herself and accept the proposal she'd received from Mr. Nicholls. Stop trying. Stay home.

They were half an hour from Keighley. Charlotte would be back in the parsonage soon, the reviews would come in soon, and they would destroy her—destroy her chance of marrying George and of writing a new novel, or at least of getting it published. She knew she was a prickly and passionate woman, and deplorably plain. A genius, she believed, a good

Christian and worthy enough, but no more likely to get what she wanted than anybody else.

A widow sat across from her eating bread and cheese, crumbs falling on her rusty mourning. Presumably there were people who could risk their best clothes to the soot and rigours of travel, but the widow was not one of them nor was Charlotte another. When George Smith had seen her off at the station, she had been acutely conscious of her old cloak and limp dress. If *Villette* failed, this might prove to be the last time he'd see her. He would remember her this way.

"Would you like some, dear?" the widow asked, holding out a slice of thinly buttered bread.

Charlotte shook her head in curt disdain before remembering herself. "Although it's kind of you to ask."

# 6 Suffolk Street, Pall Mall East, London

*Opening Exhibition of the Society of British Artists, 1838*

O ctagonal rooms like card tables. Too many people, too much art. As Richard sidled through the crowd, he remembered his dislike of sharp elbows and damp woollens. Of exhibitions in general. He was keeping away from his own paintings, knowing what it looked like to linger beside them, although of course he'd checked as soon as he'd arrived that all three were hanging a respectable distance above the floor. Not too far above it, not too choice a spot. That would showcase his father's influence rather than his work. He murmured his apologies as he pushed toward his friend Phillip in the corner, aware that last year's efforts hadn't sold and pretty sure these ones wouldn't either. His train was approaching the station but hadn't yet arrived.

"Don't linger, Johnny," he said, shaking Phillip's shoulder. Phillip hadn't been able to tear himself far enough from his painting to let anyone else get a look.

"A lot rides on this, Dadd."

"No, it doesn't." Shaking his shoulder again as Phillip was about to protest. "It doesn't."

Egg came up and, seeing the lay of the land, helped him steer Phillip into another room. The man was pale. He had to stop this. Richard probably had to stop a couple of things, although he'd decide what they were later.

"All right now?"

Another crowded octagonal room, this one with yellow walls. The Duke of Wellington could congratulate himself. He'd been the first to paint his gallery yellow at Apsley House: the Waterloo room, magnificent with spoils. Richard had got in once when the family was out of town, pinching himself, admitted to the precincts of the Iron Duke, even if the Duke opposed everything that Dadds and Radicals held dear. Richard had been transfixed by a Flemish masterpiece by Bruegel the Elder. The canvas was nearly as crowded as today's exhibition, the details so meticulously picked out they pinned the eye. Pin-pricked it.

Crowds both excited and unsettled Richard. Maybe that's what he needed to get over. Either that or learn to use people the way Bruegel had.

"What have you seen that's good?" he asked Egg.

"One William Powell Frith," Egg said. "He's leaping and bounding."

"Isn't he just?" Richard asked fondly, and glanced over at Frith's sketch, which showed a boy reading. "*Sketch of a Boy Reading.* I praised the title. But I don't mean just us. Who else should I look at?"

The other students at the Academy called them a clique, and they'd thrown it back, calling themselves The Clique, enunciating the capitals. Dadd, Frith, Egg, Phillip, O'Neil. They worked together always, and sometimes splurged on a chop at dinner. It was a bad time to set out as an artist, with the economy stalled in recession, but Richard's father said it was always a bad time to set out and predicted they'd survive.

Now Egg looked around the room to remind himself what he'd liked, then pulled up short when he saw a fashionable paunchy man a half-dozen years older than they were.

"Do you know who that is?"

"You sound rhetorical."

"John Forster, the critic. He knows everyone."

A slight dandyish long-haired fellow came to stand beside Forster.

"He certainly does," Richard said. Charles Dickens. He was only twenty-six years old, but everyone in the room knew who he was, and the public was rapidly learning. What the dickens, what the devil. He seemed a source of light.

"I know him," Richard said.

"Forster?"

Richard reminded himself that he was party to secrets which had to be kept. The Dickens family had lived in Chatham when Richard was very young and his father had known the elder Dickens well. The town chemist knew everyone, of course, and their secrets, although in the end everyone in town knew more than they wanted to about the orotund John Dickens. His father said that Dickens *père* wasn't a tall man but a lumbering one, as florid as a lord or a publican, genial and popular, standing everyone drinks, at least at first. His father enjoyed telling Dickens stories now that Charles was growing famous. Behind closed doors, of course. How John Dickens had trained up his boy like an organ grinder's monkey, lifting him onto a table at the Mitre Tavern to sing and dance a jig. Charles would have been eight, nine, ten. It was beneath him, Richard's father had said, John being a well-paid clerk at the Admiralty. He had to take in more than three hundred pound a year. Three fifty.

"You remember, of course," his father had prompted, and Richard's brother Stephen nodded, looking dubious as he made the connection.

"That was him? Charles Dickens? Not really. The human monkey?"

Richard thought he'd been too young to recall. Now, as he watched Dickens bow to an admirer, he caught a glimpse of a slight fair boy on a table bowing to applause, his lips parted and his wide eyes dazzled. His mind might have been inventing an image to go with what his father had said. But possibly it wasn't.

"You're staring," said Egg. "How do you know him?"

"Forster?" Richard asked, collecting himself. "He's often at chapel, a Dissenter like . . ."

"Everyone in town a *Unitarian* like your father."

"Like me," Richard said.

"I thought you'd stuck with the Established Church," Egg said. He wasn't particularly religious, but something gentle in him loved constancy.

"The manufacturers have started collecting," Richard told them.

"Manufacturers," Phillip repeated, really too nervous to be here.

"The ones in Leeds. Manchester. Dissenters with money. Quite a few of 'em," Richard said. "We should all of us convert." Taking in Forster. "I *have* met him."

Had Forster overheard? Strange how one could sense being talked about, even with the back turned. Richard would have to paint that, the alert posture, a hawk's sideways cock of the head. It was a way to link groups within a crowded Bruegelian canvas, having someone talked about by one group while he listened at the fringes of another.

Forster turned and recognized Richard, heading over.

"Dadd the younger," he said, shaking hands.

"The middle, perhaps," Richard said. "I believe you've met my elder brothers."

"But you're the one does the painting," Forster said. "I'm told you've got a pair of 'em here. People speak of you highly."

It wouldn't do to ask whom, although he burned with it, and Forster knew that. These exhibitions were filled with gamesmanship, and the rules said that Richard had to give an urbane smile. "As they do of my friends, if I may," he said. "John Phillip. Augustus Egg."

"Augustus *Egg*," came a nasal voice, surprisingly unbeautiful, and before they could take it in, the author was with them. "Charles Dickens," he said, smiling at Egg. "We should form a club of the indelibly named." Turning to Richard, who was fascinated by the sprig of geranium in the author's buttonhole. "And you, sir?"

He called himself to order. "Richard Dadd, I'm afraid."

Dickens's eyes threw out sparks. "Father Dadd and Mr. Egg—you stay with me. Mr. Phillip, I'm afraid you'll have to join my friend Forster while we three of us confab over changing our surnames. One needs to be rather less tergiversated. Forster, is that a word?"

"No."

"Truly?"

"Tergiversate. Evasion of straightforwardness. Intransitive verb."

"The problem is, Dadd, Dickens, Egg—we're rather double-dealing. When I'm sure we don't mean it."

"Nor does Phillip," Richard said. "Although he's been known to fillip a peppercorn across the room."

Dickens's eyes widened in delight.

"To be fair," Richard said, "only when agitated."

The author leaned in confidentially. "While Forster forced her, poor girl. At least he would have, if he wasn't such a gentleman."

Seen close, Dickens had brilliant greyish hazel eyes, like verdigris on copper.

"Right," he said, stepping back. "The matter's settled. We'll all five of us change our surnames to Smith."

The last line of a story. He seemed ready to go, scanning the crowd. Richard didn't want to let him.

"With our smithies," he said, and Dickens turned back, still amused, but also something deeper.

"Then what shall we say?" he asked, holding Richard's eyes. "Martin?"

Startled, Richard wondered if Dickens recognized the Dadd name and Martin connection in Chatham. Surely not. It was simply another everyday name. Smith, Jones, Taylor, Martin.

"House martin," he parried. "The bird?"

"Coward, Clamp, Rutter, Leech, Pitt, D'Eath." Dickens rattled them off without pausing, his mind a cyclone. "Curley, Hatch, Stout, Last, *Shakespeare*. The alternatives an't endless," he said. "Oh dear."

"Brummel," Richard suggested, glancing down at Dickens's gaudy waistcoat.

"Oi, ve vant to be a Beau," Dickens teased, broadening his accent. "I know: we'll all be Pickwick. There's our club."

"I love Pickwick," said Egg, and Dickens beamed at him, no other word, before spotting someone across the room.

"Maclise!" he called, and turned back to bow courteously. "If you'll excuse me."

Dickens was gone, Forster steaming off in his wake. They left an audible absence behind them.

"My goodness," Egg said. "What was that?"

John Dickens had left Chatham owing money to half the tradesmen in town, including Richard's father. They next heard of him in London a few years later, when he tried wheedling credit from Uncle Henry Martin, who had taken the lease of a chemist's shop in the straggling new suburb of Somers Town. After the uncle had hung out his sign, neighbouring tradesmen warned him off known spongers, including the indelibly named John Dickens, by then an undischarged bankrupt. A local baker told Uncle Henry how he'd got Dickens packed off to debtors' prison three years before, after he'd reneged on a forty-pound loan, a sum his family was slow to repay. After being released from prison, Dickens had installed his wife and children up the road in Johnson Street and was still sniffing around the neighbourhood for credit the way a fox sniffed out hens.

It was during the notably dry summer of 1827 that the elder Dickens had first jingled into Uncle Henry's shop. Dickens didn't recognize the uncle, but he was the same bluff, talking man Uncle Henry had known when he was apprenticed to Richard's father in Chatham. The uncle reminded Dickens of both the acquaintance and the debt, and after a stuttering moment—John Dickens spoke with a thick tongue—Uncle Henry had the pleasure of watching him retreat. Imagine the uncle's surprise when Dickens arrived back the next morning, as proud as a dog with a rat in his mouth as he offered to pay off his debt to Richard's father at five shillings on the pound.

"You'll not get a better offer, young man," Dickens told him. "At least from me."

Uncle Henry had been charmed into letting Dickens run a small tick, never sure he'd settle it, especially once Dickens was evicted from Johnson Street for not paying his rent. The local trade expected him to flee the neighbourhood, but Dickens only moved his family a few blocks south, taking up residence in the Polygon around the corner from Uncle Henry's shop. Sometimes Dickens paid his tick, or part of it, and Uncle Henry said that in any case the man's talk was worth a small risk, the price of a box at the theatre. There was also the fact John Dickens had children, and more than one was sickly. Uncle Henry's predecessor in the shop had loaned Dickens money when a little daughter fell ill of the smallpox and had been kind enough not to call it in when she had died.

Yet that wasn't true of all his creditors, and Richard could see that the young Charles Dickens must have spent his youth hiding from the *rat-a-tat* of bailiffs at the door. The worst of this occurred a dozen years ago, but his father's imprisonment and bankruptcy was hardly something the famous author would want known, and Richard wondered if the mention of *Martin* had been a test to see what he knew and whether he would spill.

Spotting his father at the gallery entrance, Richard elbowed over.

"You've met someone," his father said. "Perhaps not for the first time."

Richard leaned against the doorjamb behind him. "I find I don't like knowing so much about a person I really don't know. I suspect John Forster likes the feeling, but I don't."

"Now you know why I left off being a chemist," his father said. They both watched Dickens laugh with the painter, Daniel Maclise, whom Richard admired. "The worst part is the way the clientele expect you to sympathize, despite everything you know about their most intimate concerns. Or because of them."

That was a thought. "Dickens expects you to sympathize with him, rather," Richard said. "That's the tenor of his writing. You're going to love this. You *must*." The boy dancing on the table at the Mitre Tavern, avid for applause.

"Well, he's right," his father said. "We do." Envy all over his face. Richard glanced back at the time in Chatham, not long ago, when his father had decided to be an artist.

"I don't envy him," Richard said, although as he watched Dickens, he wasn't sure what he felt. Fear, perhaps, of what one could become if successful, what the famous became. And not, he could see, unawares.

Cobham Wood. Richard was fifteen when he set up his kit under the benign eye of his teacher, Mr. William Dadson.

Up ahead was the grey stone mausoleum raised by a former Earl of Darnley. Bluebells flowered around it, and their sweet grainy scent tickled the nose. It was a pleasantly brisk spring day with the sun breaking through.

Yet Richard was in agony. His father was whistling on a stool beside him, taking lessons alongside him, having heard the call of Art.

His father would be painting in watercolours. It had cost Richard years to earn a promotion from pencil and chalk, and he felt ten kinds of woeful to watch his father set up as if he knew what he was doing. His father had no eye. His compositions were poorly framed and badly executed, always too much earth or grass or sky. Old Dadson must have let him use watercolours only because of his neatness with materials. You could see the chemist in him, Dadson had remarked early in their joint lessons. Deft hands. Said it gave him confidence in the nostrums mixed under the sign of the Golden Mortar.

His father hadn't liked that.

Good.

"So what should I attack today?" his father asked, once he'd set up.

"Whatever you want," their teacher said.

"What are you going to attack?"

"Whatever *I* want."

What was the mystery? They were at the mausoleum. One painted what was there.

It was a challenge, though, since the mausoleum was empty. In the previous century, when there was no room left in Westminster Abbey for the Earls of Darnley, the architect Wyatt had designed the Cobham mausoleum for family burials, but it had never been consecrated and no one was planted there. In Richard's mind, this made it more ghastly than a graveyard, since in a grave you knew the body was there, or at least a skeleton, and in any case the shucked hull, which implied that something had shucked the hull; the soul had cast off flesh and bones and gone to heaven. These things followed one from the other in a way that reassured a chap, even if one didn't like to picture the actual act of shucking, particularly when it concerned stepmothers.

A mausoleum empty of bodies, however, opened up the idea of bodies empty of souls. Richard had been worried about that ever since his father had started calling the Bible a myth. If the Bible were myth and Jesus not the Son of God but a historic figure, as some of the more advanced Unitarians claimed, there didn't seem to be any guarantee of heaven or even of God himself. Instead, you were left with atheism and blankness and terror.

Richard had been having nightmares. He'd no sooner close his eyes than find himself stumbling around in a deep black cave with no idea how to get out. Worried and searching, he'd scramble over half-seen boulders and slippery gravel. Monsters were after him, and he knew they were minotaurs but couldn't see them and grew breathless trying to get away. Then the roof and walls would start closing in and Richard was terrified, trapped, wanting to run but unable to move a finger. A weight on his chest. Hag-ridden. Suddenly the ground dropped out and he was hurtling down down down toward oily black water, about to hit when he woke up gasping.

He'd find himself sitting up in bed, his brother George sleeping stolidly beside him, trying to tell himself he was lucky. They said if you hit bottom, you died. And what then?

One Sunday last winter, after a particularly bad night, Richard had snuck off to the service at St. Mary's Anglican.

Sitting in the last pew, he'd been able to take solace in the choir and incense, if not the active eyebrows of his father's profitable hypochondriac, Mrs. Haberdasher Lambert, who'd seen him as he came in and kept turning around for a new look. At the end of the service, Richard beat it for the door. But Mrs. Haberdasher Lambert grasped his shoulder from behind, flinging him around and trapping his hand in a deadly clasp as she welcomed him back to the Established Church. Richard found himself babbling something about his mother having come here, honouring his mother, all of that, which Mrs. Haberdasher Lambert accepted with a sentimental squint of her eyes before releasing him, sore and humiliated.

It had been a piece of luck, mentioning his mother. Richard had stumbled on the one excuse that left his father unable to forbid him from going back. The nightmares wouldn't stop, but Richard liked church well enough, especially the music, and not even Mrs. Haberdasher Lambert's repeated squints kept him from going to St. Mary's most Sundays.

The mausoleum, though. The problem with painting the mausoleum was that Richard *didn't* like it, a piece of confused architecture the size of a barn but taller, girded round with Roman columns and topped with an Egyptian pyramid. What was the building's relationship to earth and sky? Richard supposed the pyramid could be thought of as drilling a hole into heaven, but since it had never been called upon to send souls there, that made it rather useless. He wondered if he might paint the mausoleum as useless and forlorn, even though Lord Darnley kept it in good tick. He would like to portray it as un-haunted. A menacing blank. He had no idea how.

"What have you got?" his father asked, appearing behind him. "Nothing yet. Well, carry on."

After a winter spent painting together, Richard knew his father would appear behind him regularly, never able to focus on his own paper, as if he'd grown so used to popping up to wait on clientele in the shop, he couldn't stay in one place for any length of time. It was a lesson on the importance of concentration, Richard supposed, and he tried to take it, honing in on his paper. Grey Portland stone, a milky sky, cobalt bluebells that cared for nothing but themselves. He was rather proud of his bluebells.

"What do you think?" he heard his father ask old Dadson. "Richard, what do you think?"

Going over reluctantly, Richard took a sideways gander at his father's effort. He hadn't painted the mausoleum, like a boy at school wanting to be different and wearing his hat pushed back and his trousers slouched. Instead, he'd painted a confusion of bluebells with a thin band of cloudy sky above them. Mainly the eye was drawn to a pair of small joined eyebrows squashed beneath a cloud.

"Pigeons," his father said defensively, seeing them stare.

"Are there pigeons?" old Dadson asked.

"There were."

"And they were important pigeons," Dadson said.

Richard managed not to smile but couldn't help wriggling with embarrassment.

His father went silent for a moment, then said, "An interesting fact from a local farmer. In the old days—and I'm speaking of the *very* old days—they kept pigeons in what they called culver houses. Not dovecotes, you see. Tall culver houses made of clay with hundreds of nests hollowed out of the inside walls. Mr. Colley remembers hearing from his grandfather, who probably got it from his grandfather, about circular ladders they used inside to get at the birds. They were kept for winter meat, you see. By the gentry. A plague on the farmers, flocks of pigeons feeding off their corn."

Richard didn't know what to say, while old Dadson looked steadily at his father.

He wasn't that old. Mr. Dadson and Richard's father were about the same age. Friends, he supposed. The teacher spoke gently. "Knowledge is a bulwark against many things, Robert. But you can't let it get between you and art."

His father looked stunned.

"He means . . ." Richard said, knowing exactly what old Dadson meant but unable to rephrase it.

His father looked from one to the other. "In any case, you'll have to excuse me," he said, and turned abruptly into the woods for a piss.

Old Dadson put a hand on Richard's shoulder.

"The hardest thing, I think," he said, keeping his eyes on the father's effort. "*The hardest* is to have an artistic temperament but no artistic talent."

He glanced at Richard, and when he saw he'd understood, old Dadson smiled.

"It's not bad, I find, to have a little talent. The world probably likes you better for it. Buys your engravings and so on. One has a nice life of local approbation, and silver clanking down often enough to feed the beastlings."

Mr. Dadson was currently showing his engraving of *Rochester Castle from the Old Bridge* in the window of his shop. Richard blushed like a boy, embarrassed at being treated as his teacher's equal but also delighted. He had no idea what to answer, although apparently he didn't have to. Mr. Dadson gripped his shoulder playfully and shoved him back in his seat.

"Now get to work, genius," he said, as Richard's father strode out of the woods, his hat filled with mushrooms.

"I don't imagine the gamekeeper cares if one takes mushrooms," his father said.

*Genius*, Richard thought. *Genius. Genius. Genius.* He felt overwhelmed with love for both his father and his teacher. *Draw your mushrooms*, he wanted to say. *Put down the paintbrush, pick up a pencil, and dear old Dadson will teach you how to sketch and shade. Then you can draw specimens from your museum! Illustrate a catalogue! You could manage that!*

"Should I paint them?" his father asked, looking into his hat.

Behind him, a gust of wind blew across the bluebells, bowing them down like a great hand sweeping, the colour changing in ripples. If there were no hand of God, the world would lose a fine way of seeing. He wondered if his father was an atheist and how he could live with it, or if the problem was that he couldn't.


L ying in bed after the exhibition opening, too exhausted to sleep, Richard was troubled by a comic song, "The Dog's Meat Man." A couple of lines of doggerel carked at him like a costermonger's cry.

> *And for a quart of peppermint away she ran,*
> *And drank good health to the dog's meat man.*

It came to Richard gradually that Charles Dickens had sung that song on a table in the Mitre Tavern. Richard's father had never told him that, so it might be a true memory. He could hear a man's voice singing it. Couldn't get free of a comic's reedy tenor he'd heard once at a theatre. But behind the man's voice a child's treble voice grew louder and shriller, soon overtaking the man so Richard could hear the child over-emphasizing words on the down beat the way that children do. *The* dog's *meat* man. *The* dog's *meat* man. Dog's *meat*, dog's meat *man*.

A small sickly blond boy with a thin nose and loose lips jigged his knees as he warbled. Richard could see him now, and they were in the Mitre all right, the tired old plaster slumping on its walls, and there was Mr. Tribe clapping time, Mr. Tribe being the landlord of the inn as well as the proprietor of an express coach that ran from the Mitre to London. This meant he was also Charon, as the room became a barque to ferry souls across the River Styx . . .

A barque. Richard realized he was dreaming, although he wasn't quite asleep. Neither waking nor sleeping, he felt adrift in a fluid, dangerous place. Liminal. He tried to thrust out of it as if thrusting up from the river floor, pushing off, spiralling up, holding his breath until he broke through the surface and found himself awake.

Richard sat in bed for a moment, then shook his head and got up to splash water on his face, glad of the cold floor beneath his feet.

"What is it?" asked Stephen, a much lighter sleeper than George.

"Barmy dream. Mr. Tribe as Charon."

Stephen chuckled sleepily and sank back down. But Richard pulled a chair over to the window and looked out at London, where a waning moon scraped over the chimney pots. He'd been here for more than four years, although he scarcely believed it. No more apparently did Dickens, who kept dipping into Chatham when writing his serials, despite having lived on the Medway for only six or seven years. His *Sketches by "Boz"* and *Pickwick Papers* had made the entire Dadd family howl as they read each new episode at night, recognizing lampoons of several old neighbours. Richard's father kept looking for a chemist he might have inspired and professed himself relieved each time they didn't find one, although lately he'd grown less interested as they read their way through the new novel, *Oliver Twist*, and it proved to be set largely in London.

Maybe that was what Richard found disturbing about Dickens: that they hailed from roughly the same place and station, yet Dickens was becoming so famous. Maybe it was simply that he was famous. Richard and his friends all wanted to be, yet he found it distasteful to make oneself into a performing monkey, whether in the Mitre Tavern or at an exhibition like today's, where Dickens had put himself as thoroughly on display as the paintings. None of Richard's friends wanted to be like that, possibly excepting Frith, who'd been scrounging since his father died last spring and his mother had been obliged to sell their hotel. Frith would do what it took. He had to.

And what did that do to the art? The question hadn't really occurred to Richard before seeing Dickens, or seeing him again, with his long hair and dandy's clothes and that sprig of geranium in his buttonhole. Well, what had desperation done to Frith? So far, it had made him better. *Sketch of a Boy Reading* was his best work yet, title aside. Nor did it seem to hurt Dickens's work, at least so far. Yet after you became famous, what next?

Too many steps at once. Richard only twenty years old and had yet to sell a single painting. He watched the moon set behind the rooftops and listened to the restless night, the murmur of London sounding like the ocean, and told himself to forget about Dickens and go back to bed.

# In Which Richard Visits
# Number 4, Upper Seymour Street,
# Somers Town, A Chymist's Shop,
# as It Was Spelled in London
## *1838*

T he next morning, Richard set out to visit his brother Bob at their uncle's shop near Euston Square. He wanted something, although he didn't know what. After a quick glance at the exhibition, Richard set off around the block, turning into the Haymarket and shouldering his way into the mob, becoming another of the bright-eyed cynics who for twenty centuries had trod the pavements of Londinium. A messenger boy shoved past in a cloud of odour, and Richard hadn't gone two steps further when a delivery man bawled down at a sweeper, "Mike why you filthy son of a—"

*Cark.* The man's nasal Cockney indignation reminded Richard of his dream word, cark. Onomatopoeia, he believed. It was drizzling and the gutters reeked of dung, but he was happy enough. Even a chap who didn't like crowds could enjoy the dodge of London. The artful dodge, he supposed, remembering *Oliver Twist*. As he elbowed his way north, Richard began whistling young Dickens's tune, hearing the child's voice in his head.

> *Near the Hungerford Market, not long ago*
> *An old maid lived a life of woe*
> *She was past forty-three, and her face like tan*
> *When she fell in love with the dog's meat man.*

"There's a gay tune, my pretty lad," an old costermonger called.

"Thank you, mother. Just mind you don't bank my handkerchief."

"It's the hurchins as does that, love. I'm arter what you've got them fingers on in yer pocket."

Ribald laughter. Seeing no one he knew, Richard pulled out his hand and pumped it obscenely at the costermonger, making her howl. Reaching the top of the Haymarket, he thought of turning east and cadging an ale from his Uncle Picnot in Leicester Square. Useful to have uncles scattered across London in hotels and fruit stalls and tobacconist's shops, all with delicacies on offer. The uncles had held a family confab four years ago after Grandfather Martin's funeral, filling the late grandfather's cottage to debate how best to profit from the ballooning economy. Ballooning at the time. Richard's father had proposed they invest their profits in elevating the quality of their stock, taking aim at the luxury trade, which guaranteed custom when the balloon inevitably punctured and the economy plunged back down.

"The Good will always be pinched and the Poor die in droves," he said. "But the needs of the Few will *ever* be fulfilled."

"Not recognizing chapter and verse," said Uncle Charles Martin, "I would postulate that's one of your own, Robert."

Uncle Charles wiggled his famously moveable ears, his signal of amusement. The uncle was an otherwise static man, a reader and religious type who dressed more like a preacher than a prosperous tobacconist in Southwark. Most of the Martin uncles were like Richard's father in having pleasant countenances, strong legs and maturely greying hair: men who looked well behind a counter, like a guarantee of quality in their goods. Yet grave Uncle Charles stocked excellent cigars and always treated his brothers and nephews when they made the trek south of the river, which (along with the ears) gave him standing in the family.

"I believe the Good Book has somewhat different advice," he went on, "Matthew telling us we should not 'be likened unto a foolish man, which built his house upon the sand.'"

"Trade is always built on sand, Charles," his father replied. "The trick is keeping your feet as it shifts."

In the end, his father's logic prevailed, and he took over Uncle Picnot's water-gilding business while the uncle opened his promising hotel. During this past year's recession, the luxury trade had, in fact, kept their heads bobbing above the flood. But only barely, and Uncle Charles was bolting, investing his remaining capital in the lease of a chemist's back home in Strood, while Uncle Picnot, well. Reaching the top of the Haymarket, Richard glanced east toward Leicester Square, sniffing for his uncle's ale. But he gave a self-denying shrug and continued north, saving his uncle a shilling.

Crossing into Regent Street, Richard found less of a crowd

and more ladies, nosegays of paintable young ladies window-shopping in their bright spring cloaks and hats. Ducking under one of the porticoes, Richard enjoyed the smoothness of the flagstones under his boots. He was conscious of walking smartly as he had a look at the ladies, who had a look at him— at least until a party of officers rode noisily into the street. The ladies vibrated toward them, becoming pond fish swimming to the curb to be fed, taking in the officers' uniforms, their mustachios, their military pensions.

Richard told himself to stop. His father expected him to be a gentleman and he had nothing but trade in his head. Nor had he any idea how the species known as *ladies* saw the world. He suspected his sisters weren't a model. They screeched up and down the stairs chasing their guinea pigs and pugs and brothers, no doubt feeling the lack of a chaperone like the heavily upholstered lady he now spotted among the girls. On the chaperone's arm was a slender young lady who looked especially paintable. A small pink mouth and almond eyes that flashed as he walked by, prompting Richard to give what he believed to be the requisite bow as her friends giggled silently behind their gloves.

Ducking into the side streets, aiming northwest, Richard soon found himself treading on straw, a sick house presumably behind it, the invalid's nerves protected from the rattle of hoofs and wheels. He doubted the man heard them, not if he were truly ill. Richard never heard a thing when he was painting well. He said a friendly prayer for the chap's recovery, or the lady's, meanwhile restraining an impulse to cross his fingers like a pagan in Berengrave Lane. *Not getting me any-time soon.*

"Fine warnuts! Who'll buy me fine warnuts?"

75

Richard looked ahead to see street sellers tumbling toward him in a many-coloured tidal wave, the girl at the front jiggling her basket of walnuts. A peeler must be herding them on from some impromptu market nearby. What street had he wandered into? He didn't want to be where he was. Even at a distance, the costers emanated a fertile stench of spoiled food, like a badly kept kitchen. When he met them, Richard put his hand in his pocket to hold onto his shillings.

"Whelks. Whelks! Beautiful whelks! A penny a lot!"

A flower seller grabbed his trousers, looking up with appealing eyes, but he detached her quickly. "Hep out a good girl," she insisted, thrusting out her violets as she pattered along beside him. But Richard was distracted by a richer smell.

"Chestnuts all 'ot! Chestnuts all 'ot! *All* 'ot chestnuts!"

He stopped the chestnut seller and flipped him a penny, burning his fingers as he took the charred cone of paper. Realizing he'd wandered off course, Richard turned a circle as he tried to orient himself, finally spotting the Euston Arch above the buildings to his right. How did it get so far east? Eating his chestnuts, he angled back toward the arch, gateway to the station and the churned-up suburb of Somers Town. Uncle Henry had been deeply grieved by the construction of Euston Station over the past three years. He'd had to endure the sight of his friends' houses levelled across the street and acres of fields ploughed under beyond it—fields where his boys had grown up playing—as thousands of scavillmen worked loudly around the clock churning his world into mud.

Navvies; they called them navvies in London. Richard's brother George was a scavillman back home at the Chatham shipyards, their father's disappointment, a sullen lad and a loner who seemed destined to sink back down into manual employment, although Richard still cherished some hopes of George, who had his depths.

Meanwhile the army of navvies had hurt his uncle's custom and ruined his sleep with their shouts and fights and thieving, the once peaceful suburb resounding with English outrage and Scottish brays and the burr of homesick Irishmen; navvies of all shapes and sizes striving to be heard above the metallic clank, clank, clank of hammers, the earthen thud of picks, all of them blackened and sweated by the fires burning for warmth and the gaslights hissing out dead-white illumination, every man jack of them smelling of smoke and onions, such great ghostly clouds of smoke drifting among them that they may as well have been working in Vulcan's forge. Aunt Hannah Martin had grown drawn and his delicate little cousin, another Mary Ann, had started coughing in a worrisome manner, although Uncle Henry's boys had liked the mess well enough, sneaking into the lines of tracks being laid south toward the site of the train shed even as the shed started rising from the terminus, a marvel of iron two-hundred-foot long.

Mostly it was finished now, his uncle's shop left facing silent brick walls where neighbours had once stood chatting. At least the locals could congratulate themselves on one victory, the rail company having agreed that locomotives would be detached at Camden Town and the trains pulled into Euston by horsepower, sparing Upper Seymour Street the nuisance of engines and allowing the familiar whinny of living beasts to rise over the station walls.

Arriving at Euston Arch, Richard looked up at what they assured him was the highest structure in London, seventy-two-foot tall. Stopping, he asked himself how he would paint it. Not technique. How did it make him feel?

Proud, he found, not awestruck. It had taken more than two thousand years, but English civilization had finally progressed beyond the level of the Romans, having harnessed steam and speed and power. A Roman citizen snatched from the time of Caesar would probably recognize much of contemporary London, the houses and carts and all the pretty girls chaperoned by matrons, the dashing self-important officers and the costers hefting their baskets and no doubt the meaning of the costers' incessant carking if not the words.

Yet the Roman would surely be awed by Euston Station, as Richard wasn't. They'd arrived at a new age, faced a blank canvas, and as he strode onward, jingling into his uncle's shop, Richard couldn't have been more hopeful about the new heights that England would reach and (despite the fact he hadn't sold a single painting) the summit he would attain himself.

Bob was at the counter of the chymist's shop, as it was spelled in London. The uncle was unsurprisingly absent, Uncle Henry being the least consistent of the Martins.

"Here he is. Not haunting his paintings at the exhibition," his brother said.

"I dropped in for a quick look. How are *you*?"

Bob shrugged. They had always been companionable, their roles within the family too different to admit rivalry. Bob was the responsible older brother, his manner calm and his whiskers admirable, the one who would eventually be left in charge of the family, a burden he accepted gracefully.

Richard was their lottery ticket. He was permitted more freedom, but whatever silver he won would have to be shared with the others, and Richard accepted that, too.

"I met Charles Dickens yesterday," he said, taking a stool. "Does his father still come by?"

Bob shook his head. "The uncle finally cut him off. We see him in the street sometimes. His younger boys are in school not far away. Though Boz has been here. Charley Dick. But a week ago, in fact."

"What? Buying ink?"

"Strange day. He came in to pay his father's debts, which were getting elderly. I was at the door when I saw him heading up the street, stopping in at all the shops."

"So you've met him."

"Reminded him that we'd known each other back in Chatham. Just as well he stopped here earlyish. I showed him the ledger, and he paid in full. At which point I told him, 'You know, you need only offer seven shillings on the pound.'"

"And did he laugh?"

"Looked daggers. I thought, *There's an angry man*. He don't like being played."

"I suppose an author is more used to being the player, moving his characters about and all that."

"You came here to talk about Dickens?"

Had he? Probably, despite telling himself when he'd set out this morning that he wanted to see his brother. "Although if I've learned one thing at the Academy, people mainly want to talk about themselves."

"Which knowledge would have come sooner and cheaper if you'd gone into trade."

Richard smiled. "I doubt I'll see Charles Dickens again," he said. "I have an idea he'd recognized the Dadd name, and the Martin. We probably know too much about him for his comfort." Thinking for a moment, Richard added, "I'll see him, of course. But I don't expect he'll know me."

"I don't expect he shall."

"But as an artist, you know, how does one avoid *being* him?"

There, that was what he'd come for. Bob considered his question silently, cocking his head and failing to arrive at an answer.

"Perhaps I mean, is he what success looks like?"

"Cleaning up after the father? There's virtue in that."

Their eyes met, and they chuckled.

"Well, my God, there are lumps in it, too," Richard said.

"In what?" Uncle Henry asked. He came out of the back parlour holding a letter, his hair as wild as ever. He was the youngest of the Martin uncles and given to schemes, distractions, flights of fancy that he abandoned almost as soon as he took them up. The uncle was only a few years older than Bob and their father took a quasi-paternal role toward him, especially since the uncle had been his apprentice back in Chatham. They were often at loggerheads, but could also be counted on to defend each other from anyone else's criticism, Richard's father being the first to say that Henry was as canny as he was capricious. He'd brought his shop through the Euston debacle when more than a few of his neighbours had gone to shutters.

The uncle shook Richard's hand across the counter. "A visit from the genius."

"He won't be another Charley Dickens, though," Bob said. "Not enough of a dandy."

Richard supposed his clothes were sufficiently fashionable for a student, so Bob might mean his work. "My first critic."

"Who? Charley? Has he been back?" the uncle asked. "A bad move on his part, paying off the father's tick. John can ring up more credit now the trade knows Charley's going to clear it."

"Who's the letter from?" Richard asked.

"Oh," their uncle said, scanning the page as if he hadn't read it. "Your aunt's brother Harry, the one in Canada. Sarge went up to visit him but decided to go back to Utica, in New York. He says it's become home."

Two of Aunt Hannah's brothers had immigrated to America, Henry and Sargeson Verrall, after canvassing the family to help with the fare. They'd sailed for New York City but afterward moved restlessly northward, stopping here and there, Harry liking the sound of the Canadian town of Chatham in the newborn county of Kent. Richard found it odd to contemplate the doubling of Chatham and Chatham and Kent and Kent when neither could be anything like the other. More of Egg's duality, he supposed, but this time he didn't like it.

"I'm thinking of emigrating myself."

Richard was startled, and turned to find Uncle Henry speaking to Bob.

"Not before you've worked out your articles, of course. And I'll give you first refusal on the shop." Seeing Bob's look of politely repressed horror, their uncle added, "Yes, well. That's why I want to leave. I thought the railways would be a boon, but they've blocked off custom. Of course, Hannah won't hear of going."

Another pigeon thrown in the air and shot down all in one motion. However, Richard supposed the Verrall brothers were useful, trying out America the way he was being tried in the world of Art.

"Lottery tickets," he said, thinking aloud. Bob and the uncle looked at him as if he were cracked. "I only mean that Harry and Sarge have been taking a gamble. But if it works, they'll be able to share the wealth with anyone, as it were, who helped buy their tickets. Even if you never emigrate yourself, they could take one of your boys."

"Truth," Uncle Henry said.

"John Dickens won the lottery with his son."

"I see what you're saying, but John got his luck without buying a ticket," Uncle Henry said. "I'm not claiming he's a bad man. When his children came down ill, he'd sit up the night when the mother wouldn't dream of it. He wasn't shamming when he told you that, as he *would* tell. I'd see it in his face. Puffy, you know. Stick a finger in his cheek and it wouldn't come out. Bladder case, with a tendency toward dropsy."

The uncle contemplated John Dickens's health.

"But if there wasn't some drama or crisis with his children, well," he continued, "his attention was elsewhere, wasn't it? His older boys ran wild, as the youngers do now. He sent young Charley to the Wellington House Academy around the corner. Not exactly the King's School in Rochester, is it? I'd see him to and fro, shabby as a mudlark. The father kept the boy alive, but whatever young Charley has achieved, it's on himself."

"Though he paid off his father's tick."

"Well, it's his father," Uncle Henry said. "And you know all about *fathers*." Chuckling, he sent upstairs for coffee, which they drank in peaceful contemplation of his apothecary jars.

R ichard first learned they were removing to London in the fall of 1833 when Uncle Henry had showed up unexpectedly at their old home in Chatham, having got up with the stars, he'd said, and walked the full forty miles from his chymist's shop in London.

"Aside from the occasional ride from a farmer," he admitted, when Bob picked a piece of straw from the back of his jacket.

Afterward, their father and the uncle had closeted themselves in the parlour. Richard and his brothers only had to exchange a glance to agree that Uncle Henry was in trouble and needed a loan. They hadn't thought much about their father's recent visits to London or the way he was stepping down from local positions, not seeing any connection to the family confab about the luxury trade. They'd assumed their father was simply taking a rest after finishing his work as secretary of the Chatham Reform Society, the Reform Bill having been passed in Parliament the year before, granting the vote to middling men like their father and gaining Parliamentary Borough status for Chatham. As for his museum, the fact he was training a new curator only meant that their father was bored. He chaffed Uncle Henry about being flighty, but they were more alike than not.

"So," their father said, as he and the uncle arrived in the sitting room that evening, preceded by heavy footsteps up the stairs. Richard had grown nervous by then. The extended meeting raised worries that their father was hard pressed to guarantee the uncle's loan. He might be facing financial problems himself. They might lie behind the London visits, which Richard had added up on his fingers. Not to mention all this stepping down.

"So," their father said again, and left another silence.

"Sir?" Bob asked, and their father nodded firmly.

"We're moving to London. It's arranged. I'm buying my brother Picnot's business. Robert, your uncle has agreed to formally sign your articles"—Uncle Henry giving Bob a wink—"so you'll finish your apprenticeship in the capital.

Stephen," he said, finding him in the corner, "you'll apprentice with me in the gilding shop. George, my boy, you'll be staying in the shipyards. Carpentry, I think. Richard, it's time. It's art for you in London." The father paused to enjoy the prospect, then remembered Arthur and John. "School, of course, for the little chaps."

Richard felt the room expand. London. And art school? He'd been worried that old Dadson's limitations as an artist would curtail his own advancement, not yet having seen that William Dadson was an excellent teacher, which used a different muscle.

"But what about us? What happens to us?" Mary Ann had asked, and Richard looked over to see his sisters vibrating with unease. "What happens to *me*?"

"Well, my dear," their father began, "the capital will provide you with many advantages." He stopped, looking silly about what these might be.

"But we have friends here. I might *marry* here." Mary Ann's wail hung in the air. Their father looked aside, smiling uncomfortably.

"It'll be all right. Your Aunt Hannah is there," Uncle Henry said kindly. But Mary Ann burst into loud sobs and fled the room, slamming the door. The fire leapt at the draft of air and crackled mercilessly.

Mary Ann's complaint became Richard's first intimation that success had its drawbacks, its wormwood. Aunt Hannah had arrived to help, a sensitive lady, slight and gentle. You'd think Uncle Henry would have known himself well enough to marry a practical woman, but Aunt Hannah was a pale dove cooing, *There, my dear. There, there.* So sweet was the aunt, so gentle, that her efforts quickly failed. Mary Ann grew bitter, pushing her complaints to the centre of their removal from Chatham.

Or putting Richard there. It soon transpired that Mary Ann blamed Richard for the move, believing the rest of them were being sacrificed to his artistic career. He didn't see it: George was a self-sacrifice, while Bob and Stephen were palpably looking forward to London. But he couldn't convince Mary Ann that the brothers weren't just putting up a good front, especially since she wouldn't talk about it directly, pointing out that she hadn't said a word.

"Not a word," she would tell Aunt Hannah, often quite loudly.

Even on their last day in Chatham, as she packed up the kitchen, Mary Ann had expressed herself mainly with a *clatter clatter clatter*. Richard and Stephen were waiting at the table, hoping in vain for dinner. *Clatter clatter rattle.* A pause and Mary Ann said mournfully, "I could have married here."

Richard noted the change from *might* to *could have* but decided against saying that she could just as well marry in London. Mary Ann was a handsome girl. Her features were a little too big for her face, but her eyes were a striking dark blue, her skin creamy and smooth, and she wasn't yet twenty-one. Bob defined her as marriageable, although Richard was aware of bias. His brother had no wish to inherit a houseful of old maids.

"It really isn't my fault, M.A.," Richard told her.

"Did I say a word?"

"I would have thought it was mine if the old man hadn't gone crazy for art. Surely you can see how much he likes the prospect of framing on his own account. I know that's not the whole of it, but don't you think I feel a bit of a burden, that to some extent he's living perhaps a little, well, vicariously?" As she glared at him: "If you know the word."

His sister threw an earthenware plate to the floor, where it shattered into thick wedges. They all looked down at it.

"That's your fault, too," she said.

Unfortunately, Mary Ann proved to be right. The sisters were lost in London. They made few friends, while Aunt Hannah seldom visited, preoccupied with her sick little daughter. Meanwhile, Richard prospered. After their father took possession of the framing shop, he got to work improving his stock of artist's supplies, bringing Richard along to the dank warehouses where pigments were sold, the air muggy with linseed oil. He took Richard when calling on the hob-nobs at the Society of British Artists, which had its exhibition hall only a few doors away. Painters competed to hang their work at the Society's fashionable exhibitions and, as his father said, someone had to frame them, "and someone else might want to exhibit there one day."

Poor Mary Ann. Poor old Dadson: Richard soon saw the difference between provincial artists and the professionals in London, witty men and keen observers, especially of their rivals. Historical painters came into the shop. Watercolour men. One day the bell tinkled and Joseph Mallord William Turner himself walked in, small and scruffy, but speaking with confidence of Paris, Rome, Florence—"too many Italians"— and meanwhile knowing exactly what he wanted in terms of cochineal.

His father soon boasted a group of artist friends, his closest being David Roberts, a heavy-featured Scotsman and former president of the Society. Richard grew used to finding

Roberts smoking his pipe in the back parlour, feet up on the fender, cup of coffee at his elbow. It was Roberts who set Richard his goal of applying to the Royal Academy Schools. A dubious squint at his scrawlings: "Yuh might just manage."

Richard's father was so pressed after refurbishing the shop that he couldn't pay for Richard to attend Sass's preparatory academy, the usual route. Instead, Roberts sent him to the British Museum, ordering him to copy the museum's casts and drawings. Once a week or so, Roberts would hold out his hand for Richard's sketchbook and criticize his work—"Now that bit's good, but don't get yuir hopes up"—sometimes calling in his friend, the marine painter Clarkson Stanfield, a kinder and more handsome man.

"It's hardly the same as studying with Sass, is it?" Richard asked Mary Ann, and immediately felt petty. Having professional artists criticize his work probably advanced him faster than any second-rate academy. And look what happened. Two years after they arrived in London, Clarkson Stanfield was elected a member of the Academy, which allowed him to recommend candidates to the Academy Schools. Stanfield recommended Richard, and he was accepted before the ink had dried on the letter.

A s he left his uncle's shop, Richard was still brooding about fame. Not that the subject was entirely problematic, since if he were famous, he'd have his own studio—boxes of top-notch cigars to treat his friends—a pleasantly efficient assistant whom he'd know precisely how to direct without embarrassment—undraped models, their strong thighs—*not* that he could think about that here (Where was he?), picturing himself instead at the centre of a salon of admiring artists—"Please, Stanfield, allow me to return the favour"—never the least bit supercilious, unlike that *geranium* Dickens—until Richard stumbled over his boots, a blush rising furiously over a chin and cheeks which he was reminded hadn't yet formed a secure relationship with whiskers. Not a single picture sold, and he had the brass bollocks to concern himself with *fame*.

Richard's contempt for himself must have burned on his face. Meeting his eyes was a painted girl whose own eyes widened. It was evening now, and he was back in the Quadrant at the foot of Regent Street, bereft of young ladies at this hour and given over to the painted frails. The poor girl, mistaking the focus of his contempt, folded her shawl over her face and drifted away, leaving Richard wanting to do the same.

Yet the question wouldn't go away. Over the next few months, he occasionally saw Dickens across the room, surrounded by an expanding coterie of admirers. It was easy to avoid him, especially since Dickens seemed intent on doing the same. But there was no escaping the author, with new chapters of *Oliver Twist* published each month in Bentley's magazine. They said *Oliver* wasn't doing as well as *Pickwick*, which Richard heard with a nasty sort of pleasure he disliked in himself. But it was still selling in the tens of thousands, and his sisters were among the fanatics, finding the story of poor orphaned Oliver to be so sweetly pathetic they fell onto the latest *Bentley's* the instant it appeared in the shops, hurrying Oliver home, pattering the dear little fellow upstairs and settling him down for a series of crackling reads in front of the fire.

Stephen did the honours, having the best voice in the family, his mixture of growls and comic cadences taking Oliver from the workhouse to his entrapment by the criminal boy-stealer Fagin. Richard always intended to excuse himself but never quite managed, leaning against the doorframe week after week as if he were about to leave. One day, as he followed Oliver's inadvertent escape from Fagin, it occurred to him that critics weren't entirely correct when they accused Dickens of painting in black and white. In fact, he painted shadows while eschewing shadows, an artistic versatility, a mastery, a challenge that made Richard wonder if Dickens might be speaking to him after all, despite their mutual silence.

What did Richard hear? For one thing, that John Dickens must have let his son run as wild as Uncle Henry claimed. The author knew the tricks and twists of London streets as well as any criminal: its characters, its stews, its dodges and thefts, everything he needed to pitch young Oliver into an escalating series of traps. The younger Dickens was making use of his neglect, turning it into fame.

Richard didn't have that goad. He'd always been fortunate, the death of his mother aside. He'd been coddled, as Mary Ann still pointed out. His sister was twenty-four now, forgetting her mending as Stephen read onward, biting her knuckle, far too concerned with Oliver's fate. Poor Mary Ann had never had a proper suitor in London. Or, to be optimistic, she hadn't had one yet. Bob invited his friends home, but none had given her more than a nervous glance before finding it necessary to explore the other side of the sitting-room door, the stairs, the street. *Bad luck*, Bob kept saying. Listening to the saga of *Oliver Twist*, Richard began to suspect that his own luck might be just as foul.

Which was to say, good luck might be ill luck to an artist.

"'He!'" Stephen cried one night, as the evil Fagin rediscovered Oliver. "'Could I mistake *him*, think you? If a crowd of devils were to put themselves into his exact shape, and he stood amongst them, there is something that would tell me how to point him out. If you buried him fifty feet deep, and took me across his grave, I should know, if there wasn't a mark above it, that he lay buried there. Wither his flesh, I should!'"

Such anger. Bob had seen it. Richard heard it, and began to suspect Dickens's neglect had bred a fury so powerful it propelled Oliver's story forward like a steam engine, giving his writing such speed, such an indelible sense of combustion, that he became the first truly modern author, filling a void no one had realized was there, the apotheosis of the age.

Richard was left with serious doubts about his own chance of rocketing. Here he'd been preoccupied with fame when the real danger was failure. As he tied his cravat at the mirror the next morning, he saw a blandness in his features he'd never noticed before, and his smile—*smile*, he told himself—struck him as limp, when Dickens's looked feral. He began pausing as he painted, worried that he hadn't any anger in him, no chip on his shoulder he dared you knock off, no sense of neglect to nip his bollocks and give him a raging, urgent sense of momentum.

Some days he felt so low, he wanted to lay down his brushes, hide under the covers and *give up*, the word failure, failure, failure beating a tattoo in his brain. He paced his room in the Suffolk Street attic, angry at himself and obscurely humiliated. *Richard Dadd: Watch Him Plummet to Earth—From a Height He'd Never Reached!*

Richard refused to let himself fail, not without a fight. When a lecturer pulled out the cast of a murderer's bound hands, he drew muscle and bone. He sketched every model they were given in Life Class, even when a guardsman proved too drunk to hold a pose, his foot slipping off the rung of his chair. Richard spent long hours at his easel hacking out a still life, a portrait, a scene from a play, and after a visit to Plymouth, he worked up his sketches into a series of seascapes and landscapes. Yet he wasn't sure that all this effort added up to anything, and when he finally spent a morning at the end of October laying everything out in the attic, his squares and rectangles looked like a mad chequerboard on the floor. Nothing added up, and he couldn't begin to understand why.

"It strikes me as incoherent," he said, having called in Egg and Frith for a critique. His friends walked in heavy boots around the echoing attic, picking up sketches, watercolours, bending to look at Plymouth oils propped against the wall, where the chequerboard turned oddly vertical.

"But this is wonderful work," Egg said, going down on one knee in front of a seascape. "You're making such progress."

"There might be some good bits," Richard said, picking up the picture to bring Egg back to his feet. "But they're probably accidental."

"Why are you being so hard on yourself?" Frith asked. "I shouldn't."

Richard had never explained about Dickens, knowing the absurdity of comparing oneself to the apotheosis, even though Charles was only five years older than he was and their families remained tied. As Uncle Henry had predicted, John Dickens found his way back to the shop. Also as predicted, Charles had turned up to pay off the new debts. Then he'd surprised them, turning vile as he paid, seeming to grow taller and darker and thinner as he threw down his money, calling Uncle Henry a species of Israelite for allowing his father credit *when he knew*.

"It's probably better to be hard on oneself than on other people," Richard said. "I need some assistance here, lads. Come on. Tell me what's lacking. I can't make it out on my own."

But his friends were hesitant, and as he looked over their shoulders, Richard saw that Egg was right: his work was progressing, at least technically. In fact, he'd gone far enough beyond both Egg and Frith that he suddenly felt unkind bringing them here, as if he were rubbing their noses in it; as if he'd been given the moon and was whining about wanting a great burning ball of sun.

He picked up a still life. "The edge of this knife. I did a bad job positioning that, sticking it out at the viewer. A little too threatening, don't you think?"

"Knives *are* threatening," Frith said. "I've been known to threaten my canvas with one. Sometimes hourly."

Richard forced himself to smile and picked up a watercolour. "This one isn't anything like my sister, really. She has beautiful eyes."

He gave Egg a hopeful glance. If he wasn't going to get any help with his work, he might as well try out his suspicion that Egg liked a managing woman. Mary Ann was only two years older than Gus, give or take. But his friend's vague smile revealed a total lack of interest, and Richard was left to fumble his portrait back onto the floor.

Eventually his friends landed on a few minor inadequacies, Frith picking up a mahl stick to point them out. Richard nodded politely, and as soon as seemed plausible, he took them downstairs for tea. Throwing himself into an armchair, he abandoned his friends to his sisters, hearing the girls become too chatty for gentility, yet unable to shake the picture of his attic and its incoherent chequerboard. He had no intention of taking a knife to his paintings, not least because he'd have to go down to the kitchen to get one. But he did wish someone would give him the sun.

"Dadd, are you with us?" Frith asked.

"I'm so sorry."

"Egg's talking about going to the theatre later this week. *The Tempest*. Are you in?"

"I think I'm coming down with a cold."

"What does that mean?"

"You're going deep on me, are you, Billy? The meaning of a cold, of life, of Art." Seeing them look alarmed, Richard smiled. "Of course I'm in. I'm an idiot. I have a small complaint in the throat, that's all."

A complaint the size of the sun. But he wouldn't miss Shakespeare, who tackled life's big questions and might provide Richard with some answers. They settled on Thursday, Mary Ann offering them another slice of cake, which Egg seemed cool in declining.

# En Route to Covent Garden Theatre
## Where Richard Saw *The Tempest*
## by William Shakespeare
### November 3, 1838

It was O'Neil's idea to go to the Hummums before the play. Harry O'Neil had been born in Russia, and even though he'd returned to England when he was a child, this made him their sophisticate. They'd gathered at Richard's house that afternoon and set off early enough for the theatre to allow for diversions along the way, O'Neil and Frith talking over top of one another as they headed toward the City, the air thickening with fog. Their progress was slow but Richard still felt sweated and soon had to lean against a lamp post to recover.

"You really aren't well, are you, Dadd?" Egg asked.

He tried to formulate an answer but was distracted by O'Neil speaking behind him. Actors suffering from a cold stopped by the Hummums to steam out their lungs before a play. Why shouldn't Richard?

His friends seemed to expect a response, when all Richard felt was a foggy sort of panic. Because he'd never been to the famous *Hotel* Hummums and needed more time to work up to it, that was why. Because he had a worry about pox, even though he knew O'Neil was only proposing the Turkish steam room, not hiring a piece of baggage to take upstairs. Because he had an uncomfortable suspicion that his father opened up the occasional piece of baggage at the Hummums, and the last thing he wanted to do was confirm it by running into his father there, accompanied by one of the female sex. This seemed possible, Richard's father having sent them off by saying he was planning to go out himself and not mentioning where.

"So we'll all be swells," Richard croaked, unable to come up with an acceptable excuse.

"Are you sure an ale wouldn't do you better?" Egg asked. "Or a brandy?"

Gus seemed genuinely concerned, not looking to escape the hotel. Maybe he was more experienced than Richard, with females as well as the Hummums. Gus was a year older than he was, already twenty-two. He was also discreet, while Frith and O'Neil talked bawdily about their conquests, even though Richard didn't see how the females in question could be *conquests* when one paid, any more than he could understand why Frith boasted about the process when his tackle had nearly fallen off from the pox last year, at least the way he'd told it at the time.

"We can get a brandy there," O'Neil said, which seemed to satisfy Egg.

Walking with greater purpose, they soon arrived at the

great flat facade of the Hummums, pocked with curtained windows that wavered not quite square from the candle-light behind them. In the thickening fog and fall of night, the Hummums looked more respectable than the respectable buildings around it, not least because whores kept clear of the entrance. Some were probably stationed inside, others waiting to be summoned, and the neighbourhood's casual dolly-mops seemed to understand that adventuring onto professional ground would only earn them a black eye.

Once through the door, Richard was temporarily blinded by the glitter of light inside and disoriented in the bustle. What was the correct attitude to take if one met others one knew? No doubt a laddish unspoken *ho ho ho aren't we all going to do the unspeakable ho ho ho*. He could manage that, at least if it wasn't his father, although he stumbled as they walked down a ground-floor corridor when a door opened on a painted strumpet with her bare bubbies served above a corset like two plucked chickens on a platter. To his relief, O'Neil said something to the chamberlain about steam this time, *our friend has a cold*, and the chamberlain answered obsequiously, "An't the air that chill these days, sir?"

They walked up and down stairs as if in a dream, and Richard didn't know quite what level they'd reached when they entered a disrobing room, although it felt damp and subterranean. Attendants helped them out of their clothes as if they were swells; he'd got that part right. Presumably the attendants routinely guarded men's clothes and purses, since O'Neil made no particular arrangement. Soon they were as brazen as models, and after two more steps up they reached a great maw that opened into the Turkish bath.

Standing at the entrance, taking in the clouds of steam,

the firelight, the dim forms of odalisque males on banquettes, Richard asked himself what he was doing here, then realized how much time he'd spent lately asking after a grand purpose in life, or at least his grand purpose: *Richard Dadd, What He Should Be, If He Can Manage Anything at All.*

Well, he was in a steam room. O'Neil thought it would make him feel better and they'd brought him here; that was all. That was all, and Richard couldn't have felt more relieved. Throwing himself onto a banquette, he breathed in warm air for the first time in months. It made him cough, but in a good way. Sweat dripped into his eyes, salty on his lips, coursing down his neck and back and chest. O'Neil was right. He'd sweat out his cold and leave here feeling much better.

His clique lounged on banquettes in an uncomposed grouping. Through dimness and steam, one took surreptitious glances, both at them and at a couple of men walking by, their tackle swaying, the heat being kind to them all. Richard didn't think he showed any sign of having no experience with the female sex, although perhaps by definition he wouldn't know. There might be some physical manifestation equivalent to the Masonic handshake or similar. At least he was satisfied that he was perfectly normal otherwise, reassured repeatedly by swimming in the Medway as a boy, having brothers, drawing models in Life Class, et cetera. Allowing for their respective statures, his friends were normal as well, which was inexplicably reassuring; none of them like the gentleman nearby who spread his legs to show off a pair of enormous bollocks on which his pizzle lay curled like a cat on a wrinkled pink cushion. Richard wondered if women laughed at men's pride, whether they'd laugh at him, at least if he ever got up the nerve, and knew they probably would.

S ummer on the Medway. They dove into the golden water like arms going into sleeves. Weeds down there, swaying like shadows as you brushed them. Silt brushing up from the river floor. You swam underwater until your lungs caught fire then surfaced to gulp in great draughts of air. Down again after that into the cool warm water, kicking your way here and there, switching directions like a fish until the need came to surface *uuup* under the board where Fatty Tull lay idling, dumping Fatty into the river in a great *haw* sputter sputter choke.

*I'll get you, Dadd!*

Splashing water at each other, kicking up the river, chasing pieces of driftwood until their stomachs began to growl. Hauling themselves onto the bank, they shook off water, shook rainbows off their hair, exaggerating the shake of their bits, thrusting them out and waggling them in case any girls were watching, although (horrifying thought) not their *sisters . . .*


"H ey now!" Richard cried, leaping to his feet. O'Neil had dumped a pitcher of cold water on his head, and after the initial shock, after drawing in a great long choking breath, Richard doubled over coughing. Coughing half his lungs out, his ribs aching, Frith placing a spittoon at his bare feet so he spat ingloriously into it. Drawing in another long breath, half-standing now, hands on his knees, Richard managed to breathe slowly in and out and in again without coughing.

"There, you see?" O'Neil asked. "Mr. Henry Nelson O'Neil, Physician in Ordinary to the Royal Academy Schools. You feel much better now."

"Yes, I do," Richard said, although, in fact, he felt far worse.

It was a struggle to get into his clothes—a struggle to hide the struggle of getting into his clothes—and as they left the hotel, the slithering adhesion of cold humid air outside made Richard break into a new sweat. Evening was on them, the fog thickening. Gas lamps were reduced to faint circles, pale buoys in a dark sea that led them around corners and toward the theatre. Richard felt light-headed and knew he ought to go home, but he wanted to see the play, William Macready's staging of *The Tempest*, talk of the town. *The Tempest* was supposed to be unstageable, but the critics were saying that Macready had triumphed.

Another triumph. Since taking over management of Covent Garden Theatre last year, Macready had been mounting Shakespeare's plays as they had originally been performed, returning to the Bard's text for the first time in more than a century, *King Lear*, *Macbeth*, now *The Tempest*, Macready taking the lead to draw a profitable crowd.

They were part of the crowd now, surging toward Covent Garden. Apprentices elbowed past them, shiny clerks and stuffed bankers, an undertaker and a legion of whores, Macready having turned the whores out of his theatre, being a family man and a devout Christian, although they hadn't gone far. Females of all grade and style grew visible to every side before receding into fog, Richard's clique being far enough from the restrictions of both the Hummums and Macready's theatre to be . . . where were they? In between, he supposed. Liminal. The word had come to Richard a while ago. He couldn't remember why, but he liked it.

As the fog drew in, forms of all shapes and sizes wisped through it, leached of colour by the night, faces made mysterious by hats and shawls. An arm reached past, brushing his sleeve. Richard heard a murmur of apology, although he couldn't make out the words. He just saw bleached forms so graceful he remembered his previous *Tempest*, a ballet danced a few months past by Marie Taglioni, a piece she called *Miranda*, taking the lead as Prospero's daughter on their magic island encountering men for the first time.

Richard had gone with his father, Shakespeare being so much a member of the family they wouldn't miss one of his visits to town. They'd arrived late, uninterested in the opera beforehand, edging into a spot in the pit while Taglioni was already performing, doing one of her famous ethereal flutters *en pointe* across the stage.

*That's* why he'd remembered. Miranda was veiled by Prospero, who held a thin fabric in front of her, making it look as if she were dancing through fog.

"Hi, watch where you're ..." A boy's rude interruption. Richard truly hated crowds. The words of old Dadson came back to him. Knowledge is a bulwark. Knowledge. Bulwark. More words he liked. Knowledge as a bulwark against the liminal.

"My question is," he heard himself telling his friends, "whether Macready got the idea of staging *The Tempest* after seeing Taglioni dance it last summer."

"A question that can't possibly wait until we've run the gauntlet," Egg said, the air clutching at his sleeve with a pair of arms, a doxy hoping for his custom.

"That was all I had to say," Richard answered. "Or rather, that it's something to think about. That one might hitch onto wagons, you know."

"He's still talking," Frith said. "And I believe he's saying something."

By now they'd arrived at the theatre doors. Pushing through a last gasp of smell and men, they were finally inside. Egg had got the use of someone's box, and after finding a way through the crowded saloon, they opened the door on their refuge, taking their chairs and glancing at the stage, which was still placidly curtained.

"Now *what* were you saying that's important?" Egg asked.

The theatre was both cold and stuffy, like sick lungs. Richard told himself the crowd would soon heat it. "Did I speak?"

"About Macready getting the idea of *The Tempest* from a dance," Frith said.

Richard pushed back his hair, feeling heated. "I don't know whether he did or not. But it strikes one as possible—and it's canny, you know." He was suddenly struck by his penetration. "To pick up a subject that's found success and then amplify. Let someone else prepare the public. We really ought to think about that when choosing our subjects."

"Rather than striving to be original," Frith said. He wasn't disagreeing. Egg and O'Neil chewed on the idea. Richard was surprised to find that Phillip wasn't there. Where was Phillip? Richard hadn't seen him all afternoon, and he'd thought Phillip was coming to the play.

"Stanfield didn't tell you?" Egg asked. "Whether it was coincidence, or whether Macready stole the idea."

Richard tried to remember. Clarkson Stanfield was a close friend of Macready, although Stanfield hadn't introduced him to Richard's father. Richard supposed each discipline of artist had friends in inferior positions, Stanfield relying on the father as his gilder and framer, Macready on his dresser, Dickens probably on his printer. But artists didn't know dressers, nor actors a framer, not really *know* them, no matter how essential a framer's family believed him to be.

"Well, it's his *father*," he heard his Uncle Henry say.

"You really aren't feeling well, are you, Dadd?" Egg asked.

Richard's mind had seldom moved so rapidly. "I think I've been working too hard," he said.

"Do you want to leave? I don't mind."

Richard shook his head. "Stanfield didn't say anything about Macready stealing the idea. He wouldn't, of course, even if he thought it true. But he didn't."

"He didn't say anything about the rumours of Macready having a liaison with Miss Helen Faucit?" Frith asked, looking up from a playbill. "Who's playing Miranda tonight, I see."

Egg read the look on Richard's face: "Didn't. But then he wouldn't."

"Have you heard the story of Macready's marriage?" Frith asked, as O'Neil borrowed the playbill. "How he met his future wife up in Scotland when she was nine or ten years old. Declared her a prize little actress, trained her up and married her at eighteen. Miss Faucit is how old? Crikey. Eighteen."

"Frith, you're dreadful," Egg said.

"Besmirching the reputation of an *actress*," Phillip added. Richard was startled to find Phillip behind him. Must have come in?

"I only shade in depth to the characterization of a family man who tossed the totties from Covent Garden," Frith said, seeming unperturbed. "You're the one who's always on about multiple layers, Dadd. Stanfield really said nothing about little Faucit?"

They were waiting for an answer. "Dadd didn't say," Richard answered. "But then he wouldn't."

In fact, Stanfield had never mentioned her name, no more than he'd mentioned Taglioni's dance. The double *Tempest* was probably a coincidence, perhaps something in the air, although Richard couldn't muster the energy to retreat from his thesis. He looked out at the theatre, which was filling up quickly, legions of tiny people infiltrating the pit and popping up like jack-in-the-boxes in the stalls. Filling despite an inscription on a silver salver Macready had presented to Stanfield after he'd done a bit of work for Macready the previous winter.

*That* was a story: how Stanfield had worked up a moving diorama for one of Macready's pantomimes, a two-hundred-foot-long canvas scrolled out for patrons showing scenes from the Alps to the Channel. Stanfield had started out as a scene painter, but he hadn't done any work in the theatre since becoming an RA, concentrating on easel paintings, his marine paintings, and he'd asked Richard's father for advice when Macready requested he send in a bill. Richard's father had suggested throwing it back on the manager, asking Macready to pay whatever he felt the diorama was worth. When a cheque arrived for the satisfactory sum of three hundred pounds, Stanfield had horrified Richard's father by refusing it, telling Macready he would only accept half.

"He's doing something noble," Stanfield said. "Reclaiming Shakespeare, and at great cost, Dadd. I'd like to support him."

"But what about the salver?" O'Neil asked, and Richard realized he'd been telling his story aloud.

"It's on Stanfield's sideboard," he said, "and I was thinking about the inscription, how Stanfield 'had brought the magic of his pencil and the celebrity of his name to the aid of a discouraged and declining sister art.' 'Declining.' I quote."

Richard nodded out at the theatre, which was full now to bursting, thousands seated around them, just as thousands had packed Macready's plays all year. It made him wonder if self-pity was an intrinsic part of the artistic personality, like fat in bacon.

His friends laughed; he must still have been speaking aloud. But he thought he might be right about the self-pity. He was certainly guilty of it himself, and probably with as little reason. *The Times* always belittled Macready, but most critics cried up his *Macbeth* and said his *Lear* showed a pathos seldom seen onstage. Richard agreed, having seen both, Shakespeare being almost a member of the family.

Hadn't he just said that?


This past June. They were reading *Much Ado About Nothing*. At home, the latest act in the family's Shakespeare mania. For as long as Richard could remember, his father celebrated Twelfth Night by announcing which of Shakespeare's plays they'd read that year. When Richard was very young, his father had taken all the parts himself. At least, Richard had thought so until last year, when he'd caught a weird fireside flicker of their mother's smile on Rebecca's lips and realized their mother must have read parts as well. It came to him that he had no idea what she'd been like. She'd just been his mother, he'd never known what else. Now she was gone to flickers, and he surprised himself with a sob, which luckily the family had read as repressed laughter.

This year Richard was chiefly reading Dogberry, while

Stephen and Rebecca had been given the lead parts of Benedick and Beatrice. Everyone was put to work as soon as they reached a useful age, the girls copying multiple texts, all of them assigned multiple roles. They usually gave one night a week to Shakespeare, doing as much as they could before bedtime, and reading each play over and over during the year.

Evenings melted away in drama, their understanding of each play deepening as their diction improved, although Richard didn't think either education or locution were precisely his father's goal so much as two of the mixes in his unusually mixed motives. In London they often read on Thursdays, his father still taking the lead from the chair closest to the fire. They liked to tease that his best part was Shylock, Shakespeare's tradesman.

"Shakespeare came from trade" was his inevitable reply. "Being the son of a glover."

Stephen preferred comic roles, calling most of the male romantic parts too wet, Shakespeare's ladies being far more bracing. Bob usually handled the chief lovers, while Richard didn't care what he read, especially after he'd taken up the violin this past spring and spent much of *Much Ado* looking forward to his song.

> *Sigh no more, ladies, sigh no more,*
> *Men were deceivers ever,*
> *One foot in sea and one on shore,*
> *To one thing constant never . . .*

George's rude laughter. Not a good memory. Richard didn't want it, but he could still see George laughing *har har har* in the doorway, his brother having arrived unexpectedly from Chatham, intuiting that on a particular damp Sunday afternoon they'd be reading *Much Ado* from beginning to end. Scruffy, stocky, his eyes an unnerving bright blue against the brown of his workingman's tan, he'd interrupted Richard to scrape a chair into the circle, saying, "Well, here we are agin."

As a little boy, George had surprised them one evening by prompting Bob when he'd forgotten an entrance in their *Midsummer Night's Dream*.

There had been a silence, then a high piping voice, "'So quick bright things . . .'" letting Bob finish, "'come to confusion.'"

"'You spotted snakes, with double tongue,'" George prompted Mary Ann. When she couldn't continue, he went on exultantly.

> *Thorny hedgehogs, be not seen;*
> *Newts and blind-worms, do no wrong;*
> *Come not near our fairy queen.*

George was too young to have been given a text, only eight or nine. Looking bewildered, their father had asked, "How much of it do you know?"

"All of it," George answered stoutly.

"And what shall be your reward?"

"*Bottom*," George said, stars in his eyes.

He went on to recite the role of Bottom in a singsong, but there was a sweetness to his word-perfect memorization that seemed to relieve their father; that relieved Richard of a worry about George he hadn't even known he'd had. For another four or five years, George shared comic parts with Stephen. Yet as he grew older, as his voice dropped, as he . . . well, coarsened, hadn't he? Something in the blood announced itself. George was reverting to their family's past in the shipyards while the rest of them pulled themselves up. From an early age, he'd run with a low drunken crowd, swore, scrapped, come home with cut knuckles and black eyes. The shame of it: he stole from the till.

It was as if all that was low in their family had been concentrated into George. No doubt that was why their father sent him back to the shipyards, where Dadd and Tull cousins told them he laboured as hard as a pair of oxen but bellowed rudely at his superiors. In the end, Richard figured his brother might be broken into docility, but what then? Living a common scavillman's life with a woman they would be ashamed to know.

Yet George loved Shakespeare, and Richard still hoped something fine might froth out of him. After all, George had intuited himself home so he could read *Much Ado*, even if the part he wanted was Richard's comic sheriff, Dogberry. Richard didn't care, although he could see from their father's frown he was worried for the sisters, George already having taught them the degree of innuendo in Shakespeare, *har har har* at every mention of prick and prickt.

Richard thought Dogberry was harmless; surely that was the point, a sheriff ordering his men not to apprehend criminals, for "they that touch pitch will be defiled: the most peaceable way for you, if you do take a thief, is to let him show himself what he is and steal out of your company." And, in fact, all went well until they reached the speech about pitch, and George read his way into Dogberry's big scene.

"'I pray you watch about Signior Leonato's door, for the wedding being there to-morrow, there is a great *coil* to-night,'" he said, and his rude *coil* made time crack open. Richard caught a glimpse of Shakespeare's age, the swagger and the blood, ladies as hard as jewels and gentlemen worse than hoodlums, strutting their powerful stockinged calves, their codpieces, waistcoats and their proud starched ruffs over a floor of filth and straw.

A brief crack, then time closed. George wasn't acting; it wasn't that. It was as if he'd come from there, not just a reversion in their family to the shipyards but a changeling in time.

Richard had remained unsettled until Rebecca came in as Beatrice. With the girl's needling "'Good morrow,'" when it was evening, Rebecca lightened the room. She was the only one of them who could act, although it was true Stephen read beautifully. An oddity that the most shy and awkward among them could disappear into a role and come out breathing poetry, a painfully shy girl becoming *sweet Beatrice* when Benedick finally called her so. Watching Rebecca laugh her way merrily through her closing lines—"'I yield upon great persuasion'"— Richard wanted to tell her, *Run away! Abscond to the theatre!*

She wouldn't have to abscond. No one cared that much about a middle sister.

*Go!* he urged her silently. *Now!*

Yet afterward, as their father praised her performance, Rebecca's blink of surprise told Richard that she was the opposite of the old man, at least according to the Dadson dictum. Rebecca had artistic talent without an artistic personality, its own type of curse. What a family they were: the father, Mary Ann, Bob the rock, merry old Stephen, then Richard, George, poor old Rebecca and after her Maria, already beautiful at sixteen, her brothers' relief, certain to marry, and after her the step-guineas, still too young to tell.

Rebecca had sparkled as Beatrice, swaggered as Miranda in *The Merchant* and showed rare plangency as Cordelia the time they read *Lear*, addressing her broken father with such tenderness that Richard could still hear her keen, "'Sir, do you know me?'"

It was ludicrously unfair. Richard had been granted so much, his sister not quite enough and George next to nothing at all.

T he curtain was rising. Richard shushed his friends, unable to imagine what Macready would do with *Lear*. Which was what they were here for, wasn't it? Even though Richard had an idea he'd seen it more than once already. The first time, their father had taken a box so the sisters could respectably come to the theatre for the first true production of *Lear* since the play was rewritten during the Restoration. They'd seen the rewritten version years ago in Chatham, opening as per Shakespeare with Lear's decision to divide his kingdom among his three daughters but soon veering off, Lear's Fool cut out entirely and a happy ending tacked on, Cordelia marrying Edgar, falderal and fiddle-de-de. Macready's production was a historic event, their father said, *an* historic event with its restoration of the pre-Restoration tragedy that closed the play: the Fool dead, Edgar dead, Cordelia dead, Lear himself dead, dead, dead.

"Sounds a treat," Stephen had whispered.

The second time, Richard had jostled around in the pit with his friends. They must have enjoyed it: here they were again, and in a box this time, Egg's box, a box of eggs. Pushing back his hair, which for some reason was damp, Richard leaned over the rail to get a good look at the bristle of hunting trophies on Lear's castle walls, at the Druid circles that would rise on the misty heath when mad Lear wandered there with his Fool, Miss Horton, the actress Miss Horton playing the Fool as a beautiful hectic boy. Rain would lash down and wind howl above the crash and clash of thunder, of lightning, gas lightning, lime lighting, and soon would come the superb moment when the stage filled with nearly two hundred Roman senators . . .

No, that was *Coriolanus*, Macready's *Coriolanus*. Richard had seen *Coriolanus* last winter, and Stanfield had told them a trick Macready played: how the last three rows in the Senate were filled by boys in togas, the first row made up of bigger boys, then a row of smaller boys, then a row of even smaller boys, creating an eerie sense of recession. Of distance. Perspective, that was the word.

Except. Prospero's sprite Ariel was flying above the stage. This wasn't *Coriolanus* or even *Lear*. Richard had come to *The Tempest*. He knew that, even though he wasn't quite sure why he was there or how Ariel was flying. Liminal, he thought. Ariel was a liminal sprite, and as Richard watched her soar . . .

> *Where the bee sucks, there suck I:*
> *In a cowslip's bell I lie;*
> *There I couch when owls do cry.*
> *On the bat's back I do fly*
> *After summer merrily.*
> *Merrily, merrily . . .*

. . . and he realized (what was it?) Richard realized a hundred hundred *hundred* things, his mind working so rapidly that Shakespeare, Macready, Taglioni, all manner of brickbats and cowslips rose up before his inner eye like the stones from a fallen garden wall flying up and slotting themselves back into place.

Now he understood. Many things. For one, there wasn't any bulwark against the liminal. It infiltrated. Which was a useful thing for an artist to know.

Yet here was the puzzle. Richard was at home, and there was a hand on his elbow, and it was Gus Egg steadying him as his father felt his forehead, saying, "My dear boy, you're burning with fever. We need to get those boots off. Are they damp?" before bawling, "Stephen! Get me some leeches! Bell's in Oxford Street, and if they're not open, pound them up."

Now he was on the sofa. No time had passed, but his father was holding up a leech and Richard was saying, "Lovely little chap, like a pizzle," to the distant giggle of sisters.

It was still dark when Richard woke up, and his father sat reading in a chair at the foot of his bed. He levered himself upright, feeling quite well.

"Here you are, pater. What time is it?"

"Eight o'clock," his father said mildly, taking off his spectacles and putting the book on the bed. "Where are we, by the way?"

Richard smiled at the question, then understood. "I was quite ill, wasn't I? But I'm well now. At home. In bed."

His father continued to watch him closely. "Your fever broke just before dawn."

"Dawn? You mean it's eight the *next* night?"

"You've been asleep for almost sixteen hours."

"Good Lord." Richard lay back down, unable to work

out the timing. "I didn't pull Egg out of the theatre, did I? I remember him being here. You told Stephen to get leeches."

His father came to stand over him. "What's the last you remember of the play?"

Richard tried to think. "Ariel on wires near the beginning." Correcting himself: "No, the cowslip speech is toward the end. It's the only thing I really remember. I hope I wasn't a nuisance."

"Your friends said you seemed to enjoy the play. They thought everything was fine until it was over and you started talking as if you'd seen *Lear*. You told them Macready had been brilliant, and that Rebecca had played Cordelia with great plangency. You'd always believed she should go on the stage, and now you'd been vindicated."

"Oh Lord," Richard said, although he couldn't help chuckling. "I always have, actually."

"Gave us a scare," his father said, sitting down beside Richard on the bed. "How's your head? Any pain about the temples? The neck? What about here?" His father gently manipulated his head. "Any dizziness?"

No and no. "It's odd, though. One minute I was watching Ariel, and then I was here with Gus. I have no memory of anything between. Not even any sense of time having passed, the way you do when you wake up in the morning."

His father let him go. "You weren't asleep. You had a very high fever. I called for leeches to draw it out. The physician approved, when he came." His father looked proud of himself. "I suppose I know how to treat my own son."

"I saw something," Richard said, and his father looked mildly alarmed. "You mustn't worry. It's just that I've been flailing, and last night I realized that lacking focus means lacking a subject. There's Mr. Stanfield with his marine paintings. Mr. Turner with . . . whatever he does. But you know a Turner when you see one. His light. And I had a feeling there might be something for me in the imaginative. In Shakespeare, the greatest writers. They paint the liminal with words, and I have brushes. It's a way forward, anyhow."

"My goodness," his father said, looking far too impressed.

"I'm famished," Richard said. "Don't imagine I could have a chop."

"Anything else?"

Seeing his advantage, Richard said, "Perhaps some eggs and a piece of fish. Toast? With some marmalade, and maybe a cup of coffee."

"Mary Ann!" his father bellowed.

Richard settled back into bed, feeling pleasantly weak. "You've never thought of putting Rebecca on the stage?"

"Two artists in the family, I don't think."

"Nothing the matter with artists," Richard said, although he didn't want to argue, being more interested in his chop. Asleep for the better part of a day. No wonder he was famished.

# On the Moor
## Near Haworth, Yorkshire
### *February 11, 1853*

T he notices were good, *Villette* talked up everywhere. Charlotte's fame was confirmed; she was entrenched as a literary lioness. Yet she accepted (not yet humbly) that God had condemned her to a difficult life, so it was inevitable: a friend had sunk teeth into her novel. A former friend. Harriet Martineau had complained not only in a private letter but in a long review published in the *Daily Mail* that Charlotte's novel put too much emphasis on love. Women had other motives and Charlotte ignored them.

Stalking the moor, Anne's dog Flossy waddling behind her, Charlotte was surprised the heat of her anger didn't melt the snow. Clear a path for her and poor old Flossy. She was certain that nothing was greater in this life than love and unselfishness and fidelity. She also knew that what Harriet meant by *love* was marriage. Yet who to marry—whether or not to marry—was the most important choice a woman could make, sometimes her only real choice, if she were permitted to make it. Also a major plot point for a writer, but leave that aside.

Don't leave it aside. Harriet knew that perfectly well when she wrote her novel, *Deerbrook*, which turned on two thwarted love stories and (of course) two climactic marriages. She'd also known the power of love in her private life, even though Harriet was famously an old maid. Charlotte had recognized first-hand knowledge in *Deerbrook*, and hadn't been surprised when Harriet had told her that she'd been engaged when she was young, half a lifetime ago, Harriet being fifteen years older than Charlotte.

They'd talked during Charlotte's visit to the stone house Harriet had built for herself at Ambleside. The eccentric life she'd built for herself, rising well before dawn for a cold bath and a walk by starlight, the darkness leaving her half-blind when she was already deaf. Somehow she didn't stumble, working out her day's writing while getting her exercise, undistracted by the beauty of Lake Windermere and the high fells she knew only as black interruptions of the stars. Her torrential flow of reviews and books and political articles she managed by being at her desk before seven o'clock, not rising until dinner, and never rewriting a word.

Harriet had informed Charlotte of her unbreakable routine their first evening together by the fire, a kind but intractable look on her slightly flattened face and in her prominent wide-spaced eyes. Poached egg eyes, Emily would have said. This was two years ago. They had known each other for about a year by then, Charlotte having asked to meet her in London.

"It suits me perfectly," Charlotte had yelled into her friend's speaking-trumpet, happy to be left alone for a morning of reading and letters. They spent the afternoons together, often driving out or walking, Harriet striding along in heavy shoes and leather leggings, holding her trumpet in one hand and a furled umbrella in the other, using both to punch the air for emphasis *one-two* like a pugilist. During one of their *sorties* to the lake, Harriet told Charlotte about the engagement, her fiancé a schoolmate and friend of her brother, a young clergyman by the name of John Worthington.

A Unitarian clergyman. Harriet had been born Unitarian, the daughter of a Norwich manufacturer, although in her latest book she'd all but declared herself an atheist, which Charlotte found intolerable. The thought of no God, no succour, no afterlife that would reunite her with her sisters and mother and possibly even her poor brother. But Harriet was consistent. She had introduced Charlotte to her livestock and explained that she grew her own food, digging her taters, believing in self-sufficiency; in the atomized, individual, snuffable self, unable to count on a greater power. Silently aware that her father had been born poor on an Irish farm, Charlotte saw no virtue in digging potatoes. But she liked Harriet and especially admired *Deerbrook*, which was why she'd asked that they be introduced.

"I was already quite deaf when I met Mr. Worthington," Harriet had said, leading Charlotte downhill at a pace. "I remember being grateful to him for admiring me, which I dislike to look back on."

"I think gratitude a fine basis for marriage," Charlotte yelled toward the trumpet. "As long as both feel it."

She had spent enough time with Harriet to understand that a particular look meant neither disagreement nor judgement, but simply that she hadn't heard.

"We became engaged in the year '26. You were just a child then. He was twenty-two and I was two years older and in a religious phase, which might have been my attraction. I was also a needlewoman. Possibly he read that as a guarantor of femininity. In fact, my father had recently died and we were impoverished, and I was looking to support myself with my needle. Marriage was not a terrible alternative, and Mr. Worthington was clever. He'd taken a mathematical prize at college."

"Did you care for him?" Charlotte yelled.

Harriet paused, and this time Charlotte could see she'd heard. "Why yes, I did," she said, looking into the past, which from the direction of peoples' gaze, Charlotte always thought was located down and to the left.

"But he went mad, you see."

Another pause as they both looked at the choppy lake.

"Brain fever. He was taken ill quite suddenly, while working as a pastor in Manchester. The doctors originally believed he'd recover, but when the fever subsided, he wasn't himself. Feeble and depressed, I was told. Worse. By then, he was with his family in Leicester, and the local doctor suggested I visit to remind him of possibilities. However, my mother declined to let me go. I believe my brother James interfered, painting the insanity as incurable and the engagement as best forgotten. Mr. Worthington's depression grew bottomless, and a few weeks later he was dead."

Charlotte was horrified, drawing her collar closed. "By his own hand?"

"It wracked me, but it made me," Harriet went on as if she hadn't heard, although Charlotte was certain she had. "That's when I began to write seriously and decided against marriage as a proposition. I saw that our union wouldn't have been happy. No marriage would have made me happy, and I doubt I could have made a husband happy, although I regret Mr. Worthington's death. I regret not having seen him before he died, and I regret the breach with his family. I learned much later that someone had told Mr. Worthington's parents that all the while I'd been encouraging their son, I was engaged to someone else. That's why I hadn't come to Leicester."

Two years later, Charlotte could still see the expression on Harriet's face. A cold wind had blown tendrils of hair across her friend's cheeks, but she'd looked as if she were smacking her lips over a juicy ripe peach. Not only had one man loved her, but her fiancé's family had no trouble believing that another man would as well. Harriet had been the peach. She wasn't an old maid because of her deafness. In fact, if Charlotte read it right, she was an old maid who had loved, and whose love had been denied her, and who had gone on to a profession that suited her well.

This was precisely the story of Lucy Snowe in *Villette*. Reading Harriet's review in the *Mail*, Charlotte had realized that while she'd expected most critics to either loathe or condescend to her novel, she'd counted on Harriet to sympathize. Getting the reverse, she felt like a child who'd set her heart on one toy and been fobbed off with another. No matter that it was a better toy. She hadn't got what she wanted, when fame was supposed to give her exactly what she wanted.

Instead, as Charlotte took her exercise on the moor, she felt pecked to death by crows. Her work may have reached an admiring public, but she was harassed by her friends. Not only had Harriet betrayed her, but George Smith hadn't written a line since she'd left London, getting his editor Mr. Williams to send her the reviews. Charlotte didn't know whether she'd done something wrong or whether she ought to read his silence as her final confirmation that theirs was simply a business relationship. Her reviews and sales meant she'd given George all he wanted from her, at least for now, and he wouldn't write her again until he needed a new novel.

Meanwhile, she'd arrived back in Haworth to find that her rejection of his proposal meant Mr. Nicholls had resigned his position as her father's curate and applied to go to Australia as a missionary. Yet since her father needed time to find a new curate, Charlotte often saw Mr. Nicholls drooping his way through Haworth like a large, wet, beaten black dog. Hardly flattering when she was the one who'd given the beating. She also liked dogs and felt sorry for him, especially with her friend Ellen Nussey visiting.

"He makes a spectacle of himself, all hunched up like that," Ellen had said this morning, watching Mr. Nicholls from the dining room window. Charlotte supposed he was going into the church, but she wouldn't join Ellen and be caught looking.

"He's taking a child's funeral," she said, keeping her eyes on the socks she was knitting.

"But did he know the child?"

"A pupil at the Sunday school," Charlotte said, "where Mr. Nicholls has been admirably active. It isn't a great compliment, is it, Nell? To think so poorly of someone who likes me."

"Presumptuous," Ellen murmured, with more than a hint of

peach-eating in her tone. *She* was Charlotte's best friend, not Mr. Nicholls. This was true, although Charlotte didn't like Ellen's increasingly proprietary manner. It was something she'd noticed since her fame. Old friends tugged at her attention. They were jealous of her time and made little claims, insisting on their right to fuss over her health, to fetch tea and shawls and bring her gifts she hadn't asked for, particularly the gift of their company. She found it unpleasant, the way they'd started treating her as both superior and incompetent. That's why Charlotte had wanted to meet lions like Harriet in London, who might know better. But they had disappointed her.

It was so cold the snow squeaked as Charlotte walked. Her spectacles would have fogged so she hadn't worn them and could see almost nothing. She knew the paths. She wouldn't stumble any more than Harriet did before dawn at Ambleside. But where Harriet saw black, she saw white and dun. She saw a vast snow-ridden undulating plain. She was an ant crawling across it, a cinder, a speck. Nothing made her feel more insignificant than her inability to see what others so easily could. She *was* insignificant. One time in London she'd half-heard a woman say in a crowd, ". . . told me she's the smallest creature she's ever seen outside a fair."

The wind was coming up; she would have to turn around. Charlotte had been picked up and thrown more than once by the Yorkshire wind. Laughing in its deep hollow voice: *You think you're moving forward. But I'll set you back.*

"We've punished ourselves enough," she told Flossy, and turned home.

# Starting from Richard's
## New Studio, Great Queen Street, Lincoln's Inn Fields, London
### *March 21, 1839*

R ichard and his Clique were celebrating the sale of his first painting, a scene from *Don Quixote*. Not celebrating with the dash he'd like, but then his effort had been sold to a patron he wouldn't have chosen. At this spring's exhibition, Richard had found favour with the long-nosed comic actor W. Tyrone Power, the stage Irishman who'd last year played *Groves of Blarney* to a delirious caterwauling public.

"Kiss the Blarney Stone," Frith carolled. "Let's all go to Oirland and kiss the sainted stone of Blarney."

"I'll check the sailings," Richard said, Ireland being the better alternative, the lads also having proposed a celebratory visit to the house of Mrs. Ketchum, the aptly named bawd.

"Now he's kissed everything that moves," O'Neil said, "Frith is starting in on everything that doesn't. Advantage Frith. Stones can't run away shrieking."

His friends were lounging in his new studio, Egg and Phillip smoking a cigar, all of them drinking his treat of porter. Richard was confident it was exactly what an artist's studio should be: a cramped doorway, a hunched ceiling, its walls painted green half a century ago and every inch tacked over with drawings whose edges lifted as puffs of wind blew through the rotten sashes. It had the amusingly raffish, down-at-heels air of a defrocked parson. Richard usually slept at his father's house and, more to the point, ate there. But this was his domain, his ash-strewn castle of collapsing plaster and good north light. He'd never thought *Don Quixote* was his best work, and the identity of the buyer had confirmed it, but Richard was on his way now, and nothing could stop him.

In the half-darkness came a hum from Frith, half throat-clearing and half musical. He wavered to his feet and began singing in his best imitation of an Irish tenor:

> *A baby was sleeping;*
> *Its mother was weeping;*
> *For the husband was far on the wild raging sea;*
> *And the tempest was swelling*
> *Round the fisherman's dwelling;*
> *And she cried, "Dermot my darling, oh come back to me!"*

"The Angel's Whisper," a tremendous success for W. Tyrone Power and every stage-Irish street singer in London.

*Her beads while she numbered*
*The baby still slumbered,*
*And smiled in her face as she bended her knee:*
*"O, blest be that warning,*
*Thy sleep adorning,—*
*For I know that the angels are whispering with thee!"*

Richard beat time happily on his thigh, convinced of his friend's talent, artistic if not musical. Arguably, to use his father's word, *arguably* this was an historic gathering. His friends would rise high in the firmament, the future stars of British art. Or at least they'd join him in making a sale or two before the latest exhibition closed.

What set their clique apart was their habit of working fiendishly hard. Frith had made a long and lucrative tour of Lincolnshire during last year's long vacation, having flattered a rich farmer with such a handsome portrait that his neighbours formed a queue. Frith would soon go back to Lincolnshire, while Richard was gearing up for another sketching tour, planning a route that might take him as far north as Leeds and Manchester, home to the richest of manufacturers. He planned to drop in on family, friends, acquaintances on the way; on the family of friends, acquaintances of the friends of the family of acquaintances; indeed on anyone living a short hike from the picturesque. He would sleep in barns if he had to, which he probably wouldn't, aware that in any case that this was a passing phase, a gruelling hilarious time that would one day fuel the stories he'd tell his grandchildren: *Richard Dadd, When He Was Becoming.*

*The dawn of the morning*
*Saw Dermot returning,*
*And the wife wept with joy the babe's father to see;*
*And closely caressing*
*Her child with a blessing,*
*Said, "I knew that the angels were whispering to thee."*

Thunderous applause. Perhaps not quite thunderous with only four of them clapping, but O'Neil stomped his feet. With a flourish, Frith bowed and sank into a chair, pretending it was as comfortable as their chairs would be in future. While they were painting, Richard and his friends concentrated on the anatomical turn of a neck, the angle of a shadow, on getting their tone right, the sky right, the Thames not quite right, not a sewer, but the way it should be, trying for the same degree of understanding Frith granted his rich red-faced farmers. While painting, they were realists, one eye on their subject and one on the market. Otherwise they were dreamers. And what was their dream but a future in which success would fly them above petty annoyances, whether leaky windows, disappearing porter or buyers who were less boast-worthy than one would have wished. Not to be a snob.

"Time for Mother Ketchum's," O'Neil said, putting down his empty bottle and standing unsteadily.

"Or not," Richard answered. When he realized the others were looking at him, he fumbled for an excuse and couldn't find one. O'Neil bent down to look in his eyes, a great whiskered face leaning in, a porterous breath. What O'Neil saw made his eyes widen, and he straightened.

"He hasn't been there," he told the others, meaning more than Mrs. Ketchum's. Richard tried to think of a witty detour, but O'Neil wouldn't let go. His enraged falsetto: "Why on earth not?"

Egg and Phillip looked embarrassed, Frith amused. Being unable to lie, Richard said weakly, "I have concerns about *houses*." As Frith tried to wipe away a grin: "Well for God's sake, Billy, you nearly died of the pox, at least to hear you tell it."

"So it's the father's doing," O'Neil said. "One might have suspected."

"No," Richard said. "In all fairness."

He wondered at the exchange of looks above his head.

"It's really not," he insisted weakly.

"But here's the thing," Egg confided, and Richard looked for Gus to throw him a buoy. "The way it affects the work."

An hour later, Richard was in the lobby at Mrs. Ketchum's, such as it was. Surely Egg had been joking about the work, but the hint was worrisome and O'Neil had been persistent. Now Richard scuffed his boot unhappily on the stair as O'Neil arranged things with the thickly rouged Mrs. Ketchum. After a considerable activity of eyebrows, she named a room on the second floor, and Richard dogged up and up, expecting to meet an experienced whore in a reassuring coze.

Instead, he opened the door on an acrid yellow room that had been painted no more recently than his studio. At its centre was an uncurtained bed with a fair-haired girl splayed across it, fourteen at most. Fifteen, with a snub nose and small squinting half-moon eyes. Perhaps he was meant to think that such a young girl must be clean.

"There you go," she said, pulling down her shift to show her bare little bubbies. "Which way is it, then?"

"What's your name?" he asked.

"Florrie."

Which probably meant it wasn't Florrie. Trying to find his footing, Richard told himself that he was the man and he was in charge. The thought was so encouraging that with a warm *throb, throb*, he hardened inside his trousers, no doubt too early. Edging awkwardly toward the bed, he asked, "Can you pull up your petticoat, please, Florrie?" Thinking he might as well get what he wanted. "And just, perhaps, open your legs."

"I'm a good girl," she said. But it sounded like a rote response, and she hiked up her petticoats without any nonsense and plumped her bottom toward him. Her legs were thin, but when she opened them, he saw ripe flesh and violet. The girl was hairless, which put him back in Chatham, the time he caught a very young George in the garden with his short pants dropped and his tiny tackle firm in the process of making the toddler Maria show him what she had. Before he cuffed George, Richard had caught a glimpse of his sister's plump madge looking like a lightly clenched fist. Now, beside the whorehouse bed, he could see how the fist had opened between the girl's . . .

Richard couldn't help a muffled cry. "I'm dreadfully sorry," he said, aware of his damp smalls.

"An't the first to," the girl said, levering up on her elbows.

"I suppose that's it," he said, looking around, anxious to go.

"Pied for a *how*er, 'aven't you?" Florrie asked, swinging her legs over the side of the bed and going to a washstand, where she poured some water into the bowl and wet one rag while taking another from a shelf beneath.

"'Ere we go," she said, pattering over on her broad bare feet.

Richard felt helpless. He didn't know what to do with his hands.

"Unbutton then," she said, all business, and once he did, she swabbed down his linen as impersonally as if she were dusting a vase on the mantelpiece. Tossing the soiled rag aside, she reached further inside his flies with the dampened cloth and he found to his surprise and pleasure it was warm.

"'Ot water, innit?" she asked. "I likes me looxeries."

She swabbed him down rhythmically, and Richard drew a breath. He was aroused again, which didn't seem to surprise her.

"'Ere we go," she said approvingly, still tugging. As his trousers fell to his ankles, the girl urged him toward the bed. With an expert pull, she tumbled him down on top of her in a mess of rumpled clothes and dirty sheets. Richard was still wearing his boots, which were clapped like vices on his ankles. Yet she soon had him jouncing in and out as he knew it was done, didn't he, from seeing beasts? Although he hated, truly hated, being a beast himself. Hated it and loved it, wanting this so badly he was terrified of finishing too soon or losing his stand or in some unsuspected manner humiliating himself a second time, even though the girl was a whore and he'd never know her real name.

Then he caught sight of himself in a looking glass he hadn't noticed before, a tall glass from a gentleman's dressing room with a reflection so wavering and inexact it wasn't noticeably him. He was watching some other man in a parallel bed wapping his wife, excited to see him giving it to her . . .

"*There* we go," the girl said.

Richard drew in a breath that was half-groan and half-sob. It wasn't what he'd imagined. His friends implied triumph and this was loss. Wasn't it loss? A moment's blankness, a true blankness of mind, and Richard levered himself out of bed, pulling his pants up hastily.

"That a surficiency?" the girl asked. "Not likely to compline, then?"

When Richard shook his head and muttered, she seemed

to lose interest and padded back to the washstand, apparently on her own behalf.

"Still 'ot," she said happily, which Richard didn't find flattering. He tossed a tip on the bed and Florrie scrambled back for it. Seeing himself out, he wished he were invisible, especially when he had to pass Mrs. Ketchum in the lobby, in her rouge and taffeta and soiled feather headdress. She gave him an amused, speculative look.

"I'll just take my leave," he said, hearing himself sound foolish and turning outside without waiting for an answer. Richard knew what she would imply: that he wasn't normal. He had an idea that most men didn't care to look and watch. They didn't like it so damned much and so little. Look how he'd celebrated his first sale. Discovering he was abnormal.

Richard walked back to his studio as fast as he could. Broke into a run, pounding up the stairs to fling open his door and slam it, pacing back and forth, back and forth, before fumbling to light a candle. The flare of the match lit a sketch of Egg tacked to the wall. Richard thought very well of his friends even though he knew their shadow sides: Frith talented yet light; O'Neil helpful but bullish; Phillip as fragile as he was perceptive. Egg he'd thought faultless. Gentle Egg. Wounded Egg, feeling too keenly the harshness of life.

"The way it affects the work," he'd said. Gus hadn't been joking; he'd been making Richard a noddy. Wounded Gus, gentle Gus, was needled through with mischief. How many times had he skewered Richard while the others laughed behind his back? He couldn't trust Egg. Couldn't trust any of them: O'Neil not bullish but a bully, Frith light and buoyant, it was true—*because he was hollow.* As to Richard himself, here's genius for you: Abnormal. Deviant. Despicable.

He tore the sketch of Egg off the wall. Turning it over, seizing a pencil, Richard bent over his table and sketched the splayed whore in a few quick lines. Then he got to work between her legs, hardening as he drew the intricate folds. When he was done, he rubbed the sketch against his crotch as she had her rag, then saw what he was doing reflected in the window and cried out at the thought of what anyone across the way might see.

Swivelling—feeling entirely irritable—Richard thrust the corner of his double-sided sketch into the candle flame, holding it between his finger and thumb as the edge caught fire. The flame ate slowly toward his hand, and when it scorched his fingertips, he let it go, watching the burning paper drift and rock and stutter to the floor. When it landed, Richard imagined a conflagration. But the floorboards were so old they were petrified. The flames burned out quickly, the golden fire darkening to red and the paper to black before it turned white, turned to ashes, warm ash scattered on top of the older, colder ash from his former friends' cigars.

Half-waking, realizing what he'd done, Richard scuffed the ash beneath his boot to make sure the fire was out. No trace of his drawing remained, although he could still picture the girl's cunny in sufficient detail that he'd be able to make another. *Surficient* detail, he recalled, and began to see the humour in it. At least he'd save a few quid on visits to the bawd's if all he had to do was draw.

Outside, the parish clock struck the quarter-hour. Richard realized his clique would be arriving soon, concerned and amused. Really, they were fine chaps, the best, but they could wait until morning. Richard hadn't buttoned his coat when he'd left Mrs. Ketchum's nor thrown it off when he'd come in. Now he did it up snugly and let himself out, taking to the streets.

L ondon by night was dangerous, everybody knew. But Richard still felt slightly abstract and it didn't bother him. He supposed he was only going to Uncle Henry's shop, where Bob would be able to settle the normality question, Bob being the only one he could talk to. But he felt somewhat abstract about his route as well, figuring he'd get there eventually. Meanwhile he sauntered, passing a party of swells, a watchman, a second watchman; passed apprentices free for a late-night hour, a pair of cat-sized rats fighting over the unspeakable in a gutter, a dozen sleepers snoring in doorways and the cries of too many dying babies drifting down from the rookeries. Reached Seven Dials, hadn't he? Shrieks, slaps, commotion spilled from the tenements, not much muffled by broken windows and the oilcloth used to patch them. Danger Town. More so, of course, for those who lived in it.

"You shouldn't be here," came the voice of someone stopped just ahead. "I'm safe, but you're not. What do you imagine you're doing?"

Charles Dickens was waiting at the corner.

"Sometimes a chap wants a walk," Richard said, stopping beside him.

"Sometimes a chap wants his purse stolen or his throat cut."

"Arguably," Richard said. "But sometimes he just wants a walk."

Dickens didn't like his answer. Anyone would want to know what Richard was up to, but Dickens seemed supernaturally annoyed at being fobbed off. The moon was emerging from the clouds, making visible his silent debate about whether to bid Richard good night.

"Come on, then," he said, and Richard felt bound to follow. The great author was going to take care of him. Grudging, exasperated, but he was going to do it, and led Richard out of the rookeries.

"Where do you live?"

"Great Queen Street."

"It's on my way home."

Richard wondered if Dickens knew a true-life Fagin who guaranteed his passage through the night. Yet they hadn't walked long before a rough-looking ragged man doffed his cap and said respectfully, "Mr. Dickens." Possibly he was so well loved that the common man protected him. People said he was a walker; that he walked for hours through all parts of London well into the night, either collecting material or writing his books in his head, no one was sure.

"I'm just back from Exeter," Dickens said. "I've taken a cottage for my parents, so your uncle won't be troubled by any more demands. Or perhaps I should say, qualms about whether to give into the demands. Failed qualms."

He said *failed, qualms* as if stubbing a cigar twice. Dickens sounded belligerent, but he wasn't making any bones about knowing exactly who Richard was, and Richard decided to meet him there. He didn't want to argue.

"Scattering to the four winds," he said. "My uncle keeps talking about immigrating to Canada. He has the idea of resettling in a place called Chatham in the Canadian county of Kent."

Dickens paused, seeming to enjoy the incongruity as much as Richard. "Where's this?"

"I gather somewhat north of Niagara Falls."

"I've always wanted to go to Niagara Falls," Dickens said, for once sounding like a chap his age.

"I think they're friends, you know. Your father and my uncle."

"But surely friendship implies equality," Dickens said. "And my father was never in trade."

He walked on, making Richard catch up. The man was mercurial. Overdressed as usual in the mode he himself had named Gent. Clerks, tradesman, artisans with enough lucre for flash ready-made clothes: they were Gents instead of gentlemen. Richard didn't know quite what to make of Dickens, but he wanted to find out.

"Do you feel equal to your friends?"

"You *do* have questions, don't you?" Dickens asked, and led him silently past a block of darkened windows. It was very late. Richard couldn't think what else to say.

"I see you watching me, you know," Dickens said finally. "In theatres and so on."

Richard was glad the moon had disappeared, hiding his blush. "But surely that's what an artist does. He looks. Watches. Entirely normal."

Say it often enough and he might actually come to believe it.

"*Artists* and writers seem to try not to," Dickens said. "It's usually members of the public who stare. As if I'm a walking oyster liable at any moment to extrude pearls."

Richard couldn't help laughing and he couldn't have felt more embarrassed. He stuttered an apology and they reverted to silence, turning the corner, almost at Great Queen Street.

"It's a good question, though," Dickens said. "P'raps even a useful question. Do you feel equal to *your* friends? Forster says you've talent."

"That's kind of him, and perhaps it *is* a good question, since I have no idea how to answer it."

"How to answer modestly. If I'm not mistaken, however, you just did."

Even without being able to see Richard's face, he seemed to pick up on all manner of things one didn't intend to say, shuffling through layers of meaning like a card-sharper.

"And when people call you a genius, what do you think about it?" Richard asked, deciding he might as well. "What do you think about *them*? Do they have any idea what they're talking about? Or are they such fools you find it hard to take them seriously?"

"Good heavens," Dickens said. "A *geen*-yus, are we?"

"I meant you."

Dickens prickled with annoyance. "What precisely have I done to deserve this? Walking you home. It's a word I only ever use ironically."

"My point exactly."

"So you want to be like The Inimitable, do you?" he asked, leaving no doubt about the irony. The Inimitable Boz: his original pen name. When Richard was in Chatham recently, Dickens's old school master, Mr. Giles, had boasted of having sent him a silver snuff box engraved The Inimitable.

*Baker's bull-dogs, Giles's cats, New-road scrubbers, Troy Town rats.*

"Should I want to be?" Richard asked. "Like you?"

No one better to answer his question. They'd reached the corner of Great Queen Street. Dickens paused, crossing his arms.

"My friend Maclise told me a story," he said. "You probably know it, about Jones, the military painter."

Richard did, but Dickens was going to tell it anyway.

"I gather he looks something like the Duke of Wellington and takes care to dress like him, having a passion to be mistaken for the Duke. Liking men to salute him and so forth.

When he heard this, the Duke is supposed to have remarked, 'Mistaken for me, is he? How strange. No one ever mistakes me for Mr. Jones.'"

Dickens gave him a sharp salute and walked off briskly.

"I deny having said that," he called without turning.

Did he think he was Jesus Christ delivering parables? Yet Richard liked Dickens. Liked his friends, his clique. Hated himself. No, he didn't hate, but he no longer trusted.

Went inside.

# The Parsonage,
# Haworth, Yorkshire

*February 11, 1853*

"You've surely caught a chill, staying out so long," Ellen scolded. She took off Charlotte's cloak as their old housekeeper, Tabby, stood waiting with her slippers.

"Really, Nell. As if I don't know when to turn home."

"You were brooding over your notices, weren't you?" Rhythmically brushing the snow from the cloak. "Losing track of time. When they're not worth it. The critics. They don't create anything."

"A public."

"You already did that with *Jane Eyre*. You could publish the worst manner of plumphery and they'd buy it. In fact, they'd probably like it even better."

"Plumphery?" Charlotte laughed. Ellen was right, of course. The public would devour her plumphery, just as they devoured the worst sentimentality of Dickens. So would Ellen, having no literary taste. But Charlotte loved her.

Ellen had set the parlour aglow with candles, bringing out the scarlet warmth of Charlotte's new flocked paper and carpet and mahogany chairs. A characteristic of the rising British figure: his house grew more fashionable, comfortable, palpating with self-satisfaction—a succubus—as he shrivelled inside it with overwork and age.

Not that Charlotte had been much to begin with, and she made no claims now. Ellen had always been the pretty one. Yet as she bent to remove her work from her chair, the candle-light threw into relief the lines around Nell's mouth and the webbing at the corner of her eyes. A jolt to realize how greatly she'd faded. She'd been so lovely when they had met at school, such a sweet manner to go with her dimples and curls, and she'd invited Charlotte home to a formidable county house, the Rydings. Charlotte had assumed that Ellen would marry young and marry well.

Yet wealth was like water and could be shallow, and Ellen was the last of twelve children. There had been suitors, but if she'd had a proposal, she would have accepted it. Instead she still lived with her mother, whose death would leave her impoverished. She would be dependent on her brothers or— Charlotte was beginning to suspect—on her. Ellen's proprietary manner wasn't entirely second-hand reaching after fame. She'd hinted more than once that they could eventually take a cottage together, which of course Charlotte would have to pay for. It wasn't only George Smith who wanted her to keep writing.

To be fair, the worst pressure came from herself.

"I conspired with the servants about tea," Ellen said, meaning old Tabby and young Martha, who did all the work. Ellen was tatting a lace collar and kept her eyes on her needle. "I made my raisin cake, which should be coming out of the oven. I hope you have an appetite after your walk."

"My father hasn't come down? Has he been coughing badly?" Ellen shook her head. "I asked Martha to make him a tray."

As Charlotte got up to go to her father, Ellen sucked her lips, still having her opinions, as house cats did. Always hanging between them was something she'd once said in anger: *That selfish old man.*

Charlotte sat back down on the edge of her chair, not meeting Ellen's eyes. She disliked this silent interplay of knowing what Ellen thought, and Ellen knowing that she knew, and her knowing that Ellen knew that she knew. She supposed it was like marriage without its pleasures. Charlotte longed for her sister Emily, who'd always said what she meant. Emily would know if she should continue humbling herself to their father, giving him his tea before she'd had hers, even though his bronchitis was almost better and these days Charlotte had to answer as many letters as he did. More. Emily would also know if Charlotte should write George Smith mentioning that she hadn't heard from him. Know whether she should resign herself to a future in Yorkshire with Mr. Nicholls or more probably Ellen, who wanted to take Emily's place, and Anne's place, and couldn't, although she was sensible and loyal and quite often right, despite being taught since a child not to say anything directly. Ladies didn't.

*What do you* want *to do?* Emily would have asked.

"I'm quite hungry," Charlotte said, settling back in her chair. "I'll look in on Father after tea. And instead of sewing this evening, I should probably catch up on my correspondence. We've candles enough."

"I'm so sorry," Ellen said, although she patently wasn't, and it was hard to know whether she'd lit the room so brightly because she liked the little luxury, or because she wanted Charlotte to write to George—who would make Charlotte comfortable, and by extension make sure Ellen was comfortable—or if it was a little of the first and a bit of the second, although if Charlotte put on her writer's hat and was brutally truthful, she would have to admit she didn't really care what poor dear Ellen did or even what she hoped. She wanted her sister, and failing Emily, her tea.

An hour later, Charlotte knocked lightly and went in to find her father sitting up in bed. On his plate was a scattering of crumbs. She touched his arm gently.

"I hope you liked Ellen's cake. She baked it especially for you."

"Ellen is a good girl."

"We're hardly girls, Papa. How do you feel? I haven't heard you cough, not significantly."

"I believe I've made it through again, by the grace of God." The bronchitis was an annual worry, but he looked better than he had yesterday, and far better than the week before. "You didn't take cold when you walked out?"

"It was a dry cold for once, rather than damp. A *cold* cold, but pleasant."

"No sign of the pain in your side?"

"Listen to us, sounding like a pair of old people," Charlotte said, so her father's eyes lit with humour. "No, there was not."

In five weeks, her father would turn seventy-six, and he

still had a considerable amount of white hair and an even more considerable amount of nose, which Charlotte didn't remember as being quite so grand when he was younger. Branwell had been a miniature of their father, having inherited the nose and red hair. Because of Branwell, Charlotte had an idea of their father's percussive impact when he was young, turning heads when he strode into a room, a tall flaming torch of rectitude.

Not that Branwell had inherited the height any more than the rectitude, having been on the same scale as their mother and Charlotte. Charlotte had always held her stature against their mother; their poor mother and her first school at Cowan Bridge, where the starvation she'd suffered had stunted whatever growth her blood would have allowed.

Emily was the only one who'd been tall, her strong features so unlike any of theirs that she must have taken after someone in their father's family in Ireland, although he'd never said. Aunt Branwell had told them that Anne was much like their mother, whose faint claim to looks had been in her delicate skin and colouring, the pretty light brown hair and violet-blue eyes. Charlotte's nose, resembling a potato, might have been Irish, but the one sketch they had of their mother suggested maternal blame there, too.

Charlotte had been only five when their mother died and Aunt Branwell took over their care. It was unsettling to think that their aunt had been dead more than ten years; that Anne had been gone almost four years, Emily and Branwell lost to her for five. Their father was all Charlotte had of family. Her father. No more *them* and *their*.

"Ellen didn't go with you?" he asked.

"I encouraged her to stay. She likes a good fire."

"And you wanted your privacy."

"And she had a cake to bake."

"Have you any more notices of your novel?" he asked.

Charlotte shook her head. "Although my friend Mrs. Gaskell writes that she's being castigated for *Ruth*." This was Elizabeth Gaskell's social issues novel, the type Charlotte had decided not to write, no matter what George Smith wanted. In Mrs. Gaskell's case, the critics didn't matter. Or at least, their invective only drew public attention to the shocking subject of the novel, a fallen woman and her redemption. *Ruth* was selling like the first fruit of spring, often to people who wouldn't admit reading it. "I should have thought Harriet Martineau would go to great lengths to support her. But perhaps support isn't Harriet's strong suit."

"You mustn't brood on Miss Martineau," her father said.

Charlotte tried to be light. "I know. A Godless heathen."

"From her writings, I would say she has a man's brain and confidence," her father said, surprising her. "She doesn't represent your public, which is comprised not only of ladies who consider themselves intelligent yet small and trodden, but men who feel so, as well. I believe that sums up the majority of the population."

And Ellen dismissed him as *that selfish old man.* Where did she think they'd got their intelligence?

"I'd like to believe you, Papa."

"You should. You should," he said, and nodded at his newspapers. Taking up a magazine, Charlotte sat down and began reading to him about the new prime minister, Lord Aberdeen, in office since the end of the old year, and now being satirized as a coachman trying to steer six wayward horses with the faces of members of his cabinet.

Turn the page and there was a story about the new president of the United States, Mr. Pierce, who apparently spent much of his time secluded, his only son having died in a train wreck shortly before his inauguration this past January. The boy had been eleven years old, the last of the president's three sons. Mr. Pierce and his wife had survived the wreck, and the poor woman was reported to have swooned when she'd seen the crushed body of her child.

"The burden of office," Charlotte said, aware of heavy footsteps on the stairs.

"I would say the cost of ambition," her father replied, and raised his voice. "We might take a lesson on the impious folly of aiming too high."

By which she assumed he'd heard the footsteps, as well. A knock on the door, and Mr. Nicholls put his head in.

"Forgive me," he said, his Irish accent identical to her father's. "I only intended to leave a letter about parish business, but Miss Nussey insisted I come up."

Charlotte clenched her fists in irritation. Ellen couldn't resist an opportunity to put Mr. Nicholls at a disadvantage and had sent him upstairs for Charlotte's father to scold once more about his presumptuous proposal. A poor man having the nerve to ask for his daughter! Her father had suffered an apoplexy last year, and now the veins at his temple swelled perilously. Charlotte could have throttled Ellen, and walked quickly to the door with her hand out for the letter.

"And are you so pusillanimous as to accept direction from a woman?" her father quavered behind her.

"I'll show Mr. Nicholls out," Charlotte said.

In the dark hall, Mr. Nicholls held miserably to his lamp as if leaning on a staff. Between his height and his black

Irish whiskers, he looked like a shadowy outcropping of rock. Charlotte remembered feeling intimidated by his size when he'd arrived to be her father's curate seven years before. She and the parish had also disliked him for his physical stiffness and unbending dogmatism, not seeing at first that he was enormously shy. He was also tactless. Despite being an outsider, Mr. Nicholls had begun a long campaign to stop women from drying laundry in the graveyard and was a settled opponent of Sunday footraces.

Yet he visited the poor every day, keeping candy in his pocket for the children. He liked children and they liked him. As she led him downstairs, Charlotte remembered looking out the back window one afternoon to see him thundering along a moorland path in his clerical black, his big dog Plato barking joyously alongside as he led a crowd of raucous boys and girls ally-ally-up toward the heights.

Another time, the wife of a machinist in one of the mills had stopped Charlotte in the street to praise his fervid attendance during her son's illness, "a-praying and a-groaning as hard as ye please, Miss, wrassling with Saint Peter to pull my boy back from the ab-yiss, until we had him here again on soil and earth."

Ignoring her theological misapprehensions, as Mr. Nicholls probably wouldn't, Charlotte had put a hand on the woman's arm. She'd had to reach up, Mrs. Lundy being a strapping example, as was her son, whose essentially sound constitution Charlotte suspected was largely responsible for his cure.

"It's a great balm to have such a son," she said.

"It are, Miss," she replied. "It are. It are."

Mr. Nicholls reached the bottom of the stairs and turned miserably toward the door.

"I can't let you leave without a piece of cake for your tea," Charlotte said, and he brightened too hopefully.

"I would be . . ."

She couldn't let him be honoured. "It's not a symbolic cake, Mr. Nicholls," Charlotte said. "It's a raisin cake that Ellen made us."

He smiled slowly, then chuckled at her joke. "I'm afraid a symbolic cake wouldn't help much with my concrate evening appetite."

It had taken Charlotte a long time to discover that he had a sense of humour. Leading him into the dining room, she allowed Mr. Nicholls and Ellen to ignore each other as she cut him a large piece of cake, all of them without a doubt thinking about his proposal in just this room last December, which Charlotte wished she hadn't relayed so minutely to her friend: how shocked she'd been as big, strapping Mr. Nicholls had paled and trembled, making her an offer she'd never expected, and which she'd been touched to find was entirely based on his love for her private self rather than her reputation. After seven years in Haworth, he claimed to know her.

Once the cake was cut, it occurred to Charlotte that she had nothing to send it off in. But Mr. Nicholls had anticipated her and held out a threadbare handkerchief, his hand once again trembling. Muttering his thanks, he wrapped the cake and was off.

After hearing the front door close, Charlotte said, "That was poorly done, Nell."

"He's an ill-looking man," Ellen said pettishly. "Wooden. He's like one of the village dancers, only moving his body from the knees down. I prefer the waltz myself."

"I think him rather good-looking," Charlotte replied. "The features are strong, the nose admirable, although he hasn't a mobile face because he hasn't a mobile character. But he's kind and true, for all his faults."

They were also Ellen's faults. Neither was intellectual, which was her gravest objection to Mr. Nicholls's proposal. By this she meant they were intelligent enough, but read little and showed a limited understanding of novels, including hers. They were conventional, mulishly stubborn and as predictable as the washing in and out of the tide.

It was true she often found solace at the seashore.

Sighing, Charlotte called for Tabby to clear the table and took out her writing desk.

"My dear Sir," she wrote to George. "I do not, of course, expect to have a letter from you at present, because I know that this is the busy time at Cornhill; but after the weary Mail is gone out . . ."

Charlotte lifted her pen, unsure whether she should send another begging letter. A brief chew at her lip and she decided to finish it, since she finished things. She could decide later whether to mail it.

". . . I should much like to hear what you think of the general tone of the notices—whether you regard them as reasonably satisfactory. My Father seems pleased with them, and so am I . . ."

"Do you write to Mr. Smith?" Ellen asked, but Charlotte wasn't in the mood to answer.

# Richard Meets Manchester

*Spring 1841*

M r. Gaskell held back, letting Richard reach the door first. The Reverend Mr. William Gaskell was a courteous man, and meticulously moral. He was one of the rising figures in the Unitarian church, although he was rising without any sign of worldly ambition. Even his good looks were ascetic. A tall man with mild eyes and long pale hands.

Giving him a nod, Richard started inside, only to reel backward. Inside the hovel was a stench of rot, filth, vomit and a terrifying undertone of fish far from the sea. Richard was back smelling the fishy miasma of cholera blowing off the Medway hulks during the epidemic of 1832. His cousin William Dadd had been the first to die in Chatham, gone after six hours of shitting maggoty water. They'd burned his clothes, but nothing could stop cholera from chewing through the Medway as it had through all of England—across the Continent, around the globe—bursting through the floor of undefended homes like a fanged and scaled monster. The poor had died in the hundreds of thousands but no one was exempt or immune.

Mr. Gaskell seemed to think he was, looking down at Richard from his angular height before stepping past him toward the door.

"Isn't that the odour of cholera?" Richard asked.

"We have no more cholera than you do in London," Mr. Gaskell said. "Typhus, perhaps. Although I would say more likely," sniffing the oceanic air, "childbirth."

Mr. Gaskell was touring Richard through the delights of Manchester—the effects of the recession—Richard having come north to see his painting hung in the local exhibition. It was meant to be a brief stop before he headed farther north on a sketching tour, but Richard was trying to make the most of it. Not that he could see much through the clouds of factory smoke, nor hear much above the metallic clatter of one cotton mill after another and another and another, which together created an eerie discordant hum that sounded like the devil's orchestra tuning up in hell.

Mr. Gaskell disappeared inside the hovel, leaving Richard to follow like a boy being dared.

An old woman lay in the centre of the floor. Richard started forward to help when he realized there was nowhere else to put her. She lay on an unspeakable blanket. No sofa anywhere. Of course there wasn't. As his eyes grew accustomed to the dimness, he saw the rest of her family crouched beside a low deal table near a wall that had been rubbed shiny at shoulder level. One girl clutched a limp doll in rags, perhaps the newborn. They looked like gargoyles.

"I believe there are twenty or twenty-two people living in this house," Mr. Gaskell told him. "You'll find as many in each of the habitations through this district, and can see how things look when people are forced to sell their furniture for food.

"And perhaps," Mr. Gaskell said, addressing the gargoyles, "to sell most of the blankets we brought you."

"You'd better bring us jobs," came a man's voice. Those might have been fighting words. The man might have been a radical Chartist, rioting against the mill owners a month or two past and now hunkered here in hiding. But his voice was so weak that his statement sounded like simple fact, and Richard supposed it was.

"I'd like to bring you a job, Isaac," Mr. Gaskell said. "What we've got are blankets and food. The ladies will be bringing you bread soon, and porridge for the children."

"I've reckoned the definition of charity," said the man, Isaac, wavering to his feet and pausing there with his knuckles on the table to gain his balance. He sounded like an educated man, although he spoke in a thick Lancashire accent. Self-educated, then.

"What definition have you arrived at, Isaac?"

Another gentleman might have said this superciliously but William Gaskell sounded curious.

"Gentry providing you with what they'd like to give, when it's convenient for them to give it, instead of what you need. Because they don't ask what you need. Or if they do, they don't listen, or they won't give it you."

"That's fair," Mr. Gaskell conceded.

"Give me a job," Isaac went on, as if he hadn't heard. "Give me a job and I can buy my own bread and blankets. Get the mill owners to give me a job, instead of building themselves such fine estates and buying thousands of pound of jewels for their ladies."

Or art, Richard thought, shifting uneasily.

"They're your parishioners," Isaac went on, hectoring now. He seemed to gain strength from his words, as if words had always fed him. A bow-legged, bone-skinny, clem-jawed man of no obvious age. "There they go each week to your fine square Cross Street Chapel, commending their souls and their charity to God. Now would I belong at Cross Street, Mr. Gaskell?"

"I thought you were a Methodist, Isaac. But we'd certainly make you welcome."

"To show me off, as you demonstrate our misfortune to this young dervinity student, as I suppose. And my good day to you, sir."

Richard bowed foolishly.

"Mr. Dadd is an artist," Mr. Gaskell said, "who might, for instance, draw your house to show the conditions you're obliged to suffer, and publish an engraving. Perhaps that might reach the mill owners, or conceivably Parliament. You know that gaining ground is complex and subtle, Isaac, with action called for on every front."

"An artist," the man said. He didn't look at Richard but turned and stared at his family, as if seeing them through other eyes. All the air went out of him.

"I didn't come here to, to make you feel badly," Richard said, managing at the last moment not to say *humiliate you.*

He hadn't come here to sketch either, nor realized that was

what Mr. Gaskell wanted. Richard had arrived in Manchester the previous afternoon and taken the Gaskells an introduction from a Unitarian gentleman he'd met last year in Leeds. He'd asked where he might lodge and the inevitable invitation followed. This morning, Mr. Gaskell had offered the tour without any mention of sketching, and now Richard didn't know how to disappoint him, but knew he would. He'd found his subject, and it wasn't here.

Over the past eighteen months, Richard had settled into painting his own branch of the literary, where he was slowly making his name. Making a splash after showing his vision of Shakespeare's Puck at the exhibition this spring, singled out for notice after his painting had been hung inches from the floor, which critics lambasted as an insult and a scandal, given his *happily conceived picture*, its *EXCELLENCE*. He'd sold his *Puck*, sold several watercolours to a chap in Leeds. Now the Royal Manchester Institution was going to exhibit his *Fairies Assembling at Sunset to Hold Their Revels*. Richard was painting the liminal, the intangible, the numinous. Ethereal beings holding their revels in glades.

Well, he was painting fairies. He felt a fool in the company of an ethical man like Mr. Gaskell and a starving one like Isaac, and thought about the engravings he'd seen from the Spanish master Francisco Goya's *Disasters of War*, a series of cartoons slashing out images of his beleaguered countrymen left starved during the Napoleonic campaigns. Goya had called one *The Beds of Death*. Another *There Is No One to Help Them*. A third, showing soldiers grappling with women: *They Do Not Want To*.

Richard had recently painted *Ever Let the Fancy Roam*, after Keats.

*Ever let the Fancy roam,*
*Pleasure never is at home . . .*


Pleasure wasn't at home with Isaac. The low bleating Richard had registered as the misplaced sound of a lost lamb outside was, in fact, the frail sob of the rag-covered newborn, on earth perhaps for a day. The person on the floor he'd taken for Isaac's granddam was more likely his wife, not safely delivered. Isaac seemed to be waiting for Richard to produce a sketchbook, but he could only think, *I'm no Goya.*

*No Goya. Not great, nor shall I be.*

Astounding how the lowest person he'd ever met could make him feel so small.

Richard knew he had to cling to his subject. He'd found what he ought to paint, what spoke to him, what spoke *through* him, and if he didn't paint it he'd be no good to anyone. Better to be the best at what he could master than struggle into the seventh, eighth, ninetieth rank of those trying to recreate historic greatness, and foreign greatness at that. He couldn't do what Mr. Gaskell wanted, even though the reverend gentleman was his host; even though he was a famously rising Unitarian minister; even though he was right.

"If you would be so kind to sit for a portrait," Richard told Isaac, "perhaps we could settle on a time."

A flare of vanity on the starving man's face. This was the reason Richard hated portraiture: the painter saw too much. Layers of personality crowded one's senses, and Richard truly loathed crowds, especially the ones that jostled around inside people's heads. In Isaac's case, meeting his peculiarly wide-set eyes, Richard could see not just vanity but a perverse pride in his misfortune, which stood in honest opposition to what he no doubt considered other men's thieving prosperity; saw his rare acuity, and irritability; saw perseverance, grievance, pain and want.

Saw no particular care for the bleating newborn.

"Might as well now," Isaac said. "Having nothing what you might call *perductive* to do."

He intended the sting. If born a gentleman, Isaac would have been supercilious. Raising his eyebrows at Mr. Gaskell, Richard fumbled for the sketchbook in his pocket, but the clergyman held up his hand. They had several other stops to make. He would deliver Mr. Dadd back in a couple of hours. No doubt Isaac would be available.

"Saving a better offer," Isaac agreed.

M r. Gaskell spent the rest of the morning walking Richard along the unpaved, filth-strewn streets of working Manchester, looking down from iron bridges at streams dyed scarlet by the manufactory, at ponds stained every cheap oily colour of a tottie's finery. Mr. Gaskell showed him a nation of Irish living pond-side with their pigs; introduced him to Dissenters crammed into shambled old houses set around courtyards that doubled as cesspools. They always had to look down, picking their way through excrement, and Richard could scarcely enter the dank cellars when Mr. Gaskell insisted on descending. He would stay on the bottom step, unable to get a true count of the numbers of extraneous gargoyles the mill owners were storing down there, all of them crouching, all of their shoulders rubbing smooth lines onto the walls that looked like the trails left by slugs. They were Job, Wesley, Job again. Some seemed fond of their children. Some were drunk, including women.

Mr. Gaskell cut him loose as the church bells rang eleven o'clock, and Richard spent the next three days at his prescribed work. First he sketched Isaac, whom he posed leaning forward on his knuckles at the table as if he were addressing a meeting, which Isaac seemed to understand, pursing his lips happily. Afterward, Isaac took him to the filthy cellar of the first Job, whom he hectored—"Show some respect for yerself, man"—even though Job had washed a clean circle onto his face between the time Richard had met him and the time he'd returned. Afterward, Job passed him to Fan, and it continued, Richard led from one uninhabitable habitation to the next, wading through cesspools, descending into unspeakable cellars. He sketched some of his subjects, made quick watercolours of others. Not that he needed much colour.

All the while, Richard silently protested that *this wasn't his work* and wondered if it ought to be; whether he should try to be more useful, taking the next step. Perhaps he should at least try to be another Goya. Better: a modern-day Hogarth drawing his own version of *A Rake's Progress. A Worker's Regress?* Not that he could imagine the mill owners buying cartoons of starving labourers for their walls, or Parliament actually considering an engraved protest, although Richard was surprised how quickly he grew popular with the starvelings themselves. By his third morning, he'd invisibly become known throughout the most dangerous parts of Manchester, wandering as freely among the cesspools as Dickens, every third man bobbing his head to The Artist. It made him feel a royal fraud. He wondered whether Dickens felt the same and doubted it.

It was true Richard would be able to harvest faces and features for his real work. His *Puck*, after all, was a mischievous little chap on a toadstool surrounded by a circle of dancing fairies, otherwise known as models. The unfinished canvas of Titania awaiting him in London centred on Shakespeare's fairy queen sleeping beneath a proscenium arch made of goblins, a nod to the theatrical spectacles that partly inspired his work. His fairy folk needed faces, meaning that Isaac's wide-set eyes and Wesley's flattened nose wouldn't be wasted, and on his third day, he found something particularly compelling in a girl named Hephzibah, who might have been fifteen.

Richard had come to realize that this was the age his friend O'Neil liked girls, which explained his own apprentice encounter with slit-eyed Florrie at Mrs. Ketchum's. He'd since learned that he liked his own women older and sturdier, having explored sufficient brothels (surficient brothels) to understand that he *had* a preference, and not just for mirrors. An over-surficiency of brothels, his friends implied, raising an eyebrow. Egg was particularly censorious.

Yet nothing like that drove him to draw multiple versions of young Hephzibah sitting on a stool in the doorway of the house she shared with her father and twenty-odd others. Richard had brought her up from the cellar during a rare appearance by the sun, posing her to lean back catching its rays and asking her to enjoy it. She'd given him a look he hadn't quite seen and instantly wanted, and he set to work to frame it by quickly delineating her narrow shoulders, her thin wrists and the corded neck of an older woman, the head too big for her frame, which sometimes shook from a cough. For all this, the girl had thick dark hair, good bones, big black eyes and budding lips. He would have called her pretty if she were healthy, with some fat to her cheeks and more colour. As it was, Richard searched for a word and came up with *beautiful*. She was as beautiful as a dying rose. He badly wanted her to give him whatever he'd glimpsed.

"I hope you're enjoying this," he repeated, and again he got the look, which this time he could see was withdrawal, a glance aside, a sad smile that seemed ancient. Such weariness in a pale child, her heavy lids so much older than her pretty mouth. Her eyes were faery and he drew them quickly, bottling her for future use. After making sure he had what he wanted, one or two copies, Richard packed up and gave her the crown he'd given them all, which made her pupils dilate.

Isaac had been wretched. "Thought I was doing ye a favour," he'd said, wanting with all his pride to turn back the coin but having a family behind him. Richard put it down on the low table and left so Isaac could take it.

"Thankee, sir," a girl called after him, and as he'd stepped outside, Richard heard a slap.

B ack in his room at the Gaskells', Richard looked over his work, the sketches in his book of faces, eyes, mouths, shoulders, full portraits in pencil. With them were a few loose watercolours. Most of the work was indifferent, but in a few pieces he'd caught a glimmer and a couple were acceptable, including one of the watercolours of Hephzibah. At a different level, whether or not it was good, the occasional scratch felt useful. Not knowing what to do, Richard tore the best pieces from his sketchbook and arranged the work into subject (Jammie, Job, Job, Isaac), the useful pieces kept aside as sacrosanct, although he still wasn't sure what he meant by useful, and whether he could do as Mr. Gaskell wanted or not.

Of course he couldn't. Richard had known that from the start. He chose a few of the portraits and headed out to give his subjects each a version of himself, amused at his own condescension in signing them, which they wouldn't notice and couldn't read. Most looked stupefied as he handed them their likenesses. He realized they had never seen this before. Art. Themselves. He might have been giving them each a clockwork bird with golden feathers and ebony eyes. Hephzibah's bandy father took hers almost reverently.

"Why . . ." he said, voice quavering, unable to go on.

Afterward, Richard returned to the Gaskells' in time for tea and an apology, which left Mr. Gaskell silent. They were in the dining room, Mr. Gaskell's beautiful young wife serving from a silver pot which Richard saw through Isaac's eyes could be sold to feed dinner to a neighbourhood. After which it would be gone, and the people would still be starving.

"Perhaps what I feel," Richard said, trying again, "is that I'm not sure art serves a purpose exactly, or that it ought. At least that mine doesn't. I tend to think of artists not as troops, as it were, charged with advancing civilization across the uncivilized world, whether in Africa or, if I may say it, central Manchester. Instead I tend to think of art as a demonstration that civilization exists, the artist being thrown up by society as a marker of its maturity. I think we're rather useless in ourselves, or that I am. But if it's not entirely admirable to be useless, surely it's acceptable. God made beauty, and I'm not sure what purpose that serves, other than to make us feel both elevation and pleasure."

Both the Gaskells were listening closely, Mrs. Gaskell watching him steadily with enormous grey eyes set under masses of auburn hair. She was as tall for a woman as her husband was among men, and it was impossible to see them together without thinking of their long-limbed marital congress, or at least it was for Richard. Not that he thought of himself any longer as abnormal, having learned during his admittedly frequent visits to brothels that some houses kept mirrors because a goodly number of men enjoyed them. Instead, Richard had a feeling that no man was as straightforward as the clergyman felt he should be, and that probably included the clergyman. People wore secrets next to their skin, the Gaskells obviously among them, being the parents of two small daughters.

So many layers to the world. When he was working as hard as he'd done these past few days, Richard's mind churned through them like a steam engine. He had an idea that Mrs. Gaskell sensed this, being clever in the feminine way, her own mind having long slender fingers that reached deep into one's thoughts. He would never admit it, but Elizabeth Gaskell terrified him, despite serving a particularly delicious seed cake.

"However," she said, as her husband remained silent, addressing Mr. Gaskell's unstated disappointment as if he'd spoken aloud. "However, I'd wager they'll keep hold of their portraits long after they've sold all my blankets."

"Well, that's true," Mr. Gaskell said mildly, and Richard felt over the hump.

"When my father and I were in Leeds last fall," he said, "we heard a sermon from the Reverend Mr. Martineau. I would imagine you know him. Or at least that you know of his sister Harriet, the writer."

Mr. Gaskell nodded.

"I probably haven't got it right," Richard said. "But Mr. Martineau spoke of worship as rising not for a purpose, not for gain or a wish for change, but more purely from emotion. I understood him to say that moral power doesn't come from the will, but from an affection for God he called deep and pure and . . . I particularly remember the word *entrancing*, and which brings us to a state of selflessness and self-oblivion. No doubt I've got it wrong, but that's also how I look on art."

"My friend James Martineau would find you a remarkably acute pupil. That's precisely what he's been saying," Mr. Gaskell said. "I happen to disagree with him, and he might well split the church, since I'm not alone in believing that rational use of the mind is what brings us closer to God's grace and helps us carry out His intentions. But no doubt that's what my friend Martineau says. Your argument is entirely consistent."

"I don't wish to argue," Richard said. "All I really want to do is paint."

"And what do you paint?" Mrs. Gaskell asked, the Manchester exhibition not yet having opened.

"Shakespearean subjects. Keats. The liminal; one of my favourite words. Puck, Titania . . . fairies," he admitted weakly. "Though not sweet ones."

"Fairies aren't sweet in Lancaster," Mrs. Gaskell said energetically. She seemed entirely aware of her husband's disappointment but otherwise delighted with the subject. "There was a story in my village of Knutsford about a woman from Mobberley who encountered a fairy, although I've heard an old farmer from Mobberley say she was from Mere, which he could guarantee, having known her granddaughter. It's true, however, that at a well one night, this good wife encountered a fairy, who gave her a potion to cure her crossed eye. All was well until she met the same fairy by daylight at the market in Ollerton and thanked him for the potion, which he could see had worked. The fairy asked which eye he had cured, and when the good wife showed him, he put it out.

"You mustn't trust fairies in Lancaster, you see, especially when you encounter them by daylight."

"I drew a girl named Hephzibah today whom I thought incorporeal."

"Oh yes, the poor child. Consumption."

In Leeds last year, Richard had sat beside a man named Hammond at a dinner of manufacturers of the kind he hoped the Gaskells would host, introducing him to potential patrons. Not that he had the brass to even hint at it. In Leeds, his father had arranged things. He had come north to attend a lecture by a friend at the Leeds Mechanical Institute and brought Richard along to make some introductions. Richard was still attending the Royal Academy Schools, but at a certain point the artist schooled himself. An occasional absence wasn't noticed so much as assiduous attendance, which implied a lack of confidence, of progress, a focus. At least Richard found it convenient to think so.

Looking back at the Leeds dinner, he now saw it as the opposite of the muddy puddling he'd been visiting in Manchester. Everything Mr. Gaskell had shown him left Richard with an overall sense of lives melting like glass in a fire. When he and Stephen were boys, they'd put shards of broken bottles onto the end of metal rods and hold them to the forge of the Chatham blacksmith, the immense and easygoing Grimly. As Grimly beamed over them, they'd watch the shards melt, the long slow extending drip of glass strangely oily and more exciting than beautiful. More disturbing than exciting. Each time they did it, Richard had expected beauty, and each time he'd been disturbed.

The contrast with Leeds was instructive. Mr. Tayler's dinner now seemed to bristle with texture he hadn't noticed at the time: slick green and silver wallpaper, velvet chairs, plump pink hands hooked inside brocaded waistcoats—a competition of waistcoats—as dozens of candles refracted rainbows off acres of silver and crystal. Richard and Frith had talked about this a few years ago, how in historical art, the present bled into the past, changing what was portrayed. Memory seemed to be like that, too. Not stable, not etched in glass. Melting glass, more likely. The present melted into the past and changed it, making memory as unreliable as Mrs. Gaskell's Lancaster fairy.

However—*however*, as the lady had said—there was no question that his neighbour Mr. Hammond had won the waistcoat competition, looking magnificent in pink and gold. Richard felt modest beside him in grey, which suddenly amused him. *Why*, he thought, *modesty is another form of feeling superior to one's neighbour.*

"So it was probably at a conjunction of Reform Committees that we met," a merchant named Mr. Varley was saying to Richard's father, down the table.

"A great victory," his father replied. "The type of thoughtful progress the nineteenth century demands. As one wishes the Chartists would realize."

A murmur of fellow feeling amid the scrape of knives and forks. After only three days in Leeds, they were not only at dinner, they were liked. These were his father's people, Unitarians and Methodists, a table of Dissenters. They were richer than he was, but some had started out humbly and Richard's father was rising. Like him, they had supported the Reform Bill back in '32. Not to get the vote as his father did, since most of these men had probably already enjoyed it, but to gain seats in Parliament for the manufacturing towns.

His father had been one of the chief organizers of Chatham's greatest Reform meeting. Richard had been glued to his side during all the jostle of the tremendous outdoor forum held at the end of the Military Road, a bare-kneed fifteen-year-old among prosperous men who strode and spun through the day with the fitful energy of children. From the wings of the temporary stage, he'd looked out at a jumble of upturned faces, four thousand and more crowding forward to hear speakers like his father. Under fast skies and the gimlet watch of Redcoats, his father stepped out to second a motion thanking those members of both houses of Parliament who'd pledged to support the bill, his voice half-lost as the crowd howled its approval.

"It is my privilege to second ... My privilege," his father had roared, looking exalted, the scant hairs on his bald pate dancing in the wind as if magnetized. Seeing too many slack-jawed faces below him, Richard had understood that not everybody cared about Reform. Why should they? They weren't getting the vote. For many people here, this was just the circus come to town. For others, for worse types skulking about—thieves and drinkers, his brother George's friends—it might provide an opportunity to rampage, during which they would be as happy to loot the shops of Reformers as of deep-dyed Tories. Already this year, Richard had watched a crowd of respectable workmen lose themselves during a visit from the Archbishop of Canterbury, who'd come to town to speak against Reform. During his progress from the cathedral, hisses began, then groans, and as the men's complaints rose to a yowl, they pelted the archbishop with rocks and mud and rotten eggs that landed on his immaculate robe as thick as berries.

In the end, the Military Road crowd had stayed friendly, the bill was passed by Parliament and a subscription raised to provide a celebratory dinner for the Chatham poor. That magic night they illuminated the town, lanterns and candles lighting the dark old curving streets to the uncanny edge of daylight, the townsfolk wandering spellbound, women holding onto each other as if they might be carried away. Richard often thought about the illumination as he prepared his canvases, underpainting them a moonish white to give his fairies the faintest of shimmers.

"And what's your position on the political?" Mr. Hammond asked Richard. Samuel Hammond was younger than most of the manufacturers, with roguishly cut hair to go with his pink-and-gold waistcoat. He'd introduced himself as a flax spinner the way Richard supposed Mr. Josiah Wedgwood might say he was a potter.

"Politically, I defer to my father," he replied.

"So you mean to follow in his footsteps," an older man put in from across the table. Mr. Smart, Richard believed. A wrinkled chap with baby-soft white hair curling over his lengthy ears. "We'll see you give up this painting nonsense and take to business."

"My elder brothers have the jump on me there, I'm afraid."

"Ah," Mr. Smart replied, illuminated, a human Chatham. "A *younger* son."

"Third, I'm afraid. Painting it is."

"My own third proved himself a booby," Mr. Smart said. "I put him into the Marines. Sink or swim."

He chuckled at his joke. Richard realized he should have answered just as bluntly, *It's our fourth that's the booby. My father put him in the shipyards.* He was here to boost his career, but there was only so far Richard was prepared to bend himself in search of patrons.

"My father's conundrum is three daughters," he said. "It's what they say. The first is handsome, the second pretty, the third quite beautiful. He probably should have brought them here instead of me."

Mr. Smart shot a shrewd glance at Richard's father. "No fortune, though," he said. "Better to bring you. No man at this table would marry a girl without lucre."

"Well, here's something you might help me with," Richard said. "How does one set a value on the intangible? I won't ask about art. But here's my sister, Maria Elizabeth, a sweet girl as well as a beauty. It's true my father won't be able to give her as much as I'm sure he'd like. But doesn't she compare well . . ."

"To a rich girl brown as a wart?" Mr. Smart interrupted. "And as crusty, likely. The answer is the same as for my earthenware. A girl's worth as much as the market will bear. Your sister's an expensive proposition. A man would have to give up the prospect of money to take her, presuming he could get a girl with a fortune, which even my friend here managed. A rich girl and a handsome one, if I do say, his better half being my niece. But if Sam hadn't got hold of her, I wonder if he would have picked money or beauty."

Before Hammond could answer, Mr. Smart said, "Money. He's a good lad." Looking pointedly at the pink waistcoat. "Underneath."

The two men chuckled at each other before Mr. Smart leaned confidingly across the table.

"I liked a pretty girl in my day. Not the beauty and not the handsome girl, which I always thought should marry a bishop.

My niece'll get the whip hand of this one," he said, nodding at Hammond, who was so entirely unoffended he chuckled again. "A pretty little girl with big blue eyes and what-d'ye-call-'em, ringlets, that was for me."

"My sister Rebecca will arrive on the next train," Richard said. Now they all chuckled, and good-humoured Sam Hammond began asking about art, if Mr. Joseph Mallord William Turner was as dwarfish as they said, and whether the yellow in his paintings would fade.

"We've had a devil of trouble lately with dye rotting the thread," Hammond said. He shot an unhappy look down the table at a florid man, presumably the manufacturer of his dyes. The man seemed to feel his gaze and turned, giving him a bland smile.

When Hammond turned back, Richard said, "I wouldn't call him dwarfish, although his legs are probably shorter than he'd like."

And they were underway.

I n their lodgings that night, his father tore open a letter from London, scanning it quickly. He told Richard that his Uncle Henry had accepted an offer for the sale of his stock and the remainder of the lease on Upper Seymour Street. He and Henry had been debating whether or not he should accept. Now it was done, and the Henry Martins would sail for New York in the spring.

"He didn't get the terms I told him to hold out for," his father said, reading the letter more closely. "Henry is rash. He couldn't even wait until we'd got home to tell me. He probably didn't want to tell me to my face. But, in any case, it's done."

His father tossed the letter onto the bed. After a moment's thought, he sat down beside it, hands dangling between his knees. The room was pleasant, all one could ask. Clean linen and a good fire. But Richard was conscious of the tragic stories his Uncle Picnot had been adding to the ones Frith liked to tell about his father's inn. He found hotel rooms melancholy, like old soldiers with too many memories of war.

"The family's breaking up," his father said. "You need component parts in a family. Henry can be rash, but we need that. And I believe Bob is serious about the Clarke girl in Chatham. Now that Henry's going, Bob can open a shop and marry. That's him gone, too."

"Bob's already gone, pater," Richard said, toasting his legs by the fire. "He's been gone for quite a while, and he's still here."

"Paint that," his father said. "See if you can. We like to fool ourselves, but you can't be here and there at the same time."

"That's precisely what I paint."

His father got up irritably. "I would have thought you'd got beyond that. Sounding like a student. The world is a more practical place, Richard. You had dinner tonight with practical men. They want paintings by the inch, preferably with naked women in classical poses they can plausibly call art."

His fairies? What else did his father think they were? Not that Richard had set out to paint for the market. It was a happy accident that he'd begun to paint what was starting to sell. It was as if the age were speaking through him. He had something in common with Dickens after all, although he'd never say so, even to his father. Paint it first. Paint what you had to, and create the market for it afterward. That was his plan, and what he'd spent the evening doing. Richard was going to see Hammond in the morning, his new friend Sam having asked him to bring some watercolours to the factory. Fairies in a flax mill. They'd slip off the paper and flee.

"I know you and Uncle Henry are close, even if you fight all the time. Admit it," Richard said, when his father seemed ready to disagree.

"Henry was my first apprentice," his father said. "You haven't lost someone that close to you yet."

Everyone but Richard seemed to have forgotten about his mother.

"I never thought he'd do it," his father said. "It was a wretched offer."

Richard repressed a smile. "I find hotel rooms melancholy."

"I find them expensive."

"Well, if you're going to be like that."

"I am."

He was. Richard took out his book and lay down on the bed, boots crossed. He'd been reading Byron's *Don Juan*. Opened it to a bookmarked page.

> *What is the end of Fame? 'tis but to fill*
> *A certain portion of uncertain paper:*
> *Some liken it to climbing up a hill,*
> *Whose summit, like all hills, is lost in vapour:*
> *For this men write, speak, preach, and heroes kill,*
> *And bards burn what they call their 'midnight taper,'*
> *To have, when the original is dust,*
> *A name, a wretched picture, and worse bust.*

Richard laughed out loud.

"What?" his father asked.

Richard shook his head. Nothing.

# Richard Can Afford a New Studio
## 12 Greek Street, Soho, London
*September 24, 1841*

He'd figured it out, of course. How to be a good painter and a good chap. A great painter and a godly chap, taking into account his respect for Mr. Gaskell, which had gathered invisibly like a pure white fall of snow.

The trick was to separate the two. He'd remembered Chatham, the way his father had kept his work as a chemist separate from his labours for the Reform Bill. Life behind the counter had nothing to do with Reform, although it was true the goodwill from his political efforts flowed back, increasing his custom among everyone but Tories. He felt like a booby in taking so long to see it. But now Richard was underway.

"Just look a bit more aside for me, would you?" he asked. "You're supposed to be humble. I realize it's difficult."

Bob adjusted his pose indulgently, moving more slowly and luxuriously than he had to. Richard's first good work. He was making a sketch for the Wiltshire Friendly Society, the first step in preparing an engraving for a pamphlet promoting their schemes. Bob would be one of two men sitting together in a friendly, which is to say Friendly, fashion. Stephen had agreed to sit for the other, and Richard would pull in a pair of guinea sized brothers or cousins to represent family, possibly an aunt.

Friendly Societies struck him as the way to go, men like Isaac, or an employed Isaac, piling their pennies together so they could draw out pounds when they faced catastrophe. He could do their sketch and afterward learn how to engrave it in a pleasant hum of charity, exempt from Isaac's claim that charity was what the gentry decided to give when they felt like giving it. The Wiltshire Friendly Society had gone looking for someone, and Richard was hardly gentry.

He was happy, if he had to define. Tip-top. Richard had always prided himself on being good-tempered, but now he felt so blithely alive the nerves burred in his wrists and ankles and jaw. He was doing precisely what he ought to, his days divided into painterly works and good ones. He didn't claim to have mastered any of it, which was the next step, and one he knew would take everything he had. But he was striding along the right path, what they called the wind at his back, his young life ready to take flight. Surely it was possible to strap on wings and soar like Icarus without getting too close to the sun. To climb Byron's vapour-shrouded hill without falling into Byronic cynicism. He foresaw no limits, no hubristic fall. *Richard Dadd: Try to Stop Him.*

"Here's an idea," he said, continuing to sketch. "I need a model for Manfred . . ."

"No."

"You don't lack time."

The Henry Martins had sailed for New York in April. Bob was still searching for a suitable location for his own chymist's shop. But the exhaustion of his extended apprenticeship meant he wasn't moving quickly, even though Miss Catherine Clarke of Chatham with her what-d'ye-call-'em ringlets was giving him increasingly frequent hints.

"I don't have time for puffery like that," Bob said.

"You have time for puffery like this."

"For a Friendly Society pamphlet. Not to be featured on the drawing-room walls of the Captain of Her Majesty's Honourable Corps of Gentlemen-at-Arms."

"Impressively remembered. Although it's not a drawing room. I'm not sure what it is, actually."

They were speaking of Richard's first commission. At the spring exhibition, he'd noticed a foppish gentleman bending down to look at his paintings, which had again been hung at a contemptuous height; an exquisite fellow in tan trousers and a black coat with all the silky depth of the night. John Forster had sidled up to congratulate Richard. This was the Whig politician and fourth Baron, Lord Foley, who at the time was the Captain of What-Bob-Said. Since the baron didn't buy anything, Richard thought no more about him until a creamy letter arrived ten days later. Lord Foley wished to discuss a series of panels for his Grosvenor Square townhouse. Perhaps at ten o'clock on the fourteenth inst.?

As the church bells chimed, Richard had presented himself at the door of the townhouse, which proved to be a house the size of a town. Admitted by a quizzical butler, he was placed like a delivery on a small chair in the entrance hall, or at least where a delivery would have been placed at home, and left to admire the gilt-framed Italian paintings hung up to the corniced ceiling. He was sure he recognized a Titian. Richard tried not to be intimidated and failed.

Eventually the baron came in, wearing slippers and a dressing gown.

"The artist, the artist," he said.

"Richard Dadd, sir," he answered, standing, assuming that he hadn't remembered.

"Yes, I know that," Lord Foley said, and Richard could see that he did. A relief to find that a member of Her Majesty's government was on top of things. As footmen opened double doors, he took Richard through a series of connected rooms until they reached a gilded, niche-filled, statue-filled, unfurnished blue-and-gold chamber, overwhelming in its echoing splendour. It was, Lord Foley said, "in need of brightening." Richard had spent time planning for this crucial moment, and as Lord Foley looked even more quizzical than his butler, Richard proposed scenes from either Byron's *Manfred* or Tasso's epic of the Crusades, *Jerusalem Delivered*, elevated subjects he'd thought might interest the baron while setting the tone he wanted for his career. Lord Foley's pause made Richard think himself daft for considering his future. He should have asked John Forster for clues about the baron's tastes.

"Devilish hard to decide," Lord Foley said, no doubt a politician's default response, the first step toward changing one's mind. "Both, I think."

Richard was left to stammer, even though he hadn't yet understood that Lord Foley was hooking him for a tremendous commission, upward of one hundred painted panels. A more established man probably wouldn't have taken it. Several might already have turned him down. Richard's father managed the negotiations with milord's man of business and they agreed on a hefty fee, but his father wasn't confident Richard would see all of it, given the aristocratic propensity for living on tick, often for generations.

However—and Richard kept hearing Mrs. Gaskell say this—*however*, it gilded his name. Did you hear about Richard's commission? It would take a year, he figured. The moment his father and the baron's man shook hands, Richard started working like a fiend, beginning with scenes from *Jerusalem*. It was a quixotic job, not least because Lord Foley suggested, which is to say *required*, that a guardsman of his acquaintance model for Tasso's hero, Godfrey of Bouillon, who would lead the First Crusade against the Turks from a corner of Richard's new studio.

Richard had expected to face tollgates in his rise, setbacks—gravity—but nothing like this. Corporal Lankin proved to be a magnificent blond specimen who seemed to be chiselled in marble. This included his classical features, from which Richard had quickly despaired of extracting even a flicker of emotion.

At their first sitting, he'd dressed him in a dun tunic and plausible chain-mail.

"We're reaching back to the year 1095," Richard said. "You've sold your lands and gathered an army of Christians to march out of Europe. This is your life's work, to take Jerusalem back from the infidel."

Corporal Lankin looked calmly blank.

"You'll be leading your men into battle," Richard said, hoping that the mention of war might get a rise from a military man.

Corporal Lankin grew blanker. For all Richard knew, that was how they looked.

"Perhaps a snarl?" he'd asked.


At least Richard could tell stories. Construct stories, something a little tidier than what had actually occurred. Bob was amused, diverted as he sketched, although Egg had been concerned. Egg and Richard had been hefting some porter upstairs to Richard's new studio while he'd told Egg his story about the corporal. As they dumped it inside the door, Gus had asked, "Did he manage it? The snarl?" Ruining his Dickensian end line.

"I can get him to pose, but with effort," Richard said, flicking a finger at a cloth-covered board. "And to hold it, with effort. He keeps reverting to his marbleized standing at attention. This is going to take far longer than I'd thought. God knows, it can't take years. I'd disappear, my career in tatters. I'm aware of the possibility, believe me."

What he'd been doing that day: getting in porter for a Gaskellian meeting, another of his proposed good works, longer lasting than the Friendly pamphlet. It was time to set up a new exhibition society for younger artists, who were routinely trodden on by bigger men, their paintings hung poorly at the established exhibitions when they were hung at all. He'd sent out a general invitation, knowing he could count on his friends but having no idea how many others would turn up.

Egg was the first, met in the street outside. Now he helped Richard arrange either too few chairs or too many, a wooden cacophony, an earthquake of shoved seating.

"The idea is," Richard said, rehearsing his speech, "I put it twenty years ago, the Society of British Artists was an upstart organization, mounting exhibitions *contra* the Royal Academy. Now both are as fossilized as ammonites."

He gestured (as planned) at his father's ammonite, placed beforehand at the front of a shelf. The benefits of organizing a new exhibition struck him as obvious.

"Are they?" Egg asked. "In what way?"

O'Neil was even worse once the meeting began.

"Why are you proposing this, Dadd?"

Attendance was surprising, painters on chairs and windowsills. O'Neil had been travelling, and this was his first time in the new studio. Richard had taken the lease on far larger rooms to accommodate his commission, and now O'Neil looked pointedly from the high ceiling to the width of windows. "You're doing all right."

Egg moved restlessly. "To be fair, he's had canvases hung at shin height just as much as we . . ."

"His work always gets notices."

"We could improve everyone's chances," Richard cut in. "Set up something with more of an engine to it. More modern."

"Where?" asked one of the landscape painters. His clique was here, all save Phillip, back home in Scotland. Otherwise he'd attracted landscape painters. He'd had no idea there were so many.

"So we've decided to do it and jumped straight to the practicalities," O'Neil said.

"Surely the practicalities determine, well, the practicality of an idea," a landscape said. His name was Poynter, Richard believed.

"Dadd's right," Egg said. "It's important to position oneself at the forefront of the age. Not at the shins of the old men." Turning to Richard, "It's good of you to think of us."

Richard still didn't know whether Gus was being ironic or sincere when he said these things. Before getting his commission, Richard had joined the other members of the clique for weekly sketching sessions. They had used each other as models, and one night Richard had surprised himself by drawing Gus as a Puritan. He sometimes thought the word for Gus was *stringent*, at other times simply *observant*. One didn't care to speak about oneself, not deeply, but Egg had quickly picked up on Richard's wish for moral reform both in society and in himself. Which is to say, he'd noticed that Richard had sworn off brothels, or at least managed not to go there more than most men. He'd also let him know that he approved.

The brief silence was broken by Frith.

"Of course, one doesn't wish to antagonize anyone," he said, speaking from behind his newspaper, Billy being an example of what Richard's father had deemed impossible, here and not-here at the same time.

"A good way to avoid problems is to ask the old men for advice," Richard said. "Everyone likes giving advice. It makes them feel part of something."

"So we *have* decided to do this," O'Neil said.

"The practicalities determining practicability," Poynter insisted, and on they went in ever-widening circles, in spirals like frangible snail shells, like ammonites uncoiling, lengthening into whips and flashing out to scourge Richard's poor idea.

He'd expected circles, spirals, challenges, delay. His father had advised Richard to welcome challenges as a goad to greater achievement, and they were welcome, although not as a goad. More, he had a superstitious fear that he was succeeding too easily. Men paid for doing too well. He was already paying with O'Neil. With O'Neil and perhaps with Egg. He needed a little bad luck to mollify his friends. Richard was tip-top happy, but he was also terrified that he'd plummet back to earth just as quickly as he'd risen, revealed as nothing but puff.

So he walked. When the meeting was over, Richard had walked out into Soho, walking as Dickens did, trying to calm his over-busy mind with rigorous exercise; to evict O'Neil from his brain. He usually set out earlier in the day, when he was losing the light in his studio, counting the steps on evening marches to drown out his worries. One step, two steps, three. Sometimes he walked well into the night. Nights weren't really so dangerous, not if you avoided the rookeries.

That night Richard turned south and then west, walking along the river toward Chelsea, no idea why. Once he'd left the worst of the city behind, the riverside was pleasantly cool and smelled of trees after a rain. He could almost believe he was back in Kent. Richard's jaw loosened, shoulders dropped, his knees shambled booby loose as he tired himself out. Dickens walked to tire himself out; Richard was sure of it. A man needed sleep, and given Dickens's immense output—a new novel lately, the magazine he edited, his plays, countless *charitable* committees—he probably found sleep as elusive as Richard. A hundred panels to paint: Richard's brain churned like a mechanical loom.

He needed to find balance. To walk a fine balance, permitting himself a busy enough mind to churn up solutions to his painterly problems but not so busy that he couldn't sleep. One step, two, three thousand. A balance, let us say, between churn and exhaustion, where he might find peace.

Sometimes he found it. A few days later, walking south of the river, Richard looked up absent-mindedly and was struck by the peach-coloured beauty of the sunset. As he marvelled, a round space opened in his mind and spread without impediment into the world, turning all of life into a lofty exalted cave that at once enclosed him and had no limits. Richard felt awed by the wonder he was part of. He was passing Bedlam, and every metal paling quivered brilliantly in the coral light. At his feet pecked a pigeon, and he saw each feather as if he'd drawn it, all of them stained a rosy silver. Above him the rooftops blushed.

A panel came to him, a vision of a panel he would paint for his series on *Manfred*. Byron's half-mad hero would lie in a waking dream or dreaming sleep, in thrall to the forbidden love that powered the poem; to the woman Manfred could neither speak of nor forget. Around his head was a fog of tiny, fugitive dancing figures, male and female: the thoughts and memories that devilled him, as the spirits had decreed they always would.

> *Though thy slumber may be deep,*
> *Yet thy spirit shall not sleep;*
> *There are shades which will not vanish,*
> *There are thoughts thou canst not banish;*
> *By a power to thee unknown,*
> *Thou art wrapt as with a shroud,*
> *Thou art gathered in a cloud;*
> *And for ever shalt thou dwell*
> *In the spirit of this spell.*

The painting would be as much about Richard as it was about Manfred, but he saw now that an artist's best work was disguised autobiography. Saw that as the real reason he hated portraiture. Having to burrow into someone else's being was a diversion from the true work of mining oneself. He was all he really had to offer: his vision, the way he saw the world. *His genius*, Dadson whispered.

Richard walked on, re-crossing the river to his studio, where he slept a refreshing sleep. He woke up knowing he was a long way from painting *Manfred*, with the Crusades stretching interminably before him and Lankin such a burden. "But sometimes you keep drawing trumps," he told Bob.

Richard had solved Lankin that same morning by an off-hand mention of the celebrated pugilist Bendigo Thompson, how he'd seen Bendigo fight not long before the pugilist had lamed himself doing his famously exuberant handstands at the steeplechase races and been forced to withdraw from the ring.

"You saw Bendigo?" Corporal Lankin's face moved.

Cautiously, Richard said, "My friends and I saw him fight Deaf Burke . . ."

"You saw the 'ead butt what disqualified Burke and give the championship to Bendigo," Lankin interrupted, his carved lips opening in a smile. He hadn't kept his mouth shut to hide bad teeth. They were as regular as chalk in a box.

"Bendigo would have won anyway," Richard said. Slowly, as if trying not to startle an animal, he reached for a sketchbook.

"'E would," the corporal agreed, his posture loosening. "Not that I were lucky enough to be there, but one of me mites seen it. 'Ad Deaf Burke by the bollocks, 'e did."

As Corporal Lankin demonstrated, Richard sketched his unleashed grace.

"Did you ever see Bendigo?" he asked, wanting to keep him going.

"What I saw were a bout with Ben Caunt, one of 'em, where Caunt near strangled Bendigo by the rope." Lankin choked himself in a double-fisted grip.

"Did you really? Lucky cove."

"It were a bout for the hages," Lankin said, and started narrating the fight as he acted it out, step by step, with Richard slashing quick curved lines of lips nostrils eyes neck hands.

Now, he said, Caunt laid a punch to the belly and Bendigo answered with a cuff to the ribs. Then Bendigo fell down to the ground—"as were 'is wont."

Lankin crashed down enthusiastically, acting stunned, shaking his head theatrically, then rolling with sudden energy to evade an incensed and invisible Caunt, leaping up and cuffing Caunt's invisible ear, dancing around Richard's studio in his chain-mail, punching one-two, one-two, dancing closer and closer, until with a *Why not?* Richard threw down his sketchbook and put up his fists, so they were sparring happily.

Richard loved this. The duck and bow. The swipe of air. Both were laughing, Richard feeling the power of the corporal's swing as it whistled past him, light on his feet but not half as powerful as the guardsman, a power he liked to feel opposing him, feinting at it, left right, left right, left right, until he just barely glimpsed a fist coming toward

Blackness.


"I woke up thinking I was in Manchester," he told Bob. "On the ground, a soldier bending over me during the riot."

"A *riot?*" Bob asked.

Richard had run into a riot during his second visit to Manchester, when he'd come back south after a sketching tour of Scotland. The Gaskells were out of town and he'd gone to an inn. Forgot his dislike of inns until he'd unpacked in his room, a particularly sad old soldier with torn sheets.

As Richard crossed the lobby, planning a walk, his landlord stepped in front of him. "I shouldn't go out now, sir," he said. "Bit of trouble on the town, if I may say so, sir."

"Right. Read about it in the newspaper."

Chartists promised to disrupt a rally by Anti–Corn Law League supporters. Both groups were against the government, but the league was moderate and the Chartists were radicals. Richard's father was an Anti–Corn Law man. So were the manufacturers, calling for the repeal of the corn laws that the government used to keep bread prices artificially high, starving the poor for the benefit of great landowners like Lord Foley.

"Had you already met Lord Foley?"

No, this was before they'd met, Bob was right. But Richard *had* met Isaac, and Isaac was a radical Chartist, refusing to let the manufacturers tell him what he wanted. The Chartists had eight demands, none of them involving corn, each more unlikely than the last. The universal male vote. A secret ballot. Paid MPs. Not that all working men supported Chartism. Some just wanted cheap bread.

Nodding at his landlord, Richard went back to his room and returned with his sketchbook, waving it as he went outside.

Why had he done that? Walked into a riot. Not his subject, no real wish to sketch. Truth: he wanted rumpus. He'd been such a good chap, especially during the sketching tour of Scotland. But sometimes a man needed rumpus, he told Bob, failing to add that he didn't know any brothels in Manchester or he would have gone there instead.

Richard found empty streets. Closed shops. Quick footfalls as a herd of urchins ran past him, their sharp knees digging the air like trowels. He hurried after them and broke into a run at the first distant sounds of shouts, cries, muffled chants coming from Stevenson Square. He felt like a bead of water rolling down a windowpane, running faster and faster with more and more other runners until he heard wrenching wooden sounds amid the shouts, shipyard sounds, the groan and splinter of timbers.

Rounding a corner into the square, Richard saw a crowd of ragged Chartists swarming a raised league platform, which rocked under their assault like a ship stormed by pirates. He took an instinctive step back and was pressed against a wall by a ripple of movement around him. Sidling along the wall, he reached a barred door and stepped onto its threshold so he could see above the crowd.

Thousands of heads filled the square, pushing incoherently as northern voices yowled *Hey* and *Oi* and *Yaw*. Richard didn't see anyone he recognized, no Isaac or Job or Job or Hephzibah's bandy father, although he'd bet most of them were here. In the distance, he glimpsed police and Redcoats massed in the side streets, troops kept back by officers riding their restless snorting mounts.

Richard tried to catch his breath and couldn't. Bodies churned in front of him. Fought at the foot of the stage. A few men could raise their fists but most were packed so tightly they could only shove head against head like fighting bulls. Banners jerked above them, Chartist banners that League supporters were fighting to wrench down. *Votes for the Working*

*Man!* The letters on white cloth stretched out and crumpled as they were pushed and pulled. Stretched crumpled pushed pulled. Richard found it peculiarly bracing.

In the middle of the crowd, one banner slumped down, its stick supports cracking like gunfire. A scramble, and one man emerged with a broken stick he raised to a great jeering yowl. Yelling back, he levelled the stick and jabbed it at the crowd. Jab jab, fighting, jab jab, joust. He struck one man in the chest and the poor bugger went down bloody. In front of the stage, men ripped another banner apart. More went down, slipping underfoot to be trampled. Richard had never imagined anything like it.

A grab at his elbow. He toppled off his stoop to find a tall Redcoat holding his arm in a killing grip.

"What do you think you're playing?" the lieutenant yelled.

Richard held out his sketchbook with his other hand. He'd sketched the riot. Hadn't intended to do that.

"Fecking journalist," yelled the lieutenant.

"Artist, I'm afraid," Richard yelled back, enjoying the ruction. Men circled around them, clearing a space as if they were pugilists. Richard was about to say more when the lieutenant suddenly flung him by one wrist. His head snapped, hitting brick so he saw black stars and

R ichard wasn't in Manchester. He was waking up on the floor of his studio after Corporal Lankin had knocked him out. "My head one fat ache," he told Bob. Opening his eyes, he saw the corporal kneeling over him, such a look of horror on his face that Richard hadn't been able to help a weak chuckle.

Clearly the right thing to do. Lankin cracked a smile, and

as Richard continued chuckling, Lankin joined in until they were both laughing. The corporal gave him a hand up, clapping him so enthusiastically on the back that Richard was propelled half over. Probably just as well, given his dizziness. More stars.

They coalesced into a new panel. Easing himself upright, Richard saw a scene with Lankin's Godfrey kneeling over a fallen soldier, who would have Richard's face.

"In a commission like this, an artist likes to make one signature joke," he explained, although Lankin didn't seem to get it, not the sharpest sword in the armoury. "Hung out of the way, of course, over a door, if Lord Foley hasn't any objection."

A few days later, when Lankin arrived at Greek Street, the baron followed him in. Richard bowed, hoping to hide his surprise.

"The artist's studio," Lord Foley said, all louche ease with the guardsman reverted to marble behind him. Richard wondered if they saw each other all the time or if Lankin had gone to him particularly. The baron had looked at earlier panels only after they were delivered to his townhouse, usually pleased but once or twice raising objections, which had been warranted. A good eye. A true aesthete. He walked to the easel.

"Ha," he said, taking in Richard's fallen soldier. "Ha ha." Being one of those people with an entirely mirthless laugh, the way some dogs really barked, "Woof woof." But his eyes were lively, and he clapped Richard's back as hard as Lankin had. It needed steady legs to keep from pitching forward.

"I shall enjoy having this," Lord Foley said, taking a keen look around the studio. He ended by nodding at Lankin.

"Good job," he said. Lankin gave him a look of pure relief and relaxed, this time for good.

"So they're nancy boys," Bob said, as Richard finished his sketch. "Or at least Lord Foley is, and the guardsman is hired."

O'Neil had said the same thing.

"A baron needs an heir the way drink needs a bottle, and you say he's rich and well past thirty and isn't yet married. Something keeps him off women."

"The thought had never occurred to me."

O'Neil had pushed back Richard's hair and looked in his eyes with exaggerated concern. "I never know whether you're wilfully naive or just naive."

Now Richard told Bob, "They could be sodomites or sparring partners, for all I know. He might keep an actress in the Haymarket or an opera singer and eight little bastards in Croydon. Console a duchess, if barons are sufficiently purple to console duchesses. I have no feeling for these people."

Aristocrats. Not his subject. True, he was curious.

"Are we done?" Bob asked.

Looking through the sheaf of sketches, Richard raised an invisible glass. Bob raised one back, and for a moment Richard considered a new sketch, then shook his head, deciding not.

# Mrs. Gaskell
## Pays a Visit to Haworth
### September 1853

C harlotte worried that her friend would find life in the parsonage as barren as Robinson Crusoe's island. As bereft of interest as the American backwoods, where they had only a tattered old Bible to comfort them. Her father read prayers before breakfast, after which he retired to his study and Charlotte waited for the post. She walked before dinner and walked again after. Tea, a fire, bed. One day in the parsonage and her friend would desiccate. Ash in a cone on the floor.

Not a bit of it. When the cab door opened, the warmest of breezes blew out. Charlotte wanted to run to her side, but an unwanted visitor was just then leaving the parsonage, a would-be patron of her writing who lingered on the steps, and

Charlotte had to get him away before he realized that their arriving guest was another literary lioness he could patronize, the novelist Elizabeth Gaskell.

"My dear, my dear," Mrs. Gaskell said when he was gone, linking arms as Charlotte took her inside. She was already laughing about her adventures on the train from Manchester, where an undertaker's boy had been transporting an under-built coffin, the nails of which began popping as they loaded it, as if the lady inside wished out, "preferring first class. But I know you catch nightmares from ghost stories, and I'll stop." Peering in the dining room, Charlotte's parlour: "What delightful paper."

Elizabeth Gaskell was one of those people who changed the tenor of a house when she walked in, not by a display of egotism or by their lofty Alpine presence. Not like Thackeray and Dickens. Not like men. Mrs. Gaskell's famous charm lay in her unaffected interest in people; her entire absence of self-regard. She didn't know why she should speak about herself. She knew all about herself. She would rather hear other people's stories. A beautiful, tall, solid woman, a tree trunk, she would fold herself into whatever chair was empty, and her "How *are* you?" to whomever she found beside her was so obviously sincere, her silences so attentive, her wit so fertile, she could draw even a pedant into the liveliest of conversations. Even Charlotte.

No one called her Elizabeth. "I banish Mrs. Gaskell. You must call me Lily," she'd said not long after they'd met. Charlotte had never managed to. She loved Mrs. Gaskell but resisted giving herself over entirely to her friend, who was not only kind and moral and an admirably modern novelist but also one of the worst gossips Charlotte had met. She dashed off letters to half the country filled with everyone else's *moving* and *inspiring* stories, as Charlotte knew first-hand from getting them herself and devouring them before dinner.

The Reverend James Martineau's feud with his sister Harriet had kept them apart for so many years that when they'd accidentally seen one another last week in London, both had turned to stone like Lot's wife gazing on Gomorrah. Dickens was so far above most of humanity, such a titan, that he left others feeling diminished, and they behaved in small ways toward him. She'd heard Wilkie Collins confess to a friend that he'd taken most of Dickens's editing suggestions on a story but rejected one, even though he knew Dickens was right, impelled to deny him the satisfaction of having his way all the time. Mr. Collins being one of Dickens's closest friends.

Since Charlotte wasn't allowed to call her Mrs. Gaskell, she didn't call her anything. Nor did she tell her everything, although it would have been a relief. There wouldn't be any George Smith during her visit, apart from his role as Charlotte's publisher, the usual writerly complaints. The Reverend Nicholls, yes. He'd been secretly writing and Charlotte needed advice.

Knowing her friend would be hungry, Charlotte had ordered dinner to be ready.

"I'm afraid my father won't be joining us," she said. "He still isn't well, although he's improving. He'll be with us for tea."

"Delightful. And in the meantime, we finally have each other. How *are* you? I want to know everything."

A visit she'd planned for June had been postponed when both Charlotte and her father fell ill. Mrs. Gaskell was a martyr to headaches and the mother of six, four still living, so health was a long and intricate subject, with digressions and verbal footnotes. Charlotte was much improved, but her father. Men's need for flannel waistcoats. The ill north wind. Mrs. Gaskell was a slave to her tuppenny opiates, but she would never evangelize, every constitution being unique.

"You appear so hearty and yet you suffer," Charlotte said. "It makes me hope that appearances really are deceiving, and my constitution is stronger than it looks."

She said things like this partly to gauge others' reactions, but once they'd started in on health, Mrs. Gaskell's face had settled into a look of generalized solicitude, and it didn't change.

"I have a particular reason to mention it," she added, picturing Mr. Nicholls's whiskers.

"You're thinking of starting a new novel? Which takes so much out of us."

But the door of her father's study opened across the hall. It was far later than Charlotte had realized. Dinner was long over, and now that she was awake to the house, she heard Martha and Tabby rattling tea things in the kitchen. Mrs. Gaskell rose as Mr. Brontë came in, and Charlotte was proud to introduce her upright, intellectual father in his well-brushed black, an Anglican clergyman who was open-minded enough to welcome a Dissenter into his house, even though he disapproved of her Unitarian faith and loathed her modern opinions on the role of woman.

Neither Charlotte nor Mrs. Gaskell supported radicals who campaigned for the equality of women. Yet neither had they any use for men who believed women to be unequal. It was a lonely position, and Charlotte had found it necessary to keep a small mental list of men whose overall beliefs and actions were sufficiently worthy to balance their unregenerate feelings about the female sex, meaning that they could be tolerated, and she was able to enjoy some measure of society. Her own list began with her father, and one of her great hopes was that Mrs. Gaskell would add him to hers.

"I'm an admirer of your novels," Mr. Brontë said, always a good start. "They are moral works, I believe. My daughter Charlotte faces the same criticisms as you, madam, and my daughters Emily and Anne did, for addressing difficult subjects: the redemption of fallen women like your Ruth, and the temptations faced by impoverished ladies like my daughter's famous Miss Jane Eyre. Yet difficult subjects must needs be discussed, for without discussion, sin walks unchallenged among us."

Martha came in as he spoke, setting tea on the table.

"I would add," he went on, "if a man doesn't wish his wife or daughters to read such novels, he may prohibit them. Or rather I should say, attempt to prohibit them. I permitted my children free access to my books and newspapers, not least," he said, leaning forward in antique raillery, "because they would have read them anyway."

"Thank you," Mrs. Gaskell said, charmed by what she could see was a welcome Mr. Brontë had been preparing as they chatted, the way he prepared his sermons. She was about to go on when Mr. Brontë interrupted.

"Is that lemon cake?" he asked Charlotte. "Then you might cut me a piece. We may live in the wilds of Yorkshire," he told Mrs. Gaskell, "but every savage enjoys his lemons in season.

"A larger piece," he said sharply. "Keep that one for your appetite."

"My father is particularly fond of lemons," Charlotte said, and it was unfortunate, but Mrs. Gaskell seemed to think he would be.

After tea, after prayers, after her father had gone above, Charlotte and her friend were left alone with a good fire, the weather having turned. Mrs. Gaskell had been looking forward to seeing the heather blooming on the moors, and it had stayed late this year through a series of fine warm days that Charlotte had hoped would last for her friend's visit. But the weather had grown so unseasonably hot that it brought on a storm, great whips of lightning and long boisterous rolls of thunder racing and blasting and crackling over the moors as if fighting an airy metallic war, the gods crashing and clashing above them. Emily had loved these storms, helplessly drawn to the window, drawn outside, always in thrall to great inhuman carelessness, whether from nature or man.

In the storm's wake, cold autumn air blew in. The heather was blasted, its short season done.

"You alluded to some new writing," Mrs. Gaskell said.

"I didn't intend to. It's true I started something, but I've put it aside to think. The idea isn't quite ripe yet. I usually start and stop several times." Charlotte paused. She'd discussed her ideas with her sisters but was out of the habit. "The kernel of the story is two brothers. Adults, I thought, but when I started to write, one of the brothers decided to be a boy of ten, as you know characters do. I thought this might answer, having started two of my novels with children. But then I thought it told against me; that I should try something new. And maybe I should and maybe I shouldn't. But in any case, that wasn't what I was going to speak of. Something more romantic. But that will have to wait until tomorrow."

Mrs. Gaskell perked up, ready to demand more, to say she wasn't at all tired, the journey was nothing really. But Charlotte cast her eyes toward the ceiling, meaning her father.

She was teasing. He couldn't hear them. She didn't know the last time she'd felt this mischievous. Felt amused, felt young, planning to tell Mrs. Gaskell what had transpired with Mr. Nicholls in serial form for her enjoyment, the closest she could offer to the exhibitions of dwarves and giants in London. Poor Mrs. Gaskell, all anticipation and eyebrows, and Charlotte was determined to make her wait.

"Must we indeed?" she whispered, and Charlotte nodded solemnly, planning to take her to her father's church in the morning and say, *Here is where Mr. Nicholls lost command of himself giving me communion for the last time,* a sickening and embarrassing and mawkish display before the entire parish.

On the way back out of the village: *Here is where I found him on the day he was to leave, sobbing in anguish like a child whose dog had died, thinking I would not bid him farewell.*

In the path on the moor: *Here is where he told me that he wouldn't go to Australia, having withdrawn his application to be a missionary.*

In the gully: *Here is where he walked thirty-seven miles from his new parish to meet me, more than once, without my father's knowledge.*

What she wouldn't say: In this dining room, beneath the portrait of Mr. Thackeray you have been admiring, sent as we discussed by my handsome, genial, penny-pinching publisher, I have spent hours and hours of my waning life waiting for Mr. Smith's letters, which came sporadically after *Villette's* success and stopped without explanation in July.

Here is where I ceased writing to my oldest friend, Ellen Nussey, disliking her barrage of unanswerable questions about Mr. Smith and her mean-spirited criticism of Mr. Nicholls, who for all his faults suffers as greatly as I do from unrequited love.

Here, I am as lonely as I have ever been. Here, I have hated our inflexible routine. Here, with your arrival, I have remembered that I once loved it, when predictability was a shelter. While I was in exile, working as a governess, I crept past tall ticking clocks in tall empty hallways and said to myself, *Now they are praying, now they are walking, now they are peeling potatoes for dinner.* My sisters made the difference. Since they left me, the parsonage has fallen silent, and it is an oppressive, pulverizing silence. Life alone is a ballet without music. I hear oddly padded footfalls outside this room and don't know whether I am hearing the servants or the dead.

But music has come back with you, the music of your voice, and I understand that I must have someone with me. My father is old and I will have to leave the parsonage when he dies, and that might be soon, and I don't know what to do.

A scream. Mrs. Gaskell's door thumped open. Charlotte leapt out of bed, not yet awake in the silken grey miasma of dawn.

"My dear, was that a gunshot?" Mrs. Gaskell cried from the hallway.

Alert now, Charlotte left the room in her shawl and bare feet, taking her friend's arm and leading her back into Aunt Branwell's bedroom, the best room and guest room, usually tenanted by ghosts.

"There's nothing the matter. Only that I forgot to tell you. My father's gun. He's kept it loaded beside his bed every night since the Luddite riots, and has to discharge it every morning out his window."

"But the Luddite riots were more than forty years ago."

"Yes, but Chartists were discovered drilling with sticks on the moor during the Hungry Forties. To a man my father's age, fifteen years ago was last week."

Mrs. Gaskell's eyes lit up and they exchanged smiles, beginning to laugh, trying to stay quiet, their shoulders shaking. Mrs. Gaskell scrambled back into bed, hiking to the far side, inviting Charlotte to get her toes under the covers.

"Is there anything else I should know?"

"There's a madwoman in the attic."

They giggled like girls, Charlotte almost forty, Mrs. Gaskell a few years past it.

"What are you hiding in *your* attic?"

"Absolutely nothing. Our old clothes go to the poor. The girls' discarded toys. Superannuated chairs. Everything we have is in use or on display. Like Mr. Gaskell's great worthiness." Seeing Charlotte's shock: "I say that with the deepest respect and love. You'll understand when you're married."

Charlotte wondered what she knew but saw only general encouragement. Mrs. Gaskell—Lily—leaned back and stretched out her arms.

"When I first met William, it was obvious quite quickly that he would ask me to marry him and that I would probably accept. But should I? How to decide. You see I was a scatterbrain—even worse than I am now—but at least I knew it. So I sat down with pen and paper, telling myself to try to see what was well and truly and deeply *there*. I stared at my paper and chewed on my pen, and after a great deal of thought, I wrote down William's name and after it the one word *just*. He was a just man. Only that, and I knew what my life would be, and I chose it."

Charlotte was struck by the story and tried to see as clearly.

"You don't forgive me for taking my husband's name in vain."

"I was only asking myself to choose one word for Mr. Nicholls. We've talked about him."

"The one who went to Australia?"

"He's here, in a new parish. He felt I began to behave sympathetically toward him in the face of my father's coldness. It made him decide to stay in Yorkshire, in a parish forty miles to the south."

"And were you? Sympathetic?"

Yes and no. "He told the missionary society he was afraid he would be prevented from fulfilling his duties in Australia because of a tendency toward rheumatism."

Both giggled.

"I was planning to take you on a tour. Where he did thus and such. How he's contrived to send letters. Where we've met on the moor."

"Tell me now or I shall die."

Charlotte waited in a gully on a flat rock by a beck. It was early September and the weather was still like August, the gully humid and close. Insects were busy. Birds. Her sister Anne had always loved the spearmint-green grass tufted around the grey rocks, emerald green, a demanding Irish green, and when they'd found the colour in Bradford, in a muslin figured with leaves, Anne had exclaimed, *God is good to me*. Although generally he wasn't.

Spearmint grass and eroded banks. A romantic scene in a novel, no doubt, a lady waiting for her suitor, but Charlotte felt anxious and silly, and was perspiring more obnoxiously than ladies ever perspired in fiction. She had to take off her spectacles to clean them, and when she put them back on, she saw two sheep peering over the edge, looking mildly censorious. No censorious sheep in romantic novels either, or if there were, their wool wouldn't be matted. They would be lambs and they would gambol. In Charlotte's novels, and her sisters' novels, black clouds would roil and tumble, lightning crackle, thunder roar. They sowed a different set of clichés.

A cloud passed over the sun and in the sudden uncannily warm shade Charlotte felt breathless, sultry, *wanted*. Then the sun came back out and she felt cliché.

Mr. Nicholls had planned to set out by starlight and walk to nearby Oxenhope, where he would dine with his friend Mr. Grant. Afterward, it wouldn't take him long to reach her. They had agreed to meet at three o'clock, and Charlotte realized she had absolute confidence he would arrive when he said, despite everything that could happen in a tramp of almost forty miles from his new curacy in Kirk Smeaton. She also realized the farmers would see his long approach over the open moor and would gossip. But Mr. Nicholls had friends in Haworth and she told herself the farmers wouldn't know it was Charlotte he was meeting, not when she was hidden in a gully, less like a heroine than a lost button.

This was their second meeting after he'd left Haworth. The first one was brief, in June, and she'd left Ellen Nussey nearby while they'd talked. Afterward, Ellen had wanted—no, *required* assurances that Charlotte had sent him away definitively, and Charlotte had enjoyed letting her friend know that she hadn't, not quite.

"Hedging your bets," Ellen had vulgarly said. Charlotte knew she was right but wondered aloud when Ellen had become mean-spirited. None of it bore thinking about, and Charlotte thought about it all the time. She had become her own mother, making the type of calculations a mother made for her daughters, rounding up suitors like a sheepdog his sheep, not yet sure which one would be sheared.

A sound of tramping. The nonfictional sheep disappeared over the verge, and Charlotte rose to see Mr. Nicholls scrambling downhill, favouring his right leg. She didn't believe in his rheumatism, which hadn't been mentioned since he'd begged off Australia, but naturally he would be footsore after walking forty miles. Thirty-seven. Even though he was a demon for exercise, presuming curates could be demonic.

Charlotte hated her chattering nerves and *would* get on top of them.

"Mr. Nicholls," she said, composing her face into an expression of agreeable empty-headed blandness, as ladies were advised. And Charlotte was a lady, despite not being treated as one when she'd been a governess. Despite disliking the empty-headed blandness she was supposed to project, and often chose to. It was a cardinal point.

"Hullo then," Mr. Nicholls said. "You came."

Beaming over her, colour high, black hair windblown, he looked like a hardy young farmer. Belatedly hearing what he said, Charlotte realized that Mr. Nicholls had walked forty miles without being certain she would meet him.

"Am I unreliable?" she asked. "I wouldn't have thought so."

He agreed, but she was back in a memory of early days, rainy, sheltered in the parsonage, when Branwell had passed on tags of the Latin and Greek their father taught him. *It makes me a gentleman*, he said. *And me a lady?* The question always cardinal. *Not if you let on you know Latin*, Branny said, leaning heavily on her shoulder as she copied, a delicious weight of warm boy.

Charlotte didn't know why this particular memory had rumbled in over so many others. Mr. Nicholls was nothing like her brother, either when Branwell was young and good or later, after he had overripened. Then she caught a glimpse: *My brother is the reason I like boyish men*, she thought, *before they spoil.* Helpless before George Smith, his leg slung over the arm of a chair. Her professor, M. Héger, blowing cigar smoke into her desk at night so she would raise its lid on his scent in the morning. Mr. Nicholls, looking so young.

Charlotte disliked knowing this about herself. A lady should want a mature man who would protect her. She decided she'd been mistaken.

"May we sit?" she asked, and when they did, she had nothing to say. No more did he. They both looked away, just enough to keep the other in sight.

"It's comforting, is it not?" Mr. Nicholls asked, after a while. "To sit in peace."

"I have a busy mind."

"Well then, I'll leave you to it," he said, and got up to take off his coat and roll up his sleeves, looking even more like a farmer. He lay down on the edge of the beck and slid one bare arm slowly into it, his arm wavering in the sun-dappled water as if it were about to dissolve. Illusions made Charlotte uneasy, her eyesight bad enough without them. They made her feel vague, dreamy, disconnected from the world, and she pictured Mr. Nicholls slowly tipping into the beck, first his shoulder, then the rest of him sliding under. She saw him dissolving on the streambed, his eyes open and empty and glittering. It was the open eyes that panicked her.

"What on earth are you doing?"

"Be patient now," he said. "I'm fishing."

"Without a rod."

"His rod and His staff, they comfort me. They have to, if a man can't afford to kit himself out, and he has to fish by tickling."

Charlotte controlled her panicky breath. The nerve of him, her father would say. Poor as a church mouse and wanting your hand. He's after the money from your writing.

No Father, in all conscience, he isn't, she'd repeated many times. And there isn't that much money.

More clouds. The wind was picking up. It swept over Mr. Nicholls as he lay prone, riffling his sleeves and flipping the hem of his waistcoat up and down. Charlotte had to go closer to see him properly, and sat down on a rock at the edge of the beck. His sun-dappled arm looked so much like the stream-bed that brown trout flitted over it unawares, swimming back and forth, back and forth like restless blunt-nosed underwater dogs.

One eddied above his hand, and faster than Charlotte could see, he batted it far out onto the bank in a great cold splash that made her scream happily. A startled snipe rose beating into the air. Charlotte scrambled to her feet, brushing herself off.

"You've got me all wet!"

"Put it out of its misery, then."

Laughing. Squealing: "I cannot."

Mr. Nicholls picked up a stone and walked over to the panicked tossing fish. He dispatched it quickly, threading a line from his pocket through its gills and placing it back in a small pool behind a rock, off from the main current of the beck.

Afterward, he lay down again, slipping his arm back in the water. It was already pink from the cold, with straight black hair laid out in thin lines. Charlotte was close enough to see this and like it, standing over him.

"Won't they be warned now and shy?"

"I've never found fish to be the most clever of God's creatures. One more as a thank you to my friends Joe and Mrs. Grant, and perhaps a pair for your father's supper, and yours."

"My father," Charlotte said.

"I don't blame him," Mr. Nicholls said, with such depth that Charlotte couldn't reach the bottom of it.

"I'm all he has."

"I'm aware of that."

They were silent again, before something seemed to occur.

"Would you like to try? Or do ladies scorn it?"

"My hands are too small."

"They're delicate," Mr. Nicholls said, with improbable satisfaction. Charlotte was startled into holding out her paws and looking at them newly. The hands of a clever child.

A bossy stubborn child, not as talented as her younger siblings.

A clever child, and wanted.


"That was as intimate as we got," she told Lily Gaskell. "He asked after people in Haworth and children at the Sunday School. I told him that my father's new curate is undependable. We agreed that he should continue writing, and that I would answer."

"So you'd like him back here as curate, in any case," Lily Gaskell said. "Helping your father, marriage or not."

Hedging your bets. Was she that transparent?

"I . . ." She couldn't mention George Smith, who might still take her to London.

Lily waited.

"Wonder how you find time to write with a family, and

197

given all the obligations of a minister's wife. Do you think they cause you to censor your writing? To hold back?"

"You asked me that once in a letter, and told me not to answer. I took it rather as a comment on the quality of my work. That hold back I do."

Charlotte's runaway letters. Her runaway tongue. Yes, that was what she thought.

"I don't, you know. I do the best I can. Give free rein to what's inside me. But perhaps there's not as much inside me as you've got parcelled up in you."

"I find comparisons invidious," Charlotte said.

"Why do you write? Always a fascinating subject. It's been put about that Mr. Gaskell got me to write my first novel as a distraction, after our little boy . . . It would have happened anyway. I'm a storyteller. I'd have been an old wife at the fireside centuries ago, meting out stories and morals. Novels aren't a replacement for children, you know. Some authors say they look on their novels as their children, but I feel quite differently. The novels, the writing, is nothing but me, and my daughters are entirely themselves. But here I am, going on, when I intended to ask about you."

Why she wrote. Charlotte thought her friend deserved an honest answer but didn't know what it was. When she stayed silent, Lily said, "It has a bearing on your question about marriage. The obligations of a minister's wife. Whether she censors herself. If she writes for approval, for instance, then she probably has to, and that isn't good for the work. But I don't think that can be your reason."

"It may be my precise reason. Or a large part. Doesn't everyone wish to be loved? I've always longed for it. The problem is that I sabotage myself by writing the truth. I feel compelled. And that can cause people to hate me. Harriet Martineau." The name made her lips pucker.

"But poor Mr. Nicholls really does seem to love you."

"I don't believe he'd let me have Dissenters as friends. He's rather strict."

"One ignores husbands when convenient."

"I see no point in accepting a husband only to ignore him."

"Then you're alone in the world of women." Lily Gaskell took Charlotte's hand in hers. "Must everything be so fraught, dear?"

Jane Eyre had told Helen Burns that to gain affection from anyone she truly loved, she would submit to having her arm broken, or let a bull toss her, or stand behind a kicking horse and let it dash its hoof at her chest. Dear Jane had meant that. Charlotte had been surprised at her passion as she wrote, the clench of her teeth and the tautness constricting her chest, but both Jane and she had meant that.

When she didn't answer, Lily said, "Poor Mr. Nicholls." Correcting herself, "Lucky Mr. Nicholls." Another pause. "Poor, lucky Mr. Nicholls."

The one encapsulating word for him was neither lucky nor poor. *Trustworthy*, perhaps. *Reliable. Patient.*

"*Available* Mr. Nicholls," she said. They met each other's raised eyebrows and burst into laughter.

# In Which Richard Receives
## an Advantageous Proposition
## That Might Not Be to His Advantage

*London*

*February 1842*

L ast year. Lord Foley's ball. There had been a great fuss among the sisters about evening dress. Visits to Richard's tailor, otherwise known as Uncle Lowe, husband of his aunt Louisa Martin. Richard must have been the only man invited to the ball with a tailor in Croydon. With an uncle in Croydon. He was perfectly happy with his sixteen-shilling ready-made trousers, but he couldn't be one of Dickens's Gents at Lord Foley's ball. He had to be a gentleman, and fortunately his father would pay.

Richard had been advised to arrive not quite promptly and reached the portico amid a loud crush of coaches ferrying quality, wheels clacking against each other, exasperated coachmen cursing, horses tossing their heads and screaming. Paintings of Charon showed him ferrying ethereal boatloads of the dead across the river to Hades when it must be more like this, especially during war and plagues, multiples boats so loaded with bodies they threatened to capsize, multiple Charons cursing.

Amused at the picture, dodging the proliferation of steaming straw-smelling patties, Richard allowed the throng to carry him inside. There, the quizzical butler was loudly announcing the Honourable This-This and the Right Honourable Lord That-and-Such, suffering a fortunately brief case of laryngitis when announcing his monosyllabic Dadd self. Standing on the edge of the first great illuminated room, Richard suffered an equally brief withdrawal of confidence, worried that none of his acquaintance would know he'd arrived.

But of course he knew no one there and no one cared to know him. *I'm not here*, he thought happily. Then: *I am a good-humoured man.*

Lord Foley's townhouse was as brilliantly lit as if milord had brought in a theatrical man to flood the rooms with limelight. It picked out the lace on the ladies' gowns, which Richard would have to remember for his sisters. The ladies were a garden of restless flowers, their *rustle-rustle* silk dresses of every brilliant colour ruched and embroidered and falling into folds their dressmakers had composed as carefully as music. Gentlemen wore their trousers cut on the bias (Uncle Lowe: "We'll cut you on the bias to keep them *that* tight.") and jackets of cloth so soft that brushing past them was like stroking the fur of mythical creatures trapped beyond the latitudes, or raised in the cool lightless cellars of castles.

In one room, card games were being played with stakes that would no doubt bankrupt the corporate mass of Richard's uncles. In the ballroom, the dance was underway, each coordinated twirl of twenty and more partners so oiled and precise that artists could freeze it at any step and capture poise and symmetry. Richard rather liked dancing, but given his lack of acquaintance, he was left to tap his foot, smiling, easy, surprised at the glance from a young lady whirling past who kept facing him with each twirl, seeming to wonder who he was. As he did at times himself.

Richard didn't see Corporal Lankin, nor expect to, but picked out the prime minister being jovial across the room. Lord Melbourne, the handsome old devil. *Milord*, he might have said. *Milord, we have Lord Byron in common. I'm trying to get inside Byron's mind with the same resolution and vigour he deployed to get up your late wife's skirts. I believe she called him mad, bad and dangerous to know while he called her a fiend. You might be interested to know, Prime Minister, that I'm planning to paint spirits and fiends dancing around my Byronic hero Manfred's head, and it now occurs to me to make one a portrait of your young Lady Caroline with her pointed fox face, so well-known from the famous engravings. I'd wager Lord Foley would like that. At least I'd wager if I thought I could afford tonight's stakes.*

Here was a truth, the evening's truth: they were living at the glimmering end of elevated times. The old men gossiping by the curtains had known great poets and fought in the greatest of wars. Modern life for all its propulsion had a sense of wistfulness for what was lost. It was this yearning, this autumnal pang that Richard was trying to shade into his paintings. Yes, of fairies. Here he was in a limelit room—ignored, but in the room—with a prime minister who had known Byron and Shelley from a boy and spent his political career athwart the Duke of Wellington, the genius who had defeated Napoleon. Twice. The aged duke himself could still be seen in season outside Apsley House or the Horse Guards or the Chapel Royal on Sunday. Richard had gone looking for him after Dickens told his story (which he'd heard before), and found that the duke didn't look a bit like Mr. Jones, although it was true Mr. Jones looked quite a lot like the duke. Enjoy the paradox, he'd told his friends.

They were all Mr. Joneses these days. Diminished forms in a smaller age. A tiny queen two years younger than Richard sat demurely on the throne, a fairy creature with a porcelain complexion he would try to capture with white underpainting, at least if he were asked to paint her. He wondered if the Queen was coming to Lord Foley's ball, although he doubted he would have been asked if royalty were expected. If she'd appeared, he would have liked to tell her: *Majesty, you with your what-d'ye-call-'em ringlets. Majesty, I would pray that you be just to your people, your poor Isaac and Job and Job and Hephzibah along with your striving artists and chymists; your manufacturers who have begun to buy paintings, some of them mine, and if I might be so presumptuous, even Lord Foley, your former Captain of What-Bob-Said, for all of us must struggle to find a way through this smaller if more propulsive age, this bullet of an age, this fusillade, when it's so easy to get blasted in the rush.*

There it was. The townhouse was mobbed and loud and Richard remembered how much he hated crowds. Having completed several circuits of the ball, picking out politicians and famous beauties, his curiosity was satisfied, his eye more than satiated. He wanted to leave but knew he couldn't, not yet. Only when Lord Foley hove into view did he see his moment, slipping through the crowd until he was in a position for his host to notice him, which to Richard's relief he did.

"Excellent!" Lord Foley cried, a dark-eyed lady on his arm, a gauzy creature with bared and drooping shoulders. It seemed to be the fashion, the droop as much as the skin.

"Thank you so much, milord, for your kind invitation. An artist"—he couldn't say "salivates" before a lady—"an artist vibrates at such a show of grace and colour."

"Vibrate, do you? Sounds a hazard to the mirrors."

Richard laughed, but the lady looked uninspired. Paralyzed, overshot from the quantity of wine and spirits provided, which Richard had done his best to help dissipate.

"I'm trying to memorize details of the lace for my sisters," he said, with a polite bow which the shoulders failed to acknowledge. "Otherwise, sir, I shan't be allowed back into the house."

"Ha ha! Sisters!" Lord Foley said, with his mirthless laugh. "Sisters!" *Woof, woof.* For some reason, this was the greatest joke in the world. "Sisters!" he cried a third time, shaking Richard by the shoulder before giving him a punch and heading off. You'd think he was unintelligent, which he wasn't. But maybe stupidity was in fashion, too. Richard had so little feel for these people he would probably never know.


N ow, facing his father, Richard felt as out of place as he had at the ball. He wasn't enjoying it this time either.

"It's very kind of Mr. Roberts to give the gentleman my name. But honestly, sir, I can't oblige him. I'm simply not the man for the job."

"I hope this isn't a repeat of that tutoring fiasco, when he went out of his way to recommend you."

Earlier this year, his father's friend David Roberts had

found Richard a guinea-a-week post teaching art to two young daughters of the gentry. Sisters, fair-haired, giggling. A draining job soon made unbearable by the cow eyes the younger girl insisted on casting at him. O'Neil and Ward had told him, *Run off with her. Get the dowry. You'll be set for life.* They'd disinherit her, Richard said. As you well know. Then there's me supporting children. *Fourteen isn't that young,* Ward said. *Oh, I see what you mean.*

Luckily, she'd written him a letter which he could honourably and with all protestations of moral, et cetera, lay before the lady mother, who swept her daughters off to their estate in Berkshire before the girl's inept delphiniums were dry on the paper. Delphinia? In any case, relief. A good excuse, a new distraction conquered, and now he could get back to his real work. It was too bad about the money, but Lord Foley still owed a sum on his commission for the panels, which had been a great success and which might lead to further commissions, at least if Richard were permitted to stay in England.

Permitted to stay, as opposed to being sent abroad with a rich man making his Grand Tour of the Holy Land. The man had approached David Roberts for a name, and now Richard was being offered the position of the rich man's travelling companion, a pet artist charged with making sketches of sites the gentleman proposed to tour. Richard couldn't see it. Aside from anything else, the role of pet artist had gone stale before the end of the last century.

"With all due respect, sir, to both you and Mr. Roberts, I've found my subject."

"Fairies."

"We both know Mr. Roberts is the master of Egyptian scenes. Syria. Jerusalem." Roberts had made his own tour of the Holy Land, arriving home two years before. Since then, he'd been working up his sketches of souks and temples and pyramids, selling his oils to great acclaim and greater profit. "Anyone coming after him is going to seem a pale imitation. Certainly someone with no interest in the subject and nothing to say. When in all modesty, the critics have called the work I'm doing, and I quote, new and valuable."

"The opportunity," his father said, pacing the sitting room above the shop. He'd put Richard at a disadvantage by summoning him to his territory, where Richard was conscious of his three unmarried, shipwrecked sisters eavesdropping outside the door. "Imagine it. You'll pass through Rome and Florence, where you can study the greatest masterpieces of all time. Athens, Cairo, even Nubia. I could never take you, and Sir Thomas will. Complete your education."

"Is that why Mr. Roberts recommended me?" asked Richard, who hadn't been listening. "Because I'm no threat to his project? I won't surpass him, when another man might. Someone with an actual interest in the subject. Bells ringing inside him at the sight of pyramids and mummies."

Bells being what Richard heard when he was onto something. Mention of the Holy Land sounded more like *clack, clack*.

"You're going."

Because you'd kill to go yourself?

"Sir Thomas Phillips," Richard said, trying a different tack. "To be clear, we're speaking of the former mayor of Newport, the one who was knighted last year for ordering the Army to fire on Chartists."

"A good Anti–Corn Law man."

"I forget how many died. How many died, do you remember?"

After killing the Chartists, Sir Thomas had not only been

knighted, he'd been invited to spend a week at Windsor with the Queen, an unprecedented honour for a man of his low rank in life (a lawyer). Sir Thomas had dined with her repeatedly, the Queen making a show of gratitude to a loyal servant, fearing as she did that revolution would break out as the recession deepened, hunger grew and radicalism gripped the labouring classes. Majesty, be just to your Isaacs and Hephzibahs, Sir Thomas had not said. Poor consumptive Hephzibah no doubt dead by now and buried. Richard stifled an impulse to cross his forefingers and thumbs against the uncanny. Against Sir Thomas Phillips. The expression on his father's face said this wasn't doing any good. You're going.

What was his father planning to do: pack him in a trunk and label it Jerusalem?

"You will be at your most charming when you meet Sir Thomas. Represent the family. He has asked my friend Roberts to recommend an artist who is a gentleman, and Davie has been kind enough to think of you."

It would be beneath Richard to behave like a boor, even to a boor. To a murderer, when you thought about it.

"Truly, pater, I don't even like touring," he said. "That's you."

In fact, Richard enjoyed tours, at least of a type. David Roberts was thinking of him because of a tour they'd taken of Scotland the previous year, Richard having travelled north by coach after leaving the Gaskells in Manchester. A sketching tour with the pater and the painter, the art making up for the problems inherent in their travels—or most of them.

Stepping down from the coach in a well-swept Edinburgh inn yard, Richard had taken some bread and cheese before turning into the crooked precincts of the Old Town, where he shook out his soreness and found himself happy. He liked cities, the gilt shop-signs, the open-eyed windows and stony streets rustling with intellect and fashion. It was drizzling but not cold, or not unbearably. When he asked directions, the Scots proved courteous despite their reputation, although to his ear the speech even of educated men contained something of a cat's purr and more of its hiss. The poor were incomprehensible, eating invisible porridge as they spoke.

He dawdled his way to the hotel, knowing they weren't going to stay long in Edinburgh and allowing himself to get lost in the New Town, its identical terraces and squares. In the morning, they would be off on a walking tour designed to clear Roberts's head of the labour of making his name. Roberts had been suffering persistent megrims as he painted up his sketches of the Holy Land, meanwhile collecting subscriptions for a book of lithographs on Egypt and Syria. The Queen had agreed to be his first subscriber, months of headache right there. On top of which he'd had to oversee the fashionable marriage of his only daughter earlier in the month: Roberts's wife, as one didn't mention, being a drunkard that Roberts had long ago cast off. Here I am, he'd said in London. Eyes two piss holes in the snow.

They left Edinburgh shortly after dawn, heading first for a nearby village to visit Roberts's mither. His father had been a shoemaker. Dead these two years, Roberts said, at the drastic age of eighty-six. Nothing pretentious about Roberts, seldom mentioning his low origins but never trying to hide them. A stocky, fat-featured, shrewd, unhandsome man. He took them to a stone tenement in Stockbridge and rapped mightily on the door. An old woman answered and Roberts introduced his mither, a doughty old baggage past eighty whom he closely resembled.

"Here yuh are," she said. "Een two piddle holes in the snaw."

"A point I've made," Roberts said. As his sister got tea, Roberts told them about drawing on the walls with the end of a burnt stick as a boy, one time picturing the lions and tigers he'd seen at a wild beast show.

"You should have kept them and sold them on," he told his mither, before turning back to Richard's father. "She white-washed over my efforts, once she'd had a good look. I'd draw, she'd whitewash. Apprenticed me to a housepainter, didn't he?" Meaning the drastic father. "You were the one who liked your Davie's art."

His mither chewed her gums, perhaps her tea, which was that strong. "Och aye," she said, although it was more of a generality than an answer; arguably a belch.

Now they sat sketching the ruins of Melrose Abbey, having taken three days to dawdle down the paths and high-ways Roberts claimed to have once covered in a day. Sheltered from the drizzle, Richard drew the great heaved ruin of an abbey as a ravaged fantasy of carved gargoyles, dragons, saints, all manner of mythical creatures.

Roberts sat beside him, a rumble of instruction coming off him as he sketched. Sometimes Richard stood behind him, watching his line, Roberts being a master of architec-tural drawing. Getting a spire, he talked about going off with the circus as a lad of eighteen, freed of his apprenticeship to that mean ole sod of a house painter. One wet day's tramp from Edinburgh, their landlady of the night had called his new friends vagabonds and beseeched Roberts to return to his puir mither. But he had wanted to be a scene painter and

stuck with them a year, painting the backdrops to their eques-
trian feats, their bear tricks and ruid pantomimes, even acting
a foil when they needed a thespian, not too badly he believed.

In Newcastle, where they first set up their tent, the respectable Theatre Royal was managed by the elder Macready, father
of the current man. Macready had been guid enough to let
Roberts study an attic of dusty scenery painted by Dixon,
Dixon having been for long years the chief scene-painter down
at Drury Lane, the second best scene-painter in the kingdom.
Dixon had a hard and accurate line that taught Roberts a lesson,
although a few months later in York (he droned on) he had
studied the act-drop of an artist he believed was named Wallace
and learned much of aerial perspective that off-set the harshness
of Dixon. Around that time he had also met another aspiring
scene painter, one Clarkson Stanfield, Stanny having been
given a different perspective by the veteran painter Nasmyth,
who'd told him to take his style from nature only.

"Stanny," Richard's father said, throwing down his book. His
father no longer endeavoured a style, his stab at art unstabbed.
Instead he toted a knapsack bulging with the tools of other
aspirations: collecting jars and nets, a shotgun, chisels, pins and
wax, chloroform and tissue paper and Charles Lyell's *Geology*,
the impedimenta of a keen if confused naturalist. These days,
Richard could feel older than his father. Egypt was the old
man's latest craze, the book he'd thrown down a loan from
Roberts about the gods of the Nile, Kos and Ra and Osiris,
Lord of the Dead.

"When I was a lad," Roberts said, picking it up, "I'd little
access to books and read whatever came my way. *The Life and
Adventures of Captain Boyle. Don Quixote.*" He closed the book
fastidiously. "Although it strikes me now that the one that

had the most effect on me was a soothsaying book about the indication of moles. It told me that having a mole on my leg meant I should be a great traveller. A caution how information like that can set a boy off on his path. By which I mean, wrong information."

"And did Stanny's moles predict he'd be a climber?" Richard's father asked. The two men exchanged an eye-roll, being on the outs with Stanfield, who now spent all his time with Dickens. Dickens had collected a crew of jolly fellows around him, most of them, like Stanfield and Macready, quite a bit older than he was. Richard still ran across Dickens and found him increasingly strange, his eyes grown as unreadable as a bird's—he kept a pet raven—a geranium always in his buttonhole, his expensive flash trousers cut insistently on the bias and soft as the pelts of castle-bred myths.

"Dickens doesn't seem to spend much time with ladies, but I think he needs their approval. Perhaps he wants mothering," Richard said. "I'm sure he's good to his wife, but I've seen him in the theatre rather basking in feminine worship. I've thought that's why he chooses older friends, so he can seem boyish in their company. He seems to like older men and little children."

Richard paused, wondering if he was describing Dickens or his father. His father was nothing like Dickens, but it was true he had become more boyish lately, as if ageing backwards. Lord Wellington didn't look like Mr. Jones but Mr. Jones looked like Lord Wellington. Enjoy the paradox.

"That is acute," Roberts said.

"Well, his wife is rapidly providing him with children," Richard's father said. "From what Stanfield lets drop."

"I do love that man, despite it," Roberts said. "Stanny. We'll leave the adulation of Charley to the ladies."

Both he and Richard returned to their sketches. Richard's father stood with his hands hanging until he thought to take up his book.

"Egypt now," he said, leafing through it. "Speaking of adulation, Egypt seems to have been the origin of many, if not most, religious myths. The god Osiris descended into the underworld centuries before the Greek Orpheus, and like Orpheus he emerged back in the light, resurrected."

His father glanced uneasily at Richard.

"Like Jesus of Nazareth and the harrowing of hell," he added, half-swallowing his words, aware that Richard was more orthodox than he. "Moses being a priest of Osiris in Egypt, you know, and bringing these myths to Palestine and the Jews."

Richard shrugged him off. He'd decided to leave these things to the parsons; that they knew what they were talking about. That Mr. Gaskell did.

"There's a subject for you, lad," Roberts said. "Osiris in the underworld."

Richard insisted on being polite. "I suppose it's near what I do."

"It's not what you're doing at the moment, but subjects mature. Look at me, starting out painting scenes like this— some of my first sales—and now I'm on to the ruins of Egypt and Nubia." He barked out a laugh. "Not such a change, you'll say. Landscape and ruins. But different landscapes and different ruins. Listen to an old man: one day you'll choose to paint different figures. They don't all have to be fey."

Yes they did. At least until Richard decided they didn't. In London, after leaving his father's sitting room, Richard chafed under the threat of Egypt. He paced his studio, back and forth, back and forth, neglecting an indifferent painting. When the light failed, and in February it failed early, he put on his overcoat, planning to brave the sleet and find his friends. But the doorknob felt cold in his palm and he knew his friends would have no sympathy. He flung off his overcoat and turned in circles like a dog before flinging himself on top of the coat. *Poor Richard*, his friends would say. *Forced to visit Rome, Jerusalem, Cairo. Forced to travel in luxury. Forced to prosper.*

In fact, he hadn't liked touring, he'd loathed it; he'd told his father the truth. When they were done sketching Scotland, the pater and the painter had headed home to London while Richard went back to Manchester, planning to check in on his painting at the exhibition. And look at his mood, no sooner arriving than throwing himself into a riot. Hit me. Knock the old men out of me. He might as well have shouted it out loud. The bleak highlands he'd liked well enough, and the opportunity to sketch, but spending every moment in the company of geezers had ended up driving him mad. Their incessant instruction. The endless middle-aged reminiscing. Two travelling companions made a crowd. One would be hell.

There was also what had happened to his Uncle Henry in the mirrored Chatham in the mirrored Kent across the Atlantic. Or rather, to his gentle teacup of an Aunt Hannah. *There, there,* she'd told his sister, trying to stroke the bitterness out of her. *There, there. All will be well. A removal isn't the end of the world.*

Richard's father had received a letter from the uncle ten days before and called them home to hear it. Uncle Henry regretted to inform them that his dear wife had not prospered after their arrival in Canada West. In his absence one morning, she had sent the children on an errand, and when they got back, he wrote, she couldn't be found. A search was undertaken, and between his uncle's pinched words, Richard heard men shouting in the forest; heard a shotgun fired into the air, a wait, no answer; heard the sobbing of his little cousins huddled in their cabin. The mast-high pines swayed above them, whispering like Sibyls, while a sluggish river meandered nearby.

The next morning, they found her in the river. His poor aunt had drowned herself. She'd been unable to bear the thought of life in the backwoods. Unable to wait for her appointed time, when Charon would arrive to ferry her across. The coroner's jury declared her to be victim of a temporary derangement. Not that it looked temporary.

Uncle Henry's letter was written on the second of January. After finishing the sad story of his wife, he told them of his second marriage at the end of December to one Miss Mary Wellman, a young lady born in Michigan.

"So very soon," Mary Ann had quavered.

"He needed a mother for his children," their father said, although they knew his interest in their stepmother had gone beyond that. Mary Ann seemed about to mention this but bit her lip: *I don't say a word.* Her throat was clogged with so many swallowed words that Mary Ann was strangling.

Not that Richard said anything either. He took the letter from his father and re-read it silently, particularly struck by the fact that everything had happened within nine months. The Henry Martins had sailed in April and arrived in July. Aunt Hannah died in August and he married their new Aunt Mary at the end of December.

Now Richard's father was telling him he had to spend nine months touring. Richard didn't like the coincidence. Coincidence or omen. This before taking into account the number of artists who had died sketching ruins in the Holy Land. Over the past year Richard had read about two men on two separate tours succumbing to fever in Syria. He felt pained not to remember their names.

Sir Thomas Phillips was proposing they travel to Egypt by way of Syria. He was asking Richard to hazard his life making indifferent sketches of a subject that bored him. Much better if the lawyer subscribed to Roberts's volume of lithographs. Write his name beneath the Queen's, go back to Newport and order the army to shoot at Chartists, but miss this time.

On Richard's shelf were two books about Egypt his father had insisted he read. Richard snatched one up and flipped through it irritably until he saw the name of Charon. The historian Diodorus of Sicily, born a century before Christ, believed that both the name and figure of Charon had come to the ancient Greeks from Egypt.

So Charon had been born in Egypt and lived on through the heights of Athens and Rome well into the Renaissance, when Michelangelo had painted him. Artists still tackled him, and without having to go to Cairo. If Richard wanted, he could paint Charon right here.

Except. He was pacing a studio he could no longer afford. Lord Foley still owed part of his fee but milord's man had stopped answering queries and Richard's plans for a society to exhibit the work of modern artists (well, him, really) had come to nothing. He felt irritable and crowded and pecked, as if Dickens's raven were tearing chunks from his flesh. He feared he was going to Egypt. Didn't see how to stop it, being a good-humoured man, probably as naive as O'Neil had said, and certainly not strategic.

Richard picked up his overcoat, braved the doorknob and walked out to see his friends. *Here's news*, he would say, *I'm crossing the Styx to Constantinople, Cairo, Syria, Jerusalem.*

Unless, he thought, brightening. Unless one of you cares to take my place.

# Charlotte Receives an Unexpected Letter
# Which She Had Half-Expected
*Haworth, Winter 1853–54*

T he room in London was reserved for November the twenty-fourth. Charlotte had already begun packing for her latest foray to the capital when an uneasy letter arrived from George Smith, breaking a silence of months. It half-addressed the question she'd intended to finally resolve in London. But only half, so she wrote to his mother, and now she had her answer.

Charlotte was right, Mrs. Smith wrote back. They expected George to take a very important step, the most important step in life, one which gave his family great pleasure, pleasure which she was sure Charlotte would share when he wrote her the particulars, as Mrs. Smith expected he would once they were settled, which wouldn't be long.

George Smith was getting married. Not to her. The pain was dreadful. Charlotte's chest felt crushed, and although she could breathe, her breath was hot in her throat from the fire consuming her heart. She was cratered, burnt out, fallen in at the core. Couldn't even sit straight. Lacking any self-respect, she could only hunch in her chair and whimper.

She knew this wouldn't end. No distractions. None ahead, and certainly none today. She wasn't expected anywhere nor wanted. Too cold to walk before dinner, she told Tabby. Not hungry for dinner. She had a headache. She had to go to bed. Take her tea in bed. Hide there.

Trudging upstairs, Charlotte was bowed by the hot hollow cave in her chest and a weight on her shoulders like a rod, a sword, a bar of cold steel laid across them. Freezing steel and burning pain. It was dreadful. In one corner of her mind she thought, *At least I can still feel. I felt this keenly about dear M. Héger. I survived it before. But oh pain digs in for so long. Pleasure is brief.*

Charlotte threw herself on her bed, surprised to find the letter still in her hand. She thrust it under her pillow, crumpling it meanly. She had it by heart, anyway.

Old footsteps outside. The door scraped open and Tabby hobbled in. She had brought a cold compress and removed the spectacles Charlotte had forgotten were there.

Tha-ere tha-ere tha-ere. Tha poor he-ad.

Oh Tabby, I'm so lonely.

Then marry the curate.

"What did you say?"

"Nowt."

218

*But I heard.*

Tabby's honest old face. She'd said nowt, but Charlotte had heard a voice. The hairs prickled on the back of her neck. She wondered if Emily had come back to her. Emily had called him the curate, never giving him his name, although Charlotte hadn't heard precisely Emily's voice. She hadn't heard precisely anything, but she was certain she'd heard a voice that wasn't in her head.

Charlotte shivered, the fire inside her burning cold. She tried to control it but the shivers took over, shaking her in waves of terror, shaking her knees and silly feet. The uncanny was in the room and she was inside it. Charlotte didn't believe in purgatory but here she was, trapped in a great emptiness, unworthy of love. She panicked, seeing again the looming ceilings and the stairs unscrolling in front of her that she'd had to climb when locked in a nightmare at George's house. Mr. Smith's house, the Smith house, the smithy that hammered her into spasms.

"Tabby!"

Charlotte bolted up in bed as her stomach heaved.

Tabby was ready with a basin. Humiliation as the bile pumped out.

George Smith was going to marry a beauty, Charlotte knew it. Spit into the basin. Life was unbearable. She could write about this feeling, how it felt to be the inmate of a nightmare, a portable Bedlam. The first story she'd begun about the two brothers wasn't good enough and she'd started another about a girl. Perhaps the girl would one day meet both brothers and one would hurt her terribly. Charlotte would find this out as she carried on writing, if she were able. She might not have the energy. Might not recover this time. Love was unbearable, and she'd borne the unbearable for too long.

"Papa," she said. "I'd like to speak about something. You won't like it."

It was mid-December. Charlotte had waited a few days after receiving the letter from George Smith that confirmed his engagement. She wanted her father to feel well, to enjoy his tea and be sitting in comfort before a crackling log fire. After she spoke, he looked down at her, his chin lifted by his high cravat. He looked as formidable as the Duke of Wellington, whom George Smith had taken her to see once in London at the Chapel Royal. All that was over. She felt cold and empty and driven. She was ready not to write a new story but to live it.

"You know I've been having headaches again lately," she said. "And often it's the wind and the weather, but I think we both know that sometimes it's worry."

He waited for her to go on.

"What happens if I don't go before you?"

"God forbid. Children ought to outlive their parents."

A black hole opened at their feet and they both stared into it.

"Suppose that I do," Charlotte said, tearing her eyes away. "I'd have to leave the parsonage, and I wonder where you think I should go."

This time she insisted on waiting for an answer, and her father could only sputter, his accent always turning more Irish when he didn't wish to speak. But the money from your novels. The investments your publisher made in your name.

"The visit to London I cancelled," Charlotte said, ready to tell what she hoped would be the last lie between them. She thought she was a bad liar, talking too much, the sure sign of a lie, labyrinths of elaboration, but he never appeared to suspect her.

Her father would remember, she said, that she had wanted to go to London to look at her investments, not having heard from Mr. Smith about her position since last July. He would recall that just as she was about to leave, she had received a letter with the information she had wanted, the sum of her investments—which she detailed—a letter making the strain of a journey unnecessary.

"I'm proud of what I've earned."

"And so you should be."

"But it isn't enough to live on, even with the three hundred pounds I'd get on your death. I'd need to write at least two more novels for anything above poverty, and you know how long a novel takes me."

She allowed another silence.

"Enough to live with your friend, Ellen Nussey." He sounded even more Irish.

"We haven't spoken of it, but you must have noticed that I haven't written Ellen for months, nor received a letter from her."

Charlotte planned to tell him everything, or almost everything. But slowly. Enough to start by mentioning that she and Ellen had fallen out. It was one thing for Charlotte to be angry with Ellen. Lately, to feel she'd be happy if she never saw her again, Ellen being the only one on God's scorched earth to know the details of her folly. Her idiocy. George Smith was engaged to the beautiful daughter of a wealthy wine merchant. Of a tradesman, she noted, however rich. Miss Blakeway was nearly twenty younger than she was.

Answering George's smug, self-conscious letter, Charlotte had written: *In great happiness, as in great grief, words of*

*sympathy should be few. Accept my meed of congratulation—and*
*believe me, Sincerely yours.*

Two lines. She should have done better but couldn't. Well,
let him know what he had done. She'd written as well to her
editor Mr. Williams, shipping back a box of books and saying
he needn't send more. If she were to publish again, it wouldn't
be with Smith, Elder, and they might as well understand that
now, so they would know why.

Charlotte was angry and angry and angry. Yet she had to
tread carefully to avoid raising the same fury in her implacable
father, whom she resembled so closely in character. She might
want Ellen back one day.

"Of course, it remains a possibility. But I wonder who
would pay for any cottage we'd share." She remained mild, but
her father took her meaning, even if he chose not to answer.

Charlotte could wait.

"You'll marry, of course." It was half a growl.

"We agree," she said evenly. "I can. Mr. Nicholls has
repeated his offer."

Her father turned red, creaking to his feet, ready to shout
when Charlotte raised her hand peremptorily. You'd think
he'd never seen her hand before, the way he stared at it. She
took a look herself, her tiny pink child's nails. A small hand.
Delicate. Requested in marriage a year ago. Mr. Nicholls
hadn't wavered since.

"It is right to tell you we've been corresponding and have met
twice. I can't stand the strain of keeping secrets any longer. He
wrote after leaving Haworth"—her father turned scarlet—"and
I felt constrained, eventually, to write back and encourage him
to be strong and philosophical. He wrote back saying that my
letter gave him strength and asking me to send him another."

She almost laughed at Mr. Nicholls's transparency. She had laughed when getting the letter, but her father didn't see the joke. The veins swelled at his temples.

"It would be best if you didn't have another apoplexy," she said.

Her coolness made him sit down, stumbling into his seat, gaping at her, but slowly starting to nod, although to himself rather than her. Charlotte stayed silent until the veins subsided. Then she told him that she did not expect another offer. That she had never been pretty and now she was old and ugly. Mr. Nicholls had waited seven years for her, and he didn't love her fame, but her character. She would be candid: Mr. Nicholls would have to meet conditions before she agreed to marry him. She would like him to be welcomed back to the parsonage so they could discuss these. But she hoped her father realized it would solve many problems if she felt able to accept him.

Such as. Taking a breath. She planned to ask him to come back as her father's curate, replacing Mr. de Renzy. She allowed the name of the inadequate Mr. de Renzy to hang in the air. She would like to ask Mr. Nicholls to live in the parsonage and help her make her father's life and work easy.

"I can't imagine any other man agreeing to that. If you can, please tell me."

She made a show of waiting for an answer. Her father picked up the iron and poked the fire viciously.

Afterward, she did not say, on your death, the trustees of the church might appoint Mr. Nicholls the new parson in Haworth, and I could live out my life in the only home I have ever known.

"He has spent the past year hoping I would change my mind. Perhaps I've started hoping it myself."

"The man's beneath you," her father keened, and out spilled his objections. Having heard them so often, Charlotte was able to sit back and watch her father as he spoke, disregarding the words. In his mobile passionate face, she could see the clever ginger-headed Irish farm-boy who had grown up in a poverty he had never let them comprehend. In his eloquence, she saw how his brilliance and energy had allowed him to lever himself out of the farmhouse into life as a schoolteacher, and from there most improbably to Cambridge. No one did that, but her father had, a farm boy among aristocrats. Patrick Brunty became Patrick Bronté and then Brontë. He had known Lord Palmerston. Not well, but well enough that when Palmerston was Secretary at War, her father had been able to approach him to reconsider the fate of a man unjustly convicted of a crime. Approached him three times before Palmerston relented, William Wilberforce acting as intermediary, her father having known Wilberforce, too.

Brilliant, energetic and most especially stubborn, the ginger-headed Irish farm-boy had become a Cambridge-educated gentleman and clergyman in the Church of England. He had been recommended to this parish, which guaranteed him an income for the rest of his days. It wasn't grand. There were years when he'd had to ask his friends for loans. These had been repaid, but Charlotte didn't think he'd asked his friends to find him a better position. And now, as he spit out his disdain for the upstart Irish Mr. Nicholls—*Who does he think he is?*—she could glimpse the radical ambivalence that had kept her father in Haworth when he must have hoped for more.

He must have. Charlotte knew about hope, and also about the suspicion that one didn't deserve any more than one got. She could imagine a farm boy fundamentally believing that he should stay in his place. A clergyman believing that a godly evangelical man shouldn't desire anything more than to serve the poor, of which Haworth had an abundance. So he spent his life here in penance, both for his birth and for his ungodly insolent desire. Was that right?

Or. He might have thought he'd got what he wanted. Thought so more than once. He'd fathered a brilliant boy, a genius, whom he educated in Latin and Greek so that Branwell, as a gentleman's son, might be the one to elevate the invented family name. And when Branwell had failed, her father had found that his daughters were authors and geniuses. They had called themselves the genii from the time they were children, if only he had known. And when the genius Emily died, and poor Anne, he found that his one surviving child was among the most acclaimed of living authors. His intemperance about Mr. Nicholls—He is *ordinary*, he howled—was a cry of pride in her fame and her accomplishments and, let's be honest, in himself as her father. He wanted her to marry brilliantly, not merely for her own sake, but to gild his godly humble place in the world. He would be seen as a righteous man. He would be seen.

The word *vindication* occurred to Charlotte. *Ambition*, that was obvious. They were both overweeningly ambitious. Who did they think they were? Not content to be as ordinary as Mr. Nicholls. Still stubbornly yearning for more.

*Well, Papa*, she did not say, *now we have come to an end of that, to a place of thwarted ambition. It is only the latest disappointment and I know you feel it keenly since it's probably the last. I am not going to be able to give you everything you had hoped for. I'm not going to be able to get what I wanted myself.*

Nicholls has nothing to offer, he was saying. He is proposing to take.

"Perhaps to take your life, Charlotte. Should you risk a family? With your health as it is."

"Like the whole world, Father," she said, cutting in. "Like almost the whole of the world, we're thwarted, you and I. We're ambitious, and we're not getting everything we've wanted, in the end."

"You're not listening," he shouted, and made a show of leaving the room, slamming the door behind him.

"I do know that," Charlotte told the closed door. "And I don't even like children."

A week of upset, headaches, unforgiveable temper: she meant her own. Charlotte would not give in, but despite his stubbornness, her father was old and frail and he was the one to finally capitulate. Mr. Nicholls arrived in January for a ten-day visit to his friends Mr. and Mrs. Grant in Oxenhope. Charlotte would have gone there to see him, bypassing her father's mood, but the new year brought three feet of snow and crusted it over. She would have had to walk to Oxenhope up to the shoulders in snow, a black bonnet bobbing over the moor.

Arriving for his first visit, Mr. Nicholls was hearty and red-cheeked and abashed. After she heard him come in, her father limped out of his study and made a point of walking past him without speaking. Really, her father should have been on the stage. This was a drama he'd written, a melodrama, with himself as the lead player. Mr. Nicholls greeted her father's back and he answered with a grunt, refusing to turn, heading upstairs. Charlotte saw no point in apologizing when Mr. Nicholls must have expected this.

She had been writing letters when he had knocked,

arriving a little early. Once her father was above them, boots clomping, she took Mr. Nicholls into the parlour and cleared the table of her correspondence.

"A new novel," he said, although it couldn't look like one. She would have put it down to stupidity when she first knew him. But it was just a case of nerves. Her own made her fumble with the paper.

"I've started something," she said. "I'm not sure it's good yet. Or that it shall be; I never know at first. But I intend under any circumstances to keep writing."

Charlotte glanced up quickly from her fumbling to see his response. Mr. Nicholls's face was wooden. Ellen had been right; he often was.

"It's helped you," he said, after consideration, implying that it wouldn't always need to.

"It's who I am. And I believe I've arrived at an age where that doesn't change." Glancing up again quickly. "Have you?"

Negotiations. He knew it, too.

"Why do you write?" he asked, surprising her. The letters were safe inside her desk and Charlotte leaned on its top.

"Mrs. Gaskell once asked me that. She's one of my closest friends, although a Dissenter. I have no intention of ending our acquaintance."

"You no longer correspond with Miss Martineau, I believe. Things can change."

Charlotte hadn't anticipated this. When she'd told her father she had conditions for the marriage, she'd expected Mr. Nicholls to simply accept them. But here he was, showing a personality. She had to respect that, although the thrill she was supposed to feel at male dominance eluded her. Charlotte was tired of not getting what she wanted. She was prepared to compromise, to lower her expectations, but she expected gratitude in return. She set her lips angrily. He couldn't miss it.

"It may be cheeky," Mr. Nicholls said, "but I thought the comical portrait of Mr. Macarthey in your novel *Shirley* might have something to do with me. 'The circumstance of finding himself invited to tea with a Dissenter would unhinge him for a week.'"

She had also called him decent, decorous and conscientious, but yes, that's what she'd written, and she had hissed like a witch's cat when writing it. Her lips still tight, Charlotte asked, "And are you proud of that?"

"Of being novelized? Yes, I suppose I am." He cut her short before she could interrupt. "I know what you mean, of course. I might have arrived at the age where I am largely what I am, but I hope we're all capable of growth. I found I enjoyed being teased in your novel, which I might not have when a serious young student. Now you're telling me you wish to retain Mrs. Gaskell's friendship. In the event."

A rattle outside the door, a tray shifted to turn the knob, and Martha came in with coffee. Stifling her annoyance, Charlotte had to pour and offer him bread and jam. She had fallen down in telling Martha what to prepare and now she was serving children's food. Mr. Nicholls had boarded with Martha's parents when he was curate and perhaps she knew he liked it. Either that or she knew he didn't, and she was taking Charlotte's father's side, or her own, not wanting him to live in the parsonage.

Charlotte couldn't live her life according to servants' feelings, although it was wise to notice them. In any case, Mr. Nicholls seemed perfectly happy with his bread and jam.

"My friend Mrs. Gaskell," she said, not being hungry, "Lily

Gaskell told me that the common trope is wrong, that her novels aren't like her children. Her children are themselves, and her novels are her, and hers. She couldn't do without either."

Charlotte blushed. She was speaking about children with the one man who might father hers. The marital act was here, the famous elephant in the room. She could barely restrain herself from running upstairs. How did anyone manage courtship with the great elephant—oh, please, no, but she'd pictured it. The elephant raising his trunk.

"But does this speak to why you write?" asked Mr. Nicholls, who looked equally self-conscious. It came to Charlotte that he was likely as much a virgin as she was. Oh Lord. When she didn't answer, he cleared his throat. "Why *you* write, in particular."

Charlotte tried to collect herself. "I told her, I told my friend Mrs. Gaskell," she said. "Or rather, she told me that she believes many people write to be loved. She told me she didn't think of me as one of them. But I said, 'Yes, I think I am. I think I write in order to be loved.'"

"You only need walk in the room for that."

Charlotte was startled into gratitude. Warmth. To have someone be so kind and generous and blind and courtly and bashful, ducking his head. This didn't happen, not to her. Charlotte felt her poor heart creak open. *How sweet*, she thought. Also: *I can use that in my next novel.* It seemed possible she might love this abashed, stubborn, courtly man if he would give just a little, give everything, and let her write.

Not that he could stop her, but Charlotte was so tired of struggling.

# At the Ruins of Baalbec
## for Half a Day
*October 1842*

They descended in switchbacks down camel-coloured hills, dry weeds picking at their robes. Above them, a deep blue sky, eternity written in the scud of clouds. The light was thin and brittle with autumn. As Richard squinted ahead, he was barely able to pick out an aqueduct, a wall, a stand of Roman pillars. He'd been travelling for months after his friends had let him down, and he was finding something, or at least beginning to hope he would; feeling a species of awe each time he rode toward an ancient city he'd read about at the King's School, most of them now lying in ruins. War, crusades, earthquakes. After riding all day, he often jumped from

his horse and thought he'd hit ground during a new earthquake, but it was only his balance gone.

Today, as Richard slung out of the saddle, the earth came
up to meet him and he bowed to one knee. Sometimes the
dizziness lasted, sky, sand, images whirling above his head like
insects; like the figures he'd drawn above his dozing Manfred.
This time it passed quickly, and he stood up to sleeve the sweat
from his forehead, turning to take in the sweep of Baalbec:
the felled pillars and fallen gods, the acres of pale, uneven,
weed-covered debris. He felt all the resonance of forgotten
lives, the ancient murmur of the city on the wind.

The East astonished him. He was sure he'd find something
to feed his art, if only his patron would let him. Sir Thomas
Phillips insisted they hurry along at a clip, merely glancing at
whole countries as if they were paragraphs in Murray's travel
guide. Belgium, done. France, done. Switzerland, Venice, turn
the page. They'd rushed through Greece. Hopped a boat to
Smyrna, another to Constantinople. For God's sake, man,
exercise yourself. Richard didn't even have time to sketch.
Eight, ten, twelve hours a day in the saddle. Maybe someone
had figured out how to draw while riding a horse, but Richard
hadn't been let in on the trick.

The velocity continued, and his lack of production, but
Richard was happier since they'd reached Asia Minor. The
undulation of land. The clamouring blue of the sky. Wearing
Eastern robes and headdress, his hair and beard grown
out, Richard moved with ease through the East. He felt he
belonged here, while always remaining aware that he'd been
born in a very different place, a county of hedgerows, drowsy
fields and humid orchards, their fruit hanging like dewdrops.

Kent, the orchard of England. Picturing his uncle's ripe peaches, Richard took a long drink from his canteen.

Lower his arm and what did he see? Eight or ten brightly striped tents between him and the ruins, a caravanserai passing through. Beyond them, the pale limestone walls of an oblong fortress, the standing pillars inside the walls, something that looked like a pagan temple. The Roman emperor Constantine had built up Baalbec as a fortress, although people had been living here for ages beforehand, and their descendants were still farming the Bekaa valley.

Leaving his horse with a boy, Richard headed inside the old fortress, scrambling down an incline, his boots slipping, sliding into the former courtyard of a pagan temple, he supposed that's what it was, nudging the toe of his boot at fallen lintels and pillars, fancying himself for a moment a Roman citizen in the heyday of empire, feeling the flap of his toga, flexing his toes in a pair of sandals. But that was romantic and not very useful. What did he *see*?

The same temple he'd seen half-painted on Roberts's easel in London. Take a few steps to the left and back, and there it was: the Roman-style temple as old Roberts had been painting it, precisely from this angle. Which is to say, four years before, Roberts's boots had been planted exactly where Richard's were now. He made a joke of shuffling himself into the old man's wide Scottish stance, then deliberately, symbolically stepping out. The childhood rhyme: Step on a crack, break my father's back. Step on a line, break my father's spine.

From his own angle, Richard saw that the standing pillars weren't quite to the received proportions of Corinthian architecture. Roberts had corrected them, made them true, probably to avoid being accused of getting them wrong. But Richard was interested to see slippage in the provinces even then, only lesser men available to oversee the work, the same as in Kent today. Not that he'd needed to come halfway around the world to find that some things didn't change, and that art could change them.

I t had been raining in London, raining hard, water pouring down the windows of Roberts's studio as if they were trapped behind a waterfall. It distorted the outside world, the houses across the street jerking up and down, side to side, their windows flickering like fireflies. Trees danced their branches, leaves like brush strokes. Abstract. Quivering.

They were waiting for Sir Thomas Phillips, and as he looked outside, Richard assumed Sir Thomas would be late, waiting out the downpour someplace cozy.

"This?" Roberts asked, and told Richard that it had been raining even harder when he'd got to Baalbec. He'd taken a fever and had to stay there, establishing himself in an available hovel for far too much baksheesh. Not to worry. The ruins lent themselves to sketching.

"Sketching with a fever, sir."

"Had to get in as much as I could. Paying for the tour myself, wasn't I?"

"You must know how much I appreciate this, sir. I can only hope Sir Thomas decides to hire me."

Gratitude trowelled on to the correct thickness. Richard had a talent for trowelling, he believed. He didn't particularly respect himself for it, but he always had a sense of how far he could go, what degree of flattery he could lay on before someone suspected him of insincerity, and Roberts was smiling and nodding, sucking his lips to hide his satisfaction.

Richard walked up to take a closer look at the painting. *Run's Temple*, it was called. He was trying to figure out what Roberts was doing when a sharp rap sounded on the door. The old man looked impressed, taking out his pocket watch and tapping it at Richard: right on time.

Sir Thomas was dripping. Tossing aside his umbrella, letting Roberts take his overcoat, he squelched into the studio. Richard saw a thin erect man slightly below middle height with fair skin, a ginger moustache and hard grey eyes like pebbles. He'd prepared himself for an interrogation, Sir Thomas being a lawyer; a series of brisk questions that would lay his character bare. Now the eyes made Richard expect torture, the rack, the truth broken out of him. No, I don't really want to go, sir. You're right, sir. Not my sort of thing at all. Tried to get my friends to do it, but in the end, Frith said I had to go.

Old Roberts introduced them as Sir Thomas held Richard's eyes, then stepped back to give him a long, dubious, up-and-down look, as if Richard were a horse he was thinking of buying at the Smithfield Market. Any moment, he'd open Richard's mouth and inspect his teeth. Suggest that Roberts meant to take him for a fool, did he not.

Instead Sir Thomas shrugged, faintly but perceptibly.

"Richard Dadd," he said. "I believe a ship's captain salutes his officers when they come on board."

Before Richard could recover, Sir Tom gave him a sharp salute, which Richard would come to realize was a vanishingly rare stab at jocularity.

The lawyer turned to Roberts. "You said you'd have some idea of the itinerary."

And that was it. His new patron made no mention of the financials, which his father had told Richard to pin down.

Instead, the older men talked about Cyprus, Jericho, Nubia, probably not going as far south as Nubia, as Richard stood kicking one hoof on the studio floor, too embarrassed to mention money. When there was a pause, he could only manage to raise the subject of supplies, although surely getting them implied paying for them. Portable easel, sturdier paint box, the type of camera lucida Mr. Roberts had used on his temple.

"You picked up on that," Roberts said. "Good lad."

"Camera what?"

"A modern version of the old camera obscura," Richard told Sir Thomas. A device with calibrated mirrors that cast images on paper, allowing the artist to trace the true proportions of his subjects, or rather objects, temples and so on. *Expensive*, he said, *and finicky*. "It needs patience, sir," Richard said. "But you probably want the fidelity Mr. Roberts brings to his subjects."

"Surely you'll have enough kit to carry without that," his new patron replied. "Don't want to slow yourself down." Another stab at jocularity: "We'll pass that way but once."

They never got any closer to the subject of lucre, although Roberts promised that Sir Thomas would pay for the essentials, and he did. It turned out one needed to read between the lines with Sir Thomas. He disliked discussing the obvious, or what was obvious to him. Disliked Richard's lack of productivity, although he never seemed to understand whose itinerary was to blame. Disliked the word *patience*, disliked *slow*, preferred *hurry* and approved enthusiastically of *scenic*.

In Baalbec, hearing his patron slip down the incline behind him, Richard expected him to say, *That's a scenic temple.*

"That's a scenic temple," Sir Thomas said, a small landslide of pebbles still rattling down after him. "You might as well get it on paper."

"I'm afraid Mr. Roberts already has, sir," Richard said. "Do you remember the painting on his easel that first day? Shown from precisely this angle."

"Guarantee of quality, that."

Patiently, Richard said, "You shan't want a copy of Mr. Roberts's work for your book. The public will have seen it before. I'm thinking where else I should set myself up."

Sir Tom had mentioned his book almost as an afterthought in London. They'd been examining a sample plate for Roberts's magnum opus when Sir Tom had said, "I'll be doing one of these. Travel book. Use some of his work as illustrations."

Richard had been startled. "Mine, sir?" Nor had Roberts seemed to expect anything of the sort, although he mimed approval behind Sir Tom's back and managed to whisper to Richard soon afterward, *Means he'll pay to publish it.*

Now Sir Tom made sure Richard got to work on the temple, the patron being as watchful as he was splenetic. As splenetic as he was sunburned. They had left England in July, and after their initial dash across northern Europe, they'd raced into Greece at the hottest part of summer, where the sun burned Sir Tom's face as red as a rooster's swollen coxcomb. Only now, at the tag end of October, was the redness declining along with the heat, although his face and hands were peeling, the skin flaking off unpleasantly. To his credit, Sir Tom didn't complain. He wasn't imaginative or in the least bit charming, but he was staunch.

After leaving Greece, they'd left Constantinople and, soon enough, Ephesus. Boudroon and Dvojato were done and done, then they'd turned the page on innumerable flea-ridden villages on the road to Xanthus, Macri, Cyprus, before taking a boat to Beyrout, where they didn't linger. Hovels, encampments, one night spent near the convent of St. Anthony whose jolly monks came to visit, cowls laughing around the fire. Afterward, they cantered through a devilish wet snowstorm in the mountains, dripping like melting icicles into a village whose name he couldn't remember, although they'd stayed there only last night. All this time, Sir Thomas remained staunch, lawyerly, blistered and, at every point on their exhausting journey, passionately preoccupied with one thing: whether to buy a colliery in Wales.

During the day, Sir Tom would ride up to Richard after five silent hours in the mountains and say without preamble, *It's a gamble.* At night, he debated both sides of the question beside their loud campfire, Arabs hawking and spitting, donkeys braying, dogs howling at the scimitar moon. Meanwhile Sir Tom was forced to admit, *I am forced to admit that men can lose their shirts at mining, a risky investment on the one hand. But on the other, the making of a man's fortune if the seams pay out.*

Hunched close to their campfire, for the nights had turned cold, Richard only half-listened, sometimes remembered to nod, and meanwhile failed to understand why Sir Tom was so intent on risking his pleasant fortune in search of more. He was unmarried and without heirs, and although he was fussy about his mustachios, he looked to remain so, Sir Tom having something of the spinster about him.

Poor Mary Ann, now accepted as their father's housekeeper, had slipped from unmarried into unmarriageable. Men of status weren't often unmarriageable, certainly not when they were titled. But Richard had never seen his patron show any interest in women, although he was sentimental about children, tousling the heads of the near-naked waifs running out of villages they rode into, and scattering baksheesh.

Maybe he meant to demonstrate that he had human feelings, when as far as Richard could see, he did not. Eight, ten, twelve hours in the saddle left ample time to think about his patron, and Richard had come to the conclusion that Sir Tom was trying to cover up some central lack. His gentleman's tour, even the colliery were diversions from something Richard kept trying to put his finger on before deciding that he couldn't. Nothing there. Or at least, nothing very interesting.

A t Baalbec, Sir Tom finally ambled off, saying he would leave Richard to get his temple, which sounded like an order. *You noticed the carved panthers? Those leaves?*

"Acanthus," Richard said, although he would far rather have sketched the Syrians drifting up behind him, men from the caravanserai, a confusion of weathered faces and pretty ones, the young men in these parts often looking sweeter than the women, although the men were far less capable, from what he could see.

Richard had grown used, almost, to the jostle of crowds that gathered as he drew; art as theatre. Now, unintelligible murmurs touched his back. Landed like flies, rose like whispers from the pit as his hand moved across the page. When he'd first encountered the Eastern crowd in Corfu, he'd tried to flee, clutching his sketchbook to his chest and taking off, a gang of men and boys on his tail as if they were running after the wild beast show as it left town, hoping to get another look at the elephant.

Now he acted the artist. Leave aside the fact he *was* an artist. He acted it for the watching men as he often did for Sir Tom, amusing himself now by holding out his sketchbook, admiring his work as if he were a bad actor playing himself onstage. A case of Egg's doubling. Duality. The gap between past and present in the East was making Richard think Egg might have a point. There was such an enormous rift between the glories of the ancient world and the shabbiness of the present—Roman pillars looming over these travel-stained, vulgar, spitting men—that Richard no longer saw layers so much as two sides to the coin. Much that he'd believed was being upended, although other things were coming into focus, as if he'd put on a pair of spectacles and the world was changed.

One thing Richard had learned: he was better at figure drawing than landscape, something he had sensed at home without being able to articulate it. His instincts had been correct: he was the wrong man for a tour, at least the type of scenic tour his patron demanded. Yet he had reason to be proud of the figures in his notebook, especially a letter writer in Constantinople, an old man he'd stumbled on amid the intricate weave of carpets and filth in the bazaar. Beard, turban. The angle of his shoulders suggested a let-down of language into his hand, as milk came into nursing women's breasts. Richard didn't know how he knew that, but the idea came into his mind as he sketched, and his line grew fluent. He thought about how this would affect his work when he got home; how what he was learning here would help him focus more sharply.

Then the bull entered the china shop.

"How am I supposed to use that?" Sir Tom had asked, stalking up behind him. "Another Arab. What about . . . ?"

Sir Tom looked around at the jumbled bazaar. Nodded at a crumbling archway.

"You want to be different than other men, sir."

His patron rumbled something in his throat signifying lack of conviction. But Richard had decided that the honourable way forward was to educate Sir Tom on the value of figures for his book, the importance of distinguishing himself from his competitors, of taking what Richard could give him. It was a tactic, a make-do, but it also happened to be right.

However. *However*, as Mrs. Gaskell would say, his patron just wanted to be the same as other chaps, presumably to cover his emptiness. He wanted his colliery, his gentleman's tour. He wanted his scenic ruins, and appeared now between the columns at Baalbec, having clambered up behind Run's Temple, what a name.

"Don't mind me," Sir Tom called. Meaning, put me in your drawing.

"If you could hold that pose, sir. A great help."

Sir Thomas raised his chin and froze. Richard's ally was his patron's vanity. Whenever Sir Tom got himself in a pique about the sketches, Richard asked him to pose in Arab costume. Or lately, since Richard had come to recognize the signs of an impending explosion, when he was about to. *Excuse me, sir, but I'm struck by the way that turban sits. If I may . . .*

Sir Thomas was particularly fond of a sketch in which Richard had posed him aiming a gun. Tore it out of his notebook and soon lost it, not seeing any problem in demanding that Richard work it into a painting he could use for the frontispiece of his book. Sir Tom had no idea that Richard was referring to dead Chartists in his drawing. Had no idea what he was really up to. Richard had got in the habit of agreeing to everything his patron said while doing pretty much as he wanted. He'd never been a dissembling man before. However.

"You can't seriously be offering it to anyone else," Egg had said.

"Would you go?"

A pause. This was at Hall's, the editor Samuel Carter Hall's of the *Art Union Monthly*, always a loud and hilarious place, the walls a jumble of novice paintings and engravings, the tables piled with books and far more drink available than chairs. His house was named The Rosary. The Roguery, they called it. Richard had known he'd find his friends at the Roguery when he'd set out from his studio last February, his overcoat battened against the sleet.

Now the hilarity grated against his mood, the Irish jollity not only of Hall but of his black-eyed missus, plumping her curls by the fire; the sainted authoress of *Groves of Blarney*, in which Tyrone Power had triumphed before plunking down his guineas to make Richard's first sale. Before he was pushed into plunking by Hall's patronage of Richard and his clique.

> *A baby was sleeping;*
> *Its mother was weeping;*
> *For the husband was far on the wild raging sea . . .*

The ditty itself was no longer hilarious, not with Power lost in a shipwreck the previous spring. Richard's father had come to his studio, passing him a newspaper folded to show the report. *The Times* told him that Power was one of the unfortunates drowned when the S.S. *President* went down in the Atlantic. Power had boarded in New York, having played the stage Irishman to thunderous notices from the Yankees. His profits had bought Power passage home on the biggest steamship in the world, a floating palace, and no one knew exactly where or why she went down. A storm, an absence. Whether Richard's painting was on board remained as much of a mystery. He couldn't think why Power would have taken it to New York, but discreet enquiries showed that the family had no idea where it was.

Another gloomy omen for touring. No wonder Egg hesitated.

"But Roberts didn't ask me," he said finally.

"Isn't it pleasant not to have to make a decision?"

"He wants help in turning it down," Frith said. "Ward. You like travel."

"But Dadd ought to go," Ward said. "Plump his career."

The conversation went on as if he wasn't there; as if he were a child whose head they talked over. He ought to tour. No, he oughtn't. *I oughtn't*, Egg said. O'Neil believed that he shouldn't either.

Richard had no objection to being ignored. Or he wouldn't have, if they'd come up with an excuse he hadn't already tried on his father. His friends were like Richard in preferring to stay in London and tend to their careers. All of them were rising, finding patrons, landing commissions, racking up sales almost as profitably as he was. Their clique had become a byword for the art world's coming men. Hall claimed them as his discoveries, patronizing them in the worst sense of the word, but also thumping them up in his magazine and introducing them to potential buyers, Hall being a greasy, garrulous little man whom Richard would have preferred to avoid, although that would have meant bad notices. An adept at blackmail, in his fawning way.

Turning from his friends, Richard looked around the room: the Halls' salon of flash-dressed journalists, artists, actors, writers, Dickensian Gents to a man, although Dickens himself was touring America, at least if he'd got there.

Across the room, Richard saw Mrs. S. C. Hall open her vulgar mouth in a silent laugh. Saw Poynter, the landscape painter, gape in response. Poynter would jump at the offer of a tour but he wasn't a gentleman, and Sir Thomas insisted on a gentleman. Richard wasn't any better born than Poynter, both of them sons of tradesmen, except that Poynter wasn't a gentleman and Richard was.

*Have to prepare for the fall exhibition*, Ward was saying.

*Can't be distracted*: Egg.

"At least you'd get away from your father."

One of those sudden silences. Richard heard Frith as clearly as if they were standing in an empty church, as cold and pure as morning.

"I lost my own pater, of course, and miss him awfully. But honestly, Dadd, ain't your father a little too much in the picture? So to speak. Might do you some good to get away for a year. Is it a year?"

"Nine months."

"Pregnant, that," O'Neil said.

"Count on O'Neil," Ward said. Not all of his friends liked each other, but they also did. Richard wasn't alone in feeling divided. Might do him some good to get away from the clique, as well.

Not Frith. He would miss Frith. There was something comfortable about Billy, rocking on his heels like an older man, thumbs hooked in his waistcoat pockets. In an attack of prescience, Richard understood that Frith would live a long, successful and entirely comfortable life, not a moment of which would be spent in Syria. Frith simply wouldn't have gone, no matter how hard they had pressed. In an urbane and gentlemanly manner, Billy would have wiggled out of it. Squirmed and slipped and eeled out of it. You wouldn't have glimpsed his coattails as he left the room. Not a boot heel, not the tag end of his scarf. It was entirely possible that he hadn't been in the room in the first place. Richard would miss Frith. The way he wasn't always quite there and didn't miss a thing.

"Of course you're going," Billy said quietly, and Richard shrugged. He was; that was true from the start. But since the tour would indeed prise his father off his back, well then. Well.

Wasn't it just like Billy to give him an excuse: not to stay, but to leave.


B aalbec, done. Up at dawn the next day to a smoky camp-fire, their usual breakfast of coffee, eggs and unleavened bread, an oversized Moslem version of communion wafers, the body of the non-Christ. Richard remembered his Grandfather Martin puffing his pipe at the fireside in Chatham. *And oh the Musselman*, he'd said. It had never occurred to Richard to ask what on earth he'd meant, but now he couldn't help wondering if his grandfather had been the prescient one, understanding that Richard would travel to the East.

What an odd thought. His grandfather had probably just picked up the expression from a Navy man at the dockyards, some one-legged chap who'd battled pirates off Morocco. How strange to imagine anything else.

But Richard wasn't sleeping well. Hadn't slept well for most of the tour, and he was never at his best when he didn't get enough sleep. Last night he'd been kept awake by what he supposed was music, the strange compressed keening from the caravanserai, a line of male falsetto needling through the air and piercing his ear. It went on for so long that Richard had grown frantic, tying his handkerchief around his head and pulling his hat down over his ears, hands clapped on top. Still the wail got in, on and on and on until suddenly, in mid-phrase, on an uplift of male keening, it stopped.

L ater, in quarantine off Malta, Richard decided to write down this leg of their tour in a memo to keep with his sketchbooks, tracing their route from Baalbec to Damascus to Jerusalem and finally up the Nile, where he might have found what he'd been looking for. Or at least, what had been waiting for him. Richard had sent letters en route to Frith and Roberts and of course to his father, and he could reclaim those at home. But he hadn't covered everything, and in the four months since Baalbec, too much had faded from his memory or grown confused.

On the other hand. In his small neat ship's cabin, ink and paper on his built-in table, Richard thought about how unbearable memory would be if it stored everything, like a clerk's cubby-holed desk. There would be no end to sorting it. You'd have to paw through hours of Sir Thomas before pulling out an image of pure Eastern light. No doubt the good Lord had arranged things for the best, ensuring that the mind would empty its cubbies, perhaps while one slept, storing memories of high points from the best of days and throwing out the worst, the times when one was bored or ill.

And Richard had been ill. Not fever this time. It wasn't his fault they were in quarantine, although Sir Thomas managed to imply that it was. Most ports were under quarantine after outbreaks of fever were reported across the Mediterranean. But Richard had lost a couple of days to sunstroke in Egypt, and although he'd recovered well, he'd crossed the Mediterranean from Alexandria to Malta afterward in a strange sort of nervous depression. He wasn't sea-sick like Sir Tom but in a bit of a fog, feeling that his patron was playing cards with the captain of their ship, the stakes being Richard's soul, a liminal moment that wasn't entirely a dream, although he wasn't sure what it was, making his memory of the crossing peculiarly spotty, too.

Richard was well now, better, if a little worried about his health. He wanted to sort through the images left him. Hold them in his palm, turn them, pick the true from the false like minerals he'd mined, rocks veined with minerals, their veins beating.


R ichard is waiting halfway down the stony mountain after leaving Baalbec, having pulled his mule aside to permit a single file of mounted tribesmen to make their way up, one man after another with faces like rock, savage faces surely cut from the rock on which they ride. There are no children here and none of the sturdy-legged, capable women Richard admires. There are only men dressed in purple-and-red-striped robes, the one passing him now a young fellow with a bent nose, the hooves of his enviable horse striking the ground like flint. Richard has been told the Druse and Maronites are at war, and although he has no idea which tribe these men belong to, he has a pleasant shiver at imagining himself on a battlefield amid armies, the eternal sky bleached out above, like a winding sheet ready to descend.

In Damascus a day later, he is sketching the Great Mosque, its dome as luminescent as a pearl. Around him is a restive, ill-tempered crowd. They don't seem to like Englishmen in Damascus. Men and boys run out of the surrounding maze of streets until his audience grows to more than a hundred, many of them pushing forward for a better look, their angry, thrumming voices making him feel as if he's trapped inside a beehive. The man squatting closest to him, with long, sun-darkened fingers, fingernails broken, skin lined pale yellow in the creases, is turning over the leaves on one side of his book while he tries to draw on the other.

It goes on too long. It's been happening too often lately. Giving up, he snaps his book closed, stuffs his pencil into his blouse and stands to leave. The man grasps his ankle. Shaking free, Richard sees other men and boys edging toward him angrily. He edges away, walking a few steps before panicking, breaking into a run.

Pounding down the potholed street, boots thudding on the stone, Richard feels a blunt object hit his back, another and another, and trips over a corn-cob they've thrown. A camel ahead. No beast more ill-tempered than a camel, the Sir Thomas of quadrupeds, this one turning its long neck to snarl as he passes, all gums and blubbing lips.

Boys head the crowd behind him, fastest on their feet. He turns to see the little demons flow around the camel, a river in flood. They remain at a distance, especially the men, and he gets the idea that they aren't really trying to catch him, maybe unsure what they would do if they did, or maybe frightened of what they would have to do to him. Richard thinks he should stop and confront them, attack being the best defence, but stumbles as he swivels, turning his ankle on the potholed street. A wince of pain. He isn't hurt but he staggers.

Seeing the faces running toward him, snot-nosed boys breathing through their mouths, tough-looking men bringing up the rear, Richard doubts the wisdom of confrontation and sprints off, sweating hard, his ankle weak until, and he hasn't planned this, he runs into a square with a fountain in the wall, and Sir Thomas is resting beside it and, more importantly, their guards. Richard plunges among the guards and when they see the pursuit, they surround him like weeds when you dive in a river. Their chief guard shouts at the crowd, which looks diminished now from behind their shoulders. Most of the men have dropped away and his pursuers are chiefly boys. One remaining man shouts back, but the boys turn sulky, staring down at their toes before following them away. Richard feels giddy and laughs, earning a quick, uneasy glance from Sir Tom.

He remembers every crowd that watched him; doesn't know why. At least he *thinks* he remembers every crowd; how can you remember what you don't remember? Richard can call up at will the greatest beauties he's seen: women making bricks by treading on clay and straw; the pure pale thrust of a minaret; water-bearers waiting their turn at the wells; and one time a sunset suffusing Jerusalem unlike any sunset he has ever seen, a peachy rose tinting the entire city, so that every earthen building, every wisp of cloud in the sky, every particle in the air vibrates coral, and he stands inside colour.

From the desert of Jericho, he remembers the half-naked barbarians, descendants of the patriarch Abraham who thunder out of nowhere to intercept their party. He's riding in the rear and only hears a stir at first, but spurs forward to see a band of wild attackers galloping toward them, cocking their pistols so peculiarly close to their ears that they become the horns of devils.

Murder races toward them. But Sir Thomas's party is under the protection of a chief who rides out to meet the bandits. The sight of him stops them in their tracks, evil intentions dropping like handkerchiefs to the desert floor. Oh, I've lost mine. Never had one, myself. Their chief kisses the bandits' sheikh once on each cheek, there's a milling of horses and now they're best of friends, although Richard catches one of the bandits eying his canteen.

Maybe what he remembers most is not the crowds or the chase but the sense of being watched even at private moments, as if by a jealous Old Testament God. He's being held up to judgement. Chased toward God's judgement; that's what it is. The Arabs watch him draw, watch him eat, eyes following his hand as he raises his fork to his lips, and he's caught children watching him shit, heads popping above rocks when he thinks he's found privacy, making comments on his stool; he supposes that's what they're saying. If he took a woman, which Sir Thomas makes impossible, they'd probably watch that, too. Richard feels eternally watched and chased and judged, for if the Arabs leave him alone for five minutes, damned if Sir Thomas doesn't pop up, complaining about his paucity of work.

After paying off the bandit sheikh, they ride on to camp at the shores of the Dead Sea, waiting for the moon to rise so they can ride on further, hurry and hurry. In this topsy-turvy world, the bandit has sent four men to guard them, and his men stalk back and forth, back and forth, warming themselves at the campfire, a savage parade.

Sir Thomas's party has grown to include several Royal Navy midshipmen and lieutenants they've met in Jerusalem. He's flaunting his ill-gotten title, using it to try to secure passage on a Navy steamer from Jaffa to Alexandria. He gets the promise of an introduction to their captain, and afterward they talk idly as the moon rises above the horizon. Your Arab this and your Druse that. Sir Tom recommends to their notice a colliery in Wales, after which they mount their rested horses and ride through the misshapen volcanic strangeness of the Engaddi hills, craters mawing to every side.

And what has this to do with art? Trapped in quarantine at Malta, five, six, seven months into their tour, Richard has had so little time to sketch that art is building up inside him like steam. He feels like an engine about to explode. Wonders if it's art when you don't sketch it. If it happened when you can't remember it. Sir Thomas believes he doesn't remember what happened during his two or three days of sunstroke in Egypt, but Richard thinks he does. Certainly he remembers a great deal about crossing the sea, arguably too much, since some of it might not have happened; captain and cards and bargaining for souls. Which Richard now remembers were the souls of the ship's passengers, not his. At night his mind has become such a whirl that he can grow frightened. His hands shake as an artist's can't shake. His teeth and knees chatter.

Both hands and knees are chattering now in his tidy ship's cabin, Charon's cabin carrying him back to Europe, to Naples, to Rome. Richard is so anxious, his mind unscrolling images so brilliantly fast it's as if they're being shown him by demons. He remembers a letter he wrote to Frith confiding that *often I have lain down at night with my imagination so full of wild vagaries that I have really and truly doubted of my own sanity.*

I've got *open my mind*, yes, *opened my mind*, and mind what I say, it's uncommon good soil, so soil not your lips with the traduction or reduction of my induction in this matter.

Richard remembers his letter to the word. His words to the letter. Tries to calm himself by deciding that it's nothing but the heat of Asia Minor, the motion of the horses eight, ten, twelve hours a day; it's months of broken sleep, of inadequate food, the lack of release in women and especially in art. It's sunstroke. It's nervous depression. It's Egypt, where he saw something, and where something saw him.

But Richard has left Egypt, and he'll be fine. They've got him quarantined against sickness. Protected, he thinks, and picks up his pen.

Nothing comes out. The problem being that Egypt won't leave him.

# Dualities
## Cairo and Thebes
*December 1842–January 1843*

C airo is unlike any city Richard has seen, and he isn't sure why. Their first full day in town, he leaves the hotel after breakfast and walks out into a noisy, swarming, sand-coloured street, seeing a mosque across the way. Lacking a janizary to take him inside, he walks past it without aim or direction; content, for once, to leave agenda behind, his pace long ago slowed in compromise with the heat, allowing him to fall in with the drift of local men going about their dilatory business.

They take him into a narrow street, where upper storeys of wood and daub shade him from the sun, like the overhangs on the last few timbered houses in London. The air is dry and gritty, and as he passes squatting vendors, Richard makes out the granular stink of frankincense and charcoal and spices, scents that rise into an atmosphere of powdered dung and donkey hair. He feels as if he's smoking a cheap cheroot. His throat is parched, although his light-headedness lends the day a pleasant fizz.

When the street widens, Richard spots a great fort looming over the city which he supposes must be the Citadel. Setting out to find it, he loses himself in a maze of narrow streets, passing and re-passing the same red-and-dun stone building, or one very like it, before finally entering a great square with a noble mosque on one side. Ahead is the entrance to the Citadel, a narrow passage between two round castellated towers.

As Richard crosses the square, guides precipitate out of the dusty air to fight for his business. One man falls at his feet, arse to the heavens. Another tugs on his jacket: dignity dictating that Richard wear proper clothes, liable to meet Englishmen in a capital. A third man shouts in French, approximately, and Richard manages to beckon him forward and hire his donkey. This seems to be the done thing: a couple of other tourists are riding into the Citadel entrance. With his guide holding the reins, Richard follows them into a dark narrow tunnel, where the donkey climbs up an incline broken by several flights of steep steps cut into the living rock. The beast takes the stairs like a goat, hoofs clicking, the clicks echoing.

When they emerge, Richard finds himself in another square, broad as a plain and loud with hammering. He turns his donkey in a half-circle and finds a building under construction in beautiful veined alabaster. His guide tells him in a mangle of French, English and Arabic it is a mosque being raised by the pasha, praise be to Allah. Richard dismounts and walks past it to the edge of the hill. From here he can look down on the city, on acres of flat, hot rooftops, and hear a high-pitched hum.

Cairo sings in tenor. That's what makes the city unique, a difference in tone, of harmonics. There's none of the bass rumble of London or sullen Damascus, but a lighter call that comes, he would guess, from the murmur of musical Egyptian Arabic, from muezzins calling from the city's four hundred mosques, from the thousands of tobacco pipes bubbling out-side cafes, the blebbing of water at once lively and peaceful as men idly draw at the smoke. A nicotine city, with just that feeling of relaxed vigilance, and maybe an undertone of temper, as London is coffee and jitters and tough.

For once, Sir Thomas has allowed Richard a whole morning to himself, but it's proving hard to draw, so open are his mouth and eyes. Checking himself, he pulls out his notebook to make a pair of sketches of Cairo and then the Citadel, brief things he dashes off (not badly) before he heads back down to the city, back into the dilatory stream of humanity, where he finds him-self growing so excited by the sights he can't light on a perch, on a corner, on the corner of a fountain like a thirsty bird.

Turn one way and he sees women flitting past a mosque like shadows, all but their eyes covered in black. Turn another, and three men walk toward him with loose-jointed grace, as colourful as popinjays in their red fezzes, white pantaloons and loose free-swinging robes, one in blue, one in purple, the third in faded acid green: the Egyptian seeming to be one of those species where the male is more flamboyant than the female.

They'd got in late last night. After leaving Jaffa on the Navy ship, they steamed over to Alexandria. Despite Sir Tom's appeal to both the Bey and the British Consul, their baggage is being held there for ten days, and Richard is running short of linen, obscure political considerations holding his portmanteau hostage, something to do with the Bey's son Ibrahim and the Syrian Affair, only God and the Foreign Secretary understanding the affair, and Richard isn't sure about God. A track boat, a steamer and a train of donkeys have brought them to Cairo and he knows they won't linger, telling himself to sketch but not listening, his mind a kaleidoscope of colour and line.

Then he's struck by the rays of light in the silk mercers bazaar, vendors shrieking out womanish plaints from their stalls, the rays filtering down from breaks in the high wooden roof through the smoky, mote-dancing air. Once again, he gets out his sketchbook and the usual crowd gathers. He doesn't do as much as he should, pausing too often to gawp. But he's pleased with his work, and only stops when the sun tells him it's time to find Sir Tom.

*Mr. Riga, Mr. Riga*, he asks: the merchant old Roberts told them would provide supplies for their journey up the Nile, centrepiece of Sir Thomas's tour. Richard makes his way to a dim warehouse where he finds Sir Tom talking to a little man, round as a wheel, who wears a travel-stained English jacket over a bruised reddish-purple Egyptian robe. His patron introduces Mr. Riga, who greets Richard by touching him on the shoulder and spine before raising a hand, weirdly, to the back of his neck and cupping it there intimately.

Lowering his hand, Mr. Riga claps for a servant, asking if Richard would care for tea. This while other servants leave bags of rice and onions and cases of brandy at Sir Tom's feet, one offering him a double-barrelled gun and pouch of powder, which looks damp.

"And if I may, Sir Thomas, the question of a boat for your journey to Thebes."

"Thought I'd mentioned that. The British consul is letting me use his."

"Yes, the consul. But if I may, first thoughts aren't always best ones."

His patron gives Richard a covert glance, probably much like the ones Richard gives him, traffic on most streets running both ways.

"They aren't," Sir Tom concedes, before pulling up. "Although of course we're speaking of the consul."

"Our excellent consul," Mr. Riga says, and goes on to denigrate this tip-top man, his very good friend, who despite being British appears to be the worst sort of dastard. A murderer, really, prone to drowning his countrymen. Out of ignorance, of course, not malice, although Sir Tom still doesn't know where Mr. Riga gets that. The consul knows Egypt, which the merchant's eyebrows politely disbelieve.

As they bargain, Sir Tom straight as an exclamation point, Mr. Riga quite round, it occurs to Richard that the merchant looks like a modern version of the god Thoth, at least in his incarnation as a baboon. Richard has been reading up on the ancient religion and understands that most Egyptian gods were as lithe as the underfed modern Arab fellahs. But Mr. Riga has a baboon belly, one that demands notice, thrusting itself out as he gesticulates, stretching his robe.

"An eight-oar boat," he proposes, naming a price. "Anything more is . . ." He searches for a sufficiently dire English expression, his belly expanding. ". . . jumped up."

Richard, who has lost weight on the tour, identifies more with the god Khnum, a skinny-shanks, ram-headed god with handsomely curling horns. (He is rather vain of his long hair.) Khnum is the closest he has found to a deity of art, being the god of potters; the creator god who fashioned humans out of clay. He's also the god of cataracts and fertile soil, which has a nice resonance: art requiring fertile soil, craft and power, the push of roaring water. Richard remembers standing at old Roberts's studio window as rain poured down the panes, how he felt he was standing behind a cataract. Well, there you go.

"The consul offers twelve oars for less," Sir Thomas says, his position hardening. "Ready when we return from the pyramids. And when our baggage is freed."

"Oh, they have tried that on you," Mr. Riga says, apparently forgetting about his boat but still wishing to be helpful, or find another source of revenue. "Did not my friend the consul inform you of the proper bribe?"

"There's no such thing," Sir Thomas says staunchly, as if they haven't spent six months on tour.

"But sir, the linen," Richard says, and his patron frowns at him irritably.

T hree weeks later, they're on their way upriver, a few days outside Thebes. The consul's twelve oarsmen are rowing his boat against the current, which is fast enough that eight wouldn't have done the trick. Richard has been told that the inundation is proving powerful this year. It seems to be a polite topic in Cairo, like the rain at home, although in this case they're talking about horizontal weather: the Nile in flood.

Richard lies on the roof of the cabin, hands behind his head, happy to be carried along. The Nile is dynamic, red and swirling with eddies, and the narrow bands of fields on both banks vibrate with growth. Rinman's green for the fields, he would say, and behind the fields the desert, no transition, is a light, salty brown, mummy brown. An uncluttered palette and a restful one. Richard's mind is at rest, or approaching it.

It's no mystery; he's getting enough sleep, and his days are hardly challenging, none of the effort of riding, eyes calmed by an unchanging scene. He listens to the pleasantly tremulous song of their improvisator, a reedy man, a tenor, who sits in the prow to sing extemporaneous lyrics about the sights they pass, giving the oarsmen a rhythm; his rhymes sung out in a loud, demanding voice and translated by their captain, the *Raïs*.

Sometimes translated. Partly translated. Some lines appear to be personal and rude, possibly obscene. The occasional fellah shakes his hoe at the boat. Others shout from their fields, shrill and half-laughing, the oarsmen giggling silently, the improvisator's shoulders tight with self-satisfaction.

Now, as he finishes a phrase, the oarsmen chime in lustily, and the *Raïs* has told Richard they're repeating the line just sung. This one seems to be the end of a stanza, and the oarsmen lengthen their tremulous response into plangency, making their part into a chorus, rowing to the beat of their song the way the Roman slaves rowed their galleys. As their voices fade, the improvisator begins another verse, which the stocky captain is moved to translate as an ode to the flamingo, pointing to several birds with their heads nodding above the reeds. A tall wader, long curved beak, its plumage white with pink coverts, which Richard admires.

Sir Tom is less happy, and sits below him on deck obsessively cleaning his gun with oil and rags. This is the double-barrelled shotgun lent him by the merchant Mr. Riga, which Sir Tom takes out for game every morning as the crew breaks camp on shore. Mr. Riga must be fond of the crocodiles and ducks of his country. He's provided such a miserable weapon and such thoroughly damp powder (Richard was right) that Sir Tom takes little game, although he winged two pigeons he brought on board to keep as pets. Unable to fly, they coo and bob around the deck. Sir Tom has taught them to eat grain from his hand and can devil them for hours, throwing pellets of bread at their tails so the poor things try to fly and crash around like broken tops.

Sir Tom has to be doing something, lost when forced into idleness, happiest at speed. Hurry, man. He must have been talking to himself. Now that Richard feels better, he has greater sympathy for his patron, who might be running away not from his hollowness, but from feelings of guilt at the Chartist massacre, sons and fathers picked off mercilessly as on his order, Her Majesty's troops opened fire from inside the stout walls of an inn. Seventeen men killed, thirty lying injured, more probably hidden by their families.

In seven months, Sir Thomas has never once mentioned the word *Chartist*, arguably traumatized by the shrieks and blood and brains he must have seen congealing in the town square outside the inn. Or at least by his own near miss, shot in the hip and arm as he stubbornly read out the Riot Act.

The slugs probably came from Her Majesty's troops. Seven thousand Chartists had marched into Newport intending to break one of their number out of jail, but they weren't well armed, their leaders believing that strength lay in numbers. Out of seven thousand men, only a few carried guns, and a few more brandished the wooden cut-outs they used for drilling in the mountains. Sir Tom never mentions any of this, or his wounds, even in those moments when he jumps off a horse and crumples, or pauses halfway up a hill and his grim expression makes it clear his leg is throbbing.

It might not be guilt, of course. Sir Tom could be hurrying from the usual things. A failed romance, or a lack of romance in his life; because he misses his mother, no matter how long she's been dead; because, like Richard's father, he has reached middle age and finds himself puzzled, feeling he hasn't done what he intended, unsure what has happened and wondering how he can compensate.

The night before Richard left, he and his father had sat up, the sun fading but a stench coming off the Thames they could have set on fire. In the darkening room, the familiar furniture turned to shadows, insubstantial, as if Richard had already forgotten it. The brothers and sisters had retired and his father was talking, not about the tour but about himself, almost to himself: his start as an eager youthful chemist—with a full head of hair—doing everything he could to raise himself and his family; to help raise his country. His passion for Reform, for education, for science. He was a natural philosopher. A curator. He cured people, as good as the physician he'd wanted to be; cured Richard of his terrifying fever. Framer, gilder, a friend of artists, of art . . .

Losing the thread. Struggling to find it. Deflating.

"Nothing adds up. I've fallen short, son. No one will remember me."

Richard hadn't known that he'd expected them to. *It's up to you now*, his father had said, sombre words in a sombre light. *My fondest hopes go with you. My dearest son.* And his father had wept.


I t was the pyramids that brought Richard into greater sympathy with Sir Thomas, or at least the expedition they'd met at the Sphinx. They were visiting the pyramids while their boat was prepared for the journey up-river, and it had taken them far longer than they'd expected to get there, six dragging hours by donkey. The sand was unstable on the direct route between Cairo and Geeza, the flood not yet fully subsided, and they'd been forced into taking a circular route that meant the pyramids were tantalizingly visible for hours before they arrived, like every pretty thing a child has ever wanted.

When he'd first seen them in the distance, Richard had been staggered by their size: man-made, buff-coloured mountains dropped down in the middle of salty nowhere. He'd never imagined anything so immense, although of course he'd seen many drawings and engravings. Yet the drawings hadn't caught their size, and he hadn't expected to feel so insignificant. Astonishing that a pair of ancient pharaohs had planned to make a man feel small four thousand years later. Because they'd planned it; Richard knew it, sensing the presence of long-dead kings, their godlike cranky hubris.

As he rode closer, the effect was spoiled by the sight of tiny figures clambering up and down the pyramids, tourists everywhere, guides managing their ascent with ropes. They'd been edited out of the engravings he'd seen, the reason he'd had no idea of scale, although a true likeness would have made the whole business look silly, as if the pyramids were covered in beads. This presented an aesthetic problem, although Richard wasn't interested in solving it. He'd far rather sketch a tourist.

However. Richard would give Sir Tom his elegant triangles, and meanwhile looked forward to climbing the pyramids himself, only suffering a little from the heat as they reached a village not far from Geeza, a huddle of mud houses. It was sleepy there and pleasant. Yet as they rode into the village, a flood of guides surged out of the side streets, a tumble of men and boys pouring in from every direction. One minute, silence. The next: I show you dead kings, mister. *Trois, quatre, cinq piastres. Your servant, most excellency. Hassan. Hassoun. Merci.*

They were engulfed, the donkeys turning balky, the guides from Cairo useless, no doubt in cahoots. Richard hated these tumbles and needed to get out, Sir Tom shouting at him to hurry himself, damn it. They whipped their donkeys, shoving aside touts, trotting out of the village as fast as they could, his patron making no bones about kicking away the half-naked boy clinging to his stirrups.

It didn't help. The touts were desperate and fast on their feet. Tombs, *monsieur, monsieur*, as if he and Sir Tom were part of Napoleon's army. Mummies, excellency. Baksheesh, Richard was carried toward Geeza in a flotsam of pleas. Then he caught sight of an expedition camped below the Sphinx, a grid of tents, a bustle.

"Sir!" he shouted, pointing his whip.

The expedition would have guards, and Richard whipped his donkey toward it, the touts dissipating the moment he reached an invisible boundary ten feet behind the tents. Here, then gone. Richard didn't see any guards, then realized he'd lost Sir Tom. Didn't care, wiping the sweat from his face and neck before dismounting and leading his donkey into the encampment, hoping for help in handling the rumpus, or at least a refill of water.

The tents were near empty, a few scattered sleepers, but beyond them he found a semicircle at the base of the Sphinx rustling with Arabs and loud with discovery. The towering head rose from the desert with the broken nose and calm assurance he'd seen in drawings. Part of its chest was excavated, as Richard had expected, but he was excited to find the excavation deepened to reveal an inscribed tablet between what were known to be paws buried in the sand. There hadn't been a tablet in any of the engravings Richard had seen, and from the look of things, it had only just been dug out. On either side were piles of rubble-strewn sand, Arabs sifting through it, tossing stone, faience, shards of antiquity onto a tarpaulin. A piece of glazed pottery caught the sun as it arched prettily through the air.

Beyond the Arabs, close to the tablet, a man copied its hieroglyphs onto a large paper clipped to his easel. Richard was surprised to recognize Joseph Bonomi, the artist and Egyptologist, an Englishman despite the name. He waited for Bonomi to finish copying a hieroglyph.

When he finished, he started on the next one.

"Mr. Bonomi," Richard said, knowing he ought to wait. "It's Dadd, of the Academy Schools. We've met in London."

Without looking over, Bonomi asked, "Has he brought you in to help?"

"Who?" Richard asked, then supposed that was enough of an answer. "I'm here as draughtsman to Sir Thomas Phillips. He's making a tour. Planning a book."

"Chartists." Bonomi grunted and turned, looking unfriendly, although when he saw Richard's embarrassment, he softened. "I'm not particularly proud of how I got here the first time either. Another wealthy bugger on tour."

Sir Tom had made Richard forget that straight-forwardness existed. He looked around reflexively: Sir Tom *did* eavesdrop. Bonomi smiled again, a wolfish scholar twice his age wearing a lopsided white turban. Below it was a sun-beaten tobacco-coloured face.

"This is the King of Prussia's expedition, and your *who* is Professor Lepsius," Bonomi said, putting his brush aside. "We arrived last month."

Charged with excavating and documenting the antiquities in Egypt and Nubia; Richard had heard of it. He was going to ask about the tablet when he heard Sir Tom's voice.

"There you are. Hurry yourself. I've hired a pair of scoundrels to show us the pyramids."

His patron was standing at the edge of the semicircle. When Richard hesitated, he called, "*Now.*"

"We needn't bother with introductions," Bonomi called back, but Sir Tom had already left.

They joined the expedition at their campfire late that night, having spent the evening sliding down the square interior passages of the pyramids and being roped back up like a pair of pianos. Richard was thrilled to hear about the tablet, which Professor Lepsius said they had expected to find. But Sir Tom had been in a sullen mood ever since the uproar of their visit to the pharaohs' tombs: the dance of torchlight on walls motley with colour. Brown, black, gold, white, turquoise; a sensuous dance. What a bloody mess, his patron muttered. He seemed to want the ancients to be buried in elegant monochrome, to be marble statues, unbending as he was. He paid no attention to the campfire talk of discoveries and didn't even realize that Bonomi was having at him, although he was usually quick to sniff out slights.

"But the focus of your book," Bonomi was saying, "it has to have one. How would you describe your subject?"

"What Dadd has been doing," Sir Tom said, surely a sign of absent-mindedness. "Drawing the Arab rather than the monuments Roberts has already limned."

Limned. An impressive word; perhaps a technique, a tic. Richard wondered if barristers hung impressive words on the air of the courts where they glimmered like orbs in the august light, befuddling a witness.

Bonomi bowed his head courteously, as if convinced. "So yours is to be more a study of the races and cultures of the East. Which of the languages is your speciality?"

"English," Sir Thomas said sharply, as if waking to him.

"So, of course, what we are talking about," Professor Lepsius said courteously, "is more of the delightfully popular study of character written by Mr. Charles Dickens. I am fond of *The Pickwick Papers*, which limns, as you say, the British personality."

The professor was not much older than Richard, a man with a high forehead and humble manner, despite his famous work unlocking the secrets of hieroglyphs. In Richard's under-standing, he had been the one to propose that vowels were never written down, which apparently was critical.

When Sir Tom didn't answer, the professor turned to Richard. "Of course you know Mr. Dickens."

Stammering: "A little. I'm fond of walking out at night, and so is he. We walk together sometimes, and then, of course, we talk."

"But this is fascinating," Professor Lepsius said. "I only intended to ask, have you read the work of the gentleman."

Bonomi and Richard looked down to consider the concept of the gentleman, which Dickens was not, nor pretended to be, certainly not in private company. A Gent. He'd invented the term the way he'd invented himself.

"Dickens speaks much as he writes," Richard said. "I think that's part of what makes him modern."

"It will be an accomplishment indeed to write like Dickens," Bonomi told Sir Thomas, taking on the courteous foreign tone of the professor. This was when Richard began to feel sorry for Sir Thomas, seeing his pebble eyes widen as he understood how presumptuous it was to write a book; how audacious, how arrogant. Impossible, really.

Of course, art was presumptuous, audacious, arrogant, impossible and necessary. Art wasn't a gentleman any more than Dickens was. Art was Khnum, the dirty-handed potter, the peasant god of fertile fields, the reckless god of cataracts, and Richard found himself fumbling out something like this to the professor, not quite sure how he'd got started, and hoping he hadn't insulted his patron along the way. Odd, when he thought about it later, how he couldn't remember getting started, a beat or two of memory gone, a Lilliputian version of the night he'd taken a fever at Macready's *Tempest*, even though he felt quite well and seemed to make sense, with Herr Lepsius nodding eagerly.

"Yes, yes, the Egyptian gods, who represent such a complex human psychology that they have been preserved in so many religions over time."

"Osiris becoming Orpheus descending into the underworld," Richard suggested.

"The cult of Osiris once being solemnly celebrated by his priests, of course, in the ceremonial planting of seed and the sprouting of grain. Dead seed, as it appeared. Pronto, living grain. This, the reason there is so much resurrection mythology once we have established agricultural societies."

Sir Thomas looked even more bewildered, bordering on affronted, having sensed the implication that the resurrection of Christ was derivative of paganism, or agriculture. Sir Tom was a good Church of England man who, throughout their tour, had been offering up verses from the Bible when they passed kine and palm trees, not all of them apropos.

"'And all the women whose heart stirred them up in wisdom spun goats' hair,'" he'd said one time, seeing a flock of goats, and leaving Richard to look around fruitlessly for women, his fate for months now.

Sir Tom wasn't completely lacking. As they'd crossed a bridge one time, he'd said, "No mention of bridges in the Bible," which Richard hadn't known.

Professor Lepsius assured him, "It is likely to be a very good book, with so much new material before you. All of it, certainly, new to you."

"The professor," added Bonomi, "plans twelve volumes."


As their boat ploughs upriver, Richard spends the day drawing, passing time until they reach Thebes, where he might finally find what he's been looking for. Or, at least, where they'll turn around and begin their journey home. The scenery on the river is unchanging and his sketches aren't very good, although Sir likes them; another strike against him, poor man. Richard has never believed that contentment makes for bad art, but he knows you need a dash of tumult for the best, what he would now call an engagement with the cataract.

He also knows it's hard to balance the two, contentment and the cataract, and, in fact, Richard has had trouble with his balance lately. What he wrote to Frith from Jaffa proved to be even more troubling during his nights in Cairo and at the pyramids: *Often I have lain down at night with my imagination so full of wild vagaries I sometimes* et cetera. His brain working at engine speed, kaleidoscopic speed, frightening him, *terrifying* him into leaning so far away from transcendence, from the liminal, that he'd fallen into mere convention.

However. Richard needed a rest and he's getting it, and if his art suffers a little for the time being, so be it. He squints into a bright sun: the *Raïs* tells them it's unseasonably hot for January. Sketches more palm trees, another village. Good work that, Sir Tom says.

In fact, after three and a half weeks up the Nile, Richard is back to feeling himself, more or less. He likes routine. An un-dashing thing to learn about oneself, hardly the sign of a hero, but there you go. Every day in the late afternoon, two oarsmen drive a stake into the riverbank while another ties up the boat, and Richard closes his sketchbook like clock-work. They eat a five o'clock dinner, an unvarying soup of chicken, vermicelli and onions. When night falls, the oarsmen gather on the shore, and Richard lies on the boat listening to one man play a pipe and another beat his drum. One of the company gets up to dance, leaning on a stick as if it were a woman. The others clap as he twirls and bows, and between their clapping and the piping and the rhythmic beat of the tambour, they weave a long pulsing plaint that calms the air and leaves Richard serene.

The only worm in the apple is Sir Tom, who remains restless. He's settled on Thebes as their destination so they can spend a week at Karnak, where he's been told they'll see every style of Egyptian antiquity. The original plan was to go directly there, not stopping en route. But increasingly, he has to be doing something, and Sir Tom has ordered the boat beached for a dash to the temple of Dendera, to the site of ancient Antinoë, and later to the tombs cut into the hills near someplace starting with J, where they spent a full afternoon. He is much happier after their exertions, talking expansively about collieries in Wales, although with a recent lack of reference to his book.

Richard himself can find the stop-and-start rhythm of these detours perturbing. Each risks putting him in a Frithian state. Which is the wrong way to put it, Billy never being over-excited, while Richard was left reeling in awe at the temple of Dendera, sacred to Isis, the wife of Osiris and mother of Horus. Set above the entrance gate was a pair of massively sheltering wings, their lapis, ochre and green paint still as bright as tomorrow. Inside, wings were carved throughout, although the multiple faces of Isis had been obliterated into discs, vandalized by Christian iconoclasts not long after they were carved two thousand years ago.

Wandering Dendera, Richard had the same trouble he'd had in Cairo, unable to settle down to sketch. He saw too many possibilities. Terracotta lapis sheltering mother wings. Yet he got off a few good ones before collapsing back on the boat, observing with one small part of his brain that his thoughts were tumbling all over each other like puppies, like fever, even though he didn't have a fever; he checked.

"What's the matter?" Sir Tom asked after their exertion, their excursion, seeing Richard's hand go too frequently to his forehead. Richard arranged a reassuring smile on his face and shook his head. Nothing. When he had never dissembled before.

Tonight, after the crew goes silent, Richard brings his bedroll on deck, expecting Sir Tom to go below as he most often does, leaving him to drift off under a stupendous sky. The constellations are like notes of music risen to the heavens. The stars sing him to sleep. Richard finds their tunes more happily familiar than the plaints of the crew. Venus sings, *Where the bee sucks, there suck I, merrily, merrily*. Red Mars: *The dog's meat, the dog's meat man*. Cassiopeia: *Sigh no more, ladies, sigh no more*.

To his surprise, Sir Tom chooses tonight to bring his bedroll on deck. It's a cool night, which Richard prefers, but it soon turns out that Sir Tom doesn't, and after a deal of shifting and sighing, he returns below. Richard remains sorry for his restless patron, with his vain wish to write a book, and thinks briefly about the doubled meaning of *vain*: narcissistic, unachievable. Then he must drift off, since he wakes to find Sir Thomas back on deck.

Sir Tom is back and the boat is rocking gently toward shore. At least, Sir Tom is rocking, less and less gently, more urgently, and although Richard is half-asleep, he recognizes the rhythm, which he falls into often enough himself. He's more awake than he wants to be but takes care not to move, leaving Sir Tom to his fantasies. Then his patron turns and he feels a hand on his thigh and he thinks, *Oh, so that's it*.

Richard has friends who boarded at school, knows about the long voyages of Navy ships docked in Chatham, pictures Lord Foley and his guardsman: to whatever degree any of this is relevant; to whatever degree Sir Tom's constant scrutiny of him is relevant. But Richard isn't like that and he certainly isn't interested in Sir Tom, who is approaching his father's age, an unattractive, pebble-eyed little man, peeling with sunburn, although what is happening makes him even more sorry for his patron; obscurely, almost tenderly so.

Taking care to pretend he's asleep, Richard turns aside, and the hand is abruptly withdrawn. The rocking stops and Richard thinks, *That must be uncomfortable*, although he doesn't really care. Before long, Sir Tom clumsily bundles up his bed-roll and goes below. Richard eventually gets to sleep, although not without some rocking himself, picturing a water-bearer he glimpsed once in Lebanon, the roguish black eyes meeting his above her scarf, sturdy legs spreading open.

Over the following days, Richard continues taking care to pretend that nothing happened, although his patron seems to find that difficult and turns even more restless and irritable, seldom meeting Richard's eye, casting him even more covert glances and blasting away every morning at ducks, geese, crocodiles, pigeons, flamingos, anything that crawls or flies along the riverbank, much of it inedible.

Richard minds about the flamingos, although he doesn't say. He's sorry for Sir Tom and tired of him: a guilt-ridden man, aging and not very interesting. He's tired of the end-lessly pregnant tour—seven months now—during which he keeps sensing he's close to something and never finding it. At least they're getting close to Karnak, rowing and rowing in Charon's boat, the improvisator trembling out his obscene rhythms to peasants who curse from fields of resurrected grain.

K arnak proves to be staggering, a complex of temples as big as a city. Temple and city. Temple; city. Religion once flowed through it like a second Nile. At every turn, Richard is dwarfed by statues of gods and pharaohs. Avenues of head-less sphinxes. Two ranks of rams with curling horns, avatars of his friend Khnum that have faced each other placidly for thousands of years. Ahead he sees the sixty-foot pillars in the famous Hall of Columns. An obelisk. Wings. Falcons.

Lotuses. Richard doesn't know where to look. Stares at a great fort-like building, its windows as narrow as the embrasures of castles, slits from which the gods' words once flew like arrows.

Osiris was born here. Richard has been reading about Osiris since his night below the Sphinx. Osiris was born here, son of the goddess Nut, a voice crying as he emerged from between his mother's bloody legs, *The Lord of All is entering the light*. Osiris was both a god and the founder of Thebes, which Richard understands to mean that he was once a living man, a king who ruled four thousand years ago. The ancient historian Diodorus of Sicily seems to suggest this, writing of Osiris as the king who first brought agriculture to Egypt: grain buried then sprouting, the Lord of All re-entering the light. The ancients worshipped their pharaohs as gods, and Richard sees how they might sometimes forget how it began, that Osiris hadn't always been considered divine, just as Jesus of Nazareth once walked the earth, Jesus Son of Mary, Yeshua ben Miriam, a carpenter.

The story Richard reads and re-reads tells of Osiris and his wife, Isis, roaming the known world to bring civilization home to Egypt. Civilization apparently meaning agriculture. On his return, Osiris is murdered by his jealous brother Set, or Seth, who cuts his body into pieces and scatters them around the country. Isis sets out to find the scattered pieces and bandage them together, only failing to find her husband's penis, which has been eaten by a Nile fish, the medjed.

Richard caught a medjed as they tried fishing on their way up-river: the common elephant fish with its droopy snout. He wonders if the Osiris myth is also the origin story of the medjed's snout, how he grew it from eating a pizzle. He's thinking of the way old wives' tales at home explain natural anomalies, the bluish ghostly will-o'-the-wisp rising from marshlands, a gaseous northern drift of faience that rises and retreats from night travellers, luring them on.

There once was a blacksmith named Will, they say, who was cast down by Saint Peter from the gates of heaven for his sins and doomed to roam the earth, his passage lit by a burning coal given him by Satan. Richard has heard other old wives' tales of fairy fire in Wales, how a mischievous *púca* or Puck, like the Puck in his painting, uses the evanescent light to lure travellers into danger, although he met a Welshman once who told him that the magic folk are going out of the world, revenants of the old religion leaving the land, collieries despoiling their homes; thank you, Sir Tom.

In any case. Once Isis completes her macabre work of bandaging Osiris back together, all parts save one, she crafts him a penis of gold. The gods are so moved by her devotion they bring Osiris back to life, at least for long enough that he can impregnate Isis with their son, the god Horus. After his brief and no doubt happy resurrection, the gods send Osiris back to the land of death, where he becomes lord of the underworld.

Horus goes on to murder Set or Seth, his uncle, much as Hamlet murders his uncle Claudius in Shakespeare's play, which Richard had seen performed by Macready not long after they'd moved to London. He'd had a seat at the front of the pit, just below the stage, where he was close enough to make his first theatrical criticism: that Macready was too old to play Hamlet, not just because of the thickly caked greasepaint, and Richard could see every streak, but because of the moment Hamlet knelt down before his mother, Queen Gertrude, and his knee gave an audible crack.

Wandering Karnak, Richard amuses himself by considering what the Osiris myth says about the way a good wife makes a man's penis feel like gold. How gold is a malleable metal. The original author of the myth, and there must have been one, could have made her carve it out of stone, which is as hard and reliable as a man would like, at least at operative moments. Maybe the author was female, an old wife sitting by her fireside, telling tales as she burned camel dung for fuel.

Hearing himself chuckle, Richard realizes how hot it's getting, and that he's not quite right. Heated air wavers off the nitrous desert floor, carrying with it his intention to sketch prodigiously. He no longer feels the heat as heat, but notices how slowly he moves, his body a sluggish vessel for his kaleidoscopic mind, images of gold bluish faïence will-o'-the-wisp Hamlet sliding all over each other in a way that continues to amuse him, until it doesn't. *My imagination so full of wild vagaries that I have really and truly doubted of my own.*

Panicking, Richard dashes into the Hall of Columns, seeking shade. It's cooler in here, a roofless temple where many of the supporting pillars still stand, some at an angle. Now that he's beneath them, he can see that each is close to seventy feet high, as tall as a schooner's mast. It would take a dozen men clasping hands to circle any one of them. He breathes in and out steadily, trying to master himself.

This isn't the right place for that. Richard has seen Roberts's sketches of the colonnade and should have known he'd feel dwarfed both by the pillars and the growing prestige of old Roberts, whose collection of engravings is the talk of the English community in Cairo, and whose signature he has seen on tombs throughout Egypt, R-O-B cut in rock beside scarabs and Roman graffiti.

Breathing deeply, he tells himself to look out through his eyes, not in. Examines the images, the hieroglyphs circling the mast-high columns. He follows a line of them around the nearest pillar, examining a circle of green fronds and brown-headed cobras, above which are wide blue lines—he has to step back, craning his neck to see them—several blue lines on either side of a circle of symbols, above which (stepping back farther) he sees gods and pharaohs, including the black-skinned Osiris, always pictured with black skin once he becomes Lord of the Underworld.

As he takes in Osiris, Richard backs into another pillar. It proves to be standing at a whiffed angle and he darts quickly away, noting the marshy ground beneath his feet. The temple is unstable. The columns have stood for millennia encased in sand, but after the recent excavations, they won't last much longer. He pictures the columns leaning in further, the pediments of gently coloured lotus flowers bowing toward each other, softly touching each other, the black-skinned Osiris, who is four times his height, leaning down as if interested in what Richard is saying, or isn't saying, since he isn't saying anything, although the entire hall vibrates with attention and begins tumbling slowly toward him, the pillars toppling and whirling . . .

Dizzy. He's only dizzy. Bending down, Richard fights off his faintness. Unseasonably hot, he hears the *Raïs* intone, or was it Charon, looking down at the pale nitric sand and a fly circling lazily above it. When he's more sure of himself, Richard stands up, pushing back his sweated hair, and then he doesn't know what's happening, for the hall is bathed in light.

In brilliant, coruscating, lambent light, as gold as ripened fields under a warm September sun. The shadowy, sun-streaked hall vibrates, the air carolling in a high abiding vibrato. Air dancing; motes dancing in shimmers of light. And in this light, as pure and happy as a child, he understands everything.

Osiris, the progenitor of all religion. He has formed Moses his priest, and Orpheus in the Underworld, and Jesus harrowing in hell. He is also Richard's fairies and pucks, Puck and all his faeries leaving the soft green land of Britain to enter an afterlife from which they too shall be reborn. They *shall* be reborn, as the others have been, seeds planted in the earth, planted in the rich and fertile soil ploughed by Khnum, as a man ploughs his seed into a woman, and she opens her legs to thrust her new son bloodily into the light.

Religion is the story of generation, he knows that now; of God making generations, one generation following another, which is why there is no death, why there is fertile everlasting rebirth, and he sees it is his work; it is the work of art to pass along this rich, arable secret for the next thousands of years.

"The Lord of All is entering the light!"

It is spoken. Richard hears it. He hears the voice as clearly as he hears the burble of shorebirds on the Nile. His hands shake. He is vibrating with shock and dizziness, and hears it again, just to one side.

"The Lord of All is entering the light!"

It is a priestly cry, thrilling and deep. A demonic cry, of hallowed devils attending upon the gods. Their voices start calling around him, Lord of all, all, all, like birds calling to each other from opposite banks and trees of many heights. Behind him, in front, deep to one side, shallow to the other, a cry of exultation.

"The Lord of All is entering the light!"

Then a thrumming low voice. "Join me."

Richard understands everything. Myth, life, art. He will join Osiris. He is in ecstasy. Ecstasy. Ecstasy.

And lifts his face to the sun.

# Honeymoon and Haworth
### 1854

The sublime. Waves thundering on the rocks below, breaking into high arcs, dark water shattering into sprays of white and yellow foam. Nothing but salt and water between here and America. All the power of the Atlantic beat against Ireland, waves tormenting the base of the cliff, the force resonating up her spine.

Charlotte sat tucked in a rug, watching the ocean as if it were a play and preferring it to most of the plays she had seen, not that there were many. Nor was she the person who had seen them. She wasn't Charlotte Brontë anymore. There was no more Charlotte Brontë, just as there was no more Emily, Anne or Branwell Brontë. She was Mrs. Arthur Nicholls.

Charlotte Nicholls, Charlotte B. Nicholls, C. B. Nicholls. She tested the names like a schoolgirl trying out different signatures, remembering the night she had written out a married name before erasing it so furiously that she tore the paper, the only time she was Mme. Charlotte Héger.

She might not be Currer Bell anymore either. Charlotte Brontë could be her pen name, since it wasn't her own. Everyone who cared knew that Charlotte Brontë was Currer Bell, anyway. This presumed she would write another novel, which was a bewildering prospect only three weeks into her marriage. She was on her honeymoon, a tour of Wales and Ireland. Everything was upended and she felt different in a way she couldn't define. Charlotte searched for the word. Happy.

That wasn't quite right. She felt more like the Atlantic. And if there was enormous, unsuspected pleasure in the rhythmic beating in and out; if, after an initial week of shock and pain and fumbling, her married body glowed like dark blue water where the sun's rays entered it, there was also something deep and solemn about being so irrevocably tied to another's happiness.

Her husband loved her. This was a great responsibility, which Charlotte hadn't seen before. She had only thought about what he owed her. Prickly. Armed with sarcasm and her superior intelligence, she had expected to have to fight him to get it.

Yet her husband turned out to be tactful and gave her what she wanted, often without making her ask. Charlotte would rather have stabbed herself than meet her Brunty or Prunty or O'Prunty connections, whatever they were called, her father's many brothers and nephews and cousins who, as far as she knew, were all low farmers in the north of Ireland. But he hadn't even made a dig about how it would be better to avoid them, much less insisted on carrying her north with a clergyman's stiff admonition of duty. He could have used a familial visit to put her in her place, or try to, agreeing with her prickly, misguided inclination to make their marriage a contest for dominance. Yet he hadn't said a word, not even hinted, even though he would have won the first marital round.

Nor had her husband boasted about his own family, which Charlotte had assumed was as low as hers. Then he'd introduced her to his elder brother in Dublin and a courteous, well-informed man bowed back; a sharper, keener-eyed version of her husband, manager of the Grand Canal between Dublin and Banagher, their home village; successful and busy, everything an elder brother ought to be.

And when he took her to his uncle's house in Banagher, where he had been raised, Charlotte was staggered to drive up to a gentleman's country seat, a respectable stone residence multiple times the size of the parsonage in Haworth. The aunt who met them cordially in her drawing room proved to be a gentle, modest lady raised in London, his cousins very pretty, well-bred girls, and during their visit, the servants and tenants, of whom there were many, congratulated Charlotte on marrying the best man in the county.

This was her husband Arthur, as she was learning to call him: a strict churchman, it was true, but also unboastful, tactful and happy to give her what she wanted. When she had asked him to leave her alone on the cliff, he made no objection, wrapping her securely in the rug before retreating, and only saying once, as she edged toward the precipice, "Charlotte, it makes me a little uncomfortable to see you get so close."

Charlotte wasn't stupid. She knew there was more than one way to gain the upper hand. From the corner of her eye, which was always on him, she could see that Arthur was getting restless, bored with a scene she could have watched for hours, his mind perhaps not quite so thoroughly stocked that he could spend the afternoon pawing through it. In her sympathy, she didn't think twice before lifting the rug to indicate her readiness to leave. He leapt up to take it and fold it. He would get what he wanted. But she had got what she wanted, too.

"Shall dinner be ready at the hotel, do you suppose?" she asked.

"Yesterday's dinner might be ready by now."

Their hopeful innkeeper had become a shared joke. Charlotte could see how a marriage would develop a double history that would cast single life in the shade. Maybe she could write about marriage. A thought quickly cancelled: Arthur wouldn't like it.

Besides, it was unlikely to thrill. The story of a happy marriage would be undramatic and the portrayal of an unhappy one could only end with an improbable change in one partner, likely the man, which was trite. Either that or it would end with his death, which might provide religious uplift but was still dispiriting. Widowhood was many things, but it had never struck her as earned or lucky, and it couldn't be called a reward. Charlotte was thinking of poor Anne's *Tenant of Wildfell Hall*, which didn't work and hadn't sold.

Yet as they strolled back to the hotel, Charlotte amused herself by trying to think how one *could* write about marriage. It was a challenge, and she liked the challenge of being able to satisfy herself, first of all, and afterward her public and publisher. By which she didn't mean George Smith.

On her final visit to Lily Gaskell before her wedding, Charlotte had found an excuse not to bring Arthur, hoping she and Lily could talk. Now that she had decided what she was going to do, she needed to figure out how to do it. Lily was both a clergyman's wife and a writer, and they had such comfortable talks.

Yet as the housemaid ushered her inside, Charlotte felt uncomfortably conscious of the size of the Gaskell residence, intimidated as never before by its mullioned windows, the expensively papered walls hung with engravings, the many chairs and sofas grouped on so many Persian rugs, most of them occupied by a flux of visitors.

Charlotte was bewildered by her discomfort until she remembered that the Gaskell residence was comparable in size and standing to George Smith's townhouse. During her previous visits, she'd been half-thinking of herself as the future mistress of the London house. She would live on the same scale, and belonged here.

Now that she knew she would almost certainly live out her life in Haworth, her future husband being likely to succeed her father in his perpetual curacy, the Gaskell residence loomed larger and more prosperous than before. It was also accusatory: you *don't* belong here.

Sitting on the edge of her chair, legs dangling, Charlotte realized the extent to which one saw things not as themselves but in comparison, so that even settled objects like houses grew or shrank according to a person's ambitions and prospects. Which raised the issue of the changing ways one looked at people. And how they looked on her.

"They told me you'd arrived!" Lily cried, sweeping in.

Yes, the future wife of a curate, when you are the wife of a reverend minister, even though he's Unitarian.

"I'm *so* glad to see you." Plumping down beside her.

The question being whether you see me as something less than you did before my engagement.

"I've been so looking forward to one of our talks. Many of them."

"So have I," Charlotte said, although in the end, they only managed one evening alone. Not that Lily had neglected her, making sure that Charlotte was well occupied while she attended to the many duties of a clergyman's wife: holding or attending committee meetings, visiting the poor, taking care of her husband, her daughters, her household, with its numerous servants and milch cow, possibly even writing a story for Dickens's magazine, since she'd mentioned that he'd asked for one, although the five pages of big mannish scrawl Charlotte saw her write looked more like a gossipy letter. She hoped Lily hadn't written about her engagement but knew she probably had, getting many of the details wrong.

"Well," Lily said finally, "here we are."

They were in her bedroom on the last night of Charlotte's visit. The summer sun was low in the sky, the mullioned windows meticulously clean. Lily hadn't had time to eat and the maid had brought her a plate of cold mutton, which she devoured as they spoke. Charlotte had declined.

"I couldn't do it," she said, not meaning the mutton, as Lily understood.

"I can't always keep up this pace myself," she said. "I wish I could learn to live at a sensible walk. I either gallop or collapse on the couch."

"I collapse even after being sensible. I can't do any more

work in the parish than I do now. Nor do I plan to. I hope that doesn't create dissension in the, in the marriage."

"Half the time I'm galloping off in the wrong direction. Sometimes I'd like to embrace either side of my life from birth till now," Lily said, holding her hands two feet apart, "and *squeeze* all the time I've wasted out of it. I'd still be eighteen."

Charlotte pictured doing that, and had trouble coming up with a figure, at least an acceptable one. Ten. She'd be ten years old, which wasn't encouraging. Nor did she care for the deeper implication. Lily had the verve of an eighteen-year-old girl. Was Charlotte really a child of ten? That might explain her helplessness about marriage.

"I'm sorry," Lily said. "I wasn't listening properly. My mind is working like a mill today. You're wondering whether you could have a family on top of your duties in the parish and still be able to write."

"Perhaps I wouldn't want to write. It might be a relief."

"You were worried the last time we talked that being a clergyman's wife would make you censor yourself."

"I was worried that it wouldn't."

Both of them smiling. Lily finished her mutton, and Charlotte could see she wanted more. She hesitated about whether to call for another plate but decided not.

"I won't be able to sleep on too full a stomach," she said, as if they'd talked through each step.

"You're happy," Charlotte said, making Lily look at her sharply. "You're too busy, but I think you're happy."

"I suppose I am. I've had . . ." She paused, probably thinking of her two dead children. "However. I'm a happy-tempered person, yes."

"I'd like to be happy. I'm gambling on it. I may lose heavily."

A cat fight outside A window heaved open downstairs and there was a splash, a servant throwing water. *Does fer yuh*, she called.

After a moment's silence, Charlotte said, "I find my duties in the parish a burden. And please don't take this the wrong way. Your girls are sweet, but I don't like children. I'm gambling on something that I think you have, a happy marriage." She raised her eyebrows at Lily, who gave a complicated shrug.

"Yes," she replied.

"I think it, it's a word I think of. That a good marriage *imbues* the rest of one's life. Duties become pleasures. And I've heard people say they don't like other people's children, only their own."

"I don't like all children. Some are dreadful brats, and it isn't always the parents' fault. Nor do I always get along with Meta." Her eldest. "But I would kill for her. Of course," she added, pursing her lips humorously, "there *are* nursemaids."

Then she seemed to remember the incomes of Charlotte's father and fiancé.

"You're gambling on happiness," Lily said, trying to recover. "That could stand as a definition of marriage."

"I don't want to have to write anymore," Charlotte said. "I don't want to feel the need. It's something like torture. I'm gambling that I'll be happy enough that it will simply fall away. I really do wonder why you write when you have so much else. Must you, really?"

"The nursemaids?" Lily asked.

It had never occurred to Charlotte that her friend wrote for money, although Lily had made a point of saying, more than once, that Dickens paid well. But of course, even a minister wouldn't be able to afford a house like this, not without a private income. She'd assumed they had family money, but perhaps not. Lily wrote a great many stories for magazines, not all of them good.

"We talked before about whether I hold back in my writing," Lily said. "Censor myself as a clergyman's wife. You were alluding to the quality of my work"—raising her hand to silence Charlotte—"and I told you I do the best I can. But yes, churning it out like butter rather works against quality. Would you be able to live with that?" Another dry look. "Or without nursemaids?"

"Would you think less of me if the quality of my work declined?"

"Does it matter what I think? Truly, dear."

"I would think less of myself." Charlotte felt a kindling of humour. "That might not be a bad thing."


In the parlour the night before her wedding, Charlotte's father had told them he was too ill to walk her up the aisle. "I'm an old man," he'd said in a querulous voice.

Ellen Nussey rolled her eyes mightily, making Charlotte doubt the wisdom of their reconciliation, although Ellen was her oldest friend and she hadn't been able to imagine getting married without her. It was hard enough to imagine getting married. And Ellen had ample experience as a bridesmaid.

Mr. Nicholls was not prone to eye rolling, but his face took on a more settled cast. He volunteered to check his Prayer Book to find who else might give Charlotte away, and she found a moment to tell him at the front door, "It's been his church for more than forty years. We'll feel his presence, and he knows that. It's not meant as a slight."

He met her eye and nodded, believing her, and returned before long to report that a friend might give a bride away.

The next morning, on the arm of her old friend and schoolmistress, Miss Wooler, Charlotte walked down the well-scuffed stones of the aisle, feeling the presence not only of her father but also of her long-dead mother in the vault, and her brother laid there, and her two elder sisters, dead when children, and her dearest Emily; and perhaps Anne was here in spirit, too, although buried where she died in Scarborough.

At the altar, she listened to her fiancé's friend Mr. Sutcliffe read the service, hearing a quarter of it, although she was awake to the solemn demand that she love, honour and obey her husband, and agreed in a steady voice, although not without silently rewriting her oath: hope to love, no doubt honour, attempt to obey, at least when he was right.

Now, almost five months later, Charlotte looked over at her dear boy reading by the fire, a husband she loved and honoured and often obeyed, at least when put to it, as he often obeyed her. She had learned that a calm and settled man brought out the best in her. Nervous intellectual types only fed her own nerves, and this included her father. She had not settled the question of her writing but seldom thought about it either. Charlotte was happy, and her health was better than anyone could remember.

Feeling her eyes on him, Arthur looked up benignly, marking his place in his book with one broad thumb. "What are you thinking?"

"That if I was on my own, I'd be working on a novel tonight."

"Have you come up with a new idea, then?"

Smiling, Charlotte ran upstairs and got the pair of chapters she'd worked on after finishing *Villette*, the story based on two brothers, Branwell and the madman. Or rather, the amended version, the one that opened on the little girl arriving at a school, a curious creature with a secret that would soon disgrace her.

Reading it aloud, Charlotte altered the awkward wording but couldn't change several basic problems. When she finished, she could see that Arthur wasn't any more impressed with the fragment than she was. This rankled in a small way, since who was he to judge, after all.

"What do you think?" she asked, forcing him to fumble out an answer he was ill-equipped to give, about how she was perhaps repeating herself by setting another novel in a school.

"I thought of that," Charlotte said. "But I think I've mentioned that I usually start a piece of writing several times before getting it right, and I'm not concerned."

"Are you going to continue, then?" he asked, and Charlotte had no answer. *When we need nursemaids?* she might have asked, although this was an area of silence. Arthur wanted children, while Charlotte was grateful to have escaped any hint of that so far and privately hoped she always would. They did well on their own. She enjoyed their pleasant round of parish and private business, especially their very private business. She didn't want to subtract anything from her new life; she was thinking of her father. Nor add anything, especially something as consuming and unhealthy as writing.

"I've wondered, lately, if one can grow too happy to write."

Arthur looked so stunned with love that her heart lurched, and Charlotte fought the urge to go sit on his lap, wanting to see where the discussion took them, and what she might catch herself saying.

"But maybe there ends up being reasons that one *ought* to write and spur oneself."

"A good moral." Arthur nodded firmly.

"I don't write to a moral," Charlotte said, noting that she was speaking in the present tense. "Dickens often does, and my friend Lily Gaskell, invariably. You *will* like Lily when you meet her."

Arthur looked doubtful but obedient.

"Morals answer questions raised by a story," she said. "'You ought to do this, to behave like that if you wish to avoid.' I don't think the job of art is to answer questions, but to explore them, like botanists travelling to far places."

"That might be why you're called an immoral writer," Arthur said, dumbfounding Charlotte. Meeting her eye steadily: "Well, if it's true, you should accept it."

She looked down at the pages in her hand and heard Lily Gaskell's voice: one ignores husbands when convenient. When it helps you stay happily married, she had meant. In finally understanding her, Charlotte felt swept into the sorority of wives.

"Do you want me to stop writing?" she asked, as she probably shouldn't have.

Fortunately, Arthur didn't seem to hear her. She had spoken in a low voice. Since she might rewrite the fragment one day, given the pressures of necessity or the rebirth of impulse or, she whispered inside, the diminution of happiness, Charlotte folded the pages carefully and took them upstairs, where she locked them in her desk.

*I am happy right now*, she reminded herself, and went back down.

# Rebirth
*1843*

R ichard is aware of humming, buzzing, a buzz. He is being
swarmed by gnats. One big gnat is named Sir Tom. It has
its hand on Richard's arm, fingers biting. Looking away from
the sun, Richard finds Sir Tom berating him, and from the
length of the shadows it appears that he has lost several hours.
He understands that time is full of holes. That's how the past
gets through.

Sir Tom is bothering him to get out his sketchbook and
get to work. You haven't made a single sketch today.

I haven't, Richard replies. I plead innocent.

What's the matter with you? For God's sake, why did I
bring you if you're never going to do any work?

That's an interesting question, Richard says. Why you brought me. He doesn't mean anything by it, trying to find a way out of this, making conversation, but he can see from Sir Tom's expression that he thinks Richard is being sly.

"There's obviously something the matter with you. Written all over."

"I suppose there is," Richard says, and because it's true, he laughs.

Sir Tom looks him over as if he were a horse in the Hungerford Market. In old Roberts's painting room. Eyes like gnats walk all over Richard's skin. Poor horses, devilled by gnats. At least they have tails they can switch.

He seems to have said some of this aloud. Sir Tom's pebble eyes have gone round.

"It's sunstroke," he says. "Your head isn't right."

"Oh, I see," Richard says. So that didn't happen on the boat. The lawyer is preparing his defence.

He must be saying everything aloud. Sir Tom starts back, looking petrified. Richard feels sorry for him, poor man, which is when Sir Tom begins to look worried.

You really are ill, aren't you, he says. My god, what's going on.


In Malta, at the end of three weeks in quarantine, Richard feels better, although he is changed. It's necessary to hide this, even though he has never dissembled before. On the boat from Thebes back to Cairo, he tried to engage Sir Tom about religion, but Sir Tom refused to accept anything he said, and failed to invite Richard on his visit to the watercolourist John Frederick Lewis in Cairo. Lewis had been travelling in the East for more than six years and kept a pet gazelle in his garden; Richard had wanted to meet him. Sir Tom's ostra-cization is still an irritant when he remembers it, and leaves Richard feeling aggrieved, a feeling that deepens every time Sir Tom says, *No more religion, Dadd*, as he does with increasing frequency when Richard tries to make conversation.

But Richard doesn't always remember. He is often dis-tracted, especially when they're finally permitted to leave quarantine; when they're in Naples, and when they're in Rome. They're once again travelling so quickly he's having trouble keeping up an appearance of his old iteration. He thinks it better to show himself as he once was, as the artist who was hired, a sketch, even though he is now an oil with a depth of field that was formerly denied him.

Rome he likes. The Coliseum, with the great slash down one side, four storeys here, then cut on the diagonal down to two and a half storeys, as if the gods took a knife to it, mistaking it for a cake. Hadrian's Bridge, the Tiber casting a softer light than the Nile. The sky, the light strike him as glories, such an opalescent quality, an atmospheric buoyancy that allows all the centuries to bloom here, as if Rome were a garden of multi-coloured stone flowers.

But it is the Vatican that draws him, the pair of feathery fountains in the piazza outside that mesmerize with the push and fall of water. He stares at them a long time, then notices the Pope across the square, attended by guards in stiff attire.

It comes to Richard that he must kill the Pope, although he hasn't brought his razor. After watching the Pope enter St. Peter's Basilica, he finds a barber in a side street who tries to sit Richard down in his chair, his whiskers and hair being as long as a gypsy's. Richard manages to convey that he wishes to buy a razor, and the barber directs him to a shop one street over. There, the cutler lays a choice of blades on a cloth on the counter, and he takes up one and mimes slitting his throat to laughter from the cutler and his apprentices. He likes the one with a tortoiseshell handle, and a test on a lock of his hair shows that it's well honed. Richard shocks the cutler by paying him the first price he asks. Leaving him the lock of hair, Richard walks back to the Vatican.

Since the Pope went into St. Peter's, it's a fair bet he's planning to come back out. Richard loiters in the square, pulling out his sketchbook to explain himself, sketching the façade of the Basilica, understanding the importance of his task. Osiris wants the Pope dead. Not precisely the Pope. Gregory XVI is harbouring a demon, Richard having come to understand that there are good and bad demons, as was known to old religions. When a bad demon gets into a man, it needs to be cut out.

The Pope emerges from the Basilica, or what appears to be the Pope. Richard strolls over as any tourist might, or a pilgrim, hoping for a better look. He will have to spit if the Pope blesses him to expel the contamination.

As he gets closer, Richard sees that the demon has taken refuge in an old Italian with a hangdog face, white hair and black eyebrows, a white robe and red cape. He gets quite close, since who could suspect an Englishman.

Yet Richard is made uncomfortable by the number of tall guards with pikes surrounding the counterfeit Pope, who seems to fear assassination. They don't look hangdog. They look hired. He tries to plan a route through them, an angle that will let him slash out with his tortoiseshell razor. Following the procession like a pendulum, he swings first to one side, then the other, and sometimes curls in like a scorpion's tail, looking for a gap.

Impossible. Gregory is too well guarded. Richard drops back, razor still in his pocket, where it will stay. He crosses his arms over his chest, notebook still in one hand. Catching the flash of white, the counterfeit Pope turns and blesses him. Given the guards, Richard crosses himself, as he has seen Catholics do, repressing an urge to spit. Then he goes into a side street and vomits, a tiny voice in one corner of his mind crying, *What is happening to me.*

F lorence. They are at the Pitti Palace when Sir Tom comes up behind him. Sir Tom is always coming up behind him. He is always watching Richard, like the Arabs.

What on earth are you doing?

Memorizing the painting.

With your eyes closed?

Take a look. Close your eyes. Memorize, he says, as if it's a formula every artist knows.

To emphasize his point, Richard shows Sir Tom his sketchbook, his quick outline of Rosa's *Conspiracy of Catiline* and beside it the note he has made on its composition: *calm expression like that of a man who has rather been forced into this conspiracy by the wrongs inflicted on him than impelled by the violence of his own passions . . .*

This insight is acute, but Sir Tom looks frightened, as he often does lately. He seems to force himself to nod, handling Richard with kid gloves.

I need to get some new gloves, Richard says, letting Sir Tom know he's on to him.

But his patron only looks puzzled and says, What for.

P aris. Sir Tom has taken a hotel suite. The rooms are not slumped like superannuated soldiers but as tawdry as old whores, which gives Richard an idea. It isn't difficult to find a whore in Paris, not that he wants an old one, and when he comes back, he feels much improved.

Where have you been?

Am I answerable for every moment of my day?

The whore has inclined Richard to bluntness, but he has gone too far. Sir Tom shoves a chair, which shrieks across the floor.

I have paid two-hundred-fifty pounds for your tour and this is what I get.

What have you got? Richard asks. He's quite curious, although he also hears a note of bravado in his voice.

Precisely nothing. No work, nothing for my book . . .

Oh, please. We're not going to revert to the fiction of a book you're entirely unqualified to write.

Going too far: so says that tiny voice in his head. Sir Tom is breathing hard, rhythmically, his face as red as sunburn. He slaps Richard, who pushes him away, and they grapple briefly before Richard shoves Sir Tom to the floor. He claps one boot on the older man's chest, seeing fear on his face and meekness following, and rage and humiliation. Richard waits for Osiris to tell him that his patron must die.

No! the small voice cries.

The razor in its case. The case in his portmanteau. Richard can feel in his arm the pleasantly fluid motion he used to draw the blade in front of his throat in Rome, and hear the hilarity of the cutler.

The small voice is weeping now. But there are demons

abroad, and it is possible that one has taken up residence in Sir Thomas Phillips and needs to be cut out.

Osiris is silent. There can't yet be a demon, although Richard is certain there will be one soon. He need only wait, pressing down with his boot.

Yet the little part of him makes Richard lift his foot and hurry to his room. Pick up his unpacked portmanteau, his battered case, sling his portfolio over his shoulder.

Damn it, Dadd. You can't treat me

Downstairs, Richard informs himself on how to ride post to London. The small voice is trilling as he gallops home.

# Someone Is Back in London
*Summer 1843*

I t is only ten months since he left. There's no change to his father's shop, nothing that he can see from outside. Having seen himself in other shop windows, and in peoples' eyes, Richard has stopped off at a barber's. Haircut, shave, and the pleasant barber has brushed down his clothes, brought in a shoeshine boy and now he looks much like his former iteration. Richard goes into the shop, jingling the bell.

Stephen is behind the counter. Gapes when he sees him, and Bob turns, and his father.

"Richard!"

His father embraces him. They all do, and Richard feels as pleasant as he looks, although he sees something in Bob's eyes that warns him that Sir Thomas has written. Of course he has. But they'll get to that later.

"How is everyone? All well? Tell me that everyone's well," he says. "I've had precious few letters reach me."

"Everyone's fine," his father says. "The little boys thriving. All of us here, save George, still in Chatham."

"The sisters? Still upstairs?"

An exchange of glances. But merry Stephen can't help grinning.

"Your friend John Phillip, the Scotsman. He came looking for you and seems to have found Maria Elizabeth."

Richard raises his eyebrows. Engaged?

"When he can afford it," Bob says.

"Well, you see? There's my tariff discharged. Now you lot have two more to go. Little tardy, an't you?" Turning to Bob. "And how's the beauteous Miss Clarke?"

"When I can afford it," Bob says. "Which won't be long."

"I've come home just in time," Richard says. Seeing a shade pass over his father's face, he adds more seriously, "Sir Thomas probably wrote that I've been ill. Sunstroke in Egypt, which lingered. But I'm quite well now."

Familial relief. He sees Bob notice his kid gloves, which he never used to wear. Bob gives them a once-over. But it's a small thing, and soon forgotten.


Once Richard is in a painting room, he sets several goals, always taking into account that he will serve Osiris when called upon to do so. First, having missed the spring Academy exhibition, he will work up one of his sketches from Syria for the exhibition in Liverpool. Second, he will prepare a drawing for the competition to decorate the new Houses of Parliament: *St. George and the Dragon*, he believes. He will have to work long hours to meet the competition deadline, and he lays in a stock of eggs and ale, the artist's friends, to get him over the hump. Third, and he doesn't want to do this, his father tells him he will have to meet Sir Thomas when he comes to town and, in the meantime, has to work up some sketches, and this is the pater's verb, to mollify his patron.

Not all is in order. Although he believes he's been acting with discretion, when he reaches the landing outside Frith's studio, making his first visit since his return, Richard hears voices. This is confusing, since he doesn't know at first which era they come from. Then he realizes it is Egg saying, "Dadd is back, and he's mad."

Richard doesn't know what Gus means. He went to see him immediately, Gus being a good egg, wanting to thank him for his insight into doubling and duality, which Gus had forgotten, explaining how it's demonstrated in the East, and telling him a little about Osiris, maybe making a joke or two about demons. But he was himself, and is himself, only done in oils instead of pencil.

"I went to see his father, and he says it's only sunstroke. A lingering case of sunstroke, and he'll be better soon, but . . ."

Tiptoeing away from Frith's landing, Richard reaches the street and runs back to his new painting room. Throwing open his door, he's immensely irritated to see an old Cliquish portrait of Egg affectionately tacked to his wall. Taking it down, he slashes a line of red paint across Egg's throat, a change that immediately worries him. He decides against pinning it back up and puts it in a portfolio, not knowing what to do after that, and deciding to go back to Frith's street and wait for Egg to leave.

He buys a newspaper there and feigns to read it. It takes a long time, but Egg walks out the door and away from Frith's building. Not receiving instruction, Richard counts to a hundred and goes upstairs to see Frith. When he knocks on the door, his friend calls, "Come in."

"And he came in."

Their ancient joke. It makes Richard feel better to say it.

Frith appears shocked to see him, but there's much shaking of hands, clapping of backs. No one better than old Billy.

"Why, old fellow, you look a little pale," Richard says. "You've been working too hard. You have to go to Egypt. That'll put colour in your cheeks. And open your eyes, too, I can tell you."

Turning to Frith's easel, as he always does, Richard sees an oil of a little model they all use, not unapproachable, posed as a dolly wearing a red mantle. Call it cherry: Richard recognizes the subject as Dolly Varden from Dickens's novel, *Barnaby Rudge*.

"Let's see if I can get this right," he says. "Dolly being 'the very pink and pattern of good looks, in a smart little cherry coloured mantle.'"

"Word perfect," Frith marvels.

They'd read it at home as the serials came out, Stephen narrating most of the numbers, but Richard taking duty when his brother came down with laryngitis.

"Dick has approved," Billy says. "Dickens."

Richard is unsettled by Frith's familiarity. Taking care to remain light, he asks after the rest of their clique, delighted to hear they're doing as well as Frith. Delighted but worried, as Richard understands he has fallen behind the crowd he used to lead. Even Frith's painting tells him this, much better than anything Billy managed before he left. He shouldn't have gone on tour. Although he also should have.

Richard has an image of a career, how the artist climbs a ladder that leans against the side of a building, taking it step by step, learning technique, aiming to reach the roof. Most fail, falling off the ladder at different levels, and some of the failures are very good artists, but weak characters. Only a few reach the roof, and once they're on top, most of them congratulate themselves on having made it. While the true artist, and Richard knows this, draws a breath and leaps for the moon.

Frith is leaping. He might reach the moon; he might not. But Richard has only a few suggestions for his Dolly, and they're minor, and both of them know it.

"And you," Billy says. "Look at you, dressed like a buck. How *are* you, really?"

Richard hears Egg in the question and takes care to answer casually. "Oh, I'm all right. I felt a little seedy a day or two ago, but I'm all right now." Holding out a hand, he says, "Although you can see I'm handling myself with kid gloves."

Billy laughs, always getting Richard's jokes, never troubling himself with cynicism or scrutinizing. That's why Richard will keep visiting, despite being unsettled by Billy's leap, which he will have to out-do. And, in fact, he continues to rap on Frith's door even when other friends have ended up with their portraits slashed and placed in the portfolio, something that has to be done but which causes him anguish. The slashed friends watch Richard like Arabs, but Billy accepts the surface as a fine place to glide, and Richard finds it a relief to *rap rap rap* on his door. Come in. And he came in, needing relief from his work.

The work is crushing and Richard can't always manage to sleep, not with all the worry. He's taken a large painting room and moves restlessly from one project to the other: his cartoon of St. George, a group of water carriers for the exhibition in Liverpool and, with Sir Tom's visit looming, a watercolour sketch for the frontispiece of the fictional book, a replacement for the scribble Sir Tom quickly lost. This one shows Sir Thomas holding the Egyptian gun, which is taller than he is, the shotgun that so often misfired. Richard has trouble painting Sir Tom without reference to the Chartists, but fortunately it's a reference he won't understand.

S ir Thomas wishes to have breakfast, Richard's father informs him. They've reached August in the Gregorian calendar, which is named for an earlier iteration of the counterfeit Pope that Richard failed to kill in Rome. When the appointed morning arrives, his father accompanies Richard to Sir Thomas's club, and a hole opens. Richard doesn't remember anything of breakfast, although when he comes to himself in his studio, both the pater and the patron are still with him, and the patron is so pleased with the watercolour portrait that Richard gathers he's acquitted himself well.

"We'll have this in oils," Sir Thomas says, and he gathers this is not for the first time. "And you *will* read the life of Wilkie?" he asks. "A well-regulated man."

"Thank you, Sir Thomas. I'm quite well now, I assure you. Under my father's care."

They beam. They're gone. Yet Osiris isn't happy. Patron,

pater. There is confusion, and demons are afoot, one taking up residence in the birthmark on Richard's forehead. He's forced to cut it off, a little bloodily.

"My god, what have you done?" his father asks the next day, seeing the bandage.

"Accident," he says. "Tripped and hit my head on the chimney."

*Cure me, leech me*, the little voice cries, although he isn't sick.

He isn't sick, but Richard knows this can't continue, and that it won't. When he goes home for a meal, and makes his way unseen into the sitting room upstairs; when he huddles in a corner behind the door, having been frightened by Bob's stuffed raven on the bookshelf; when the knowing eye of the raven prevents him from leaving, he hears his father and Bob coming upstairs talking about a physician. Mr. Sutherland; he recognizes the name. Physician to St. Luke's Hospital for Lunatics. Osiris shrieks like machinery.

"But if he says he's dangerous," Bob says.

"I might be able to take this more seriously if he'd actually seen Richard."

They pause outside the sitting room door. Doubled over as he is, Richard can see shoes through the crack at the bottom, the shadow of shoes.

"But you can understand Mr. Sutherland's point. He'll be able to keep up a front during a short consultation. He needs to be kept at the hospital for observation. And, in any case, he needs to rest."

"I'm not at all sure."

"I am," Bob says. "And I think we should settle this before I'm off."

A hand is turning the knob when there's a pause, and

Richard can just make out one of the men calling from down-stairs.

"She's early," Bob says.

"I'd better go say hello."

"God help me, her last days as Miss Clarke, and mine as a free man."

Their father is chafing Bob as they descend. Bob's wedding is the day after tomorrow at the bride's home in Chatham. She is going home on the afternoon steamer and Bob leaves in the morning. His best man Stephen is already in the Medway, having gone early to their Uncle Charles's chemist shop, which is not spelled chymist outside London. Uncle Charles now lives in Strood, where Stephen will attend a fair.

Once they're out of hearing, Richard allows himself a moan and scrambles to the sofa, where he curls up clutching himself under the raven's gaze. He doesn't know what to do and hasn't come up with an idea before he hears his father ascend the stairs and open the door. He's feigning sleep as his father comes in, stops in what must be surprise and pulls a chair closer to the sofa so he can watch him, as everybody does these days.

Richard pretends to wake up slowly, the way one does when gently disturbed. Levers up on one arm, blinking as if surprised to see his father. Tells himself to look sheepish. He never used to dissemble before, but it is now crucial.

"Oh, sorry," Richard says. "Must have fallen asleep."

"I didn't know you were here."

"I came over to beg dinner. A little under-nourished, I'm afraid."

"You've been working hard."

Richard swings his feet onto the floor, gaining time. "The tour wasn't a holiday, you know."

"Sir Thomas seems a decent chap."

"He isn't," Richard says.

With the shadow of the doctor upon him, Richard wonders if it's time to tell his father what happened on the riverboat, which would change everything. Richard would no longer be criticized for his lack of gratitude, Sir Thomas assigned all blame. It would buy him time, and time is Richard's friend, with holes and hollows to hide in. This comes as a suggestion from Osiris, although not as a demand.

But the small, half-lost, whimpering part of Richard is against this, reminding him that what happened was minor, at least for him. He felt nothing and it affected nothing. His patron made a harmless mistake, and it is not the action of a gentleman to use that mistake against him. It is not something Richard Dadd would do.

Richard Dadd the sketch, not Richard the oil, which is deeper.

"He isn't?" his father prompts.

"I've been wanting to tell you more about the tour," Richard says.

His father waits. Richard doesn't know what to do and hedges.

"I was thinking of going home for a visit." He remembers that Bob and Stephen will be in Chatham for the wedding, and that he needs to avoid them. "I've been thinking in particular of Cobham, how I rambled through Cobham Park as a boy."

"Would you like me to come with you?"

"Yes, please. Perhaps I could disburden my mind."

It occurs to Richard that he can tell him the real story,

the one his father hasn't wanted to hear about the speed of the tour and his patron's impatience and pettiness. He can talk about the duality of the experience: how these annoyances prepared him for his revelation in Karnak, or perhaps a safer word to use with his father would be inspiration. It comes to him that this might be the reason Osiris has not yet demanded the patron, or at least his demon, or why a demon has not yet taken up residence, although Richard knows he can't mention that either.

However. He can explain that his new access of inspiration means he's leaping for the moon, which is why he can seem unbalanced. He only needs time to balance himself, admitting that he's gone too far in one direction and could do with more contentment and less waterfall. No hospital, please, pater. Just give me time.

"Disburden," his father says. "Of course." They decide to leave after Bob is safely off to Chatham. Hands on thighs, his father stands.

"Pack well," he says. "Perhaps we'll go away for a few days. Bob and I have been talking about how you need a bit of a rest."

Osiris shrieks like a banshee. Richard knows at once that his father went downstairs but a demon came up. This is not his father. There has been an exchange, and it comes to him that this might not be the first time that the demon has taken possession of his father, who has spent his life trying to take possession of Richard. Richard has always known this. He once told Mary Ann that his father wanted to live vicariously. It proves to be far worse than that, although it is wise not to let the beast know he's seen through it, and seen through its hospital plan. That way it won't be on its guard.

"A few days would be nice," Richard says.

When the time comes, he packs very carefully, including the passport he has run out to get. The razor goes in as well, although there's a small interior gibber and it comes out. Goes in. Comes out. Goes in, out. In, out.

In.

At Cobham village, the demon impersonating his father is well remembered, and beds are found in a cottage. The demon's plan seems to involve the morning, since it wants an early night. But Richard insists on going for a walk that evening, and a moment comes when the demon is forced to relieve itself in a hollow. This allows Richard to come up behind it with the razor, hoping this will end quickly.

It proves surprisingly difficult to kill. The demon fights back. Calls his name. They are falling to the ground and wrestling. The razor blade flies off into the grass. But Richard is younger and stronger, and he has also purchased a rigging knife. When that goes into the shoulder, the demon is weakened. One, two more thrusts to the chest and the demon goes limp. There is blood. There is ragged, wet breathing. There is silence.

Richard thinks of throwing the remains into a ravine, but for some reason he is sobbing and can't. For some reason, he pauses to do up the demon's flies and button its coat over its wounds.

Then Richard gathers himself and runs into the fields, realizing that he is stained and will be questioned on the roadway. He puts a hand on the stile and leaps it, leaving a bloody print that will tell them, *I am gone.*

# Cobham, Kent
## *1858*

D ickens paused at the other side of the stile, looking back
at his friends.

"From here, he made his way to Rochester, where he was
noticed in the streets at ten o'clock at night. He asked at the
Crown Inn if he might wash his hands, and when the little
chambermaid removed the wash-stand basin, she found the
water to be dark, whether from blood or dirt she couldn't tell.

"He ordered a post-chaise to take him to Sittingbourne,
and then on to Dover, where he hired an open boat to Calais.
From Paris, he travelled south by coach, telling the coachman
he was bound for Marseilles, although he later told his doctors he had intended to kill the Emperor of Austria.

"But it was in the coach, as it travelled through Valence, that he pulled out a new razor. And with it, a keen new blade."

The murder had become one of Dickens's set pieces, acted out after he walked visitors from his new residence in Gad's Hill to the site of the killing in Cobham. He'd been collecting details: the razor, the knife, Robert Dadd's buttoned-up black suit coat, the murderer's white kid gloves; polishing his performance as he gave it to a series of guests, refining his cadence, heightening the drama and leaving out only the perilous fact he had known the family from a boy.

"Meanwhile, the next morning, the body was found right *here*," Dickens said, leaping back over the stile to throw himself on the ground, closing his eyes. "The corpse discovered by two passing butchers on their way to market. At first they thought a chap was sleeping it off, the murder having occurred directly after the venerable fair in Strood."

Opening an eye to check their reaction, Dickens found himself looking into the stricken face of Gus Egg, who must have been closer to Richard Dadd than he had known. Poor Gus hadn't an unkind bone in his body, although his lungs were becoming such a concern that Dickens was urging him to go to Morocco for the winter. Egg didn't want to, but Dickens intended to prevail.

"I'm sorry, Gus," he said, sitting up. "But we can't make life so unspeakably solemn that we're tempted to be murdered ourselves."

Francis giggled; his middle son.

Egg remained bowed, looking as if he were carrying the body on his shoulders. "A man's life was taken here, Dick," he said. "And poor Richard's effectively lost."

A stir from Dickens's young friend, Yates. "You knew him?"

Gus winced.

"And see him still?"

"He prefers not."

"But what happened, Father?" Francis asked.

His boy was accompanied by two young friends, who rounded out their party. Unbearable curiosity on their faces. Seeing how it was, Gus walked to the stile.

"The butchers," Dickens said, standing and brushing himself off, "were an uncle and nephew by the name of Lester."

He usually said, by the serviccable name of Lester, relying on the rhythm of a sentence to carry his signature humour. But Gus was listening, and best the humour be battened down.

"I spoke with both of them not long afterward, when I happened to find myself in Rochester. They told me they'd called on the local constable to report what they'd found, the constable being a tailor by the name of Dawes charged with enforcing the law in Cobham, the local worthies presumably feeling him capable of taking a man's measure—and I'm sorry, Gus. I keep doing it, don't I?"

But Gus had become absorbed by the stile, patting it with a flat hand. Dickens allowed his reins to loosen, and a smile to enter his voice, and his essential questions: Isn't life awful? How can we bear it?

"Having been made aware of the butchers' wish to get their beef to market, Dawes waved them on without asking any questions, although not necessarily without any beef. He then proceeded to the murder site, where the body was being guarded by a shepherd."

Relaxing into his story. "I doubt my friend Inspector Bucket would consider Dawes a suitable candidate for Scotland Yard. Following his coolness toward the idea of questioning the butchers, he displayed a curious insensibility to the handprint on the stile; which is to say, it escaped his notice completely; and he went on to cleverly avoid finding the razor, the weapon being unearthed by one of the inquisitive villagers busy trampling the hollow into mud, and any evidence into oblivion. In short, Constable Dawes did everything in his power to let the murderer make his escape."

"But surely there wasn't any mystery," Yates said. "They knew it to be the son."

"But think of it, Yates. The son might have been murdered by the same hand, and his body carried elsewhere. Or the poor chap might have been mortally wounded and crawled away to die."

"We hoped so," Gus murmured, listening after all.

Egg had never spoken of the murder, but it was obvious he knew more than most, possibly more than Dickens. This was galling in its own right. But Dickens was thinking about writing another novel placed on the Medway, and an author needed particulars. An author was cruel. Art was.

"How did it happen, Gus? I'm afraid you remember too clearly."

When Gus hesitated, Dickens left a pause, looking at him steadily, always aware that his eyes were variously described as piercing, pulverizing, mesmerizing. Even as Egg's reputation bloomed, his stamina had declined, and he'd grown susceptible to bullying. Dickens could dislike himself, and did so more often than others knew. Yet this was the way he secured his particulars, which the public devoured, as it devoured him.

"Dadd's sister Mary Ann was worried about the excursion," Gus finally said. "She'd stopped trusting him, believing that he hadn't been himself since he'd got back from his travels."

Apparently the sister had tried to persuade her father not to accompany his son to Cobham. But Mr. Dadd, as Gus still called him, said that something was weighing on his son's mind, and he believed that a quiet week in Kent would help him discover what it was. Richard had always been the favourite. His eldest brother, Bob, had wanted to admit him to Mr. Sutherland's lunatic hospital, Richard's landlady having heard shrieks in his painting room and been frightened away by knives waved under the door. Mr. Sutherland believed that Richard was dangerous, but their father wouldn't hear it, or listen to his daughter, and so he took Richard to Cobham.

Mary Ann had remained worried, however, and wrote her brother Stephen, who was staying with an uncle in Strood. She asked him to find their father, and quickly. But the letter had arrived too late.

"I presume you know about the second tragedy."

"Did you always call him Richard?" Dickens asked, preferring to narrate tragedies himself. "You say Bob Dadd, but never Dick."

"Not like your Mr. Dick in *David Copperfield*," Gus said. "I've always assumed Mr. Dick is a portrait of my poor friend. Richard Dadd: Richard Babley, the madman who can't bear to hear his full name spoken. I hope poor Richard has become as gentle as his portrait, living out a form of life in Bedlam.'"

"What?" Yates asked. "Dadd is the original?"

Dickens had given Mr. Dick a head curiously bowed, like a schoolboy after being beaten by a Creakle, and a strange kind of watery brightness in his eye, and had made him answer each question with a single, literal-minded, declarative sentence. He had David Copperfield's aunt Betsey Trotwood say, as she contemplated adopting him, *Now here you see young*

*David Copperfield, and the question I put to you is, what shall I do with him?* And Mr. Dick replied briskly, *I should wash him.*

He had also made Mr. Dick disturbed by any mention of King Charles the First, and especially of his head, or at least of the lack of it following his execution, while at the same time compelling him to write the king into a lengthy memorandum he was constantly writing. Finally Betsey Trotwood suggested that each time he found it necessary to emit the late Charles, like a puff of steam that needed escape, he ought to write him down on a separate page; pages which Mr. Dick made into a kite to fly with David Copperfield.

King Charles, he had Betsey Trotwood say, *That's his allegorical way of expressing it. He connects his illness with great disturbance and agitation, naturally, and that's the figure, or the simile, or whatever it's called, which he chooses to use.*

Dadd, he would say, had a posture as curiously bowed as a schoolboy after a beating by a Creakle, and his eyes a strange kind of watery brightness. He emitted Egypt and the god Osiris like puffs of steam, and as for Mr. Dick's one simple declarative—the first time Dickens had visited him at Bedlam, Dadd was able to respond to a question with one solidly built sentence followed by a long string of loosely associated concepts, like the tail of a kite, except that a kite made sense.

How do you do, Dadd?

How would you do, if you were held at Her Majesty's pleasure? Her pleasure being a pleasure for her husband to satisfy, aha, aha (his odd mirthless laugh) although all love's pleasure shall not match its fecking woe.

Yet Mr. Dick was a beloved eccentric, a favourite of readers, while Dadd gorged on food until he vomited, then shoved his way back to the trencher without washing the vomit off. He flung chamber pots, threw tantrums, had the vocabulary of a drunken horse trader and, at least during his first years in Bedlam, would attack other inmates so viciously, they were at risk of infection from man bites.

The relationship of an author to his characters could not be understood simply. If anyone reading *Copperfield* had met Dickens's parents—and fortunately they had not—they would have recognized John Dickens in the bombastic ah-ah hopes of a momentous new stage in the life of a man expressed by the criminally sanguine debtor Mr. Micawber, and recognized Dickens's mother in Mrs. Micawber, always ready to acknowledge her husband's faults and improvidence, while declaring it was not in her nature to desert him. But of course these were his parents bent to his needs as characters, which contradicted one of the most salient features of his parents' true characters: that they had never once bent themselves to satisfy his childish needs, but thought entirely of themselves.

An author painted individuals, but he didn't do portraits. His characters were such intrinsic parts of his books' design, and his design so much an expression of his nature, his temper and even his philosophy, that they may have started in the knowledge or investigation of other people, and probably did, but they were also, or became, aspects of his own character, whether of his fears, his scruples or his needs; so that when Mr. and Mrs. Micawber redeemed themselves and disappeared handily to Australia, were they his parents or were they his fantasy?

I've always assumed Mr. Dick was a portrait of my poor friend.

A man's life was taken here, Dick.

Sometimes he despaired of anyone ever listening to themselves.

"There were two weeks of confusion before Dadd was known to be in custody in France," he said. "You must have seen the newspapers. The crime of the year, and the butchers dining out on it when I met them in Rochester. Mutton, as I recall."

"You'd met him, Dick," Egg said. "You must remember. Forster introduced you to Richard at the same time as we were introduced, at a British Society exhibition. Dickens, Dadd, Egg. The tergiversated names. We were, we were buoyant."

Egg's first smile since they'd reached Cobham.

"I met him once or twice afterward," Dickens said, "walking at night. He was a good-looking chap back then, wasn't he? Poking his ambition about like an umbrella."

"It must have been quite a combustion," Yates said. "You and he. It's a wonder the cobbles didn't up and follow."

"Well of course they did. Or perhaps they were thrown at us by females. Yes, I think so."

"You left him in France, sir," his son said. "With a razor."

"He's told me," Dickens said, "during visits to Bedlam . . ."

"You've visited Bedlam?" Yates asked.

Keeping an eye on Gus, he said, "Not far outside the Forest of Fontainebleau, Dadd became attuned to the position of the stars in the constellation Ursa Major. By then it was late at night. He could feel the spectral presence of the god Osiris and understood that if two of the stars moved nearer together in the heavens, he was to slit the throat of one of his fellow passengers in the diligence, a man whose collars he began playing with as the poor chap tried to sleep.

"The fatal moment arrived. The stars drove closer together. Dadd fell upon the man with his razor, grappling"—Dickens couldn't resist fending off his powerful right hand with his desperate left—"slashing once, twice, three—four times before Dadd—was finally—overpowered. The Frenchman was pathetically wounded, but survived, and on the night of the thirtieth of August, 1843, unknown to his family, to the British press and the oblivious Constable Dawes, Richard Dadd was seized into custody in France."

"He apologized to the poor man he injured," Gus said, "and turned over all his money for his care." He spoke in a quavering voice, as if he were praising a lost sweetheart. They had been young together. Dickens had few friends remaining from when he was young, not always his decision.

"Dadd spent most of a year confined to an asylum in Clermont. The French physician, to whom I had occasion to write, said he was largely delusional, expectorating frequently to rid himself of demons—spitting, Francis—and spending hours staring at the sun. His pupils contracted to pinpoints but his eyesight seems to have been undamaged, although he told the physician that the garden took on a reddish hue, a tint he called Jerusalem.

"A quiet, enigmatic, undemanding young man, the physician wrote. *Réservé, énigmatique et peu exigent,* although by the time he was brought before the magistrates at Rochester, he had become excitable, as you might recall from the panoptic coverage in the newspapers."

"Must we do the trial, Dick?" Egg asked.

Dickens bowed, feeling like a child deprived of its sweet. The parade of witnesses. Dadd's hectic interpolations. I tell you I didn't do it! Oh, what stories! No, oh no! The water was very dark, the little chambermaid said, but I could not tell with blood or dirt. I took one of your towels, Dadd called. I took it because it had blood on it. Said the surgeon, I found bruises on the wrists. Cried Dadd, I used no more force than was necessary! The pleura, lining the interior of the ribs, was punctured in two places. I only stabbed him once! I tell you I did not do it! I never did! No, no!

"Perhaps I may say that Dadd was committed to the assizes. But he was never tried, being certified under the Criminal Lunatic Act and interned at Her Majesty's pleasure in the Royal Bethlem Hospital. It was August the twenty-second, 1844, fifty-one weeks to a day after the calamity."

A silence, before Francis asked, "What caused his madness, sir, do you know?"

"Sunstroke," Egg said.

"Blood," Dickens answered. "Please let me tell them this part, Gus, or I shall explode, which would be messy. Two days after the murder, the family on tenterhooks, Richard's whereabouts not yet known, there descended a second tragedy. Dadd's younger brother, George, stumbled into the family home on Suffolk Street, naked, soiled and babbling, perfectly unaware of his father's murder, his brother's culpability or indeed of anything at all. Gone quite mad. Imagine the anguish. Within one week, a marriage, a murder and two brothers moonstruck.

"George Dadd was committed to Bedlam, where he's since spent fifteen years in the incurables ward. Having never committed violence, he's in a different wing of the hospital than his brother, who takes his place among the criminally insane. They profess, I'm told, no desire to meet. Nor would George Dadd so much as meet my eye when I asked to be introduced. A stocky, sullen, apish young man with a degenerate aspect, or he was ten years ago. The superintendent tells me he'll carry any weight of coals and is liable to pull a volume of Shakespeare from his pocket, which he can give by heart."

"Dick, this is damnably painful."

Seeing the tears in Egg's eyes, Dickens pulled up short. "I do apologize, Egg. Here I am, carried away by story."

Some said he lacked human feeling. His former wife would claim so. It was their recent separation which had brought Dickens to Gad's Hill, buying the house he had often passed on walks with his father during their brief happy years in Chatham. He'd said how much he'd like to live in it, and his father had told him that he might one day, if he worked very hard; John Dickens never having considered for an instant that he might work very hard himself and by this clever stratagem adequately house his family.

Yet it had all turned out for the best. Dickens felt young again at Gad's Hill, even if he couldn't be seen in public with the girl he now spent the best part of his time with. He had his children with him, excepting only his eldest son, who insisted on supporting his mother. As Dickens told friends, at some risk to the boy's back.

After improvements, the house would be a formidable place to write, and it already hosted entertainments: quoits, croquet, cricket, leapfrog, all manner of picnics and donkey rides, his garden a fairground, himself the ringmaster; his eyes, they said, piercing, mesmerizing, pulverizing and bleak.

W hen Dickens next visited Bedlam, he found the criminal ward altered. Superintendent Hood had removed the bars and cages, as he'd previously done in the common wards, introducing windows, light, plants and greyhounds trained to be watchful as they comforted prisoners. Dickens felt sentimental about many things, but murderers were not among them. As he toured the ward, he disliked seeing vicious jolter-heads rewarded with living conditions more pleasant than those enjoyed by the deserving poor, presuming these, in fact, existed.

"Excellent work, superintendent," he said. "Almost worth committing murder to toss up here."

"I'm aware of the criticisms," said Hood, a younger and more hopeful man. "Your friend Dadd speaks of artists as being rather useless in themselves, thrown up by society as a marker of civilization. Give him time, and he'll speak of God making beauty—or the gods, in his schema—and say he doesn't know what purpose beauty serves either, other than to elevate society and give pleasure. By the same token, lunatics aren't of any use in modern mechanical terms, yet I think it a measure of civilization that we treat them humanely, and that doing so is another means of elevating humanity."

"Then I disagree with both of you," Dickens said. "Believing that the purpose of art is to improve society, which is also the purpose of incarceration, as it lessens crime by providing a deterrent."

"I might ask you what would have deterred Dadd, with a mind so disordered. But here we are at his cell, where he is expecting you." Speaking more simply: "Aren't you expecting Mr. Dickens, Richard?"

In fact, Dadd was staring at the wall, and as Hood tactfully withdrew, leaving a warder at the door, Dickens took another chair and waited. He noticed a new book on Dadd's wall shelf (not one of his) and the same strange fantasy on his easel he'd seen for years, an intricate and only partially completed painting of a fairy scene, at the centre of which a woodsman with his back to the viewer raised his axe, ready to strike a small object.

Dickens now wondered if the woodsman was Dadd, his recently painted hair being cut in the Daddsian style. The small object had unmistakeably become a nut; the colours were both muddy and roseate. He remembered the French physician's note that after staring at the sun, Dadd said he'd seen the world as reddened, a colour he called Jerusalem, presumably an artist's pigment.

When the silence had gone on long enough, Dickens got the book.

"Mrs. Gaskell's biography of Charlotte Brontë," he said, flipping through it.

"Met her," Dadd said.

"Which one?"

"Both of 'em," Dadd said, glancing at him shyly, before looking away. "Gaskell's wife up in Manchester. Currer Bell came in for a visit."

It seemed Dadd might be in one of his more talkative moods, even if his comments were to be directed at the wall.

"She came here, did she? Unexpectedly enterprising of Miss Brontë. Or Mrs. Nicholls, as she became, to her peril. What did you think of her? I'm curious."

"Why else would you ask?"

"Point taken."

"Tiny. Fairy. Clever. A cat. Meaning a barn cat. A hunter."

"More like a cat scratch, I'd say."

Aha. Aha.

"Mrs. Gaskell," Dickens said, sitting back down, still leafing through the book, "once spread a rumour that I'd bought an entire service of gold plate for my table. Wrote it hither and yon, all across England. I don't quite trust her book."

"Perhaps she was speaking metaphorically," Dadd said.

Dickens had to laugh, and heard that his laughter had a different quality than the hoots in the ward outside Dadd's cell: the titters, the screeches, the mechanical *ha ha ha* that rose and fell. He wouldn't have predicted that laughter could sound both so healthy and so ill.

"She died," Dadd said.

"Charlotte Brontë. Yes, she did."

"How?"

"Ah. You didn't finish the book. Can you take this?"

"Murdered? Knife? Razor?"

Growing excitement. Dickens glanced out the door, finding that his guard had been drawn to a chess game at a long table across the ward. He felt titillated to be left on his own with an agitated lunatic.

"Nothing of the sort," he said, bluff as an old sea captain, and getting up to look more closely at Dadd's painting. At the top, he was startled to make out a tiny portrait of Dadd's father, the highest figure in the composition, wearing his apothecary's apron and standing behind a counter.

"What's this here, then?" he asked.

"Soldier, sailor, tinker, tailor, ploughboy, apothecary, thief." The old nursery rhyme. Dickens picked out each figure as Dadd mentioned it, the tinker sharpening a knife behind the apothecary's back. Macabre, that. Of course, Dickens had a large collection of tinkers eternally sharpening their knives behind his back. They were called critics.

"About seven or eight months into her marriage, Mrs. Nicholls was expecting a happy addition," Dickens said, still looking at the painting. "But her health had never been good, and for some ladies, the added physical burden proves too much and breaks the constitution. She couldn't keep her food down and developed a fever which weakened her rapidly."

Dadd didn't move, as if trying to take this in.

Dickens thought of Elizabeth Gaskell's fury. Quite by chance, he had run across her in London not long after her friend had died. They'd met in the City, pausing amid the shove of newsboys and clerks and the delivery men with their clopping Percherons. Mrs. Gaskell's voice carried well above the racket. She was as used to chairing meetings as he was.

*They should have written me*, she said. *I would have come and put an end to it and saved her.* Leaving him saying, *No, no, no, Mrs. Gaskell. You forget yourself. I don't believe that's ever a solution.*

"Oh, your *beliefs*, Mr. Dickens," said she, a minister's wife. "How convenient that they never seem to inconvenience you."

Another reason he mistrusted her book was her animus toward the bereaved husband and father. It made a good story, however.

"It's a tragedy," Dadd said, still facing the wall.

Well. If one accepted the classical definition of a tragedy, a hero brought down by a fatal flaw. Thackeray had once said that Miss Brontë only wanted a Tomkins she could love and who would love her. She had found one, and she had died.

"I've moved back to the Medway, you know," he said. "To Gad's Hill."

"Why would I know?"

"I only meant to say that one is drawn home. The biography

tells us that Miss Brontë married her father's curate, which would have allowed her to stay in the parsonage in Yorkshire had she outlived her father. Perhaps this was the fatal flaw that caused her tragedy. A love of home. A weakness for it."

"Charlotte Brontë, Currer Bell. CB, CB." Taking a sly glance over his shoulder, "Charles Dickens, David Copperfield. CD. DC."

Dickens heard his laughter sound less confident. Dadd reached for his violin and, after a few bars of introduction, began singing lyrics Dickens hadn't thought about in years.

> *Near the Hungerford Market, long ago*
> *An old maid lived a life of woe*
> *She was past forty-three, and her face like tan*
> *When she fell in love with the dog's meat man.*
> *The dog's meat, dog's meat, dog's meat man.*

As he played, Dadd hopped out a hornpipe, raising his knees: a spectacle which left Dickens swinging between amusement and uneasiness, as if pulled by opposing tides.

Dadd stopped abruptly. "That was you," he said.

"It was me, was it?"

"Dancing on the table in the Mitre Tavern."

Dickens had no answer.

"You are a very strange man," Dadd told him almost companionably, although still without looking at him. "So many secrets. John Dickens, running tick with every tradesman in Chatham and Somers Town. The baker putting him into Marshalsea Prison. Him putting you into a blacking factory." Every word rang like a chime. "You're afraid of anyone knowing these things, but you write them in your book. You don't wish to be known, but you move back to the Medway where everyone knows all about you." In wonderment: "You are a very strange man."

"Well, yes, I suppose I am," Dickens said, there being little other answer. "And you're quite mad, you know."

He was conscious of the warder not being outside and got ready to defend himself. But after a long pause, Dadd laughed, *Aha, aha,* and Dickens sputtered out something that was either laughter or a sob, thinking of the girl he wished to protect. They knew all about her, too. And judged her, unfairly.

*They* were tradesmen, eyes wide open. Tailors knowing which shoulder was lower, which side one dressed on, and how enviably; bakers indulging a sweet tooth, barbers pulling it, chemists commiserating insincerely the periodic need for silver nitrate against a lower drip; all of them understanding what a man coveted and what he needed; which trinkets he used to bribe women and which necessities he failed to provide his children. Dickens had never liked tradesmen, nor trusted them. He'd never trusted anyone, including himself.

"And what are you hiding in plain sight?" he asked, going again to Dadd's painting, his eye on the squib of the murdered father.

Dadd didn't seem to notice what he was looking at.

"Shakespeare," Dadd said. "And seeds."

The canvas was certainly thick with Shakespearian fairies, and the fairy folk were dwarfed by grass heads and fallen seed pods. Dickens supposed the grass was meant to give scale to the painting, showing how tiny the magic creatures were.

"The seeds will sprout," Dadd said. "Once they've been ploughed under."

"That being their tendency."

Nodding, Dadd jabbed his thumb awkwardly at the canvas, threatening the paint.

"You mean to show me the woodsman," Dickens said.

"Feller. The fairy feller."

Another jab.

"He's about to strike an acorn with his axe."

"Nut," Dadd said.

"All right, a nut."

"Nut," Dadd whispered. "The goddess Nut, mother of Osiris of the Underworld. Break her open and Osiris comes out. The Lord of All enters the light. The feller strikes his master stroke, and she will open."

Dickens leaned in for a closer look, considering the feller, which indeed had Dadd's hair.

"You've painted him as not having struck yet. Poised, but not having struck. Is that how you wish things were? Unstruck?"

Dadd looked confused. Too much at once. He shook his head like one of the Percherons in the City, pawing his boot.

"It has already happened," Dadd just managed to say. "This is what happened. It shows what happened, as art is meant to." Hand sweeping the canvas. "Four thousand years ago."

"Or fourteen," Dickens said. Then, seeing his face, "I apologize, Dadd, I'm confusing you."

"There is no Da, Da, Da . . ."

"Richard. I apologize, Richard. Art has its uses, does it not?"

"Four thousand years ago. And today."

Both looked back at the painting, which wasn't to Dickens's taste.

Struck by something, Dadd fumbled for a brush, his box of paints.

"I suppose I should let you get on with it," Dickens said, and Dadd didn't answer.

Watching him prepare his tools, Dickens knew what Dadd didn't: that his family had been destroyed. Perhaps it was Dadd's fault. Perhaps it was blood. It wasn't only Richard and George gone mad. There were the stories of Dadd's youngest sister trying to strangle her baby, which she said wouldn't stop crying. This was Maria Elizabeth, the beautiful wife of Dadd's old friend, the painter John Phillip. Just recently, poor Phillip had been forced to put his wife into a Scottish asylum, which she was convinced was the fault of the royal family. Phillip was reported to have broken down after doing so.

Two older sisters, left unprotected by their father's murder, scraped out a living as companions and nursemaids. The painter Frith had hired the eldest, Mary Ann, as a governess, meaning to be charitable, but Frith's children had found her gloomy and he'd been forced to give her the sack. The second brother, Stephen, was said to live under a blanket of guilt, his health delicate. Only the eldest and youngest lived normal lives. Like his father, Bob Dadd was a chemist and the head of a large family, while the two younger half-brothers had immigrated to America, where both were chemists as well and had their own large families. One was even said to paint.

Dickens looked again at the top of Dadd's canvas, the apothecary figure he remembered from Chatham: Robert Dadd, with his bemused and bookish face. This was what had happened to his children, nine of them. The one he had felt to be a genius, his favourite, his murderer, hummed as he prepared his paints. *The dog's meat, the dog's meat man.*

"I'll come by another time," Dickens said. "Maybe you'll be finished your picture by then."

But Dadd didn't seem to hear him, and continued to hum, and hum, and hum, until the vibration echoed through the madhouse, and followed Dickens out.

# Author's Note

If I have the genealogy right, I am Richard Dadd's first cousin-in-law five times removed. My husband, Paul Knox, is directly descended from Richard's uncle, the chemist Henry Martin, who brought his family to Canada in 1841.

I knew my husband's grandfather, Cecil Martin, who knew one of Henry's sons—his great-uncle Theodore Martin—who, in turn, had known his cousin Richard in London when he was a boy. So there are echoes as well as artefacts in the family, including a marvellously bad painting of a river done by another of Henry Martin's sons, also Henry, that hangs above my desk. I wonder if young Henry took painting tips from his cousin Richard before the family left Somers Town. If so, I'm afraid he didn't learn much.

I owe enormous thanks to my mother-in-law, Mary Martin Knox, the family genealogist, for her research into the Dadd and Martin families. Over many years, she turned up a king's ransom of detail, which has proved extraordinarily fruitful. And there are still many volumes of her research into other branches of the family to explore.

As well, I owe thanks to Colin Gale, curator of the Royal Bethlem Hospital Archives (now the archives at the Bethlem Museum of the Mind) who extended every courtesy to me during several visits and showed me all the good stuff. I'd also like to acknowledge my debt to Dadd's biographers, David Greysmith, Patricia Allderidge and most recently Nicholas Tromans, and to editor Margaret Smith for her awe-inspiring work on the three volumes of *The Letters of Charlotte Brontë*. Frances Lowndes and Paul Mylrea were very kind hosts in Baalbec Road, London, as I explored Dadd, Brontë and Dickens sites, museums and archives throughout the U.K.

My great thanks go to the good people at ECW Press, including copy editor Crissy Calhoun and especially my editor Susan Renouf, who is always a fount of help and kind encouragement. Finally, as always, I owe an inexpressible amount to my son, Gabe, and husband, Paul.

LESLEY KRUEGER is a novelist and screenwriter. Richard Dadd's first cousin-in-law five times removed (if she has the genealogy right), Lesley drew on family information unknown to biographers in writing *Mad Richard*. The award-winning author of six books, she lives with her husband in Toronto. Find her online at LesleyKrueger.com.